Daughter
Twin *of* Oaks

Books by Lauraine Snelling

Hawaiian Sunrise

A Secret Refuge

Daughter of Twin Oaks

Red River of the North

An Untamed Land   *The Reapers' Song*
A New Day Rising   *Tender Mercies*
A Land to Call Home   *Blessing in Disguise*

High Hurdles

Olympic Dreams   *Close Quarters*
DJ's Challenge   *Moving Up*
Setting the Pace   *Letting Go*
Out of the Blue   *Raising the Bar*
Storm Clouds   *Class Act*

Golden Filly Series

The Race   *Shadow Over San Mateo*
Eagle's Wings   *Out of the Mist*
Go for the Glory   *Second Wind*
Kentucky Dreamer   *Close Call*
Call for Courage   *The Winner's Circle*

LAURAINE SNELLING

Daughter of Twin Oaks

BETHANY HOUSE PUBLISHERS
MINNEAPOLIS, MINNESOTA 55438

Published by Bethany House Publishers
A Ministry of Bethany Fellowship International
11400 Hampshire Avenue South
Minneapolis, Minnesota 55438
www.bethanyhouse.com

Printed in the United States of America by
Bethany Press International, Minneapolis, Minnesota 55438

Library of Congress Cataloging-in-Publication Data

Snelling, Lauraine.
    Daughter of Twin Oaks / by Lauraine Snelling.
        p. cm. — (A secret refuge ; 1)
    ISBN 1-55661-839-5
        1. United States—History—Civil War, 1861-1865—Fiction. I. Title.
PS3569.N39 D38 2000
813'.54—dc21   00-008414

DEDICATION

To the Brown Family and

all the others at Family Circle.

Y'all made our visit the highlight of the trip,

and your help on things southern will carry on.

Thank you for the hugs and joy-filled love.

Donny, Jenny, Sarah, Jonathan, Rebekah, and Suzanne,

you make our lives richer, and we thank you for that.

LAURAINE SNELLING is an award-winning author of over twenty-five books, including fiction and nonfiction for adults and young adults. Besides writing both books and articles, she teaches at writers' conferences across the country. She and her husband, Wayne, have two grown sons, four granddogs, and make their home in California.

ACKNOWLEDGMENTS

My thanks goes to the Historical Societies of Wyoming, Kansas, Missouri, and Kentucky. People there know how to research and taught me much. So many compilations of diaries, letters, and other books helped me research both the era and the area. My special thanks to Tom at Joseph Beth bookstore in Lexington and to Bryan S. Bush, who wrote *The Civil War Battles of the Western Front* and let me run my plot line by him at the Old Bardstown Civil War Museum and Village, where he is assistant curator. The folks at Fort Laramie, Fort Kearney on the Platte River, the Oregon Trail Museum in Independence, and the Wilson Creek Battlefield in Missouri all provided more blocks to add to my building novel.

I am blessed to have some of the best editors and readers who keep my time lines clear and my facts straight. Sharon Asmus and Helen Motter are two of God's gifts to my writing, along with all the others at Bethany House who work so hard to publish these books.

Husband Wayne says he never knew he wanted to know so much about the Civil War, but with each book I've written, he has contributed more and more in the research and development of the stories. Thank God for someone who remembers where places are on the map and where he read whatever it is I need at the moment and loves to travel the backroads to find all the sites mentioned in our research.

Thanks to all my readers who let me know how much they enjoy my books. Without readers I couldn't do what I love—write stories. I'd hate to have to go flip hamburgers at McDonald's. What a mighty God we serve.

Hugs and blessings,
Lauraine.

PROLOGUE

Midway, Kentucky
Spring 1860

"Jesselynn, what you doin' wit dem britches on?"

Jesselynn Highwood scrunched her eyes closed as if by not seeing Lucinda's scowl, Lucinda couldn't see her.

"You heard me, chile." Lucinda moved silently in spite of her bulk, a habit acquired during years of slave training. "What yo' mama gonna say?"

"What Mama doesn't know won't hurt her." Jesselynn spun away from the restraining hand on her arm. "You don't have to tell her every little thing, you know." *And besides, I'm not a "chile" any longer.* Sometimes Jesselynn thought she should have accepted one of those suitors who'd come callin' on her daddy, just to get out from under both Mama's and Lucinda's thumbs. Jesselynn squared her shoulders. "If you must know, I'm goin' down to the stables to ride Ahab for his morning works."

"Young ladies don' ride stallions, young ladies don' wear britches, and . . ." Lucinda drew herself up to her full imposing height by sucking in a lungful of air. "Young ladies don' disobey dey mama." She let a silence lengthen for effect. "'Sides, what happen to that lazy pup Abe? Dem horses him responsibility for running 'round de track."

"His arm still isn't strong enough from when he broke it. You know that."

Lucinda's harrumph said she might know it but in no way agreed.

Jesselynn continued, ignoring her mammy's mutterings and knowing she could be accused of impudence. Lucinda could be as stubborn as one of those old field mules at times.

"Zachary's at school, Adam is too heavy, and we all know I can get more out of those horses than anyone else." Jesselynn sneaked a peek from under the tan porkpie hat she wore pulled down over her brow. Lucinda hadn't budged. The frown on her shiny black brow looked deep enough to plant tobacco in.

"Dey's other boys down in de quarters a'wantin' to ride. Now you just get yo'self back up dem stairs and change yo' clothes before yo' mama come down dem stairs. State she in, you want her to feel worse?" She pointed back up the carved walnut staircase with one hand and reached to turn Jesselynn by the shoulder with the other. Miriam Highwood, coming close to term, spent much of her days lying down either in bed or on the lounge in the parlor. Feeling so ill with this baby forced her to depend more on others, her eldest daughter especially.

Jesselynn glared at the old woman with all her sixteen years of practice but turned and made her way to the first landing, her back straight. She refused to allow herself to stomp on each tread as she wanted to. She had outgrown that at least. *You should have known better than to come down the front stairs*, she scolded herself. Out the window by way of the live oak tree would have been better. Joseph needed her down at the stables. She'd have to talk to her father about this again. He had said she could ride. But she had to be honest. He hadn't said she could ride Ahab—in britches.

Even he had bowed to her mother's edict that Jesselynn was no longer a child, that she was close to marrying age, and it was long past time for her to learn to act like a lady.

"Piffle." Jesselynn knew that if she didn't get down to the barns quickly, the entire day's routine would be in an uproar. What was all the ballyhoo about women wearing pants after all? It certainly made more sense than those bulky skirts and hoops and petticoats—and confining corsets. After all, she had nothing that needed squeezing in or pushing up. Because she was tall and wore britches and a hat that hid her sun-kissed hair, she'd been taken for a boy more than once. She peeked down over the banister. Lucinda hadn't moved from her guard at the newel-post, and the glare she sent upward made Jesselynn continue on to her room. She plopped down on the edge of the bed. Outside she could hear the robin's morning song, echoed by the cardinal's. Everyone, or rather, everything was outside but her.

She crossed to the window and pushed aside the lacy curtains. No one was in sight. Lucinda had stayed at her post, or at least was still in the house. Jesselynn pushed the window higher and bent to crawl out, reaching with one leg for the thick branch she'd used as an escape hatch for years. She found her footing from long practice, hand over hand guided herself down the tree, and dropped from the last branch to the thick lawn.

Young ladies shouldn't have to go out their windows and down the tree, either. She threw the thought over her shoulder as she trotted down the dirt road to the stables. *One of these days I'll have a plantation of my own to manage, and then we'll see who rides what.* After all, that's what all well-bred southern gentlewomen did, marry and manage their husband's house as well as a good part of the plantation. She knew there had been two young men asking her father's permission to court her. But when her father asked her about them, she'd shrugged and shaken her head. They were just boys, after all. He hadn't insisted.

"Piffle. I'd rather ride than be married any day." Ignoring the thrust of guilt that reminded her she should be at her mother's side for the day's instructions, she trotted past the slave quarters, a row of small houses with gardens in back. She knew her father provided better houses for the slaves than most of the plantation owners. And while some of the younger slaves had been in the classroom with her, she wasn't supposed to know that he taught all his people to read, write, and do sums too. It was against the law for slaves to read, but Major Joshua Highwood was a farseeing, godly man who believed the law was wrong and he had to follow his own conscience. Jesselynn argued that slavery was also wrong, but so far he hadn't written the manumission papers for his slaves.

She missed him when he was gone, as he had been the last week, off to Frankfort, trying to keep the South out of war. Or at least Kentucky. Both of her brothers, Adam, the elder at twenty-two, and Zachary, at nineteen, were all-fired sure the South would win the war in a week—three at the most.

She'd heard so many rantings of the wonders of southern chivalry, she was sick of it. Why should the women just smile and say how wonderful the men were? How glorious to go off and fight—for what, she wasn't sure after eavesdropping on their near-to-fisticuffs discussions. She had a feeling many of the hotheaded young men weren't too sure either. The glory of fighting was all they could talk about, how they would run right over the enemy. Maybe they didn't think about getting shot, injured, or killed. Men's wounds wouldn't be much different than a deer's, for pity's sake. She'd cried buckets the first time she saw a deer that had been shot. The bullet hole that tore open its heart still showed up sometimes in her dreams.

It was all a conundrum to her. She smiled to herself—that was her newest word. She liked to be able to use a new word three times in the next day. Then she would remember it forever—or so the boys' tutor had said. After Adam and Zachary went off to school, he'd stayed on to teach the three younger girls, another of her father's wars against the mores of the day.

"Hello, handsome," she greeted the fiery red, or blood bay, stallion, Ahab, who bobbed his head and nickered as soon as he saw and heard her.

"How you this mornin', Missy Jess?" The soft voice of Joseph, their head groom, floated out from the stall where he was giving the stallion one last brushing. "This ol' son surely be ready to run."

"Good. I am too." Jesselynn inhaled the fragrance of clean horse, which was better in her mind than any perfume, even those made in Paris. She rubbed the stallion's ears and smoothed his black forelock. "You been behavin'? You know I got in a mighty lot of trouble this mornin' to come ride you, so don't you go givin' me any sass, that clear?" The Thoroughbred nodded as if he understood every word.

Joseph gave her a leg up. "If'n I din' know better, I'd think you was a boy, up der like dat." Joseph shook his head. "What this world a'comin' to?" He led the prancing stallion out to the half-mile track, all bounded with white board fences and dug every week to keep the sand loose so as not to injure the legs of the Thoroughbreds that trained on it. Twin Oaks Farm had turned out some of the top winners at Keeneland Track in Lexington, and buyers came from all around the South when the Twin Oaks' yearlings went on sale every November.

Jesselynn let the old man ramble. He'd been the one to pick her up after she fell off her first pony. Her brothers had been laughing too hard to help. She lifted her face to the sun, barely peeking over the horizon, too new to burn off the morning coolness. Why would anyone want to waste this perfect part of the day in bed? Of course that was why she was able to sneak out the way she did. Her mother slept so poorly of late that she no longer rose at first light. Her two younger sisters liked to lie abed, then, though they were barely old enough to put their hair up, play at dressing up and weddings before joining Jesselynn in the schoolroom. When Jesselynn had called their preferences "rot" and a few other choice phrases, Miriam Highwood had admonished her eldest daughter to never again use those words—a southern gentlewoman did not even *think* them.

Life was a conundrum, it certainly was. After trotting once around the track to warm the stallion up, Jesselynn leaned forward and stroked her mount's neck. "Okay, old son, let's see what you can do. You need to be really tough for the running of the Futura next month." She leaned over his withers and loosened the reins. Ahab leaped forward, gaining speed with every stride. Fence posts blurred and other horses being worked by young slaves in training flashed past. She pulled him up when she saw the entrance to the track flash past the second time.

Her eyes watered and her heart sang. Bit by bit she eased him back down to a hand gallop and then to an even canter. She'd pulled him down to a trot before they stopped in front of Joseph, who waited with stopwatch in hand.

The five-year-old stallion tossed his head, speckling her chest and face with globs of foam. Jesselynn wiped her eyes and brushed the bits of white away. "He did real fine, didn't he?"

"Yessum, dat he did. I surely do wish you could ride him at de track. We'd have us a winner fo' sho'." He checked the stopwatch again and chuckled. His grin flashed white in the sun against his dark face.

"Maybe that can be arranged." Jesselynn leaped to the ground and started walking the horse out.

"Now, don' you be gettin' any ideas, chile."

"Oh, I wouldn't do that." The words may have been correct, but the expression in her green eyes told the old man she was cooking up a scheme. Everyone knew what good schemes she brewed.

Hounds baying made her look toward the long oak-lined drive. "Father's home. Come on, horse, let's get you washed down and . . ."

Joseph took the reins. "You go on up dere. We takes care of Ahab here." The groom nodded toward the house.

Jesselynn shot him a smile of gratitude. He never broke her father's rule that when you rode the horse, you made sure he was cared for, no matter if you were half starving or bleeding. But today was different. Something was in the air—they all sensed it.

She found her father slumped in a rocking chair on the shaded front portico. He'd leaned his head against one of the white pillars and closed his eyes. The lines of fatigue etching his face made him look much older than his forty-five years. He looked as though he'd been days and nights without sleep. Love for him welled up in her heart, so painful it brought tears to the back of her throat. The thought of a world without her father was beyond comprehension.

She sank down on her knees beside his chair and laid a gentle hand on his arm. "Father, what is it?"

He covered her hand with his own. "War, my dear. There will be war, and there's nothing more I, or anyone else, can do to prevent it."

CHAPTER ONE

Twin Oaks Farm
Mid-September 1862

"You have . . . to get our . . . horses out of Kentucky. You're . . . the only one left who can." Major Joshua Highwood, brought home by his slave Benjamin after they'd been wounded in the battle at Kingston, lay in his own bed, being eaten alive by gangrene. He raised himself up on one elbow. The struggle to get closer to his daughter's face brought sweat to his brow and an even greater weakness to his voice. "Jesselynn, I told you to take them away two years ago, and you didn't do it." He sank back on his pillows and closed his eyes, every breath a struggle. The stench of putrid flesh permeated the room. "I know . . . far too much to ask . . . of a young . . . woman."

Jesselynn felt as if she'd been stabbed through the heart with one of her father's swords. "I know, but Adam and Zachary said . . . and you were already off fighting . . . and Mama so—oh, Father, forgive me." At this point she wasn't sure which Father she needed forgiveness from most, heavenly or earthly.

"I know child. I do. T-too much . . ."

She leaned closer to hear him.

"Your mother, right there at the foot of the bed. And a man in white standing right behind her." He rose up, a smile breaking over his entire face. "I'm coming, my dear. Only a moment." He lay back and turned his head to look directly into Jesselynn's tear-filled eyes. "Promise me."

"Yes, I will, I will. Oh, Father, don't leave me." But it was too late. She could tell he'd already left her. All that remained was his broken body and the smile he wore to greet the woman he'd loved since childhood.

Jesselynn laid her head on the sheet and let the tears she'd been holding back for two long years pour forth. She cried for the father just gone to meet his God and his dear wife. If Jesselynn hadn't believed in a life after death, she surely did now. She cried for her brother Adam, who was killed in action, and for Zachary, if alive. Only God knew where he was. She cried for the man who'd captured her heart and then been ordered out before they could marry, he, too, a casualty of the tragedy they called war. But mostly she cried for her mother, who'd died not long after the birth of baby Thaddeus. No longer could she hold the grief at bay.

"God, it is too much. I cannot bear this, I cannot." Heavy, pushing her down like a huge man with strong arms, the weight of her grief seemed to crush her beyond repair.

With her tears finally spent, she pushed herself to her feet, staggering about with a weakness beyond belief. She'd have to tell the others. She paused. The keening from the slave quarters had already begun, so the word, in a way known only to the black slaves, would pass from one plantation to another. One by one the house slaves tiptoed in to say good-bye to their master. Tears flowed freely, and Lucinda left the room with her apron over her head, sobs shaking her rounded shoulders.

Jesselynn thought about going to wake her little brother, Thaddeus, the son born not long before Major Highwood left to prepare for war. Poor child might only remember meeting his father when the man was too ill to do more than pat the boy's cheek. She chose to let him sleep. Tomorrow would be soon enough to tell him that they now had neither mother nor father. While he was too young to understand, he must be told. She sank down in the leather armchair in her father's study. Here was where she'd been conducting what little business the plantation had done since the war started. She'd shipped tobacco last fall, but this year, thanks to the drought, the crop looked meager. Picking and drying should start soon. That first November they'd had their annual yearling sale too, netting a goodly sum that carried them through. There would be none this fall. Both armies in the war were conscripting all the horses they could find.

"Take the horses and leave," her father had said. *How can I? What about Thaddeus? Go to Uncle Hiram's? I don't know the way.* Thoughts

raced through her mind like the foals romping in the springtime. Surely her father didn't really expect this of her. He'd been ill, that's all. It had been the ravings of a dying man.

But she had promised.

She and the remaining slaves had been hiding what horses they had left in case a patrol came by and demanded all the horseflesh available. So many men and fine animals used for cannon fodder. Even Adam, on his first and only leave, couldn't get over the mind-less brutality of war. She'd never forget the look in his eyes that said he'd faced the devil himself, with his fellowmen caught in the cross-fire. He had never come home again. Was buried in some unmarked grave, she supposed. All she knew for certain was that he'd been identified as killed in action. She sometimes wondered if his slave, Sammy, had died too or had run off to fight for the North. Know-ing the name of a battle site wasn't important to her either. They were all casualties—sons and fathers, brothers, cousins, and friends.

If she left, what would happen to Twin Oaks? Who would care for the slaves remaining? Who would oversee the harvest, the spring planting? Maybe she could come back in time for that. Surely the war would be over by next spring. Surely.

"Can I get you anythin' else, Missy?" Lucinda, with her dignity pulled around her like the shawl she wore in the winter, stopped just inside the doorway.

Jesselynn shook her head. Since her mother died, Lucinda had appointed Jesselynn head of the household and deferred to her ac-cordingly. Sometimes Jesselynn wished for a scolding like former days. More often she wished for her mother's lap, a place of refuge where she could pour out her hopes and fears and be comforted by that loving hand on her head. But no more. And now Father was gone too. "You go on to bed. Tomorrow will be a busy day with neighbors coming to call. I'll send one of the stable hands 'round with a note, not that there are many left to come calling. I'm sure Reverend Benson will conduct the funeral on Friday. He was sur-prised Father lived this long."

"You not gonna wait for de young missies?"

Again Jesselynn shook her head. "They're safer where they are. Carrie Mae will have her wedding at Aunt Sylvania's, and Louisa is more help there in the hospital than she ever could be here." Jesse-lynn propped her head on her hand and rested her elbow on the rolled arm of the chair where her father had so often done the same.

If she thought about it, she could still smell his cigar smoke. But it was a dream. He hadn't sat here smoking for over two years. Ever since he left before the war began. A fire that had been smoldering in her breast unbeknownst to her flickered, and a thin flame reached for air. The war—always the war. How could a loving God countenance something so destructive?

"Have some lemonade, Missy. Might be you feel better wit a cool drink." Lucinda crossed her arms across her bosom.

Jesselynn gave in. No matter how hard she tried to make life easier for this woman, she failed every time. If Lucinda believed lemonade would be a help, it would be. And she'd better get used to it. "Thank you, and then you go on to bed."

The harrumph that floated back to her told her exactly what the woman thought of going to bed before her mistress.

What would she do about Lucinda and the other house slaves? Could they stay here, or would some lowlife steal them and sell them down the road?

Jesselynn rose. The decisions to be made were too momentous to undertake sitting down. Crickets sang outside the window when she stopped to peer into the darkness. "God, what am I to do?" She waited, but no answer seemed to be forthcoming. Who could she ask for advice? Her mother would say to ask the Lord. She just had. Her mother would say to wait for an answer. She hadn't—unless you called five minutes waiting. Perhaps He'd give her an answer in a dream overnight. Her father always said, "The Lord guides His children in mysterious ways, but He guides them." Tears choked her throat. She'd never hear either of their beloved voices again.

She thanked Lucinda for the lemonade and, after blowing out the lamp, carried her glass up the stairs, sipping as she went. Lucinda was right. A cool drink did help, even when watered by a renewed burst of tears. They were never coming back. None of them.

———————

She came down in the morning to find her father lying in state in the parlor, resplendent in his best uniform, which had been cleaned and patched so the bullet holes no longer showed. Lucinda and her helpers had created a long table by covering sawhorses with boards and draping them in black. Her father appeared to be sleeping peacefully, a pleasant dream giving him a slight smile. She remembered the glory of his face just before he died. Had the man in white been his Savior?

She crossed the hall to the study and sat down at the desk, then began writing: a note for one of the slaves to carry around announcing the death, letters to the dear sisters so far away, and a note to Reverend Benson reiterating her request for a simple burial service to be performed the next afternoon.

A longer letter went to her father's brother, Hiram Highwood, who owned a large horse farm in southern Missouri. Had her father ever written his brother, as he said he would, and asked permission for them to take the horses there? They had never received an answer if he had.

The more she thought about it, the more certain she felt that she should keep her promise to her father. Surely no soldiers that far away would care about the few remaining horses of Twin Oaks. Missouri seemed at the western edge of the world, even though she'd read about California and Oregon. Gratitude welled up in her heart for a place of refuge. Missouri it would be. Far out in the country, away from all the scouting patrols of either blue or gray. Safe until the end of the war. She called Meshach to harness a wagon and take the letters to Midway to mail and pick up supplies at the general store.

The singing and wailing from the slave quarters continued all through the day as local friends and dignitaries came to pay their respects. Lucinda and her helpers kept the dining room table covered with food, much of which Jesselynn was surprised to discover they still had in the larder. Lucinda had been known to work miracles, and this seemed to be another one. When Jesselynn tried to catch the black woman's eye, Lucinda looked the other way. Some things Jesselynn had learned to leave well enough alone, and the kitchen was one, even if she was the mistress now.

Jesselynn joined a group of men to thank them for coming, and listened to their talk of the war.

"I knew Kentucky shoulda seceded, along with the other states. But at least we are in Confederate hands, where we belong," one man was saying.

"Those bumbling idiots in Frankfort—they don't have no idea what we all want," another added.

"You mark my words, there'll be fighting even in Lexington if we don't watch out. You want soldiers battling right here on our lands?"

One of the men turned to her. "I'm sorry, Miss Jesselynn, this isn't polite conversation for womenfolk to hear. So sorry about Joshua. We lost a fine man."

"Thank you." She nodded, glancing around at the men gathered. "Thank you for coming." She stepped back. "Now, if you'll excuse me, I . . ." She had to leave before she told them what she *really* thought about the war.

"If Governor Hughes would . . ."

"Get that nigger lover out of the White House . . ."

Their discussion followed her across the room to a gathering of women.

"Jesselynn darlin', how are you holdin' up?" A slender woman, her hair now silvered and wearing black mourning for her own son, put her arm around Jesselynn's waist.

Jesselynn swallowed and forced a smile to lips that would rather quiver. "I'm fine." She could feel tears threaten to erupt. *Fine? What do you mean fine?* If she didn't get out of here she would make a spectacle of herself. "Excuse me, please, I think . . . I . . ." She nodded around the circle and fled.

She kept the sobs at bay by walking to the rose garden, all the time ordering herself to behave, to be brave and act as her mother would have wanted. She blew her nose, returned to the house, and picked up a tray of small cakes before returning to the front portico. Offering food kept others from getting too close.

Through sheer will, Jesselynn kept a smile on her face, feeling like a ghost in the black dress of mourning. Thaddeus clung to her, refusing her suggestion that he go out and play with the neighbor children who came calling with their parents. Finally she had Ophelia, the boy's nursemaid, come and carry him off for a nap. He was far too young to understand what was going on anyway.

"Thank you for coming. No, I haven't heard from Zachary. Yes, it was a miracle Father was able to come home to die." Her answers became rote, leaving her mind free to run through her plans. Thank heaven her mother had instilled in her gracious manners and a backbone of iron, both required of a woman of her station.

By the time the last carriage and wagon rolled down the oak-lined drive and the last horse and rider trotted after, she felt like lying down on the floor and wailing, just as she could hear Thaddeus doing. Ophelia carried him down the stairs, his tear-streaked face flushed and sweaty.

"I can't make 'im stop cryin'. He won't shush fo' nothin'." The slender woman with skin the color of strong tea patted his back, but the child pushed away from her, his attention focused on Jesselynn.

"Come here, baby." Jesselynn stepped forward and took him in her arms. Like a fledgling coming home to roost, Thaddeus buried his face in the softness of her neck. She propped him on her hip and patted his back with her other hand. "There now, you mustn't treat Ophelia so. You hurt her feelings." A sniff greeted her teasing voice. "Come, let's have a smile." She kissed his cheek and blew back a lock of soft golden hair. Would John's and her child have looked like this—a cherub right off a Raphael painting? Jesselynn closed off the thought. John Follett was dead, like so many others. She thought of the discussions she'd overheard that afternoon between several of the young women. She agreed with them. There wouldn't be many men of marrying age left in the South when this war was over.

Besides not being the world's greatest beauty, she had an annoying habit of speaking her mind, something no southern gentleman tolerated well. She knew what she looked like. Skin that freckled when out in the sun, where she'd spent much of her time planting, hoeing, and, lately, harvesting the garden. Sometimes she helped in the fields when necessary. While John had said her hair was the color of honey fresh from a beehive and her slightly tilted eyes when laughing sparkled like dewdrops on spring green blades of grass, she had a hard time believing that now. The mirror told her that her hair looked more like straw and her eyes more gray than green of late. There hadn't been much to laugh about for the last two years. Too, she'd been graced with a figure that lacked the prerequisites of womanhood. Instead of blossoming, it remained stick straight and nearly flat to boot. Her mother always said it was her chin that would get her in trouble—square and determined. She'd learned to not lead with it, thanks to her brothers. Boxing lessons had *not* been for the girls, but Jesselynn had watched and let her brothers practice enough on her that she learned the basics. Learning to shoot a rifle had come about the same way, but much to her brothers' delight and consternation, she could outshoot both of them. Bagging a squirrel leaping from limb to limb brought her high accolades.

She buried her face in the little boy's tummy and made splattery noises to hear him laugh. If only she could switch from tears to tickles as fast as he.

"You charm him like nobody else." Ophelia now wore the relieved smile of someone who'd turned her charge over with gratitude. "He don't know him daddy gone."

"He didn't know his daddy at all, more's the pity." Jesselynn tickled Thaddy's tummy when he raised his shirt. And again. One thing with this one, once you started something, he kept it going long past anyone else's desire. Jesselynn enjoyed the game as much as he. How could she take a child this young with her to Missouri?

It wasn't as if they were going to load up the carriage and travel in comfort as they used to. Would Ophelia go along? She'd been trading flirty glances with Meshach, formerly second to Joseph down at the stables. Jesselynn had appointed him overseer of the fields and the hands who worked them. Though Meshach *could* manage the plantation while she was gone, he would have to go along with her to Missouri. There was no one else she trusted to keep them safe. And Ophelia would go anywhere if she thought it would give her time with Meshach.

Jesselynn gave the boy in her arms an extra squeeze and handed him back to his nursemaid. A headache had started at the base of her skull and was working its way around to the front. "Too much thinkin'," Lucinda would say, but as far as Jesselynn could tell, thinking never hurt anyone. In fact, her father had spoken highly of it, for both men and women, including his wife, daughters, sons, and slaves. Why did every thought weave its way back to her father? And every time, tears followed the same thread.

She sniffed and dug for a handkerchief in the pocket of her black silk mourning dress. After blowing her nose, she forced a smile onto lips that would rather tremble and took in a deep breath. "Well now, Ophelia, let's light the candles in the parlor, and after supper we can all gather there and I'll read from the 'Good Book,' as Father called it. We will rejoice that he has gone home to be with his Lord and my mother. At least, we will try to rejoice." She led the way into the kitchen, where one of Lucinda's grandchildren was snapping beans.

"Henry, go on down to the quarters and tell everyone we will have a hymn-sing tonight after supper."

"An' don' you dawdle." Lucinda's admonition made him pick up his feet even faster. "Supper be ready soon, and, Missy, you needs to rest up a spell. Ophelia come git you when we's ready."

Jesselynn nodded. Did she look as bad as she felt? She mounted the stairs to her room and collapsed on the rose-sprigged counterpane. White lace suspended by the four posters of the bed created a roof above her head. She'd tied the mosquito netting back this morning as she had every morning for years. All her life she'd gone to sleep in this room except for the times she'd been visiting a friend or relative. She'd never been farther than Lexington, twenty miles away, and that only for the races at Keeneland. Would life ever be the same again? She rolled her aching head from side to side. Stupid question. Of course, it never would. While today was bad, tomorrow would be even worse.

"Dust to dust, ashes to ashes..." Reverend Benson poured a handful of rich Kentucky soil in the shape of a cross on the pine box. "In the name of the Father, Son, and Holy Spirit, amen." He signaled the mourners, and together they turned and filed out of the iron-fenced family plot. A live oak, centuries old by the size of it, shaded the final resting place of Joshua Highwood, his wife Miriam, and the two children who died before the age of five. Two field workers remained and began shoveling the dirt back in on top of the box.

Jesselynn heard the thuds echo on the wooden cover. She would return in the evening with a spray of roses from the garden and dust grass seed on the mound so it wouldn't be so harsh. The graveyard had become a place for rest and contemplation for many of the family members. Squirrels raced through the overhanging branches of the oak, pelting the ground with shells, while birds sang their courtship arias. A camellia bloomed in the spring, dropping pale pink petals over the graves. Through the benevolence of Mother Nature, helped along by the women of the Highwood family, the burying plot had become a place of peace in spite of the sadness.

Jesselynn looked back again. This too she would be leaving, her parents, grandparents, and great-grandparents, along with various uncles and aunts and more cousins than she cared to count. Her family history. *Please God, don't let anyone ransack this sacred place as they have others.* She breathed the prayer and clutched her Bible in trembling fingers. God promised to watch out for orphans, and now that's what they were.

Coming out of her reverie, Jesselynn recalled her manners and stopped the preacher before he could climb into his buggy. "Won't you stay for a cool drink and some of Lucinda's lemon cookies, Reverend Benson?"

"Why, thank you, Miss Jesselynn, I most certainly would." The white-haired cleric placed his Bible and prayer book on the seat of the buggy and turned to follow his hostess to the portico, where she gestured him to one of the rocking chairs. He settled himself with a sigh and pulled the clerical band away from his perspiring neck. "Thank the good Lord for shade, breeze, and a tall glass of lemonade of Lucinda's secret recipe. I've sat here many a time and enjoyed all three." He looked across the braided rug to the young woman in the opposite chair. "Your father sat in that chair, telling me of his dreams for his family and for Kentucky. What a loss for all of us." He shook his head. "Such a waste."

His gentle voice made Jesselynn fight the tears again. She had made it to this point of the day without a tear shower, but if he kept on like this, another wasn't far away.

"What do you plan to do now?"

His question caught her up short. She couldn't tell him they still had horses on the plantation, for someone might ask him, and he'd be obliged to tell them. She was sure he didn't lie well, as neither did she. But she had to start practicing sometime, and now was as good a time as any.

"I-I'm not sure." That part was certainly the truth. "I might go visit my aunt in Memphis." Jesselynn cleared her throat. "She's been ailin'."

"Is that where Carrie Mae and Louisa are staying?"

"Ah, no. They're with Aunt Sylvania in Richmond." Truth again. Maybe that was the trick, mix truth and stories, so one couldn't tell where one began or left off.

"You are fortunate to have family to turn to. I know these years have been terribly hard for you."

"But no more than for all the others around here. The war is draining everyone, and as my father so frequently said, 'It will get nothing but worse.' If only heads like his had prevailed instead of those foolish hotheads who thought we would win the war in a matter of weeks." Pictures floated through her mind of her brothers cheering the news of Fort Sumter being fired on, thinking war was glory and honor instead of death and destruction. While some of their friends and relatives were Union sympathizers, like her father, most of the young men she knew talked secession. She brought her attention back to the man beside her.

"Yes, even if God is on our side, war is—"

Jesselynn tossed her manners over the white-painted railing, interrupting with a decidedly unladylike snort. "You don't really believe that drivel, do you?

"What is that, my dear?"

"That God is on our side? This is war, Reverend Benson. God is on neither side. He is stepping back to let us destroy each other, and when we're finished, He will need another flood to wash the blood away—the blood that brothers fighting brothers shed." She clenched her fingers over the curved arms of the rocker. "This is no holy war, Reverend." She turned at Lucinda's throat clearing. Looking at her old mammy's face, she knew she'd overstepped the bounds of propriety.

"Excuse me." Jesselynn pulled a handkerchief from her sleeve and rose to her feet. "Please make yourself comfortable, and I'll be back in a few minutes. Ah . . . pardon me. I-I'm not myself." She took three steps before Reverend Benson made it to his feet.

"I'm sure if you feel that way, there is no more use for me here." He clapped his hat on his head and thundered down the three steps. "Good thing your mother and father weren't here to listen to such sacrilege. All our brave boys fightin' for our very existence." He glared at her one more time. "I do pray you will come to your senses, Miss Jesselynn."

Whatever had gotten into her? Ignoring the sense that she should make things right, she entered the study and closed the door, willing herself to calm down. She could feel her heart racing, pumping blood to her face so that hours spent in the sun couldn't have made it hotter. She took several deep breaths, bracing her hands on the flat surface of her father's desk. Well, so much for propriety. She'd practiced lying, gone on a political tirade, and deeply offended her pastor, all in a few short minutes.

She was glad he left. The thought of facing him again made her cheeks burn hotter. What would her mother say to this?

"Missy Jesselynn!"

She raised her head. The call came again. She could tell by the panic in the tone that the child calling her needed her *now*. She spun around and hurried to the back steps.

"Missy Jess, Yankees comin' up the drive. Dey's gonna murder us all." The child's eyes rolled white in his round black face.

"Nonsense. You run to the stables and make sure the horses are hidden. Go now!"

The little boy took off as if the Union soldiers rode right on his heels.

Jesselynn took a deep breath to compose herself and walked back to the front portico. Sure enough, a group of horsemen were riding up the drive. Even if she hadn't been warned, from this distance she could see they wore uniforms of blue.

CHAPTER TWO

"Lucinda, go make more lemonade."

"Yessum."

Jesselynn looked around to find Meshach striding through the door as Lucinda hurried back to the kitchen. She knew the smile she gave her black field overseer went no further than barely turned-up lips, but she knew too that he understood. Or else he wouldn't be backing her up like this.

She whispered without moving her lips, "The horses?"

"Safe."

Her heart settled back to only double time. The Union soldiers trotted up the circular drive and stopped their horses ten feet from the portico steps. *At least this man has the manners to not ride all over the lawn.* The last officer to come calling hadn't been so courteous.

"Evening, ma'am." The officer in charge tipped his hat. "I'm Captain James Dorsey of the United States Army, and there have been rumors that you might have more horses to sell to the Union army." He patted the shoulder of the sorrel Thoroughbred under him. "I appreciate Roanoke here. He comes from Twin Oaks, I believe."

Jesselynn cocked an eyebrow. "Sell, sir? I don't recall evah receivin' the money promised when *that* group was taken." She deliberately deepened her accent, speaking more slowly, giving herself more time to think.

The man had the grace to look uncomfortable. "I'm sorry to hear that. I know a requisition was turned in."

"Seems, then, there was a break somewhere in the line between requisition and payment. I could surely use the money that officer promised." She nodded to the black bands circling the white pillars. "As you can see, we are in mournin' over the death of my father, so if there is nothin' else?"

"I'm sorry to hear that."

He repeats himself. He must be uncomfortable. My mother would offer them lemonade and cookies. But then my mother is dancing on the clouds of heaven with my father, and I'm the one left here.

"Would you and your men care for some lemonade?" she said and heard Meshach suck in a breath behind her. "I trust y'all would find these chairs more comfortable than your saddles." She indicated the rocking chairs and padded lounges grouped so invitingly off to either side of the front door.

The captain tipped his hat again. "That we would, and we appreciate your hospitality." He nodded to the officer mounted to his left.

"Dismount!" The crisp command cut through the settling dusk. Doves cooing in the magnolia trees by the house set up a startled cry, and a flurry of wing flapping spoke of their agitation.

At the rattle of sabers and jingling harness, a black-and-tan hound came growling around the corner of the pillared white house with teeth bared, the hackles raised on the back of his neck.

Jesselynn felt like doing the same but kept her best company smile in place. She could barely hear the ratcheting song of the cicadas above the beating of her heart.

Meshach crossed the porch in silent strides and, murmuring to the dog, took him back behind the house. Within seconds the man was back, always standing to the rear of Jesselynn but an imposing presence nonetheless.

Jesselynn knew he would do everything in his power to protect her should there be any aggression on the part of the Union soldiers. All five of them, spurs and sabers clanking, strode up the two wide steps and took a seat.

Her face a mask of resentment, Lucinda passed around a tray of glasses, already sweating from the September heat. Ophelia followed her with a plate of cookies left over from the funeral.

Neither of the women responded to the polite thank-yous from the blue-coated men.

"I appreciate your hospitality, ma'am, but I have to ask again. Do you have any horses remaining here at Twin Oaks?"

Such audacity when this is Confederate country. She glanced toward the horses being held by one of her own slaves. "Those were the last, other than a team of mules we use in the fields and to pull our wagon. Would you take everything that helps to keep us alive?"

"No, ma'am, I don't want to do that, but I'm sure you wouldn't mind if I send a couple of my men to search the stables and barns?"

Jesselynn smiled sweetly. "Why no, sir, we wouldn't mind that one little bit. But this time, please leave the hens alone. Took them three weeks to start layin' again after your last visit."

A snort from one of the men made her smile more widely. "Other than that, we have nothin' left to hide."

"You understand, this is not my . . ." The captain stopped and nodded to three enlisted men. "And don't disturb anyone or anything not connected to the horses."

A considerate Yankee. Now, if that isn't an oxymoron. In spite of all that had gone on, Jesselynn still enjoyed using a new word when she could. Now was a good opportunity. As the three left the portico, she nodded for Lucinda to pass the tray again. "Please, help yourselves. Not many bl—" She cut off the term "bluebellies" and reframed her sentence. "I reckon not many of those from the North have an opportunity to taste Lucinda's secret recipe for lemonade."

The captain's eyes twinkled, but he answered gravely. "Then we are all the more grateful that you would share this with us." He lifted his glass.

Lucinda harrumphed behind Jesselynn's chair. Without looking, Jesselynn knew the expression on the woman's face was anything but pleasant. The thin cry of a restless child floated down from the open upstairs window.

"Excuse me, please. My little brother has had a terribly hard day, and I must go to him." Jesselynn stood as she spoke, causing the Union officers to rise also. Again she was surprised at their manners. The patrol who came before had shown none.

"Please, Miss Highwood, accept our condolences on the death of your father. And of course you must see to your brother."

Jesselynn almost choked on her smile. If it hadn't been for the war, her father would still be alive, along with her brothers. And this man had the gall to offer condolences? "Well, I reckon I must say thank you, sir. I'll return as soon as I can. Please, make yourselves comfortable." *Mama, if you only knew what your training is costing me.* With a glance at her two slaves that conveyed an order to not only remain where they were but to behave properly, she left the porch in a swirl of skirts. While she no longer wore hoops due to the war, she had donned extra petticoats that morning, so she was closer to fashionable dressing than at any time in the past year.

After all, an old maid like herself didn't need to dress in her finest, as if there were such gowns available any longer. She'd dyed two of her dresses black when her mother died and kept them for mourning. She had already put them to repeated use what with all the funerals in the vicinity.

"Thank you, Thaddy, for getting me away from them," she muttered as she swiftly climbed the curving walnut staircase to the second floor.

"Lynnie." His cry came more pitifully. He had yet to be able to say her full name.

She pushed the door to his room all the way open and crossed the woven reed rug to lift him from his net-draped crib. "Hush now, baby, I'm here."

He sniffled into her neck and stuck his thumb back in his mouth. "Eat supper?" He sniffed again.

She patted his back and swayed from side to side, calming him with the rocking motion. "Not yet, but soon." She stroked the soft golden hair from his sweaty forehead and kissed his flushed cheek. Crossing to the basin, she held him with one arm and poured tepid water into the bowl from the matching pitcher painted with pink roses. Then dipping a cloth and squeezing it dry, she wiped his face around the hand attached to the thumb in his mouth.

"Daddy home?"

"No, dear, Daddy's gone."

"To war?"

"No." Tears clutched her throat and watered her eyes. "Daddy's gone to heaven to be with Mama and Jesus." Sometimes she wished he didn't talk so well. Or that he was older and could understand. How do you explain death to a baby little more than two years old? Especially one who had now lost both his parents and never knew his mother at all. She set him down on the changing table and checked his diaper. "Good boy. You are still dry. How about tryin' the pot?"

Anything to keep from going back down to the portico.

"Good boy." She praised him when she heard the tinkle in the chamber pot and, after dressing him again, could think of no real reason to not join the officers down below. Other than that she didn't want to. She refused to think of them as guests. At least her mother had not had to deal with army officers on conscription forays. *But you would have known how to behave and would have charmed them so that they would have forgotten all about the horses. Oh, Lord, please help me. We can't lose the rest of the breeding stock or Twin Oaks stud will be no more.*

Sometimes she wondered if the Lord really cared about the carnage going on, let alone the horses. As her father had said in the beginning, this was a fight between brothers, not between warring nations. Sometimes she wished she'd been able to leave as her sisters had, to get away from making decisions here, to get away to safety. Which was the reason she had sent both Louisa and Carrie Mae to Richmond to be with their aunt Sylvania—to keep them safe from marauding soldiers.

She carried Thaddeus down the back stairs and left him playing on the kitchen floor with Lucinda's two grandchildren. She'd rather stay and play with them and the kittens than go back to being the hostess. She stepped through the front door as the three enlisted men returned from the stables.

"Nothing there, sir." One saluted as he spoke. "Except for the two mules like she said and a milk cow."

"Please don't take the cow. My little brother needs the milk." She tried to keep a note of panic from her voice.

"We aren't in the habit of leaving women and children destitute." The captain rose to his feet. He set his glass back on the tray Lucinda held and nodded his thanks. "Sergeant," he said, giving a silent order.

"Mount up!" The command cut through the air, all official once more.

Captain Dorsey set his blue felt hat back on his head and touched two fingers to the brim. "Ma'am, sorry to inconvenience you regarding the horses. But just in case you happen to find any running loose, we will be on the watch."

Was that a twinkle she caught in his eye or a trick of the light? Jesselynn didn't take time to ponder the thought. "I'm sure you will be, and if there were any horses running loose, why, Captain, what a surprise that would be to all of us." *As if we'd let our horses run loose!*

The men mounted, and the captain tipped his hat again. "Good evening, Miss Highwood, and I am indeed sorry about the death of your father. From everything I hear of him, he was a fine man."

Jesselynn swallowed hard. The tears she'd kept reined in all day now threatened to break loose. "Yes, sir, he was." She watched the straight-shouldered, blue-clad backs as they trotted their horses down the long drive. Speaking of fine men, she had a feeling she'd just met one. If only he'd worn gray instead of blue.

She shook her head and turned back to the house. As soon as they'd had supper, she needed to finish the letter to Uncle Hiram and begin the thank-you notes to those who'd left gifts today. How soon could she possibly leave? Who would she take? Who would stay? And who would protect those who remained behind?

She'd just sat down to the table when one of the young hands skidded through the door.

"Rider comin', Missy."

"Friend or . . ."

"Sojer, I thinks."

Jesselynn dropped her napkin on the table. "Blue or gray?"

"Too dark." But the boy shook his head. "Bad 'un, I specs."

"Benny, what do you mean?"

Quiet as a shadow, Meshach took his place behind her as soon as she stepped on the porch.

The horse's front feet nearly clattered on the first step as the rider yanked his mount to a stop.

"So, they didn't find 'em, did they?"

The sneering voice of their ex-overseer sent shivers chasing up her spine.

"I was watchin'."

"Find what?" The thought of Second Lieutenant Cavendar Dunlivey of the Confederate army keeping a watch on Twin Oaks made her want to take out a gun herself.

CHAPTER THREE

"My father told you never to set foot on this place again."

Dunlivey shook his head, his smile sinister in its beauty. "Yer *father* ain't here no more, Missy, and I come to get what is rightfully mine."

If only he was as handsome inside as out. The thought made her choke. All she could see now was evil. Jesselynn kept her hands away from protecting her middle with a burst of anger that she refused to let show. That was what he wanted, to see her cringe. She clamped her teeth together to keep the words she wanted to scream at him inside until she could speak civilly. Dunlivey had abused the slaves, stolen from her father, and then asked for her hand in marriage, claiming it was his right, since he had done so much to keep the plantation running. He knew every inch of the land.

She raised her chin, tightening her backbone at the same time. "If you don't leave now, you may never leave."

She heard a gasp from behind her while at the same time she felt Meshach move a step closer. She knew he carried the rifle at his side.

"Think yer better'n anyone else, that's what," Dunlivey said in a threatening voice. "But now I got you. Givin' succor to the enemy, you was." He narrowed his eyes and leaned slightly forward in the saddle. "I aim to get me those horses, Missy, and I aim to get you right along with them." His words hissed worse than a water moccasin. "Those slaves you try so hard to protect will work for me again, I promise you. Or they goes down the river. Bring in good money, they will."

"You want I should shoot him now?" The click of a hammer drawn back sounded loud as a rifle crack in the stillness. One of the other slaves whimpered.

"No, then we'd have to bury him, and I don't want to soil our hands handling varmints like him." She watched as the fury built within the man and exploded.

Yanking his horse back, he screamed at her, froth erupting in spittle that bathed his mount. "I'll get you, all a'you, if it's the last thing I do."

"I reckon it just may be that if you don't turn and head on back the way you came. Next time we catch you on Twin Oaks land, there won't be any talkin' first."

"Next time, Missy, I won't be alone. This time was a warnin' outa the goodness of my heart."

"I sincerely doubt your body contains such an organ." She beckoned Meshach, who raised the gun. "If you've forgotten, we're all trained to shoot." She nodded to her slave. "Make sure you hit him in the heart so we can keep the horse."

Dunlivey's glare was so filled with hate, she almost stepped back. She wanted to run and hide, but she kept her place.

He spun his horse, applied spurs, and tore down the curving drive. "The South needs those horses of yourn, so now you can be shot as traitors." His diatribe trailed behind him.

Jesselynn blinked at his final scream that seemed to echo through the trees. Traitors. Was that what they were, simply for trying to keep something that would ensure their livelihood when this terrible calamity was finally over? *Who'd believe it?*

"Dat man be the hate-fullest man I ever knowed," Lucinda said with a huff. "Never in my life be so glad to see someone daid."

"That's not the Christian way," Jesselynn said, turning with a gentle smile. "At least that's what Mother would have said."

"Yo' daddy shoulda shot him long time ago." Meshach shook his head. "Some men born mean and jus' get meaner. He one." With dusk faded to night, Meshach could disappear into the darkness as long as he didn't smile. "He might could have a accident 'tween here and town."

"No. There'll be no killin' around here. This war has done enough of that." Jesselynn turned and entered the house. "We have some figurin' to do. Dunlivey will *not* get our horses." *If only I had done what Daddy said back in the beginning, we'd have all the horses left,*

not just the few. Why, oh why, did I listen to those brothers of mine? "The war'll be over in three weeks. The South can't be beaten. God is on our side."
"Ha!"

But who am I to take the horses out of here? A woman traveling with five Thoroughbreds? Fine bet that I'd get anywhere. Entire plantations have been lost on bets less than that. Oh, God, what am I to do?

After putting Thaddy to bed, she returned to her father's study, positioning the lamp so she could work at his desk. Though she'd been managing the plantation since her mother died and the men were at war, deciding to leave it was the most difficult decision she'd ever had to make.

"Oh, Lord, who should stay? Who will keep them safe? Who should go with us? Should I take them all?" While waiting for answers, she penned another letter to her sisters, describing the funeral and ordering them to stay where they were. There was nothing they could do at Twin Oaks. She didn't tell them her fears for their home. Other great houses had been burned to the ground, and no one knew for sure who was responsible. The South said it was the northern soldiers who burned and looted and vice versa. She had a feeling the burnings were more the work of scum like Dunlivey. He wore the uniform of the South. Why hadn't he been ordered elsewhere like her father and brothers?

They could only hope Zachary was still alive, since there had been no word of his death. She shuddered at the thought of Zach being confined in a Yankee prison. The rumors they'd heard were near impossible to believe.

"Remember," she wrote, "our God is in His heavens and taking care of us here, no matter how terrible things are. All He asks is that we love and trust Him. I trust Him to care for you and for all of us here, and to bring us back together again soon." After signing the letter, she studied the words while the ink dried, wondering if she'd written the last more for herself than for them.

The lamp was flickering by the time she'd gotten through the thank-you letters from the funeral. As she stuffed the last one in the envelope, tears threatened to overflow her burning eyes.

"Daddy, why? What am I to do?"

Lucinda pushed open the door, shaking her head. "Missy, you git yourself on up to bed. De roosters be crowin' befo' you close yo' eyes." She laid a hand on her young mistress's shoulder. "Things always look better in de mornin'."

35

Jesselynn shook her head. "I don't see how. I really don't see how." Nevertheless, she blew out the kerosene lamp and followed Lucinda and her candle out the door and up the stairs, neither one of them needing the light, they'd trod these familiar halls and stairs so many times.

A breeze fluttered the white curtains at her window and the mosquito netting that had been let down to curtain her bed. Using the light from the moon, she undressed and slid between the sheets, grateful for the cooling breezes of approaching fall.

"Father, in your Word you promise to be a father to the fatherless and a husband to the widow. I need the guidance of a father and the wisdom to know what to do. You say you will both guard and guide. All of these people here depend on me—for everything. And I have nothing. I couldn't sell the plantation if I wanted to until we prove whether Zach is dead or alive. Besides there is no one to buy it anyway."

"*Get the horses out.*" She could hear her father's voice as if he were in the room with her. And she had promised. Was a promise made on a deathbed really a vow? After all, she was just a girl. Well, eighteen and once betrothed might be considered basis for womanhood. Others her age were married and had children by now.

"*Get the horses out.*" She flipped over on her other side. "*How* do I get the horses out?"

There was no answer but the breeze billowing the curtains and the call of the nighthawk foraging for insects.

———

"Britches, that's what I need!"

Dawn had barely stained the horizon lavender when she threw back the covers and brushed aside the netting. She dug in the back of the chifforobe and pulled out the trousers she used to wear when exercising the racehorses. Some more digging yielded the long-sleeved white shirt. But she knew she'd outgrown her boots. Donning the pants and shirt, she stood in front of her mirror. From her neck down, she'd pass as male. But her hair.

Scooping it up she pinned the rich mass on top of her head. A hat. Without making a sound, a skill she'd learned years earlier when exiting by the live oak, she strode down the hall to Zach's room. Surely between her two brothers' gear, there was a hat that would cover her hair. Or one of her father's would do.

She located the tan felt hat hanging in her father's closet. The odor of pipe smoke and shaving soap brought back every memory of her father. She crushed the hat to her breast and fought the tears that threatened to overwhelm her. Hadn't she already cried enough?

But no matter. The tears overflowed her lashes and rained down her cheeks, spotting the tan felt like raindrops. She buried her sobs in the bed pillows lest anyone hear and come seeking to help.

There *was* no one to help.

No one. The responsibility was all hers.

God, where are you? You were here when Mother died. Why have you deserted me now?

Birds broke the dawn hush with their morning gossip. A rooster crowed. Another answered. A horse whinnied.

Jesselynn leaped to her feet. Was it one of their horses, or was someone coming? She dashed to the window, but the long curved road remained empty.

She grabbed a handkerchief from her father's dresser drawer and wiped her eyes and nose. Ignoring the desire to let the tears flow unchecked, she sniffed and looked in the mirror. Repinning her hair, she set the hat in place, but every time she tried to pull it snug, a loop of hair drooped from the confining band.

"Fiddlesticks!" She whipped the hat off her head and jerked out the pins, letting the curls tumble down her back.

She stared in the mirror. Could she do it? While her sisters were truly lovely, she knew her hair was her best feature. Thick and glossy with curls that were the envy of both her sisters and her cousins. She glared at a chin that could only be called stubborn and eyes that still wore the red marks of her tears. At least she no longer had the milky skin so prized by ladies. Her face, neck, and arms had picked up a golden hue from working in the sun, even while wearing a hat. At least the freckles had run together to a tone of tan.

"It has to come off."

"Missy Jess, dat you in dere?"

Jesselynn rolled her eyes. Leave it to Lucinda. She glanced down at her shirt and britches. Might as well get the caterwauling over with. Touching her forehead in a one-finger salute, she strode to the door and jerked it open. "Get the scissors."

"What you aimin' to do?" Lucinda looked her up and down, shaking her head and moaning, "What yo' mama think?" over and over.

Jesselynn paused. What if someone came calling and she had no hair? She'd give the whole plan away and someone sure as shooting would notify the authorities. Cutting her hair would have to be one of the last things she did before leaving.

"I'll change right away. Just trying to make some plans," she said, pulling off the shirt and pants and tossing them on her bed. She knew better than to let Lucinda know ahead of time what would be happening. While the older woman would try to cover her feelings, her sniffs and sad eyes would announce clearly that something bad was about to happen. The speed with which news traveled from the big house to the slave quarters was nothing short of miraculous as far as Jesselynn was concerned. She donned her dress and let Lucinda button it up.

"Breakfast ready half hour," Lucinda said.

"Good, that'll give me time to check on things at the barn. Let Thaddy sleep as long as he can. Yesterday was mighty hard on him, and I don't want him sick again if we can help it."

"Yessum."

"And, Lucinda, I think it is time to bury the silver."

"I 'specs so." The tips of her knotted kerchief fluttered as she shook her head. "I been feared dis was comin'."

"Well, at least we had things nice for Daddy's funeral." Jesselynn swallowed her tears again. All she had to do was say his name or think it and her eyes burned clear back of her nose. She choked back a sigh too. Pretty soon she and Lucinda would be crying on each other's shoulders again if they kept this up.

"Dem Yankees take ever bit dey see."

"If what I've been hearing is true, it's not just the bluebellies that have been raiding the plantations. Thieves are thieves no matter what color the uniform. Dig the holes in the rose garden like we decided, and make them plenty deep enough so no saber can find them."

"Yessum. I takes care dat."

"Good. We'll eat as soon as I get back. Bake up those two hams hanging out in the coolhouse too, please."

"Dem's de last."

"I know." Jesselynn headed for the stairs, tying her straw hat under her chin as she went. "I'll be back as soon as possible." The sun had already burned the mists off the hollows when she reached the stable doors. Meshach had Ahab, their oldest stallion and son of the foundation of the Twin Oaks stud, crosstied in the hard-packed aisle so he could be cleaned of the mud from the hiding place.

"Leave him dirty. In fact, take him back and get him filthy, him and all the others. We need to disguise them somehow."

"We leavin' den?" He dropped the brushes in the bucket.

"Tonight."

"Ever'body?"

"Oh, how I wish we could stay." She unclenched her hands at her sides. "But we can't. We'll leave the house slaves and the field hands and just take the horses. I hope we will be able to come back in time for spring planting."

"Who take care dem?"

"I reckon they'll have to take care of themselves. You think Joseph can make sure the tobacco is picked and dried? I'll write and ask Embers to take care of selling it when he does his." Tod, the eldest Embers son, had come home minus a leg, but at least he came home. His father didn't.

"Dat work. I tell dem shifless niggers to get da work done or . . ."

"I wish I could leave you in charge here, but Benjamin and I can't protect the horses alone. Maybe, if things go well, we can leave them safe at Uncle Hiram's and come right back."

"Daniel good tracker. You take 'im?"

"If you think so. Lucinda will manage the house slaves and gettin' the rest of the garden put by."

"You takin' Marse Thaddy?"

"If only there were some way to send him back to Richmond to the girls." She shook her head and moved to stroke the stallion's neck. "He's so little to take along." But she knew in her heart she couldn't leave him behind. She'd never forgive herself if something happened to her baby brother. The thought of Thaddy made her think of her older brothers. Adam so young and already cannon fodder. The tears that hovered so near the surface threatened to overflow again.

"That means we take the wagon. Can you train one of the mares to harness so we can leave at least one mule here?"

"Today?" His eyebrows shot up.

"By dark."

"Lawsy, Miss Jesse, she might spook easy."

"We'll trade off as we go and get them all broke to harness. No one looks at a horse pullin' a wagon." She rubbed Ahab's ears and stroked down his cheek. "We'll get you through, old son, we will." She studied the bright white star between his dark eyes. "Better dye all their white markings and do everything you can to rough up their coats." For the first time in her life, she felt sad at the beauty and spirit of the Twin Oaks' Thoroughbreds.

Back at the house, she took the portico steps in one leap and entered the dining room just as Lucinda was setting the platter of ham and eggs in the center of the table. While Lucinda still hovered, the remainder of the household slaves took their places at the table. Jesselynn had decreed she didn't want to eat alone, and since Lucinda insisted on using the dining room, they all ate together. Meshach took his place just in time for the platter to reach him.

Jesselynn bowed her head and paused for the settling. "Heavenly Father, we thank thee for this food prepared by loving hands. Bless this day and keep us, thy children, safe from harm. Please, if Zachary is still alive, watch over him and bring him home again. In Jesus' name we pray. Amen."

She'd almost said her father's name too, as she had at all the meals in the two years he'd been gone. But now they knew where he was, in his heavenly home, along with his beloved wife and eldest son and all the other saints gone before.

Sometimes she envied them. Their troubles were over, while she had a feeling that hers were about to get worse.

An hour later, she had an inkling of how bad "worse" could get. After hours searching for the secret drawer her father told her about in one of his more lucid moments, she finally found it. When she discovered how to open it, the manumission papers she thought her father had signed were blank. He hadn't signed them as he said he had. Why? Was it all delirium? What could she do now?

CHAPTER FOUR

"Oh, Lord, what am I to do?"

As she was beginning to think was usual, no answer came forth.
Who can I ask for advice? She ran the list of neighbors through
her mind, but none of them could know she still had horses. Besides, she'd already offended most of them with her forthright views
on the war. *Why can't I keep my mouth closed like Mama would have?*

"So who can I get to look after things around here for me?" *God,
if you'd bring Zachary back, at least part of my burden would be solved.*
She felt the tears burning her eyes again. All she wanted to do right
this moment was to lay her head on the desk and bawl.

The picture of Cavendar Dunlivey screamed its way into her
mind, jerking her upright. His vow branded itself on her brain.

"You will not get the horses, nor me or my people." A shudder
made her teeth rattle at the remembered evil in his eyes. Her stomach clenched, and she tightened her jaw.

"You be needin' somethin'?" Lucinda appeared in the doorway.

"Ah, no. Thank you." Jesselynn's heart hammering against her
ribs like steel on an anvil, she forced a smile to lips too dry to
stretch. *Lucinda. How can I leave Lucinda?*

But how could she take her and the other slaves who'd been
part of her life since she was born? Her father had not traded in
slaves. He'd inherited them from his father, and when children were
born in the slave cabins, they became part of Twin Oaks. None had
ever been sold, although several had been hired out to work for
another planter. Tom the blacksmith was right now over at the
Marshes' fixing machinery. Sarah, who had healing in her hands

with herbs, often served as a midwife around the parish, and Aaron, whose woodworking skills rivaled those of fine furniture makers, had spent the last six months at a cabinet shop in Lexington.

As her father had, Jesselynn gave those who worked out a part of their wages. The remainder had helped keep Twin Oaks going.

Could she sign the papers, copy her father's signature?

She drew paper from the drawer and uncapped the ink bottle. Using one of his letters, she drew over the signature with a dry quill over and over to get the flow and feel of his hand. Then she tried it with ink. And tried again.

Bit by bit the signature drew closer to that of her father's. Sweat trickled down her spine, and once a drop from the tip of her nose blurred the last line.

"Fiddlesticks!" She felt like hurling pen and pot across the room. Getting up, she strode to the window and looked out across the tobacco fields, the large leaves rustling in a breeze. If only she could stay until the field was picked and hooked across the rods in the barn for drying.

A horse whinnied, then the sound was cut off, most likely by a hand clamped on the muzzle.

She spun back to the chair. She had to leave tonight. Before they were discovered.

Tying her hair back, she returned to the desk. She wrote on both fronts and backs of precious paper, on old envelopes, and on the empty pages at the back of the journal she kept for housekeeping expenses and for recording the amount of preserves made, meat smoked, and eggs laid.

Her hand cramped. Again she rose and went to stand at the window. The sun stood directly overhead.

Lucinda appeared in the doorway. "Dinner ready." She glanced at the mess of papers by the desk and back to Jesselynn.

Jesselynn closed the walnut doors to her father's study and followed Lucinda to the dining room, where everyone was already gathered. When she took her chair at the head of the table, they all sat and bowed their heads. No one laughed or whispered or shifted on a chair. The song of a mockingbird followed the cadence of her prayer. At the amen no one moved, they all sat staring at the plates before them.

"Is there somethin' here that I'm not aware of?" She looked up as Lucinda set the platter of corn bread in front of her, the old woman's eyes gazing straight forward. "Lucinda?"

"No, ma'am."

Jesselynn felt like looking around to see who else the solemn-faced woman could be speaking to. "Where's Thaddy, Ophelia?"

"I let 'im sleep." Ophelia looked as though someone had whipped her, her eyes staring out of her drawn face.

"All right." Jesselynn slapped her palms on the table. "What is goin' on here?"

Button, Lucinda's youngest grandson, jumped and started to wail. Ophelia shushed him, giving Jesselynn a look that screamed pure terror.

Jesselynn looked down the table to Meshach, who was studying his plate as if to memorize each green bean and corn kernel. Arms rigid, holding herself up as if all strength had drained from her legs, she turned slowly to look at Lucinda.

"What . . . is . . . it?" The pause between each word lasted seconds that crawled like hours hoeing tobacco.

"You goin' to leave us." Lucinda tied her apron in knots.

Jesselynn sank down in her chair, sure now that the escaped strength in her legs would never return. She should have known better than to think she could keep something like this a secret.

"I thought we would talk about this later today." The weakness traveled up her body, making her head float like a magnolia petal on the water. "I . . . I'm tryin' to do what is best for all of us. Go on, eat your dinner, and then we'll talk."

"You not goin' to sell us to dem slave traders." Lucinda's words snapped Jesselynn's head around.

"Lord above, whatever gave you that idea? Of course I'm not goin' to sell anyone. I'm tryin' to puzzle out how I can set y'all free."

"Don' wanna be free. Wanna be here, like always."

Jesselynn looked around the table to see all the heads bobbing. Lucinda indeed spoke for them all.

"I understand, I guess, so eat your food and then we'll talk." She knew she was probably the only woman in the parish, nay, in the entire state of Kentucky, who planned on discussing her plans with her slaves. She looked at the faces before her. Not too many others shared the dining table with black faces either. Such a thing hadn't happened while her mother and father were alive. White folks ate in the dining room, and the others in the kitchen or their cabins.

A collective sigh rose, and then bit by bit, normal mealtime chatter picked up, starting with Ophelia and passing around the table from one to the next.

Jesselynn forced the corn bread, sliced string beans, and fried ham past the lump in her throat. Even the redeye gravy over new potatoes had a hard time going down. How could she explain to them what she needed to do? Meshach knew. Thoughts beat in her head like a broody hen beating off anyone come to steal her eggs.

"You don't like de ham?" Lucinda paused in the gathering of plates.

"No, it's fine. I just . . ." Jesselynn handed her plate up.

As soon as the table was cleared, everyone looked at Jesselynn. The time had come. Lucinda sat down and took a little one on her lap.

The silence vibrated like a plucked guitar string.

Oh, Lord, help me. Please give me the words.

"Y'all heard Dunlivey yesterday." At their gasp she knew she'd started on the wrong tack. She took in a deep breath and began again. "When my father died, he made me promise I would take the horses out of Kentucky before the soldiers, either gray or blue, could conscript them, er, take them away. If we lose the horses, we will have nothing to start over with again after the war. Joseph and Meshach have been hiding them, as y'all know, but Dunlivey knows this place. If anyone can find them, he can."

A gasp leaped from mouth to mouth.

"So, I will do as my father said. I promised him, and a promise is a promise."

"Where you go?" Lucinda continued as speaker for all.

"I can't tell you that. Not because I don't trust you, but to help keep you safe. If you don't know where I've gone, then . . ."

"Den we can't tell no one."

"That too."

"One thing I can do to keep you all safe is give you your freedom papers. Then no one can sell or buy you." Chatter started, but she raised her hands for quiet. "You don't have to leave here. I will pay you wages for stayin'." Where she would get the money, she had no idea. Other than the tobacco crop. "Life will go on like always here. You all know what to do, many of you better than I do. Then when the war is over, we will raise horses and plant tobacco and soybeans and other crops, just like we always have."

She hoped they believed her words, because right now all she could think of was leaving. She, who had never been beyond Lexington, had to find their way to Uncle Hiram's in Missouri.

"Who goin' and who stayin'?" Lucinda rocked the child she held to her bosom.

"Good question. I'd take all of you if I could, but we have to travel fast and at night so we don't get stopped." Fear tasted like blood in her mouth.

"I wisht I shot Dunlivey right 'tween the eyes." Meshach muttered so quietly Jesselynn barely heard him, but the gasp from Lucinda confirmed her suspicions.

"There'd only be others." Jesselynn looked from face to face. Tear-streaked, shaking, eyes pleading, all of them were her people, her family. Leaving them defenseless—the thought made her eyes burn, and the tears running down Ophelia's cheeks called for her own tears.

She sucked another deep breath into lungs that refused to expand. The lump in her throat grew. "God will keep us all safe. The Bible, it—" She could go no further. "Excuse me." The chair rocked behind her as she left the table.

"De wagon loaded," Meshach said from the doorway to the study.

Jesselynn finished the final signature, each one appearing more like her father's as she wrote out the twenty manumission papers. Her hand cramped, and she was nearly out of ink.

"We'll leave an hour after full dark. No one should be on the roads then." She folded and slid the last sheet of paper in an envelope and wrote Meshach's name on the front. "Here."

He crossed the faded oriental rug and took it from her. "I don' need dis."

"You might."

"Joseph out here like you said."

"Good. Bring him in."

In a moment the two black men stood before her, one as tall and broad shouldered as the other was skinny and stooped. Both of them clutched their hats in their hands, wringing the life out of the brims.

"Joseph, keep this someplace safe." She handed him his envelope.

"Laws, Missy, I . . ."

"Now, Joseph, as a free man, you can leave Twin Oaks if you want, or you can take over Meshach's job as overseer and make sure the tobacco is harvested and dried." *Please, God, let him stay.*

"Where would I go? Dis my home."

Relief attacked the stiffening in her spine. A momentary slump, a swallow, and she smiled around her clenched teeth. "Thank you, Joseph. Between you and Lucinda, I know you can keep Twin Oaks together. With the garden and the hogs to butcher, you'll have enough to eat." *If you can keep it all out of the hands of either soldiers or scum.* "We will leave you guns and lead for hunting." *And to keep off the scavengers.*

"Supper ready." Ophelia, a white cloth tied around her head, spoke from the doorway.

Jesselynn scooped the remaining envelopes into a pile and straightened them. She'd give out the rest at the table and down in the cabins.

When she entered the dining room, her gaze automatically noticed the empty sideboard. No three-branched silver candlesticks, no shiny servers. Lucinda and her helpers had done as instructed. Her father's picture no longer hung on the wall, nor did her mother's. Samuel Morse had painted them both years before.

Supper passed in a flurry of tears, instructions, and questions, many of which had no answers. Thaddy sensed the tension and insisted on sitting on Jesselynn's lap, crying and shaking his head when Ophelia tried to take him.

"Ophelia, I want you to come with us to take care of our boy here."

She glanced down the table to where Meshach was eating as if nothing untoward were happening. "I goes."

Jesselynn followed Lucinda into the kitchen. "I have a mighty big favor to ask you."

Lucinda turned, arms crossed over her ample bosom.

"Lucinda." The words wouldn't come. Jesselynn fought the tears and tried again. "While I want you to come with me, there's no one else I can trust to stay here and take care of things. You are free now. . . ."

Lucinda's harrumph said more than a string of words. "Don't need be free. Twin Oaks my home."

"Mine too." *Oh, God, why do I have to leave?* "Please, Lucinda, will you take care of things here for me?" Jesselynn knew if she let the tears come, they'd both be crying. "Please." Her whisper barely squeaked around the lump in her throat.

Lucinda wiped the tears from her eyes. "I never see you again."

"No, we'll be back in time for spring planting."

Lucinda shook her head slowly from side to side as if a great weight lay atop her knotted turban.

God, I can't stand this. You know how often she has been right. She listens when you speak and hears what you say. Please, please say we will come back.

"I stay. And I pray for you ever day, and for us." She swept her arm to the side, including all those to be left behind.

"Thank you. I will write."

Lucinda nodded.

Jesselynn stood still a moment before heading for the door. She paused, looked back. "Winter will go fast and when spring comes, watch for us."

They began loading the wagon after dark.

"Food all in de wagon. I packed a carpetbag for de baby. Yo' dresses in de trunk." Lucinda wiped her eyes with the corner of her apron.

"Thank you." Jesselynn couldn't bear to tell her right now that there would be no need for dresses. "Just in case anyone is watching this place, we must go on like nothing is changed. Those of you who stay here, you have to do the same." Jesselynn looked at June, Lucinda's daughter, whose skin wasn't much darker than her own. While June was more rounded, they were about the same height.

If she could become a boy, surely June could become her.

"June, come with me."

"Yessum." Eyes rolling, the young woman rose from the table where she'd been plucking a chicken.

"Now, there's nothing to be afraid of," Jesselynn said as they mounted the stairs. "I have an idea that might make things look normal around here. After I'm gone, I mean."

"Don' want you to go." The whimper lashed at Jesselynn's shoulder blades.

"I know. I don't want to go either." She crossed her room to the chifforobe and pulled out the other of her mourning dresses. "Put this on."

"Can't do that." June took three steps back, folded hands

clasped to her breast. The shaking of her head made her kerchief shudder.

Jesselynn breathed deep and sighed. "Yes, you can. You and I are about the same size, and if you wear my clothes and a straw hat like I always do, anyone watching this place will think I am here." *And not come hotfooting it after us. Anything to buy time.* Every time she thought of Dunlivey watching the big house, she wanted to hide under the bed.

"But you be gone. I can't be you."

"Please, June, for the sake of everyone at Twin Oaks, try the dress on." She held the dress out until June reached for it as if she were being told to put her hand into flames. Jesselynn dug in the chest of drawers for a camisole and petticoat and handed them to the shaking woman beside her.

"Come now, you and I used to play dress-up together, remember? You've worn my clothes before."

"I know, but dat was playtime. This for real thing."

"Just be glad I'm not making you wear that corset."

When June finally stood dressed in the black silk dress and a white apron, Jesselynn looked at her with eyes slitted. "You fill it out far better than I do." She motioned to her chest area. Taking the straw hat off its peg, she clamped it onto June's head. "Sure do wish now I'd worn a sunbonnet. That way no one could see your face at all." She stepped back and, hands on hips, nodded. "Go ahead, look in the mirror. What do you think?"

June fingered the material of the skirt. "I think I done gone to heaven, dis here stuff feels so fine." She smiled at the woman in the mirror. "Pretty dark for a nigger like me."

"Don't use that word, June. You are a beautiful free woman who is doing Twin Oaks a big favor."

Tears pooled in June's eyes and one slipped down her cheek. "Thank you, Miss Jesselynn, from de bottom of my heart." She smoothed the silk over her bosom and down to her waist. "I do my best till you gets home again."

Several hours later, Jesselynn was wishing Lucinda were half so cooperative. She breathed in wind for a sigh big enough to blow the woman down and let it out slowly. "Lucinda, no matter what we all think and want, I have to take the horses to Uncle Hiram's in Missouri like Daddy said. I promised. You know that." While Jesselynn thought this discussion had been taken care of in the kitchen, she was learning otherwise.

"Oh, lawsy, my baby get herself kilt fo' sure." Lucinda threw her apron over her head.

"Lucinda, please get the scissors."

One dark eye peeked over the white hem. "Why?"

"Just get them, please."

Jesselynn had tried on two pairs of her father's boots before Lucinda heaved her bulk back up the stairs. By stuffing the toes with cotton and wearing two pairs of socks, it looked like she had footwear more in keeping with her new life. Now for the hair. She pulled out the seat to her mother's dressing table and sat down.

Handing Lucinda the comb, Jesselynn sat with her eyes closed. "Cut it off short like a man's."

Lucinda took the scissors and comb, all the while muttering and shaking her head. She stepped back. "I can't do dis thing. Hair like dat, no way, Missy. Lucinda won' be party to such goin's on."

Jesselynn's eyes snapped open. She straightened her back and narrowed her eyes, sending sparks bouncing off the mirror and catching her mammy full force. "Will you help me or won't you? I *have* to save the horses, for without them we will have nothing after the war is over. You know what marauding soldiers would do to a young woman traveling with fine horses like ours."

"Laws, Missy, I can't cut yo' hair." Tears bubbled from her dark eyes and tracked down her cheeks.

Jesselynn spun on the bench seat and reached for the scissors. "I'll do it, then."

"Den yo' look like, like . . ." Lucinda shook her head. "I do it." Tears flowing, she cut the heavy tresses off at the neckline, then lifted it in sections with the comb and snipped some more.

Jesselynn gritted her teeth against the hurt as she watched her hair fall to the floor. John had loved her hair, said it reminded him of shimmering silk in the moonlight. All her life she'd had one vanity, and now it lay in pools around their feet. She closed her eyes, pretending it was her mother standing there as she'd done for so many years, combing her daughter's hair and telling stories of when she was a young girl.

Oh, Mother, if only you were here now to tell me what to do. I've needed you so these last years. Immediately she felt guilt jab her in the ribs. Poor little Thaddy had never known his mother. At least she'd had one for seventeen years.

Lucinda's repeated sniffing and harrumphs broke into her reverie. Jesselynn turned enough on the walnut bench that she couldn't see in the mirror.

"Hold still, lessen you want to look like a sheared sheep." Lucinda sniffed again. "Good thing yo' mama ain't here. Dis nigh to break her heart."

Better a broken heart than . . . But Jesselynn didn't want to think of the coming days either. How could she leave Twin Oaks, the only home she'd ever known, and head across country without her father or her brother or . . . ? She sucked in a deep breath and let it out as a heavy sigh.

Lucinda stepped back. "Dere."

Jesselynn looked up into her mammy's tear-filled eyes. "I'm sorry, Lucinda, dear, but I just can't see any other plan. Do I look like a boy?"

"Maybe if you use walnut dye on yo' face and hands and keep a hat on yo' head." She squinted her eyes. "Maybe dye yo' hair too."

"That's a good idea. Good thing I'm not as endowed as some of the others." She pulled her camisole tight across her chest. "I won't miss the corsets, that's for sure." She thought of the whalebone contraption hanging from a hook on her closet door. Up until yesterday for the funeral, she'd pretty much given up wearing one, as she'd had to do more of the outside work. Even though Joseph ran the stables and barns, someone as big as Meshach had needed to oversee the tobacco planting and hoeing, the haying, and the grain harvesting. Could Joseph really take care of the tobacco picking? She'd planned to start that next week.

Could she trust the slaves left behind to keep things going? Perhaps one of the neighbors would check in once in a while.

Oh, God, this is too much. I can't leave Twin Oaks. And if I do, will there be anything left to come home to?

"Missy Jess, you all right?" Lucinda bent down to stare into her mistress's face.

Jesselynn nodded. "I will be. God will uphold and protect us." She wished she believed that as truly as her mother had. If God had been protecting them, why did her mother never recover from childbirth and her father and brother die in the war?

I will never leave you nor forsake you.

"Funny way you have of showing it."

"What dat you say?" Lucinda stopped on her way out the door.

"Nothing. Just muttering." Jesselynn got to her feet and ran her fingers through her hair. It barely covered the tops of her ears. She shook her head, and bits of hair flew free. But long tendrils did not slap her in the face, and her head felt strangely light. Maybe this wouldn't be so bad after all.

She returned to her own room and, after donning brown britches, a belt, and a white shirt, dug in the back of the closet for her porkpie hat, the one she'd worn when working the racing stock. It fit much better now that it didn't have all that hair to hold up. She eyed the two, broad-brimmed or porkpie. Of course she could take her father's straw hat . . . but she shook her head. Young boys didn't wear plantation owner hats.

She stared into the mirror. Did she look enough like a boy? She switched to the broader brimmed hat and pulled it lower onto her forehead. That was better. By lowering her chin, she could hide more of her face.

She'd have to deepen her voice too. When had her brothers' voices changed? Fifteen, sixteen? Earlier? With all that had happened in the last two years, somehow small facts like that had slipped away. She looked back in the mirror. How old did she look? She twisted her head from side to side. *After I dye my hair and skin, will that help?*

Whirling, she ran to the stairs, her boots clattering as she descended. "Lucinda?" She lowered her voice and tried again. "Lucinda!"

Lucinda came down the lower hall. "Comin'."

Jesselynn turned her body as if to study the empty space where her father's portrait had hung.

"Yessuh?" Lucinda stopped in the doorway.

"Is Miss Jesselynn to home?"

"Yessuh. Who I tells her is callin'?"

"Jonathan from Creekside."

"Wait here." Lucinda began to climb the stairs.

Jesselynn waited until Lucinda was halfway up the stairs before she looked up. "That's right kind of you, ma'am, but you won't find her up there."

Lucinda stopped with one foot on the upper riser. She looked down over the shiny walnut banister, rolled her eyes, and shook her head. "Well, I never . . ." Heaving a sigh, she came back down the stairs. "Such a trick to play on ol' Lucinda."

Jesselynn breathed a sigh of relief. If she could fool Lucinda, anyone else would be easy.

"Let's get the dye, all right?"

"Lawsy, what dis world comin' to?" Lucinda continued to shake her head as she made her way toward the back of the house. "I boiled up some walnut husks an' we see what happen." The sniff at the end made Jesselynn wonder if tears weren't clogging her mammy's throat as they were her own.

Jesselynn gathered the last of her things, her father's journal, and the precious ink bottle. When she walked by the mirror, she didn't even recognize herself. Were her hair not so straight and brown, she might have passed for one of the mulattos. She brushed walnut-colored hair back, but it fell forward onto her brow. Her hat would have to keep it back.

The grandfather clock in the hall struck eleven as they gathered for a final prayer. Sobs from some of the house slaves broke the silence as Jesselynn bowed her head. "Heavenly Father, we commit our lives into thy hands. Keep those of us on the road safe and those at home as well." She stopped and swallowed hard, trying to clear her throat and keep the tears at bay. She knew if she broke down, there would be such wailing that it would be heard clear to Lexington. "Please set your legions of angels in charge over us all. If it be thy will, bring Zachary safely home again." Oh, how she wanted to pray for God to take care of Cavendar Dunlivey in a permanent way. "Protect us from those who set to do us harm, we pray in thy holy name, amen."

"Missy Jesse?"

She whirled and, taking a step forward, glared up at Meshach. "You mean Marse Jesse!"

"Yessum—ah, suh." Meshach studied the wrinkled brim of his hat. The sound of a nighthawk called from the front portico. "Dat mean all is clear."

"All right." She turned to the others. "Now, you all know what you have to do. You will all refer to June as Miss Jesse, even when inside the house, in case Dunlivey makes it through those posted as guards. Everything will go on as usual here. If someone comes calling for me, say that I am indisposed or gone to town or something." She looked around the circle to make sure everyone nodded.

"All right, Ophelia, go get Thaddy. You and he will sleep in the back of the wagon."

"Yessum."

"What?" She spun on the slave as if to strike her.

"Yessuh." Ophelia ran up the stairs without looking back.

Dear God, if we manage this, it will be a miracle for sure.

CHAPTER FIVE

On the trail
September 18, 1862

Unlike Lot's wife, Jesselynn knew she didn't dare look back.

The squeak of the wagon wheels sounded like children screaming as they passed the two stone pillars and turned onto the road from the long drive of Twin Oaks. She didn't need to see the copper plaque posted on one to know what it said. TWIN OAKS. Established 1789 by Joshua A. Highwood. The two trees from which the plantation garnered its name stood sentinel at the junction as they had for longer than her family's memory. Story had it that her great-grandfather had picnicked under those trees the day his land grant was signed and delivered. His journal had described them as "two oaks, nearly perfect a match in size and shape, huge and majestic beyond description, offering shade for the weary, a home for birds and squirrels, and enough acorns to raise an entire herd of swine."

How his heart would break if he could see us now. Jesselynn wiped a tear from her eye with the back of her sleeve. *It's just too much—Father dying and now my having to leave. What will Zachary think when he returns? How can I do this? God, you are asking too much.*

She blew her nose and pressed the bridge between thumb and forefinger, anything to stop the tears. If her people—she refused to call them slaves any longer—if her people knew how she felt, they would not be able to go on.

Except perhaps Meshach. Since she'd given him his papers, he had become different. Always straight and broad shouldered, he no longer looked down at the ground when talking to anyone. He held his head high and looked a person in the eye. His speech too had changed some, but God help them if he called her "missy."

She flicked the reins for her team to pick up their feet. The mare on the right still hadn't quite gotten the idea of teamwork in wagon pulling, but at least she was willing. Ahab had not taken kindly to the harness, so Meshach was riding him. The mule didn't seem to care who pulled with him.

Why hadn't she thought to break them to harness earlier? She shook her head. Why so many things? Like her father had said, "If only you'd obeyed me two years ago . . ." The memory reopened the lacerations on her heart. Could one die of a broken heart?

"Riders up ahead," Daniel, who'd been riding point, whispered out of the darkness.

Jesselynn immediately pulled off the road under the bordering tree, the wagon wheels crushing brush as they hid. Thank God there was no stone wall or fencing here. She leaped from the wagon and ran to her horses' heads, clamping a hand over each muzzle so they wouldn't nicker.

Her heart made so much noise, she had a hard time listening for the riders. Grateful for the darkness, since the moon had yet to rise, she strained to hear, knowing Meshach and Daniel were near and doing the same thing. Benjamin would be ahead somewhere. Thank God she'd thought to give Thaddy a few drops of laudanum so he would sleep through anything. What if he cried out? Only soldiers or scum would likely be on the road at this hour. Once they were farther from home, they could disappear in among all the normal traffic. After all, what was one more wagon loaded with despair?

The clop of hooves, the jingle of spurs and bits, sounded like five or six horses. While one man said something, blood thundering in her ears kept her from picking out his words. The smell of tobacco smoke overlaid the fragrance of crushed leaves and bark. Her eyes ached and watered from trying to peer through the darkness. One of her horses stamped a foot.

Now she knew what a deer felt like when it suspected danger. Her mind wept *Oh, God, help us. Please help us!* over and over till she thought she would scream. They waited what seemed like half the night from the time they could hear even the faintest sound of the riders.

"Go now," Meshach said right next to her. She hadn't heard him moving at all. Her heart leaped back up in her throat, and she clamped a hand to her chest.

"Oh." Leaning her forehead against the warm neck of the mare, she waited for her heartbeat to settle back down and her knees to regain their strength before she climbed back up in the wagon. Right at the moment, she wasn't sure she could make it.

"Marse Jesse, you all right?"

"Yes, thank you." *At least I soon will be.* She patted the mare's neck and, in spite of nearly tripping over broken brush, got herself back up on the wagon seat.

"Oh, Mi-Marse Jesse, I skeered so bad I 'most wet my drawers." Ophelia's whisper made Jesselynn smile, then start to chuckle.

"Me too, Ophelia, me too."

A giggle from behind added to her chuckle, and by the time they had the wagon back up on the road and running straight again, all of them, except for the sleeping child, were choking, trying to keep from laughing so loud that any other stragglers out on the road might hear them.

Sheer relief, that's what it is. Jesselynn could no more cap the gurgling laughter than fly back home to Twin Oaks. *Twin Oaks.* She sobered as if she'd had a bucket of water doused on her head. Had that been Dunlivey returning to watch over the home place?

Watch! Ha! Spy! That's all he is. A spy, and one cruel beyond measure at that.

She flicked the reins, and the horses picked up a fast trot. They clattered over a stone bridge, echoes bouncing from the low stone walls. Before long they turned west onto the Lexington/Frankfort Pike and picked up the pace, needing to be off the pike before sunrise and miles from Twin Oaks.

Her eyes burned as if she'd been standing in the smoke from a fire, and her rump ached from the hard boards by the time Meshach cantered back to them just as the birds made their first twitterings. The sun had yet to reach the horizon, but already she could see the features of the landscape. The trees grew taller as they drew closer to the Kentucky River, and the gently rolling hills sported pastureland with plots of trees. Stone fences, their flat capstones set on a slant, looked like gray medieval fortresses in miniature. Mist hugged the hollows. Horses whinnied. Roosters heralded the rising sun.

"Dorsey up ahead. We takes a road off to de left," Meshach said.

She nodded and rubbed her eyes with the tips of chilled fingers. Tomorrow night someone else could drive the wagon and she would ride. She heard rustlings in the wagon bed behind her.

Ophelia yawned and climbed over the supplies until she sat beside Jesselynn. "We stoppin' soon?"

"Soon." They both kept their voices low so as not to wake Thaddy.

Jesselynn turned on the road Meshach had indicated and saw Daniel waving at her a hundred or more yards ahead. In spite of the weariness that dragged her down, she wished they could keep on going. Farther out, maybe they could travel some during the day, when they and their horses wouldn't be so easily recognized.

Although looking at the team in front of her, she doubted anyone would believe the mare pulling with the mule was the dam of four Keeneland Derby winners. Two of her progeny were at stud already. And paid for handsomely in spite of the war. They were probably dead on the battlefield by now if the armies had had their choice. Unless others had already done what her father had told her to do two years ago.

"Dey's water here and even pasture fo' de horses."

Daniel rode beside her, showing the way after they left the narrowing dirt road.

"Meshach say we be safe here."

"Good."

Mockingbirds trilled their morning arias when she stepped down from the wagon with a groan. Squirrels chattered from the oak trees, informing them and the world of the invasion.

Jesselynn stretched, kneading her lower back with her fists and leaning from side to side. There was indeed water. A creek burbled over moss-covered rocks and around knobby roots. Out in the open, where the sun was already stretching golden fingers across the grass, the blades sparkled green, like a welcome mat sprinkled with diamonds.

Ahab snorted at their arrival and dropped his head to graze again, his front legs hobbled so he couldn't run or even walk fast.

Meshach came out of the trees with an armload of dried branches and dumped them by a fire pit that showed others had used this glen for respite. " 'Phelia, you get dem fryin' pans and such out of de wagon. Since you slept all night, you get de breakfast."

"Do we dare start a fire?" Jesselynn listened for any nearby farm sounds. Only the creek's gurgling and the birdsong broke the early morning silence.

"I think yes. We off de main road a mile or so, and de next farm way down over dere." He pointed to the west. "Can't see de clearin' from de road."

"How did you find this place?"

Meshach studied the dusty toe of his boot. "Don' ask. Just say I heard tell of it."

"Oh." Was this one of those places where runaway slaves could stop in safety? And had her people ever thought of running off? What did they talk about down in the quarters when the marse wasn't around?

"Lynnie?" Thaddy's voice came thinly from the wagon bed. "Lynnie?"

Jesselynn trotted to the wagon and lifted her little brother out of his nest. "Shush. You musn't talk loud." She kissed his cheek, pink from sleep, and settled him on her hip. "Come, let's go."

She sent an inquiring look Meshach's way, and he nodded.

"Just stay close."

When trees and low bushes screened them from camp, she pushed down his diapers and let him pee in the creek, much to his delight. Then while he threw twigs and pebbles in the clear water, she relieved herself, thinking immediately of the niceties of home. She would have had a pitcher of warm water to wash with, one of the household slaves would have emptied the slop jar, and breakfast would have been ready when she descended the stairs. But that was home, and this was now.

Dipping her handkerchief in the water, she used it to wash Thaddy's hands and face.

"Cold." He pulled away, scrunching up his face. "No more."

"Be a big boy, Thaddy."

"Go home now?"

I wish we could. Instead she knelt down in front of him and, laying her hands along his cheeks, looked deep in his eyes. "Listen to me, Thaddy, and listen good. Call me Jesse from now on, you hear me?"

"Lynnie."

"Not anymore, little brother." She shook her head. "Not anymore, and don't you forget it. Now, what is my name?" She dropped her hands to his shoulders and shook him gently.

His lower lip came out, and his eyes narrowed. At that moment he looked so much like his older brother Zachary that she blinked.

"No. Jes-sie-lynn," he said slowly.

Jesselynn sighed and rocked back on her heels. Right enough, she'd approached him the wrong way. One thing this child didn't lack was southern backbone. He'd go along nice as you please until . . . She'd come up against that *until.*

How much do you tell a two-and-a-half-year-old child?

Seeking to corral her thoughts, Jesselynn picked up a stick with a caterpillar attached. She handed it to Thaddeus, sure that it would distract him for a moment while she thought what to do.

He held on to the stick and giggled as the fuzzy caterpillar humped his back feet up to his front.

"Thaddy, how would you like to play a game with me?"

He studied the now extended caterpillar.

Jesselynn sighed and got to her feet. Dipping her handkerchief again, she washed her own face and hands, ran damp fingers through her shorn hair, and set her hat back in place. They were ready for the day, and all she could think of was a hot meal and a soft bed, or any bed for that matter.

She took her little brother's hand. "Bet you don't know what my new name is."

"Jesselynn Marie Highwood." He glanced from the stick up to her, then grinned. "Jesse. Me new name?"

She let out a sigh of relief. *Not a bad idea.* How could this child be so smart? "Sure, what would you like?"

"Meshach."

"Ah, that's a good name, but it already belongs to Meshach over there. Think of another." They wound through the trees as they talked, Thaddeus all the time careful to keep his caterpillar on the stick.

"Joshwa." He stopped walking and looked up at her. "My daddy gone to heaven name, huh?"

Her eyes flooded. Pain gripped her heart. She sank to her knees and pulled Thaddeus into her arms, hugging him close so he couldn't see her tears. "That's a fine name. One I'm proud to call you by." She sniffed and relinquished him when he squirmed.

"Oh, my catepiwar." He looked around on the leaf-strewn ground. "Find him."

Jesselynn rocked back on her heels just in time to see that the caterpillar had been smashed by her knee. She fluffed some leaves over it and, rising, pulled him to his feet. "We'll look for another one later. See, Ophelia has breakfast about ready."

"Want my catepiwar." The lower lip jutted out and his face screwed up in what Jesselynn knew could give rise to a wail fit to raise the soundest sleeper.

"You eat, I'll look. Come, Joshua, tell everyone your new name."

His face cleared, and he ran to stand by his hero, tugging on the man's pants. "Meshach. Meshach."

"What you wants, little marse?" Meshach picked Thaddy up so they were eye to eye.

"Me new name. Like Jessel—Jesse." He glanced over his shoulder to see her approval. When she nodded, he smiled and turned back to his holder. He thumped his chest. "Me Joshwa."

Meshach nodded slowly. "Yessuh, that a fine name. We all call you Joshua, little marse. How dat?"

"Good." Thaddy pushed back. "Eat now."

Jesselynn took the plate Ophelia brought her and sat down on the wagon tongue. "Thank you." Looking around at the sun-dappled ground, the hobbled horses grazing on the open glen, her people sitting cross-legged on the ground or on a hunk of wood and laughing softly while they ate—it all made her think more of a picnic than a flight for their lives. Or at least their horses' lives, she corrected her meandering thoughts. Her mind skittered away from thoughts of any of them really being in danger. Only the horses.

A crow flew overhead. His raucous announcement that there were strangers in his woods sent shivers up her back. What if they were indeed running for their lives?

She shook her head. *There you go, borrowing trouble*, she scolded herself and returned Ophelia's smile as she picked up Jesselynn's plate. One hint of superstition like that and they'd all be moaning and crying like death was at their very door.

She stared into the dregs of her cup. What she wouldn't give for a cup of *real* coffee. The ground chickory looked like coffee, but the semblance ended there. However, it was hot and not too bitter when laced with milk. If only they had brought the cow. Instead, she hoped to buy milk along the way. Surely there would be farmers with a gallon or so of milk to sell. The cow could never have kept the pace she hoped to set, not and produce milk too.

She emptied the sludge in the bottom of her cup out on the ground and got to her feet. One good thing, britches beat skirts any day for the walking and climbing around she needed to do to check their supplies.

"You take de bed under de wagon"—Meshach nodded to the pallet laid out—"and sleep now. We all take turns."

Jesselynn nodded. Somewhere along the line Meshach had assumed the leading role here, and if she weren't so tired, she'd talk to him about that. Right now, thoughts in any kind of order were beyond her.

———————

She woke with the sun in the western sky and the sound of gunfire.

CHAPTER SIX

"Why'd you let me sleep so long?" She kept her voice to a hiss.

Meshach shook his head. "You needed sleep." He cocked his head, listening. "Dey goin' away." He nodded toward the east.

"You're sure?"

"Um. Been lis'nin'."

"Where's Benjamin?"

"Scoutin'."

Jesselynn glanced around the campsite. Ophelia and Thaddy were sound asleep on a pallet under a full-branched oak. Ahab raised his head, studied the sounds from the east, and dropped his muzzle to graze again.

"Ahab better'n a watchdog."

"Prettier too." The guns were indeed going the other way; even she could tell that by now.

"We cross the ferry at dusk tonight." She wasn't sure if it were a question or an order.

"Yes, Marse." A smile tugged at the edge of his full lips. "Benjamin say river low enough to swim horses. Only take wagon on de ferry."

"We could save money that way."

"And be safe."

Jesselynn knew it was her turn to smile—and nod. She reached back under the wagon to pull out her boots. Wide awake as she was, she might as well write in her journal. Someday someone might want to read what happened on their way west.

That afternoon when they pulled out, Jesselynn sat on the

wagon seat beside Meshach, and Ophelia rocked a sleeping Thaddeus in her arms. As they drew nearer to Clifton, where the ferry crossed the Kentucky River, she pulled a sheet over his face and kept on rocking.

Jesselynn swallowed to keep the fear from knotting her tongue and strangling her throat. Would someone be watching for them? They waited while the ferry, nothing more than a flat raft, was pulled from one side of the river to the other by a hawser attached to a single tree and pulled by a mule. When they unloaded, the mule on the east side of the river took over, and the ferry returned.

A woman approached the wagon. "That'll be fifty cents."

Jesselynn dug the coins out of her pocket and handed them over. *Maybe we should have swum the whole rig at that price.*

"Thankee."

Meshach nodded. "Welcome." He slapped the reins, and the team walked up the ramp placidly as if they did so every day.

Jesselynn let out a sigh and felt her shoulders slump. So far so good. As the ferry glided to the other side and bumped against the bank, the man on that side shoved the planks in place and off they walked.

Meshach nodded again and touched the brim of his hat as they drove up the bank and onto the westering road. A mile or so later, Benjamin and Daniel rode up on wet horses, leading the other two.

"We did it." Jesselynn slapped her knees and let out a decidedly unladylike whoop. "Okay, Ahab, my turn to ride." She leaped from the wagon and beat Benjamin to the saddle, slinging it and the pad over the stallion's back with smooth motions. Once bridled, she mounted and grinned at her people. "Now, let's get outa here."

After looking toward Jesselynn for permission, Ophelia settled Thaddeus on the pallet and climbed up on the wagon seat, her smile pure pleasure at being able to sit closer to the man with the reins. With Meshach driving the wagon, Jesselynn nudged Ahab forward, and the trip took on an entirely new meaning for her. All the years she'd halfheartedly obeyed the strictures of young womanhood, she could now hear Lucinda as if she rode right behind her. *"Young ladies don' wear britches. Young ladies don' ride stallions."* And, oh, if she could only hear her mother speaking again, telling her to speak softly, to walk not run, to work before taking pleasure.

But she couldn't, so she paid attention to what she was doing. The horse she rode wanted to run. That's what Ahab had been bred for, and he fought the bit and the strength of her hands. If only she dared let him run for a while, just to top him off, but she knew better. Nothing in the world would attract more attention than the two of them racing down the road.

She brought him to a standstill and patted his sweat-dotted neck. "All right, old son, you can do this the hard way or the easy way, but I'll warn you right now, it's going to be my way." The stallion snorted as the other members of the party pulled on ahead. He twitched his tail and shifted from foot to foot.

Jesselynn tightened the reins and kept up a murmur that would soothe any fractious critter, two-legged or four. Ahab sighed and, flat-footed now, shook his head, his burr-filled mane slapping from side to side. She ached to clean him up, but the rougher he looked the better. Gone was the sparkling white blaze down his face and the rear off-white sock. His coat, dyed with walnut husks like her hair, looked rough and patchy, no longer that striking blood bay of days before. Even the river bath hadn't removed the dye, another worry off her mind.

Joseph and Meshach had done a good job on all the horses. By tomorrow perhaps Ahab would tolerate the harness. Meshach had worked him under it in the afternoon.

She let him trot until they caught up and no longer had to fight her horse and the fear that rose at every sound. Horses whinnied when they passed a farm, and dogs barked, but no one ordered them to stop. She rode alongside the wagon, glancing over to check on Thaddeus—or Joshua, as he now insisted on being called. How their father would have loved to hear "Joshwa," as the boy said it.

They'd ridden for several hours when she heard a horse galloping their way. Benjamin pulled to a stop in front of them. "Sojers ahead."

With woods on both sides of them, they hurried along the road, searching for a place to get the wagon through the trees. Jesselynn rode ahead, her heart pounding louder than the sound of her horse's hooves. Since it wasn't full dark yet, they needed to hide quickly. Her heart hammered until she saw a lighter place between trees. She beckoned to Meshach on the wagon.

"They're just up ahead. Hurry."

They'd barely cleared the opening when she heard the horses coming toward them. All of them had dismounted to cover their horses' muzzles.

God, please make them blind. Surely our tracks lead in here. She could feel Ahab come to attention as he shifted his front feet. She kept one hand firmly over his nose and the other clamped to the reins under his chin.

Horses and riders passed, then wagons.

Mosquitoes buzzed and drank their fill, for she had no hands to slap them. Sweat trickled down her back, her legs, her forehead. The wet beads burned her eyes, eyes that already ached from staring through the darkness, wishing for a night so black they couldn't be seen.

Was it the entire Confederate army passing by?

Where were Daniel and Benjamin?

She needed a drink. To cough. Her throat tightened. She swallowed. She tried clearing it softly with gentle pressure. She clamped two fingers over her nose to keep from sneezing. Ahab shifted.

The canteen on her saddle might as well have been in Lexington. Now that it was truly dark, she wished she could see.

An owl hooted off in the woods. A mockingbird sang his night song. No matter how hard she strained, she could no longer hear the jingle of harness nor the clump of hooves.

She sagged against Ahab's shoulder and finally coughed. Her shoulders ached, her fingers too. The bones in her legs felt about as stout as newly washed chitlins.

When she swallowed, the fear tasted metallic, as if she'd chewed a patch of skin off the inside of her cheek and it bled.

"You all right?" Meshach spoke right by her shoulder.

She jumped as if he'd leaped from behind a wall and shrieked "boo" as her brothers used to do to tease her. Clapping a hand to her racing heart, she swallowed again. "I-I'm fine. How are the others?"

"Thaddy sleepin'. 'Phelia done good wid 'im."

"Good." Jesselynn fumbled for her canteen. She felt like pouring it over her head but instead took only a few swallows. "Hold Ahab and I'll be right back."

"Don' go far."

"No, I won't."

Back in the saddle they waited what seemed like hours for Benjamin to signal the all clear so they could drive back up on the road. How many miles had they sacrificed? It felt like half the night. They picked up a fast trot and kept the pace until the team was blowing and even Ahab had worked up a sweat. In spite of the jolting, Thaddeus slept curled next to Ophelia on the pallet of quilts in the back of the wagon.

First light lent its silvery sheen to the woods and farms as they trotted along the road, now searching for a place to spend the day.

"How far to Bardstown?" Jesselynn pulled back to ride by the wagon.

"Don' know fo' sure." Meshach studied the area around them. "Maybe git dere tomorrow night. I think we bypassed Lawrenceburg."

"We've got to lay up soon." A dog barked off to the left. Farmers would be heading for milking and fieldwork at any time. If they came upon a racing farm, the horses would be out on the track for morning works.

Jesselynn shook her head at the thought. No, they wouldn't. Most all the horses had already been conscripted, and while she was sure other farms were hiding what horses they could, no one would dare use the tracks.

The dog continued to bark, setting the next farm's watchdogs to doing the same. They had to find a place to camp.

From the looks of things when they topped a long grade, their wood cover had about been overrun with farming. Tall barns with slatted sides that could be raised to let the airflow dry the tobacco outnumbered the horse barns crowned with cupolas.

Did they dare ask for refuge in a barn?

Jesselynn shook her head again. That would be a last resort.

The rising sun gilded the treetops, setting fire to those that had begun to don fall dress.

"De sojers get us?" Ophelia raised her head, fear widening her eyes.

"No, you and Thaddy just go right on back to sleep." Meshach smiled over his shoulder, his voice reassuring.

Jesselynn wished she could believe him. Her eyes burned and her head felt as if it might fall right off her neck. While she loved to ride, and britches made riding astride possible, riding for pleasure and riding all night to escape were two mighty different things. Her rear hurt, her shoulders ached, and even Ahab was drooping. She had to nudge him sometimes to keep up an even trot.

She felt jiggled to pieces.

The sun broke from the horizon and bounded into the sky.

God, hide us. You say you are our refuge. Help us find a place to hide.

Panic tasted as bad as fear. Ahab's ears pricked forward. A lone rider was coming toward them at a good clip.

"Benjamin come."

Jesselynn knew Meshach must be right, but it was several seconds before she was sure herself.

Benjamin waved, beckoning them to speed up, then turned back the way he'd come. They picked up their speed, but breaking into a canter would attract more attention. Jesselynn rode back to the wagon.

"Here, you take Ahab and the filly with you and get out of sight. A young man with a wagon and one slave won't attract as much attention."

"No, Marse, I not do dat."

"Yes, you will." She swung to the ground just in front of the team, causing them all to stop, harnesses jingling in protest. She handed the reins up to Meshach and mounted the wagon wheel. "Now hurry."

Meshach hesitated one more heart-stopping second, his dark eyes snapping fire and his jaw carved in rock.

Jesselynn held her breath, at the same time reaching for the team reins. "You know I'm right." She kept her voice low, trying to guard against Ophelia starting to whimper and wake Thaddeus.

When the big black took the stallion's reins and jumped to the ground, all the air left her lungs and she sank onto the wagon seat. Within seconds he had untied the filly, mounted Ahab, and galloped after Benjamin.

She could feel his anger carried back to her on the wind. But his years of slave training had held. Marse was always right. She clucked the team into a trot and followed the two she could barely see ahead. A man on a horse cantered past them, calling a greeting as he pulled even. When he went on without saying any more than that, Jesselynn felt she could breathe again. Had her voice sounded low enough for a young man? Slurring her words helped somewhat, adopting the softer sounds of the slaves instead of her own more perfect speech. Her father had insisted those in the big house speak properly, in spite of their Kentucky drawl.

About a mile farther, Benjamin sat his horse by the side of the road, and as soon as Jesselynn answered his wave, he trotted off down a side road. Since a loaded wagon was coming toward them, she kept her chin low as she gently pulled the team down to an easier turning pace. The man driving the wagon looked familiar, but she refused to look over her shoulder. She was sure the man was the overseer of the Tarlander Plantation to the east of Twin Oaks, but evidencing any interest could catch the other's attention.

Thank God Ahab and Meshach were out of sight. He'd worked for Tarlander more than once and would surely have been recognized.

"Was that who I think it was?" she asked Benjamin when he waited for her at a bridge crossing a wide creek.

"Yessuh." Benjamin shook his head. "Dat close." He turned his horse. "Not far now."

They gathered in a small clearing bordering the creek, where Daniel awaited them. He was already gathering sticks for a fire.

Jesselynn reached behind her to help a groggy Thaddeus climb up on the seat. "You been a mighty good boy. I'm right proud of you."

"Hungry?" He reached up and wrapped his arms around her neck. Burrowing into her chest like a little gopher, he repeated with more insistence. "Hungry. Want milk."

Jesselynn sighed. Where would they get milk? Other fresh food too, for that matter. Her eyes felt as if they'd been rolling in the Sahara Desert, and her rear felt permanently glued to the hard seat.

"I git some." Benjamin remounted his horse.

"You'd best take the mule, then," Jesselynn said.

"Oh." He dismounted with a nod. " 'Phelia, you got a jug?"

Meshach unhitched the team and removed the harness from both horse and mule, then slipped a bridle with short reins on the mule. "You hurry."

After handing Benjamin a couple of their precious store of coins, Jesselynn climbed over the wagon wheel and, when her feet felt solid ground, leaned against the wheel until her knees no longer felt like buckling. She propped her head on hands crossed on the iron wheel rim, thinking only of her bed back at Twin Oaks. The mosquito net draped just so, clean sheets cool to the skin, a mattress that molded to one's body and let sleep come like a welcome visitor.

Not like a sledgehammer against rocks.

At this point, however, the sledgehammer and rock base would be appreciated. But they had to eat first and take care of the animals. Good thing Ophelia could sleep during the night, so she could be awake with Thaddeus, who was at the moment running from tree to tree, peeking out and giggling as he dodged Ophelia's reaching hands.

Jesselynn wasn't sure who was having more fun, the boy or the woman just grown beyond girlhood. She watched, wishing she had the stamina to join in. Every bone and muscle creaked and groaned when she left the wagon-wheel prop. Meshach already had the horses all hobbled, and Daniel was starting a fire to cook breakfast.

She should be helping. She should be telling them what to do. After all, that's what the mistress of the plantation did—set the tasks for the day and then make sure everyone was working. Somehow there seemed to be a shift in positions here, and at the moment she didn't much care.

She dragged her protesting body over to the creek and lay down flat on her belly to get her face close enough to the water to wash it without too much effort. Skirts would have prohibited such an action with the ease she accomplished it. Britches were definitely more accommodating. The cool water on her face made her dunk again. She clutched her hat in one hand and swished her face back and forth in the water, scrubbing with the other hand. Her hair dripped water in her face, and it ran down her neck into her shirt when she twisted to a sitting position. Now for her feet.

Thaddeus ran up as she finished untying her bootlaces. "Me too."

Jesselynn grunted as she jerked her boots off and wriggled her toes.

Thaddy recognized a lap when he saw it and climbed in. Reaching up, he patted Jesselynn's cheek with one chubby hand, at the same time inching down her legs toward the goal.

"Wait a minute, wiggle worm." She reached for the buttons on his shoes. "You can't go in the water with your shoes on."

He giggled again, the merry sound flirting with the birdsong from the trees above.

"All right." She set him on his feet and gave his bottom a pat. "Now hang on to my hand and . . ."

Thaddeus already had his toes in the meandering water, giggling even louder. He leaned forward to catch a floating leaf.

Jesselynn snagged the back of his britches just in time. "I said wait." She set him on his feet, ankle-deep in the water. He squished his toes in the smooth gravel and leaned forward again. This time she held him steady with a firm grasp of his suspenders so he could splash water, and wade, and not tumble in.

"Coffee."

She turned at the call and loosened her grip just enough for him to sit splat in the shallow water. "Thaddy!"

"Me Joshwa." He held up his hand and let the water trickle down his arm, making him giggle again.

"Come, let's go eat."

"No." He slapped his palms on the water surface and chortled at the spray.

Jesselynn groaned. She could tell by the look on his face that he wasn't ready to be taken out of the creek. And when Thaddeus wasn't ready to be moved, his roar would be heard clear to the Mississippi.

"Ophelia has bread and jam for you."

"No."

"Butter and sugar on bread?"

"No." He slapped the water surface again.

How did he get so spoiled? But she knew. No one wanted to say no to a motherless, and now a fatherless, little boy or make him unhappy. There was too much sorrow in his life already. But she didn't dare leave him for one minute either. While the creek was shallow on the edges, the center clipped along at a good pace, and she hadn't really checked to see how deep it was. But babies drowned in buckets, and though Thaddeus surely didn't consider himself a baby, if he fell flat out, the current might keep him from getting to his feet again.

She waded out and, rolling up her pant legs, stood in water to her knees. Her mother might just as well have been watching from behind the trees, her voice came so clear. *"Jesselynn Highwood, young ladies do not show off their ankles like that, nor their knees. For shame."* For a minute, Jesselynn wished for both her mother and Lucinda. She snatched her thoughts back from memories of home as if being stung by bees. "Only look forward, girl. Only forward."

"Huh? You talkin' to me?" Ophelia stood on the creek bank.

"Ah, no. To myself." Jesselynn took in a deep breath and let it all out. Now that she thought of it again, her aches hadn't really gone away. "Come on, Thaddeus, we are going for breakfast now."

He looked up at her, eyes squinting to judge if her face matched her tone. When he saw it did, he raised his hand and stood when she took it. "Up."

She swung him to her hip. "You're all wet."

He patted her cheek. "Water good."

She turned at the sound of a horse cantering toward them. If it wasn't Benjamin, they could be in a heap of trouble.

CHAPTER SEVEN

Richmond, Virginia

"Wounded comin' off the train."

Louisa Highwood settled the patient down against the meager pillow. She'd been holding him up so he could take a drink of water. "I'll be back soon as I can," she told him.

"Thankee, Missy." His mountain dialect no longer felt strange upon her ears. These days she was grateful when the men that entered her wards could talk. Leastways that usually meant they weren't slipping through death's door.

"I will be back." The gratitude blazing from his eyes caused her to lay a hand on his shoulder. "Soon as possible."

He nodded, and his eyes drifted closed.

While Louisa had volunteered at the hospital to read to the wounded and perhaps write letters home for those who couldn't, in reality, she'd become more of a nurse's helper in the month she'd been there. The soldiers called her an angel of mercy. God knew this place needed huge doses of mercy.

At first the older nurses had tried to protect her from the ghastly sight of male bodies ripped by shrapnel and blown apart by bullets. The stench alone was enough to make a stalwart man blanch. They kept her from the operating room, but life on the wards was one horror story after another.

Keeping a smile in place took a chunk of her will. Sometimes she bathed wounds with her tears when there was no medicine available. The Yankees blew up enough railroad track to keep supplies low. A sailing ship had run the blockade to bring in much-needed supplies until the Confederates regained ground and rebuilt the tracks.

She spent much of her time washing faces ravaged by pain and bringing cooling cups of water. Walking swiftly down the center aisle, she promised to be right back to all who called to her. An empty bed made her shut her eyes and swallow. John, the man who'd occupied that bed yesterday had not gone home, at least not to his earthly home. The letter he'd shown her from his wife told about a son born after he went to war.

Like Thaddeus at home. Twin Oaks, where what to wear that day had been the morning's main decision, where her older sister Jesselynn tried to get Louisa and Carrie Mae to help her on the plantation after Mother died, and Daddy and her brothers had ridden off to war. Maybe if she'd been more helpful, Jesselynn wouldn't have banished her to Richmond.

"Hurry, Miz Highwood, we needs you." The call came from one of the helpers outside. It was their job to bring the stretchers in, if they could find a place, that is. In the meantime, heat and flies and untreated wounds added to the death toll.

Louisa wiped her hands on an apron already stiff with blood and other unmentionables and wished she had time to stop for a drink herself. Pushing hair the color of honey-laced molasses back in a loosening chignon, she paused only a moment at the top of the steps. Real air. At least compared to that inside. Using the back of her hand, she dried the sweat—she no longer referred to the rivulets as perspiration—from her broad forehead clear down to her slightly pointed chin. She'd been told her eyes were her best feature, amber with flecks of gold, but right now all she could think was that they ached and she had no use for long lashes. She never batted them at anyone anyway. More than once she'd been told with her slight figure that she wasn't strong enough to help lift heavy men, but she knew there was strength in leanness, and she used it well.

"Over here." Jacob, taller and stronger than most of the free black men who'd been hired to assist, reminded her of Meshach back home. He moved from stretcher to stretcher, cloaked in a gentle spirit and a heart that ached like hers at the carnage.

While the doctors tried to keep her out of the maelstrom of incoming wounded, Jacob recognized those who needed her hand to give them strength. Joining the ebony-skinned man, she looked down at the stretcher and the man whose field bandages were now soaked and crusty with blood. Either the doctors or the bullet had taken one leg off below the knee and bound both the stump and the man's head, leaving only part of his jaw visible. His right arm was taped to his body to protect better than a sling.

She knelt in the dust and laid her hand on the man's heart and felt the strong beat. "Let's move him into John's bed. That's the only one left on our ward."

Jacob nodded and beckoned another assistant to help him.

While there, Louisa checked the man behind her but knew before she even touched him that he was beyond help. Death had won again. She moved down the row, her low murmur as soothing as her touch.

"Am I in heaven?" A soldier squinted against the sun's glare. " 'Cause if there's angels around, can't be hell." He coughed, and pink drool leaked from the side of his mouth.

Oh, God, why do you let this continue? Louisa had long ago given up the dream of an easy victory for the South. There was no glory in war. Her brothers had lied to her and to themselves. She beckoned to another freeman and pointed at the dead man. "Take him over there, and bring this man to my ward. I'll find a place."

They did as she said while she turned to the muttering man on the next pallet.

"What are you doin' out here?" The man, outlined by the blazing sun, stopped behind her.

Why, I'm pourin' afternoon tea. What all did you think? She bit back the retort and rose to her feet. She still had to tilt her head to see his face, shielding her eyes with her hand. Between his size and the fiery aura surrounding him, he might have been God himself.

"This is surely no place for a woman of your tender years. Get on home now."

He had to be new. Most of the other doctors were so grateful for help that they ignored her obvious age. Or lack thereof.

"I'm sorry you feel that way, sir, but my—the men need water, and usually I'm reading to them or writing for them. Surely that is within the bounds of Christian charity. Christ himself said—"

"I know what Christ said, miss, but He wasn't in the midst of a military hospital."

"No, sir. His battle was much bigger." She kept her voice gentle, hoping she sounded more like her mother than the harridan she'd been accused of one day. She backed away, knowing that if he sent her home, there would be nothing she could do about it—today. And she wanted to get inside to help with the man Jacob carried in first. There was something about that man.

"Doctor, over here." The call caught his attention, and Louisa hurried for the ward.

"He just wants to protect you," one of the older women said in passing. "You mustn't take it to heart. If I didn't need you so bad, I would never let you help here like you do. It isn't seemly, I know, but these are terrible times, and 'seemly' seems not so important any longer."

"Thank you." Louisa heard one of her patients calling. "I must go."

Between her and Jacob, they had the two new men cleaned up and resting on fresh sheets before the doctor arrived on the ward. Louisa held the enameled pan to catch the discarded bandages, which would be taken out to the washroom and boiled clean, then rerolled and used again. The man in the bed groaned but never regained awareness.

"Just do what you can. The longer he stays unconscious, the better off he'll be. Then the pain won't kill him at least."

"What about his head?"

"Not as bad as it looks. Head wounds always bleed profusely. He won't be so handsome as before, but the bullet didn't puncture the skull. Not sure if we can save the eye or not. Hardheaded man, he." Captain Tate, one of the few doctors who thanked Louisa instead of trying to chase her away, finished tying off the bandages around the head of the wounded man and got to his feet, his knees creaking with the effort. He looked down at his patient. "He's one of the lucky ones. No more war for him. If you can keep him alive, he'll go home."

He took the basin from Louisa and handed it to Jacob. "See that this makes it back to the caldrons, boy." He checked the arm stub of the man in the next bed and then looked up to his standing helper. "Lead on, dear Miz Highwood. I heard you have another new recruit."

"Down here."

When the doctor left the ward, Louisa took her water pail out to the pump in back of the hospital and nodded to the helper who leaned on the pump handle and began the requisite number of pumps to bring the cool water up from the well.

At least the hospital had a well, and a clean one at that.

"Thank you." She picked up her bucket and stopped, staring up at the tall windows on the second-floor wing, her ward. Seen from the outside, the brick walls and white-painted window trim gave no hint of the suffering inside. But when one opened the door, a miasma of moaning, despair, and the stench of putrefying flesh smothered the air, making it not only imprudent but impossible to draw in a deep breath. The September heat lay like a featherbed over the building, trapping the heat in the bricks. Even the leaves of the elm trees hung limp, too tired to rustle.

She'd become adept at shallow breathing.

The cries for help, for God, for home, were a different matter.

At least she could bring water.

"Miz Highwood, ain't it time for you to git on home?" One of the men who could now sit up nodded toward the dusking window. "Not good for you to be out after dark. Ain't safe."

"Thank you, I'm about to go. Aunt Sylvania always sends one of her servants to fetch me." Her aunt had given up trying to keep Louisa from the hospital, and now that Carrie Mae's wedding was drawing nearer, she had other things on her mind besides a niece who might have coined the word "stubborn."

Louisa set her pail down on the bench designated for it and glanced around the room. So much more to do and never enough help. If only she could get Carrie Mae down here, but the day she did come at Louisa's importuning, she'd fainted dead away at the sight of the men on stretchers waiting to be seen by the doctor.

"You comin' back?" one of the other men whispered as she walked the middle aisle, stopping to adjust a sheet, a pillow, touch a shoulder.

"First thing in the mornin'." She stopped at the man lying in John's bed. She couldn't think of it any other way until they at least knew this man's name. But he never stirred when she touched his hand. If only they could keep him alive long enough to find out who he was.

She studied the line of his jaw. What did he look like under those bandages? Would he recognize himself in the mirror when he awoke? What was there about him that seemed familiar?

"You got the purtiest hair, ma'am." A soldier who looked too young to shave tried to raise his head but winced and let it fall back. "Please don't think I'm bein' forward."

"I won't if you promise to rest and get well."

He shook his head with the barest motion. "Them nightmares. They make sleepin' purt near impossible, but I'll try." Eyes, circled and crisscrossed with red and sunken back in his skull, pleaded for her touch.

She took his hand and patted it. "I'll bring my Bible with me again tomorrow and read you some."

"Thankee, Miz Highwood. You git on home now."

Louisa stopped at the doorway and looked back. How many of them would still be there when she returned in the morning?

CHAPTER EIGHT

Morgantown, Kentucky
September 23, 1862

"Town up ahead, mile or so." Meshach trotted Sunshine, the mare, alongside the wagon.

"Can we go out around it?" Jesselynn straightened her shoulders. She'd been nearly asleep.

"Night dark like this make no nevermind."

Driving through a town, no matter how small, brought out the knots in her stomach. "How far ahead is Benjamin?"

" 'Bout half mile. He waitin' on us."

There'd have to be a direct confrontation on a moonless night like the one they were driving through for anyone to even get a glimpse of them. They didn't know anyone this far from home, so how would anyone know them? Besides, they'd only be sounds, dark as it was.

"What do you think?"

"Go on through. Save time. I tie up to de wagon and drive. Dat way someone see us, dey not 'spect some nigger stealin' de hosses and wagon."

Jesselynn thought of her team. Even Ahab looked more like a workhorse now. He was tired enough to plod along, head down, the arch gone from his neck and the lift from his tail. The horses had begun to take on the nondescript look needed to keep them safe in the daylight, let alone the night.

What to do?

A dog barked off to their right. Another answered, but there was no excited yip of a dog coming to see who they were. They were just doing their job, announcing someone going by.

"All right." She tightened the reins with a soft "whoa," and the wagon squeaked to a halt. They needed to get some grease for the wagon wheels. So many things she should have thought to bring. So many she hadn't been aware they'd need.

Meshach stripped the saddle from the mare and tied her to the tailgate along with the filly.

"We's a'right?" Ophelia's sleepy voice came from the pallet where she and Thaddeus slept each night.

"Sho' 'nuff, sugar, you g'wan back to sleep."

If only I could crawl back there and sleep too. Jesselynn felt like rubbing her rear. Riding horse or hard bench, either way her rump hurt by the end of the night. Never had she thought that walking would feel good. Or that running would feel better. But not with someone chasing them.

She scooted over and Meshach clucked the team into motion again. "Where's the rifle?"

"Right behind us."

Jesselynn reached back and grabbed the stock, then settled the gun at their feet. Better safe than sorry, as her mother had always said. But then Miriam Highwood hadn't been fleeing across the state of Kentucky either, not that she wouldn't have if it were necessary. But no way could she picture her mother donning britches. She would have worn an old dress and shawl, but no britches.

Once she'd opened the gate in her mind, thoughts of home scrambled through like runaway sheep. How were Lucinda and Joseph doing with the plantation? Was the tobacco all cut and drying? With the drought, the leaves were small anyway and drying in the field. While the fugitives had only been on the road a few days, it felt like a month and another world.

The final question leaped into her head like the wolf that chased the sheep. *What about Dunlivey? Did he come back?*

She shivered at the thought. He could be trailing them already, and he wouldn't have to hide during the day. He could travel as long as he pleased.

But he's in the army. He can't just leave like that. This thought brought her a measure of comfort. So easy in the dark of night to dream up bogeymen, and Dunlivey surely was the king of those. An owl hooted right over their heads, leaving her heart pumping and her hands shaking. Maybe it was a good thing Meshach was driving. Ahab would feel her fear.

She could hear her brother Zachary's put-out voice. *"Quit acting like a girl, Jesse, or you can't come with us."*

Or her mother. *"Jesselynn, you must be a lady. You are too old for climbing trees any longer."*

Or Lucinda. *"You break yo' mama's heart, actin' like dat."*

This was a night for voices.

"All quiet up ahead." Benjamin trotted up to the wagon side, seeming to come out of nowhere.

"Good."

When they drew even with the outbuildings of the town, Meshach slowed the horses to a walk. While they could see the outlines of the buildings, not a candle lit a window nor a sound spoke louder than the clop of the horses' hooves and the squeak of the wheels. Maybe the town had been abandoned. Had there been fighting in the area?

Where in thunder were they?

She didn't realize she'd been holding her breath until she felt light-headed as they left the town behind without incident. Jesselynn sucked in a deep breath and let it out on a sigh.

She swatted at a mosquito, tired of the incessant whine about her head. The long sleeves of her shirt and long pant legs saved all but her neck and face. As dawn neared, a breeze picked up, and the mosquitoes left.

The sky lightened slowly like a shy bride hiding her blushes. Birds twittered and fluttered, trying out voices roughened by the night. A cardinal burst into song as the sun pinked the clouds. A rooster crowed, cows bellowed from the farm off to the side of the road, a horse whinnied, and Ahab pricked his ears.

The road started down a hill, and off in the distance they could see the steam rising from a river that glinted between the trees.

"Stopping somewhere along the river?" she asked.

"I s'pose. Benjamin find us a good spot." Meshach raised his head, sniffing the breeze. "Some'un cookin' bacon. My, that do smell good."

Jesselynn sniffed. "You're making that up."

"No, suh. Close yo' eyes and sniff again."

She did as he said, and a smile stretched her cheeks. "You're right. Bacon and eggs and biscuits. Lucinda's biscuits. Now wouldn't that be fine?"

"We might could buy bacon and eggs. Gots to get milk fo'

Thaddy, but . . ." He shook his head. "No one makes biscuits like Lucinda." It was his turn to sigh. "I sho' do miss her good cookin'."

"When we get to camp, you want to find a farm and get us some supplies? Or I could do it."

"Benjamin will. Lucinda tan my black hide if she hear we let you go off by yo'self."

Jesselynn started to argue but chose to leave it alone. The farther they got from home, the less hold Lucinda would have. She nibbled on her bottom lip. You'd have thought Lucinda was mistress of the house instead of her.

Please, God, let us see Lucinda and Twin Oaks again. Guilt caught her by the throat and squeezed. How many days since she'd read her Bible, either to herself or to the others? How long since she'd thanked her heavenly Father for keeping them safe? Did it really make any difference?

After Benjamin signaled them to the stopping place, she dug a few more coins from her leather drawstring bag and handed them to him. Soon they would be down to gold pieces, and those she could never give to a slave. It would be far too noticeable.

"Get milk, bacon or ham if they have some, and eggs." She paused to think. "And ask if they have any vegetables they can spare from their garden."

"You wants grain for de horses?"

She shook her head. "They'll have to do on grass. I'm sure Uncle Hiram will have plenty of grain to fatten them for the winter. Take the mule."

"Yessuh." Benjamin grinned at her. "Not Ahab, huh?"

"You git." Meshach stripped the harness off Ahab and draped it over a wagon wheel. "And hurry. We's hungry."

"And tired of mush." Jesselynn scooped Thaddy up in her arms and gave him a whirl around hugs and kisses on both cheeks, making him giggle.

"More." He patted her cheeks with both hands. "More Jesselynn."

"More who?" She stopped whirling and adopted her sternest face. "What's my name?"

Thaddeus looked down, one finger on his lower lip. "Jesse."

"Good boy. Now say it again."

"Jesse." He pooched out his lower lip. "Jesse!" His finger now pointing to his own chest, "Me Joshwa."

"All right, Josh*wa*! Let's go wash in the river."

Cold water has a way of waking one more fully. By the time she'd removed her boots and stuck her feet in so she and Thaddy could wade, feeling was returning to her legs and posterior. She looked across the water to see two deer drinking in the shallows. But when Thaddy slapped a stick on the water, they vanished into the shadows before she could point them out to him.

Catching Thaddy by the hands, she swirled him around as she waded out to her hips and then dunked them both. He shrieked with laughter until she heard Meshach announce breakfast behind her.

"Good. Come on in. The water feels fine." Dripping, she turned, Thaddy in her arms.

Ophelia appeared from behind Meshach. "Missy Lynn." Her eyes and mouth showed her shock.

"Don' call her dat!" Meshach lashed out at her, his laughter turned fierce in an eye blink.

"I's sorry." Ophelia cringed like a puppy about to be whipped. She looked at Jesselynn. "I know, Jesse. I jes' fo'git."

"Then don't call me anything at all. If we make mistakes with just us, that is one thing, but little mistakes can lead to our being caught, and if we're caught, you might be raped or killed or sold. Keep that in mind."

"And think, 'Phelia. Think! You got a brain under dat kinky wool, so use it." Meshach frowned at Ophelia.

Jesselynn looked at Meshach, shock making her hands tingle. He sounded so like her father he could have been standing there. How many times had she heard Joshua Highwood say the same thing to one of the slaves? He expected them to think, fully believing that God gave those with dark skin every bit as much intelligence as those with light. Needless to say, other planters didn't agree with him and frequently told him so, so he'd no longer shared that information.

The fear of *uppity niggers* permeated the plantations like miasma hovering over a swamp. But even though it became illegal to teach slaves, Highwood had continued and, therefore, so had Jesselynn.

The song of a cardinal broke up the exchange, and Meshach shook his head once more in Ophelia's direction before returning to the fire, where Benjamin was dismounting with the supplies. The cardinal's song had become their signal so that no one ended up at the wrong end of the rifle.

Within minutes, Ophelia had the bacon frying, and the perfume of it brought the others back to the campfire. Jesselynn, with Thaddeus on one hip, grabbed a dead branch on the way and pulled it up to the fire. She swung her baby brother to the ground and began breaking sticks off for the fire, motioning him to do the same. Gone were the days when small children were carried everywhere on the hip of their slave and played with continually lest they cry and be unhappy. At least with those of Twin Oaks.

"My, that smells downright heavenly." Jesselynn sniffed again in appreciation. They had used up their bacon, along with the rabbits Benjamin and Meshach managed to snare. If only there had been more in the storehouse at home for them to bring along, but she couldn't see letting those left behind be without food either. So they had split the stores, knowing that the money would need to be stretched until it pleaded for mercy and then stretched some more.

They would be eating squirrel and rabbit at home too, unless someone got a deer. She jerked her thoughts back to the matters at hand just in time to scoop Thaddeus up and away from the fire.

"No! You don't touch the fire. You know better." At the sternness of her voice, he screwed his eyes shut and puckered his mouth to let out a wail. "No, stop that. You are not hurt." She gave him a bit of a shake to catch his attention.

"I take him." Meshach dumped some more wood down by the fire and reached for the child.

"No, he has to learn to mind." She grasped the chubby chin and looked right into Thaddy's blue eyes, so like his father's it made her heart hitch. "When I say no, I mean no, and you have to stop what you are doing right then. Without another move." He blinked and stuck a forefinger in his round mouth. "You hear me?" He nodded, never taking his eyes from hers.

"Me be good."

"I know you can be good." She hugged him and kissed his cheek, tasting the salt of a tear that trekked downward. "And you must be." *For all of our sakes.*

"Sit yourself an' eat." Ophelia handed her a plate with one hand and took Thaddeus with the other. "I feeds him."

Jesselynn knew that she should do that herself and let Ophelia eat too, but like a bolt from the sky, her knees nearly collapsed, setting her down with more of a thump than she'd reckoned. Her plate tipped alarmingly, but she righted it before her two fried eggs slipped over the edge.

"Bread! Fresh bread?"

"De lady, she gived me dat." Benjamin's smile near to cracked his face. He pointed to a sack behind the log. "Dey's carrots, an' beets, an' some beans, 'longside de milk an' such. She one nice lady. She say we by Morgantown on de Green River."

"I set snares. We have rabbit stew fo' supper." Meshach handed Thaddeus another piece of bread to dunk in his milk.

Thaddy smiled, a white trickle off the side of his lip. "Good." He waved the bread, brushing it against Ophelia's cheek so she ducked back. That made the little boy chuckle and wave his bread again.

A leaf floated down and hovered in the smoke before drifting off to the side. The sun slanted through the thinning branches of the oak tree to her back. Jesselynn inhaled the scents of autumn— leaves falling to decay and make rich leaf mold so that the land might sleep and sprout again, fried bacon, coffee, the shoreline of the sleepy river, oak branches fired to coals.

If she closed her eyes, she could pretend they were on a picnic and that later they would drive home and . . . if there was any home left.

Better to keep her eyes open. She drank the last of the coffee, tossing the dregs into the fire, then rising, she set her cup and plate in the wash pan steaming over the coals. Staggering to the wagon and taking the pallet out felt beyond her strength, but she did it anyway and collapsed without a blink. Some time later she felt someone pull her boots off and throw a mosquito net over her, so she mumbled a thank-you and sank back into the well of sleep.

Her favorite dream returned.

The shade of the oaks lining the long drive to Twin Oaks dappled their faces as she and John Follett strolled the length and back.

"I talked with your father." John took her hand and tucked it around his bent elbow so he could press her closer to his side.

"I know." Surely he could feel her heart thumping clear to her fingertips.

He stopped and, turning her to face him, took both of her hands. "I . . ." He cleared his throat and tried again.

She felt as if she were swimming in his eyes, stroking deeper to reach the fine soul she saw shining there. No suitor had ever made her feel like this.

"I love you, Jesselynn Highwood, and I want to marry you, the sooner the better." He didn't have to say before the war, but she knew what he meant. He squeezed her hands. *"Tell me you feel the same."*

"I do." Oh, how she longed to say those words in front of the minister.

He kissed her then, her first kiss, and the sweetness of it made her yearn for more. She nestled into his chest, both his arms around her. Such a safe place, like the nest she'd never known she searched for.

Turning her face up to his, she kissed him back, her parasol tipping over her shoulder and shielding them from any spying eyes. If Lucinda caught them . . .

"Jesselynn." The voice no longer matched that of the man in her dreams.

"Jesselynn!" The hand on her shoulder brought her back from her euphoric dream. She sat upright and banged her head on the wagon bed.

"What? What's wrong?"

"Bluebellies crossin' de river."

Chapter Nine

On the banks of the Green River
September 24, 1862

"Hide the horses," Jesselynn ordered.

"Did dat." Ophelia sank back on her haunches, her eyes wide.

"Where's Thaddeus?" Jesselynn rubbed the spot on her head as she crawled out and sat to pull her boots back on.

"Sleepin'." Pointing to another pallet in the shade of a tree, Ophelia's hand shook.

"Good." Jesselynn dug under the mosquito net for her hat and clamped it back on her head, feeling as if she became a young man in that single motion. No more Jesselynn, who'd enjoyed being kissed under the oak trees. She was Jesse, younger son of Joshua Highwood, on a mission.

She could hear laughter, horses splashing, men calling orders. How far from the ford had she set up camp? She glanced up to see the sun way past the high point. It was later in the afternoon now. Would they dare cross the ford at dusk with Yankees in the area?

Of course the soldiers could be miles up the road by then. Or they could camp just on this side of the river.

"Go on as if nothing is wrong," she whispered to Ophelia. "We have every right to be here, and as long as the horses are hidden . . ."

"But dey might cotch me." Ophelia looked like a rabbit who wanted nothing but to bolt back down its hole.

"Not with me here." She reached back in the wagon bed for the rifle they kept under the seat. A rifle and one pistol. Not much ammunition if they needed to frighten off a rover or two. Meshach wore the pistol tucked in his waistband.

She watched Roman, the mule, grazing in the sunlight, his long ears swiveling to keep track of the noises around him. When he raised his head, looking off to the north, she held her breath, only releasing it when the animal dropped back to cropping grass. A blue jay flew overhead, announcing its displeasure at the invasion of its territory.

The wait continued. Her mind raced through the things she should do if a blue-coated soldier rode into their camp. Shooting him would be stone-cold stupid, unless he tried to take a slave or a horse. Could she pull off her disguise as a young man? She'd already figured what to say about their traveling. Going to Uncle's for a visit, that's what. Was there a law against traveling?

She scrubbed her palms down the sides of her pants. Wet hands did not a sure shot make.

Silence felt like the kiss of heaven. She swallowed and patted Ophelia on the shoulder. "We'll be all right now." Birds twittered and flitted in the trees. A dog barked some distance away. All the normal sounds of woodland life carried on.

A bit later Benjamin and Meshach led the horses out of the woods and hobbled them again to graze. Roman nickered when his friends returned and fell to grazing again. Peace lay over the campsite.

Benjamin slipped out of the woods moments later. "Six, eight sojers on a patrol. Dey not lookin' for trouble."

"I surely do hope not." *But they always need horses.*

"Think I try fo' a mess a fish." Meshach slouched against the wagon wheel.

"Did you sleep?"

"Enough. Benjamin better sleep now. Daniel too."

Ophelia set about scrubbing vegetables for the rabbit stew, the savor of the cooking rabbit already tantalizing Jesselynn's taste buds. She dug in the sack for a carrot, since she had slept through dinner, and supper wouldn't be until near dark.

Carrot in hand, she took out her father's journals and flipped to the blank pages. After all the years he'd kept a journal, she had decided to follow suit when he went off to war, and she had kept them up until their flight. But now there would be no account of food put by or crops harvested unless Lucinda or Joseph thought to keep records at home. Hers was about their journey. She sharpened a quill and shook the ink bottle. Soon she'd need to make ink.

Jesselynn snugged her back against a tree trunk and, with journal on her knees, set to her task. After filling in the date, she swiftly described their travels through the nights, the patrols they'd avoided, the money they spent, and now the condition of the mares, who would soon need grain.

She watched them grazing so peacefully, then went back to her journal. If they had brought everything they might need, they would have had three wagons, not one. She fingered the Bible she kept in the leather satchel with the journals. Tonight she would read to them all before supper. She couldn't keep her eyes open long enough in the morning. How long would it take her to get used to staying awake all night and sleeping during the day? And feel rested?

She woke with a crick in her neck and the ink bottle unstoppered. The sun glowed red on the tree trunks as it sank toward the hilltop. Rubbing her neck, she stuck the cork back in the ink, mentally scolding herself for being so lax. She looked around the campsite and saw Thaddy playing in a pile of leaves, Meshach cleaning a harness, and Ophelia stirring the cooking pot.

Her stomach rumbled as the fragrance of the stew drifted past. Pushing herself to her feet took more energy than she thought possible, but once she had stretched and yawned, she could bend over to pick up her satchel and stow it back in the wagon. Scratching a mosquito bite on her neck, she wandered over to where Thaddy played with a carved wooden horse in the dirt and leaves.

Meshach had been busy.

"See horse?" He held his toy up for her admiration. "Good horse."

"That he is. You been eatin' dirt?"

He shook his head, but his mouth showed otherwise.

"Come on, let's go to the river and wash."

"Play in water?" He boosted himself to his feet, rear first, horse clutched in one fist. With the other he reached for her hand and together they strolled toward the water. The trip took longer than usual as Thaddeus admired three sticks and two patches of leaves, giggled in a flickering shadow, inspected a burl on an oak tree, insisted they walk around the *other* side of a tree, and found two rocks that went in his pocket.

Carrying him would have been ten times faster, but not as entertaining. Thanks to her sharp eyes, they watched ants carrying crumbs back to their soil home and a beetle digging for whatever beetles dig for.

When he sat in the water, she let him splash while she took off her boots. How wonderful a swim would feel. But if it washed the walnut dye out of her hair, she'd have to boil more husks to make new, and that took too long for this evening's entertainment.

Gold still streaked the river that looked more like a big creek with wide beaches and gilded the outlines of the trees on the far side. Fording this so they needn't go into town would be easy. The water didn't appear to be up to the horses' bellies even. They'd have to pitch or tar the wagon bed before they got to a river where they had to swim the horses. So many things to think of.

She rubbed her forehead. Most likely she'd slept a cramp into her neck, which caused the headache, not the thinking.

She studied the far shore. Upriver some cows stood drinking in the shallows, so obviously there was a farm there. Downriver all she could see were trees, some still green, others touched with fall paint. How far had the Union soldiers gone before camping? Or had they headed north to Louisville? If only she had any idea what was happening with the war.

"Jesse, look."

She glanced down to see Thaddy, water running down his arm, holding up something shiny. Bending over, she grasped his waving hand. A gold button, once closing an army uniform, lay in his palm.

Was it Union or Confederate? And how had it come to be here?

"My button." Thaddy grasped her rolled-up pant leg and pulled himself upright, reaching for the treasure.

"All right. But keep it out of your mouth, you hear?" He nodded and closed his fingers over the button.

"Mine."

"Put it in your pocket, then, so you don't lose it." She watched while he did so, then looked out again to the riverbanks.

A rifle shot popped in the distance and then another. Someone hunting or—

The barrage that followed answered her *or*. The shots came from the northwest and far enough away to keep her from running to hide, but if there were both gray and blue ahead of them, perhaps they'd best stay right where they were.

The volleys continued, a bugle blew, then silence fell. One more shot erupted, and that was it. She waited, but even as the sky shifted from fire to ember gray and the evening star peeked out, only the sound of birds gossiping off to sleep broke the stillness. A fish jumped and smacked the water on return.

"Come an' eat." Meshach spoke from off her right shoulder.

She hadn't heard him arrive. She looked down to find Thaddeus covered with mud from the hole he'd been digging in the bank.

"Oh, Thaddy." She shook her head, grabbed him up, and, holding his arms, soused him up and down in the water to wash the mud off. His giggle brought smiles to both her and Meshach. "Now we'll have to get you in dry clothes again."

"So, do we stay or go?" The question had been chewed on by each of them, with everyone but Jesselynn saying go. The thought of running into either patrol made the hair on the back of her neck stand at attention. They could lose everything.

"I take Roman and go scout." Benjamin leaned forward. "No one sees us."

"All right." She shook her head, wishing she felt braver. Here in this copse and small meadow with the river at their door, she felt safe for some inexplicable reason. The other side of the river spelled danger.

While they waited, she helped Meshach check on the horses, digging dirt and a rock or two out of their hooves and inspecting for any harness galls, all the while listening for Benjamin's signal. When it came, the sigh of relief originated in her toes and worked its way upward.

"No sign of sojers. Road clear." He swung off Roman and joined them in the firelight. "I followed a road some an' see signs a patrol go dat way." He pointed to the north. "But de road we take is clear."

"Good." She stood and dusted off the back of her pants. "Let's go, then."

Within minutes they had Ahab and one of the mares harnessed together, Jesse riding Domino, the younger stallion, and Meshach driving the wagon. As they headed out, she glanced back to the clearing, seeing the glint of the river through the tree trunks. Was it wrong to want to hang on to a moment of peace?

When they reached the ford, she waited on the bank for the wagon to go ahead. Glancing upriver, there appeared to be a log floating in the middle.

"Meshach, you see that log?" She raised her voice to be heard over the splashing horse hooves. Water was past their knees and heading for belly-deep. Would the wagon have to float?

"I sees it. Come on across." The horses were pulling the wagon into shallow water. Jesselynn nudged Domino into the river. He snorted and tossed his head but at the pressure of her legs continued forward, ears flicking to catch her encouraging words. He snorted again as they drew level with the log.

What she'd thought was a log. Where the face should have been, only a black hole gaped at the sky, and the gray-clad soldier floated on past. Jesselynn kicked her horse forward, her stomach fighting the urge to erupt.

CHAPTER TEN

Richmond, Virginia

"But I have to go back to the hospital. The men need me."

"It's just not proper for a young girl like you to be working in that . . . that place, and you not even married. I don't see how the doctors ever let you in the door." Aunt Sylvania had said these words far too many times before for Louisa to pay a great deal of attention. Nor would she tell her aunt that the doctors and officers understood her to be a widow and several years older than her actual age. They knew her as Mrs. Zachary Highwood. Adopting the name of her missing brother had seemed like a good idea at the time.

And it still was. Getting a wedding ring hadn't been difficult, since she'd taken her mother's out of the strongbox at home. She kept it on a chain around her neck until after she left the house.

Louisa smiled gently at her aunt, whose chin had a tendency to quiver in righteous indignation. Out of the three girls of her family, only one did as any proper young lady would. Carrie Mae sought and found a fine young man to marry. No matter that he was missing part of an arm. His old family heritage more than made up for that, and being a successful lawyer had nothing to do with how many arms he had. In fact, his loss made him a more sympathetic character in the courtroom.

Louisa knew all this and understood Aunt Sylvania's concern, but . . . that was the word. *But.* What about the suffering right down the street? *What if Father were to come to my hospital and there was no one there to give him a drink, read to him, or write letters home if he couldn't use his hand? Or Zachary?* She already knew that Adam was beyond her care. She hoped he and their mother were enjoying each other's company and looking out for those left here on earth.

"Louisa, you are not listening to me." The spoon clattering onto the saucer let Louisa know that she had missed something important. When had she gotten so adept at appearing to be listening when her mind roamed off elsewhere?

"I'm sorry, Aunt. What was that you said?"

Sylvania sniffed, setting the ribbons on her morning cap to fluttering. She *tsked* with more force than necessary, another indication of her rising indignation.

Louisa laid her fork down on her plate and gave her aunt her full attention. Excuses would not help. Life here was so different than at Twin Oaks. Why, oh why, had Jesselynn sentenced her to so-called safety with Aunt Sylvania? Until she'd found a place at the hospital, the boredom of society in Richmond had more than once brought her to tears. As the capital of the Confederacy, Richmond held more balls and concerts and soirees than she ever planned to attend in a lifetime. Playing at dressing up and attracting beaus those years at home were vastly different than reality. Such a waste of time. She kept herself from shaking her head just in time.

"I . . ." Sylvania paused, beetling her brows at her niece. "I believe it is time for us to have a small soiree. I hear young James Scribner has returned from the war, and I believe you and he would . . ." She paused again and lifted one eyebrow.

Louisa forced a smile, making sure that both sides of her mouth lifted and, along with a nod, encouraged her aunt to continue. *Oh, Lord, no, please not another one. Now I have an idea what the slaves felt like on the auction block, but at least no one has checked my teeth.* "Are you sure you have time for that, what with gettin' ready for the weddin' and all?"

Long-suffering looked at home on Sylvania's time-spotted and wrinkled face. "I will manage. Your happiness is of utmost importance to me." Another sniff followed, and this time the bit of cambric touched the tip of her rabbity nose.

Louisa used every bit of training her mother had instilled in her. Her eyebrow stayed where it belonged. "Thank you, Aunt, I'm sure it is." *Why can't Carrie Mae get up early enough to distract her?* Thoughts of what she would like to do to her sleeping sister took her mind off on another trail.

"More biscuit, Missy?" The soft voice at her shoulder made

Louisa turn with a smile. Abby, her woolly hair covered with a white kerchief, held out a basket covered with a white napkin, the fragrance going before it.

"Thank you, I will. These are even better than Lucinda's at home, but I know you will never tell her I said that."

"No'm." The smile that caused dimples in her ebony cheeks made Abby chuckle too. "I knows Lucinda be one fine cook."

"Yes." Louisa took a golden brown biscuit and set it on her plate. *If only I could take some of those with me, they might tempt Sergeant Wilson's appetite.* But she knew if she asked, her aunt would launch again into her oft delivered speech on the unsuitability of her niece working at the hospital. Louisa had it memorized—*well* memorized.

"Message, madam." Reuben, who used to be the butler but now was more man of all trades, set a silver salver, worn bare in spots, on the table in front of his mistress.

"Oh, now what?" Sylvania set her coffee cup down only the least bit harder than necessary, showing that her displeasure had not totally abated.

Louisa used the distraction to lay her napkin on her plate and push back her chair. "Thank you, Abby, I must hurry." She spoke low enough that Aunt Sylvania wouldn't hear. She kept her pace sedate as "befitted a young woman of breeding"—her aunt's words—until she reached the hall, then flew up the stairs.

Coming out of her room, she nearly bumped into Carrie Mae, yawning and stretching as she crossed the hall.

"Goodness, need you be in such a rush?" Carrie Mae patted back another yawn with a delicate hand. Her hair, much the same rich color as Louisa's but curly instead of straight, looked charmingly tousled instead of sleep flattened. Sleepy eyed, she gazed at her sister. "I suppose you're all done with breakfast too and off to the hospital?"

"How did you ever guess?" Louisa patted her sister's cheek, feeling years older and wiser. "How was the cotillion last night?"

"Last night? I barely got to bed before the sun rose." Carrie Mae yawned again. "Excuse me, oh, did Aunt mention the soiree? It is about time we returned some of the invitations, you know."

Louisa shuddered. "If she drags out one more—"

"Now, sister dear, meeting the right people is important. You know that well as anyone. What would Daddy say?"

"Daddy would say what our Lord said—a cup of water for the

thirsty, bandages for the wounded, and given as soon as possible."
She smiled at her sister, who was already shaking her head.

"I have rolled enough bandages for the entire Army of the Potomac. You think I do nothing all day. Why"—she held out a needle-roughened finger—"see how often I've stuck myself, yet that uniform still looks like it belongs on a slave rather than a Confederate soldier."

"If you could sew as well as you play the piano, there would be more uniforms maybe, but think how many hearts are lifted by your music." Louisa leaned over and kissed her sister on the cheek. "How is Mr. Steadly?" Jefferson Steadly had asked Carrie Mae to be his wife after a minimal courtship, having declared himself so smitten by her he couldn't wait.

"Oh, Louisa, I only wish for you the happiness that I've found. I believe he loves me like Daddy loved Mama."

"Then that is our wish come true for you." Louisa squeezed her sister's hand. "I must hurry. I have much to do."

"Don't forget . . ."

The rest of the sentence was lost in the rustling of her skirts descending the stairs. Unbidden, a thought of the scarecrow on crutches, as the men called Lieutenant Lessling, passed through her mind. *Hmm, he'll hardly even talk to me. I wonder why.*

She picked up the basket that contained her Bible, a copy of Shakespeare's comedies, paper, quill and ink, and a packet of lemon drops for *her men*; then setting it on the entry table, she paused at the mirror to tie her bonnet. Once she had left the house without one, and the weeks of sniffing reminders weren't worth repeating the mistake.

"Here, Missy." Abby slipped a napkin-wrapped packet into the basket. "You must eat befo' you fades away."

Louisa raised an eyebrow in question.

"Not to worry. Dey's extra for de gentlemens." Abby ducked to hide a grin. "I fix a basket for dat Reuben to carry too." She stepped back a step. "But I not does it again 'less you promise me to eat yo'self."

Louisa fought the tears that burned at the back of her throat. "Thank you. I know our Father sees in secret."

"He better keeps the secret too." With that Abby headed to the back of the house, throwing a conspirator's smile over her shoulder as she pushed against the door leading to the outside kitchen.

"You ready, Missy?" Reuben held open the door, a much larger basket at his feet.

Knowing she had extra gifts to take lent speed to Louisa's slippers as they traversed the blocks to the two-story brick building that housed more suffering than the residents of the once fine but now aging houses in this part of the city cared to know.

Louisa couldn't understand how so many could go about their business as if the yard lined with wounded soldiers on pallets didn't exist. In fact, she had heard two matrons complaining one day that the screams heard from the hospital were just not to be tolerated.

It was all Louisa could do to keep from screaming at the two of them herself.

But in spite of those few, most women supported the war, rolling bandages, sewing uniforms, taking recuperating soldiers into their homes so they could be tended, knitting wool socks, and collecting what medicines and medicinal herbs they could for the soldiers' relief. Some contributed by earning money for supplies. The Ladies Aid at the church Louisa had chosen to attend did all of that and more.

Of course Aunt Sylvania had thrown a fit at that move too. The church Louisa chose was definitely not fashionable. How would she ever meet a young man of the proper quality there? What would her dear Joshua say if he saw his youngest daughter attending a Quaker meetinghouse, of all things?

As they neared the brick edifice, the low moans that sounded like a flowing river hummed louder than the cicadas thrumming in the elm trees.

The smell met her at the door like a heavy curtain.

"Where you wants dis?" Reuben nodded to his basket.

"Right here in this closet. That way I can parcel things out." She hung her bonnet on a hook and donned the white apron hanging beside it. At the same time, she scooped two bloodstained aprons out of another basket and, bundling them together, handed them to Reuben. Unbeknownst to Aunt Sylvania, Abby had been laundering the aprons since Louisa began her hospital service. Another secret she and the slaves kept between them. How would she ever be able to help with the soldiers if her aunt discovered their duplicity?

Reuben checked the water bucket and shuddered. "I gets fresh."

Louisa nodded and smiled her gratitude. As he left for the

pump out back, she checked the contents of both baskets. Hard-boiled eggs, already peeled for ease of eating, a packet of salt, biscuits slathered with butter and honey, a loaf of bread all sliced and buttered, sliced cheese to add to the bread, cookies, and a jar of chicken soup. Surely something here would help Private Rumford take more than two bites at a meal. No matter how she encouraged him, she got the feeling that all he wanted to do was die, if not from his wounds, then of starvation.

Reuben returned and she reached for his bucket, but a shake of his silvering head made her smile again. Lately he'd taken to staying with her while she took dippers of fresh water around to the men.

"Thank you, but I don't want you gettin' on the wrong side of Aunt."

"Not you worry, Missy. Let's get goin' now."

They stepped into the ward, and silence fell like a featherbed floating into place. Greetings bounced around the room, one patient passing the news of her arrival on to the next who might not see or hear.

"Good mornin'." She began on the right side, taking turns each day so no one always received her assistance first. The man in the bed raised himself on one elbow.

"I was 'fraid you wasn't comin'." He scooted back to brace against the wall.

"Why? Am I late?" Her smile made the man in the next bed chuckle.

"I . . . I don't know. The nights are so long, seems like mornin' fergits to come." He drank his fill and lay back. "Thankee, ma'am. Just seein' you so purtylike makes the water taste pert near as good as the spring at home."

"Hey, don't spend all mornin' with that worthless mountain castoff." The laughter in the tone made others laugh, one to the point of coughing as if he might not stop.

"Now, y'all just wait your turn." She spoke to the room and held the dipper for the man in the next bed. "How are you this mornin'?"

"Toler'ble." He hawked to clear his throat and spat into a towel left by his head, a towel already spotted with red.

Louisa kept her smile intact and slipped him one of the slices of bread with cheese. "I'll be back with more water soon as I can." If only she could bring him something hot to drink, perhaps he could better fight the infection raging through his body. But he did look more alert today.

As she made her way around the room, smiles followed her like butterflies after blossoms. For those too sick to raise themselves up to drink, she put her arm behind them to give them support. Several men were unconscious, so other than laying a hand on their shoulders and breathing a prayer for healing, she passed them by. Later she would come by with a basin of warm water and wash hands and faces.

The man in bed seventeen was such. She studied the rise and fall of his chest. He was breathing well at least. "Has he been awake at all?" The man in the next bed shook his head.

"Nary a sound outa him. Not even a groan. Doc says it's the head wound."

"Is he in a coma, then?"

The nod made her wince. "Do you know anything about him?"

"No'm, not a thing." He eyed her basket. "I sure would appreciate some o' that cheese you brought t'other day."

"With bread, or would you rather have one of cook's biscuits?"

"Mighty hard decidin'." He closed his one eye, the other an empty socket with a scar that ran from his hairline to his chin. That early wound had healed, so he was sent back to the front. He wouldn't be returning to battle again, not missing a leg.

When she held out the bread and cheese, he took it, his hand shaking so the bread almost fell to the floor. With a quick hand for his advancing years, Reuben handed the bread back without looking the man in the face.

"Here you goes, suh."

When the soldier failed to say anything, Louisa frowned at him and smiled at Reuben. "Thank you. Some of us seem to have forgotten our manners."

A hoot from the men around him made the culprit flush and stop chewing long enough to mumble, "Sorry. Thank you, boy."

"His name is Reuben, and he is far too old and valuable to be a boy." The ice in her voice cooled the air around them by several degrees. She waited, one slipper tapping the floor, counting the seconds.

It took more time than she'd liked, making her wonder if her strictness with these wounded men made any difference in the way they thought.

"Ah, Frank, give in."

"Now, you dumb—" At the collective gasp, the remonstrator cut off the rest of his sentence, earning him a smile from their angel. While she was on the floor, they all knew she tolerated no swearing, crude language, or cruelty in general. Her method of punishment to those intrepid cursers changed many minds. She just ignored them, walking by as if they did not exist.

By the time she and Reuben had circled the room, one of the doctors arrived, along with an assistant who helped change the dressings. While they started at one end, she waved good-bye to her helper and started at the other end, this time with a basin of warm water, washcloth, soap, and a towel. Those who could wash their own hands and faces did. The others received her gentle touch with sighs of appreciation.

"I heard you know how to shave a feller," one of her men said, raising both his hands swathed in bandages.

"I do, but it will be some time before I can get back."

"No problem, Miz Highwood. I ain't goin' nowhere."

She smiled at his gentle joke. "Not today, but soon."

"Home? You think they might send me home?"

"That'd be my surmise, but the doctor there has the last say." No one without usable hands would be sent back to the fighting, that she knew for certain, and from the looks of him, this young man, a boy really, would be going home soon. They needed his bed for those much worse off than he. Her gaze wandered over to the man who had yet to regain consciousness. The doctor would be seeing him next.

What was there about him that drew her? She ignored the puzzlement and eased her way to stand by the foot of his bed.

"How are you today, Miz Highwood?" The physician stopped beside her, studying her face. "Child, how long since you've taken a day off?"

"Oh, last week, I think." She shot him a piercing look. "How about you?"

"Last week. Must have been last week." His smile and head-shaking said he knew they were both lying. He patted her shoulder and turned to the patient, who showed no signs of impatience at the wait, unlike some of the others.

Louisa screwed up her courage. "Do you know anything about him?"

Dr. Fremont shook his head. "No, he had no identification and hasn't been able to answer questions. I was hoping he would be conscious by now, but then maybe this is better. At least he isn't feeling any pain, and with those wounds, the pain would be severe." He picked up the man's hand and checked the pulse. "His heart is strong. He's goin' to need that."

Louisa studied the man in the bed, what she could see of him. She promised herself to come back later because, conscious or not, warm water on his hands and face would feel good. And getting the blood washed off him would make her feel good. Knowing that the doctor would not tend his patient until she left the bedside, she returned to her errands of mercy, and the next time she looked up, the doctor and his assistant had left the ward.

With all of her men washed and some sleeping again, she searched out the razor she'd hidden away behind some boxes and filled her pan with hot water again. The razor needed stropping to get an edge back on it, but she hadn't found a suitable leather strap at Aunt Sylvania's. Short of asking Reuben to buy one for her, she'd made do up until now.

"I know this is dull, so if you'd rather wait . . ." She shrugged and raised her eyebrows as she spoke.

"Ah, she at least won't cut your throat and might get the worst off," the man in the next bed advised. "I could do it but . . ." He pointed to his bandaged eye.

"That's all right. I trusts her." The man lay back and raised his chin.

Louisa used the cloth to rub the soap so she could lather his face. The act brought back a vision of her father standing in front of a mirror in his bedroom, the brush in his hand full of lather, the razor glinting in the early morning sunlight. Her nose wrinkled at the memory. The soap had smelled nothing like this, and a rag didn't lather like the brush that fit in the mug designed just for that purpose.

Father, where are you? And where is Zachary? Is someone helping Zachary this morning?

She bent to her task, the rasp of the razor against the whiskers sounding loud, as if all the men were waiting with held-in breath to see if she would draw blood. With the razor she was using, it wasn't a case of *if*, but *when*.

By the time she'd finished, she had said "I'm sorry" so often that each new protestation brought chuckles that swelled to laughter from those around. If they only knew how good it made her feel to hear them laugh, even if it was at her expense.

She wiped off the remaining lather, shook her head at the left-over stubble, and stepped back.

"Looks to me like a rat been chewin' on 'im." One of the men who'd graduated to crutches offered his opinion from the foot of the bed.

"Thank you, Sergeant Arthur. Next time you can do the honors."

"Next time I'll make sure that razor got an edge on it. Give it here, and I'll take care of it."

"Now, why didn't you say that before?" Louisa picked up her pan of soapy water, draping the towel over her arm.

"You didn't ask."

She rolled her eyes and pushed on past him. "Tomorrow you're in charge of shavin'."

"Miz Highwood, you gonna read to us again?" The question came from another who could no longer see.

"Yes, that I am. Right now, as a matter of fact." She knew that if she didn't sit down fairly soon, she might just fall down.

By the time she headed for home in the evening dusk, her back ached, her feet felt like she'd walked miles, which she had, and the man in bed seventeen still hadn't awakened.

CHAPTER ELEVEN

Western Kentucky
September 25, 1862

"Jesse, me go home."

Jesselynn picked up her little brother and hugged him close. "I know. I want to go home too."

Thaddeus patted her cheeks with both of his hands. "Then go." He turned to grin up at Meshach. "We goin' home." The smile lit up his face, and he laid his cheek against his sister's. "Go home now."

Jesselynn first tried to swallow the boulder blocking her throat, then at least swallow around it. *Home, where the hip bath can be filled with hot lavender-scented water, and I can soak for a week, then sleep in my own soft bed until I feel like waking up. Where Lucinda or one of the others will bring me coffee or tea in bed if I so desire, where the doves will coo in the tree outside my window and I can hear the horses whinny on their way to the track.*

She hid her smarting eyes in Thaddy's shoulder and rocked from one foot to the other, crooning under her breath. *Home . . . oh, Lord, I want to go home.* A shudder started in her heels and worked its way up until she clenched her teeth. All she had to do was tell Meshach to turn the horses around and head back to Twin Oaks. She clamped her teeth shut and her arms around Thaddeus. The words bubbled in her head and up her throat. *Home, let's go home.*

"Ow! Jesse, you hurtin' me." The boy leaned back and stared into his sister's eyes. He patted her cheek again. "You cryin'?"

She shook her head and, setting him down, rubbed the corner of her eye. "Just got a speck of dirt in my eye, that's all. You go on and help Ophelia find firewood so we can have breakfast."

"Home?"

"Someday." The look of such utter sadness that he sent her before he trudged off behind Ophelia made her swallow hard again. Like their father, Thaddeus could say more with one glance than most people could with their mouths in an hour.

Home, she thought as she settled down to sleep some time later. *Home . . . sometimes I wonder if I ever even lived there or if I made it all up.*

"Thaddeus. Thaddeus!"

The sound of Ophelia calling brought Jesselynn awake long before she was ready.

"Thaddeus!" Meshach had joined her.

Jesselynn rolled out of bed and slid into her boots in a motion getting smooth with practice. She grabbed her hat on the way out from under the wagon and jogged to the edge of the woods, listening for another shout.

If Thaddy is lost, I'll never forgive myself. What happened? "What happened?" Jesselynn grabbed a sobbing Ophelia by the arm as soon as she found her.

"I was . . . I was . . . oh, Marse Jesse, he be gone. Thaddy be gone. Dey snatch him away."

"Who? What?" Jesselynn gave the keening woman a shake. "Tell me, Ophelia! Tell me what happened." She could hear the others calling in the woods.

"How long ago?"

Ophelia shrugged. "I . . . he was right beside me, then gone. Lawsy, our boy be lost. Oh, Lawd, help us find 'im. Please, Lawd."

"Thaddeus Joshua Highwood, come out wherever you are." *He can't be lost. He must think we are playing a game.* But no matter how hard she listened, he didn't answer.

Meshach made his way through the woods and stopped beside her. "Dis brush be so thick, he could fall in a hole, be anywhere."

Jesselynn felt like someone had stabbed her in the heart. Not Thaddy, not her baby brother. For all she knew, her only brother. Why had she slept so long? Turning brimming eyes upward, she shook her head. "Not Thaddeus."

"We find 'im. He not get far."

"He got farther than we can see, didn't he? What was Ophelia doing? Taking care of Thaddy is the most important thing she does."

"She know dat."

"Could someone have snatched him?"

Meshach shook his head. "Can't see how. Who? Why? No one know we here."

Dunlivey. The name exploded in her head. *Dunlivey*. He would take Thaddy knowing that nothing could hurt her more. But if he'd been there, he'd have taken them all. No, that couldn't be it.

"We just got to find 'im."

Jesselynn swallowed hard and sucked in a deep breath. Fainting wouldn't help, that was for sure, but she felt so light-headed right now, she could float off into the woods. She leaned against a tree trunk. She could hear the others calling his name. They sounded so far away. Surely he couldn't get that far.

"Thaddeus, the game is over. Come out now!" Her voice didn't carry beyond her nose. She took another breath and tried again. *God, I'll do anything you ask. Just keep him safe. Bring him back. Please God, please let us find him.*

"Tha-dde-us!" Better. Taking more air in, she screamed his name.

Meshach walked not ten feet from her, alternating with her, calling the child's name.

"Shh." Jesselynn froze. Was her mind playing tricks on her?

"What?" Meshach leaped to her side.

"Shh. Listen." Benjamin called Thaddy's name some distance away. Jesselynn froze, wished she could stop her heart. It was making too much noise. She held her breath. Could that be him?

She looked at Meshach, who nodded back. He pointed off to their left.

Together they pushed through the brush, stopping every couple of feet to call and listen.

The child's crying sounded clearer.

"Thaddeus?"

"Jesse."

"Call again, baby."

"Jesse."

They changed their angle and pushed on. Meshach grabbed her arm before she slid down the embankment. At the bottom lay a badly injured horse with Thaddeus stroking his neck.

"Horse hurt bad."

"Yes, darlin', I can see that." She turned to Meshach. "You got your gun?"

He nodded. "Thank you, Lord, you takes care of our boy."

Together they made their way down the slope and, when the horse started to thrash, stopped. Jesselynn hunkered down and slipped into her gentle crooning.

"Thaddeus, baby, you come on away from there now. Come to me, baby."

"Make horse better?" Thaddeus stood. The horse tried to raise his head and knocked the boy over.

"Easy, Thaddy, come on now." But Thaddeus squatted back down by the horse's head and began stroking his nose again.

"Good horse. Be good, nice . . ."

If Jesselynn didn't know better, she'd have thought it was herself sitting by the downed animal, singing the song that quieted. The horse settled back, a rumble coming from his throat.

"He bad hurt on chest. Legs look all right. Maybe lost too much blood," Meshach observed.

Jesselynn had been cataloging the injuries while she motioned for Thaddeus to come to her. He shook his head.

"Help horse."

"Yes, Thaddeus, we will help the horse. You come away now."

"Comin'." He patted the horse's nose again and backed away. The horse lay still, but they could see how he watched the small child, as if trusting in his care.

When Thaddeus reached Jesselynn, he patted her cheek. "See horse. He bleedin'. You fix."

Jesselynn wasn't sure if she wanted to hug him or wallop him one first. "All we need is a wounded horse." She shook her head. If she could get Thaddy away, Meshach could put the animal out of its misery.

Slowly Meshach moved in on the animal, all the time singing the same song Jesselynn used so well. He extended a hand for the horse to smell, then sat down in front of it and rubbed up its white blaze. "You one fine-lookin' horse to be hurt so bad like dis. How we gonna get you outa here?"

Jesselynn groaned. With Thaddy in the circle of her arm, she watched Meshach calm the beast. The blue saddle blanket told them which army the horse belonged to. The carbine was still in the scabbard, the saddlebags tied on behind the army saddle. The rider must have been blown right off his horse.

"How long you think since he was hit?" It looked like the shell had taken half his chest off.

"Day or two. Got to clean dis up, stitch a bit, get 'im some warm water. Sure do wish we had some oats to mash."

"You want me to send Benjamin for some?" She said it with every ounce of sarcasm she possessed.

Meshach shook his head. "Cornmeal will work."

Jesselynn groaned.

"Meshach fix." Thaddy sighed. "Me hungry. Go find 'Phelia." He stood and started up the bank, but Jesselynn grabbed him before he got more than an arm's reach away.

"I'll go with you, young man. You stay with me, you hear?" She looked up to see Ophelia, Benjamin, and Daniel looking down at them, shaking their heads. Tears ran down Ophelia's face to stop at the smile that cut off their track.

Thaddeus broke away and scrambled up the grade. "Meshach fix horse. Hurt bad. Joshwa hungry."

Ophelia met him partway, snatched him up, and, clenching him to her bosom, scolded and cried over him all at the same time.

When Jesselynn broke clear of the trees, she expected to see dusk settling, but the sun hadn't moved that much at all. It just seemed like a lifetime they'd spent hunting for Thaddeus.

Ophelia had him seated on the wagon tailgate, threatening his life if he moved, when Jesselynn reached them.

"Jesse." He raised his arms to be picked up.

"You just sit there till I get done talkin' to you." She shook her finger in front of his nose. "Don't you ever, you hear me, ever go in the woods by yourself. You stay with me—"

"You was sleepin'."

"Or Ophelia or Meshach. You do not go off by yourself. Do you understand?" She clipped off each word, using the words to keep from smacking him on the behind—and hugging him to bits.

A finger went in his mouth. His head drooped. He nodded. "Yes." A sniff drew up his shoulders. "But—"

"No! No 'but.' I'll wallop your butt till you can't sit down."

"Thaddy sorry."

Jesselynn rolled her eyes heavenward. How come he already knew to say sorry? It had taken her forever to learn that. More than one lickin' as she recalled.

"Thirsty."

"Yeah, me too." She scooped him up in her arms and settled him on her hip. "Let's get a drink."

"Get horse a drink?"

"Benjamin is doing that." She hadn't heard a shot from that general area so she figured they were doctoring the horse. All she needed right now was one more mouth to feed. And one too sick to graze from the look of him. Surely they should just shoot him and get on their way.

———

Two days passed before Meshach deemed the horse they now called Chess because of his wounds ready for any kind of travel. "Will have to be slow and not go too far."

Jesselynn just shook her head and swung aboard Ahab. Chess and the filly were tied to the back of the wagon, the scabbard and saddle left where someone was sure to find them. The supplies in the saddlebags had added to their stores, and the gold piece tucked in a small pocket now resided in Jesselynn's pouch. All in all, they'd gotten good return on their time and caring.

"Keep Chess." Thaddy stroked the horse's nose from the wagon bed.

"No, Thaddy. We have enough horses."

"Chess my horse."

"Thaddeus Joshua Highwood, listen to me."

He looked up at her with a smile that came straight from the angels. What could she say?

"We'll talk about this later."

Benjamin kicked Domino into a canter in order to do his usual scouting to keep them out of the clutch of soldiers, didn't matter which color uniform. He waved once and disappeared around a bend in the road.

Jesselynn thought of the crude map the younger man had gotten in one of his scouting forays. According to the map, they were to head south for a time and then pick up a road heading west again. As the days passed, she wished at times they had followed the more heavily traveled road to Louisville, but they had decided against it. The possibility of boarding a keelboat to take them down the Ohio River and onto the Mississippi still carried far more appeal than the overland trek. But they'd have to pass the fort at Cairo, where General Grant was stationed with his army. "Army of the West," she'd heard it called.

Meshach clucked forward the team consisting of the two mares this time. Daniel rode the mule. Jesselynn glanced over her shoulder at the clearing they were leaving behind. Such a terribly close brush with tragedy. They would have to be more careful, that's all.

She pulled her coat more tightly around her. Clouds hung low and smelled like rain. Lightning splintered the sky off to the north. This promised to be a bad night if the clouds had anything to say about it.

It wasn't long after full dark that the clouds gave up and released their burden on the travelers below. Within minutes, Jesselynn's wool coat smelled wet and rain dripped from her hat brim down her neck. She turtled herself as much as possible, but the wind first nipped at her hat, then turned to tearing at it and shaking her furiously, like a dog shaking himself off. The frigid drops blew into her face, and when she tucked it into her coat, they ran down the back of her neck.

"Tain't fit fo' man nor beast," Meshach declared when Jesselynn trotted alongside the wagon. Already puddles disguised the road in a muddy stream when they climbed a rise and slid down the other slippery side. He set the brake some to keep the wagon from running over the horses and hushed Ophelia when she squealed at a slip.

They climbed another grade and were back on a westering ridge. At least she hoped it was westering. She couldn't even see Ahab's ears, let alone far enough ahead to get an idea where they were going.

The longer the rain persisted, the more she longed for home.

So her father had made her promise. They gave it a good try. How would he know if they turned around, anyway? She shook her head, her hat flopping about her ears. Maybe this was God's punishment for leaving home. Surely they'd been on the road long enough for dawn to be coming soon.

Ahab snorted and, arching his neck, whinnied before she realized what he was doing. "No!" She tightened the reins in retaliation for being jerked from her somnolence. The horse side-stepped, his entire body at attention. Something was coming toward them.

She reined Ahab to the side of the road under the over-hanging trees, praying that Meshach was doing the same. She could hear a harness jingling, and when that fell silent, a horse galloping toward them. She swung off her horse and clamped her hand over his nostrils. Others followed, barely heard above the rain on the leaves overhead and her heart thundering in her chest.

A shot and then another.

The lone rider raced by them, water splashing from the horse's hooves.

Was it Benjamin?

Her eyes hurt from straining to see what was happening.

Horse hooves fading, others charging on. Two riders splashed past, then two more. Another shot was fired, this time so close she saw the flash of the gun.

All the hoofbeats faded into the distance. The rain picked up again, as if the brief interlude had been to tantalize them. Who was the fugitive? Who was chasing him? Confederate, Union, or deserter? What lay ahead?

Her ears ached from listening, and her eyes burned in spite of the drenching. Ahab stamped a front hoof and pushed her in the back with his nose. She stumbled one foot forward, almost surprised that she'd been able to move. She felt rooted to the soil like the oak tree that kept only the worst of the downpour from her head.

"Jesse? Jesse?"

"Here." Clamping Ahab's reins tight in her fist, she followed the sound, discovering the wagon no more than twenty feet away. She stopped by the front wheels. "You think that was Benjamin?"

"Uh-huh. He run like de devil himself be after him. Patrol musta cotched him."

"Or tried to."

"Domino, he outrun army horses anytime. You watch, Benjamin be back soon," Meshach said.

"I hope so, but they were shooting at him."

"No matter, he too far 'head to get shot."

Jesselynn hoped he was as sure as he sounded. "So we wait?"

"We gets us off'n dis here road, dat's what. Daniel, you found any other trail or road?"

"I thinks so. Dey's a dark spot in de woods. You wants me to look it out?"

"An' be quick. Dem sojers might be comin' back."

Another wait set her skin to crawling under the soaked coat and dripping hat. At least Thaddy was dry in the wagon bed under the tarp. He and Ophelia were so quiet, either sleeping or too scared to make a sound. If only she could see. Another part of her mind reminded her, *If you could see, then they could see you.* Gratitude for the rain surged through heart and mind, the intensity of it turning the drops to steam. Or at least that's what it felt like.

She let Ahab listen for her. As long as he dropped his head and dozed beside her, she leaned against him, her eyes heavy but the frequent shudders from the cold keeping her awake. Besides, she had yet to perfect the art of sleeping standing up. When her horse raised his head, she clamped her hand over his nostrils to keep him from whinnying. As soon as he relaxed, she knew the arrival to be Daniel.

"Follow me." The rain nearly drowned his words.

Cold, wet, and tired didn't begin to describe the misery that made fitting her foot in the stirrup and pulling herself aboard her horse a near impossibility. When Ahab snorted and shifted away from her, she fought tears that would only add to the water funneling off her soggy hat and streaming down her face. Leaning against the saddle, she fought the despair that threatened to overwhelm her.

"Get on the horse! Now!" she commanded herself. "Ahab, stand still!" She punctuated her words with a slap on his shoulder. Instead of obeying, he nickered and took a couple steps forward. She knew he resented being left behind, and even though she couldn't hear the others, she knew he could. "Ahab, stand!" This time her voice snapped in the sodden air. Ahab stamped one front hoof but stood still until she swung into the saddle, it, too, soaking wet. The last remaining dry part of her shivered in the cold wet. Shrieking took more effort than she had available.

"You all right, Marse Jesse?" Meshach asked when she trotted even with the wagon. "We was 'bout to go back for you."

Marse Jesse indeed. Right now this *young man* couldn't wrestle a flea.

"You can git under de tarp wid 'Phelia and Thaddy."

"Thanks, but no thanks. Did Daniel say how far?"

"Over here!" The voice came from their left.

Never had night seemed so dark or rain so wet as they pulled the wagon under what smelled like an oak tree. The canopy cut off the worst of the torrent so they could hear each other talk without shouting.

"Sojers 'bout half mile ahead on de road. Farm mebbe down dis here one." Daniel sat his horse next to Jesse. "I think we be safe here."

Jesselynn could do no more than nod.

They waited out the night, huddling together under the tarp with the horses on long lines to graze on what they could find. The wind let up as the sky eased into gray. Torrents reduced to drizzle, tree trunks took on form, and one of the horses shook all over, his mane flapping like a soaked rag.

We'll never get a fire started, Jesselynn thought, trying to keep the shudders from making her teeth clack.

"We dare start a fire?" Meshach dug at a tooth with his tongue, studying the dripping landscape.

"Sojers close by," Daniel answered.

What about Benjamin? Did he get away? If I'm supposed to be the leader here, we are in worse trouble than ever before.

"Go on foot and see where de farm be." Meshach pointed back along the trail they had obviously come in on.

A bugle sounded some distance away but close enough to raise the hair on the back of her neck. Jesselynn heard Ophelia stirring behind her. At least someone had slept, and the longer Thaddy slept, the easier on all of them.

A hound bayed somewhere to the north of them. As the sky lightened, birds twittered in the branches overhead. Cold hard biscuit would be all they had if they couldn't get a fire going. A cup of hot coffee or even hot water sounded like ambrosia.

Daniel slipped back into camp like a shadow, appearing out of the trees without a sound. "Farm 'bout a quarter mile away. Dere's dogs 'round it. Saw a man go to the barn to milk."

Meshach returned from the trees carrying an armful of dry branches and pulled crackling leaves from his pocket. "Dey's under a rock." He took the tinderbox from under the tarp and set to making a fire. Within minutes the flames licking the branches brought a whole new feeling of cheer to the group.

Jesselynn felt hope climb over the despair that weighted her down.

"Is . . . is a fire safe?"

"Smoke won't go far in rain. I kin—" The sound of the bugle cut off his words as they all strained to hear anything else.

A horse whinnied. A cow bellowed. Drops smacked the sodden mat of leaves on the woods floor. Another horse whinnied, this time closer.

Jesselynn stopped moving as if someone had shouted an order to halt. The others did the same. She and Meshach reached for the rifles at the same time.

Ahab nickered. The mare did also. Benjamin rode into the clearing wearing a smile wide enough to crack his face.

"Mornin', Marse Jesse. Meshach, you kin put de guns down now."

"Benjamin, you're alive." Jesselynn dropped the rifle back down in the wagon bed and grabbed Domino's reins.

He slid off his horse and stood in front of her. "No dumb sojers gonna cotch me and Domino here. We outrun dem fo' sure."

"How'd you find us?" She wanted to check his arms and shoulders for the wounds she was sure he'd received with the shots fired.

"I puts bit o' cloth on a low branch to mark our turnin' places." Daniel slapped Benjamin on the back. "And he finds 'em."

A whimper from the sleeping pallets brought her attention back to the wagon. Ophelia was stirring a pot over the fire so Jesselynn pulled back the tarp, being careful to keep the puddling water from seeping into the bedding. "How's our boy this mornin'?"

"Hungry." He climbed up her side and nestled against her.

"Ophelia is makin' breakfast."

"Don't want mush."

"Too bad. This mornin' we're lucky to have anything hot." She glanced up at the skies that hung right about the treetops. While the gray was lighter, it was still gray and drizzling.

He clung to her more tightly, his voice turning to a wheedle. "Joshwa want bacon—and egg."

"Well, Joshwa better go on away and bring back Thaddeus, who is much more agreeable." She kissed his cheek and nuzzled his neck.

"You wet." He scrubbed his cheek dry.

"And cold. Get your clothes, and I'll help you get dressed."

"Me do it."

"Thaddy, please just do as I tell you." She took her hat off and slapped it against her thigh to get some water off it, then set it back on her head, pulling it low so the drip didn't go directly down the back of her neck. While he stood glaring at her, looking so much like a miniature version of her father that laughter warred with tears, she shifted things around until she found his clothes, dry but like everything else, carrying the feel of damp.

"Breakfast ready." Ophelia held out a bowl of steaming corn mush with a dollop of sorghum in the center.

Jesselynn pulled a wool sweater over Thaddy's curls and set him down to put on his shoes. He grabbed his stockings.

"Me do it!" The glare he gave her could have roasted a goose.

Since Jesselynn had been reared on stories of her own independence, she shook her head. *How did Mother put up with me?* "All right, *Joshwa*, you do one, and I'll do the other. Race you."

He took up the dare and tried cramming his toes into the stocking, which promptly slipped out of his hands and headed toward the wet ground. Jesselynn stopped rolling hers and snatched the sock before it hit the mud puddle. When she handed it back to him, Thaddy grinned up at her and handed the sock back.

"You do it." She nodded and within a minute had his socks on and was buttoning up his shoes. Life sure would be easier if he had boots that just pulled on or laced without a button hook.

Since puddles still dotted the ground, they ate leaning against the wagon gate and the wheels. Talk died while everyone made short work of the mush, dunking their biscuits in the coffee to soften them.

"Baby cryin'." Thaddeus cocked his head and looked off toward the west.

"There's no babies clear out here."

"Sho 'nuff is." Meshach stopped chewing to listen.

The cry came again, so sad it nearly tore her heart out. When the cry stopped, then picked up again, Jesselynn scraped the last bit from her bowl and set it down on the tailgate. "I'll go see."

"Not widout me." Meshach waved the others to stay where they were as he and Jesselynn headed into the woods. "Maybe dey's a cabin up ahead."

"Could be." A branch snapped underneath her feet. Why was she making so much noise when Meshach seemed to move without touching the ground?

They stopped to listen again, then angled some off to the right. The cry seemed weaker.

"Are we goin' the right direction?" she asked.

"Yessuh." He shot her a smile that in the dimness seemed even brighter than normal.

They stopped again, waiting, but no cry came.

A chill rippled up her back. Was this a trap to separate them all, make it easier for someone to steal the horses? She looked over her shoulder, but there were no sounds of attack from the direction of the wagons. Surely no one could sneak up on them so easily that Ophelia didn't even shriek.

She took in a breath and held it, listening so hard her ears buzzed.

A whimper. A hiccup. A cry.

Relief poured through her like a warm shower, soaking clear to her toes. There was indeed a baby. Now just to find it.

"Keep cryin', little one," she whispered as she and Meshach pushed aside branches and made their way toward the sound.

The ground dropped away at the lip of a hollow. Trees marched down the steep bank, a fallen granddaddy oak lying crosswise partway down. Mists feathered the trees and obscured the bottom, where she was sure a creek meandered downward between rocks and logs. How far to the water she had no idea. They ghosted from tree to tree, dancing with the fog that splattered when an errant breeze tickled the upper branches.

Once around the rotting log, she caught her breath.

Meshach shared her look of horror before stopping at the end of the log, just out of the child's sight.

Wearing a tattered shift and covered in mud, the child rooted at the breast of the woman lying dead in the lee of the log. From the looks of her, she'd died at least the day before. A newborn lay between her legs, also dead.

"Runaway slave." Meshach hunkered down where he was, shaking his head all the while.

"How do you know?" She kept her voice low also, not wanting to frighten the child.

"See de brand on her face."

Jesselynn recognized it now. Her father had forbidden such atrocities.

"Hey, baby, we come for you." Meshach's voice carried the same gentle cadence he used for the skittish horses.

The little one whipped around, screwed up his face, and, sitting in the muck, raised his arms to be picked up.

Jesselynn reached him first, crooning all the while, then picked him up and hugged him to her chest. "Ah, baby, how'd you make it through the night without wild animals gettin' you?" She rocked from side to side, watching as Meshach checked out the body of the woman and the dead infant. "We have to bury her," she said.

"I know." He held up a pitifully small sack. "She been on de road some time."

"And died in childbirth." Jesselynn looked around them. While in the sunlight this would be a lovely shaded glen, in the rain and fog, dismal was the only word she could think of. When she saw the scars of the whiplash on the woman's arms and chest, she hugged the baby tighter, making him wail instead of whimper.

"Think you can find de way back?" Meshach had placed the infant on its mother's chest. "Send Benjamin to help here."

She nodded. "We didn't come too far. I can call if I need."

"Or whistle like a robin?"

"Oh, I guess not." She picked up the tow sack and, with the child on her arm, made her way back around the ancient tree. "I'll have Benjamin bring the Bible."

"Yessuh, thanks."

As she climbed higher, she felt a rush of warmth down her side before she could hold the child away from her. "Well, thanks for that little gift. You could have warned me."

The boy whimpered and stuck his thumb and forefinger in his mouth, hiccuping at the same time.

"Wonder how long since you've been fed." She stopped at the top of the bank to catch her breath. He might be just beyond babyhood. She doubted he was even a year yet, but lugging him up the steep hill made him seem heavier with every step.

By this time too she was fairly certain he was running a fever. What might she be bringing into camp?

CHAPTER TWELVE

The military hospital
Richmond, Virginia

"Do you think he is ever goin' to wake up?"

"I certainly hope so, Miz Highwood." The doctor shook his head. "But every day he remains comatose, the less chance . . ." His voice trailed off. "Maybe if you spent some time talking with him, reading to him, that might help."

"You think he can hear me?"

"I've heard tell of folks who woke up knowin' things they could only have heard while asleep. Makes me think ears are more important than we give them credit for. Let's see if Corporal Shaddock there might read to him. Missin' a leg won't hurt his tongue any."

If he can read. Louisa was careful not to voice the thought. Corporal Shaddock didn't need anything else to make him feel worse. Some men seemed to handle the loss of a limb better than others, but no one accepted living on one leg easily.

She studied the man wrapped in bandages and lying so still. Who was he? Why did he seem familiar? Was it because she had seen so many bandaged men by this time, or was it something else? Could he hear them and was just not able to respond?

But he wasn't paralyzed. The doctor had made sure of that. What was keeping him in some no-man's-land?

She thought back to her early morning time reading her Bible. This soldier had come into her mind even then, and so she had prayed for him as she did for so many others. That thought led to another, as so often happened. She'd prayed for those at home too. What was going on at Twin Oaks, and why hadn't they heard from

Jesselynn after the letter she wrote telling them that Father had died?

Sometimes the urge to go home was almost more than she could bear.

Instead of succumbing to the tears that threatened, she pasted a smile on her face and took the few paces to stand beside Corporal Shaddock's bed. "I know you are awake, so just open your eyes and take this little treat I have for you."

He blinked and cracked one eyelid. "Go 'way."

"Now, you know me better than that."

"Be nice to the lady, son, if ya know what's good for ya." Lieutenant Lessling leaned on his crutches, another victim of losing a leg but choosing to make the best of a bad situation. Said he had a plantation to run as soon as they released him from "this miserable example of a house of healin'." This he repeated more than once to whoever happened to be in the vicinity.

The general in charge hadn't thought too kindly of the rebuke.

Louisa had a hard time keeping a straight face when Lessling went on a diatribe. She'd heard much worse.

"So, Corporal Shaddock, shall I go on to someone else?" Her smile made him blink twice and flush once. He was young enough that he hadn't lost the ability to blush, and his fair skin shone like a rose in full bloom.

"No, ma'am." He winced as he rolled flat on his back and pushed himself up against the wall. He tried glaring at her, but the cutting glance from the man on crutches changed his glare to a grimace meant to be a smile—perhaps.

Louisa waited until he was about as comfortable as he would be, then handed him two molasses cookies in a napkin. "Wish I could offer you coffee too, but . . ." She shrugged. "You slept through breakfast."

"Warn't neither sleepin'." The act of growling made him cough and clench his treat tight enough to break the cookies into small pieces. He opened the napkin and gave her an apologetic look. "Sorry, missus."

"They'll taste just as good, but don't you go tellin' all the others what you have there. They might get jealous."

He ducked his chin, but she could see the beginnings of a true smile stretch his lips. She patted his shoulder before bending closer. "Now if you could do me a favor, perhaps?"

He nodded. "If'n I can."

"Would you mind talking with the man in that bed?"

"But he don't say nothin'."

"I know that, but Doc said this might help. I'd read to him if I had time." She touched the Bible she always kept in the pocket of her apron.

"I don't read so good, ma'am, but I could surely give it a try if you could see fit to loan me your Bible."

Rejoicing in the spate of words from a man who hadn't strung more than two together before, she handed him her Bible. "Why don't you start with the Gospel of John? It's always been my favorite."

With the crumb-sprinkled napkin spread on the bed beside him and the Bible propped on his chest, he fumbled through the pages until he found John and began to read. " 'In the beginning was the Word, and the Word was with God, and the Word was God. The same was in the beginning with God. All things were made by him; and without him was not any thing made that was made.' "

Thank you, Father. She sent her prayer winging heavenward as she went on to the next patient.

"Shore do be fine to hear them words." The boy on the bed looked too young to begin shaving, let alone nearly die in a hail of bullets. "My ma read to us ever night."

"Mine too, when my daddy wasn't there." Louisa handed him a lemon drop. "Thought this might help that frog in your throat." While she knew the frog would live there permanently due to his neck injury, sucking on the candy would be soothing.

"Thankee."

By the time she'd finished one side of the long room, the men on the other were getting restless. The heat and the flies ripened as the sun reached the midpoint, turning the second floor of the hospital into a miasma of sickness, smells, and sweat.

"You go on, take a minute under that shade tree out there." The lieutenant stopped beside her after his self-imposed traversing of the center aisle. While she'd tried to get him to take it easier, he insisted that walking not only made him stronger but also helped pass the time.

She'd noticed that much of his time was passed assisting those who were worse off than he. "Thank you. I think I will." She wiped her perspiring face with the underside of her stained apron. "I'll get a bucket of cold water at the same time."

"You let Jacob bring the water. Better him carrying those buckets up the stairs than you."

Louisa gave him an arched eyebrow look that clearly said, "Who made you my boss?"

"Sorry." A tiny smile quirked one corner of his well-defined lips. But he didn't back down, even leaning on crutches and looming over her. "That's what he was hired for. You want to take an old man's job away from him?"

Louisa sighed. "Now that you put it that way, of course not, but it doesn't look to me like he has extra time on his hands." She glanced over to where the corporal continued reading. Several other ambulatory patients had taken up the spare spaces on the beds. *Why didn't I think of that before?*

"You can't think of everything."

Her attention snapped back to the lieutenant. "How...?"

"Your face is like an open picture book. One needn't even know words to read it." He cleared his throat. "I better get back to..." Without finishing his sentence, he turned and clump-thumped his way back down the aisle.

She watched him go. Thin—no, emaciated was a better word for his build, his shoulder bones sticking out of his thin cotton robe like angel wings. His wrists and fingers could do with a better flesh covering; the bones showed so clearly. And his face... She'd seen a human skeleton once, and it didn't look too different from the man swinging on his crutches. Yet his eyes hadn't lost their piercing blue nor his mind its sharpness. Both courtly manners and a keen intellect, quickened by a good education, were evidenced by every word he spoke. She'd be willing to bet he came into the world as officer material, and the war only honed it.

What would he do now?

None of your business, my girl. Now get on about your chores and quit lollygagging over something that has nothing to do with you. He's one of your patients, that's all. On her way out, she grabbed both buckets and headed on down the stairs.

A slight breeze made pumping the water a pleasure, and when the first gush hit the tin bucket, she wished she could stop and splash it on her face but kept pumping instead. Stopping would only prolong the effort. The clang and suck of the handle and pump sang a song peculiar to hand pumps, the gush turning to a gurgle as the bucket filled.

"You don't want to do dat, Missy." Old Jacob took the handle from her with a reproachful shake of his grizzled head.

Louisa glanced up to see the lieutenant looking down at her from the window. She put two fingers to her forehead in a saucy salute and stepped back as Jacob took the first bucket from under the spigot and set the other in place, all the time keeping the handle in motion. She dipped her handkerchief under the waterspout and used it to wet her face. If he weren't watching, she might have wiped her neck and down her bosom also. If only she dared defy Aunt Sylvania and go without her corset, the cool air could at least reach her skin.

She sneaked an upward peek, but no, he hadn't moved. *Drat and tarnation!* Taking the dipper that hung on a hook beside the pump, she filled it with water and drank, making sure that some of it dribbled down her front. The remainder she poured over her hands and wrists. She thought of plunging her hands in the bucket up to her elbows, but who'd want to drink water she'd had her hands in?

"I takes dese up now."

"Yes, thank you."

She watched him go, the weight of the full buckets rounding shoulders already curved from heavy toil. But as the lieutenant said, the man's job was important to him. She wondered whose slave he had been before and when he had been freed. Had Jesselynn freed all their slaves as she'd threatened to? Or had Father done it himself? Oh, the questions of home. When would a letter come through? Thaddeus would be so grown up by now that she would hardly recognize him, and he wouldn't even know who she was. They must be cutting the tobacco. Lucinda would have the kitchen in an uproar putting up pickles and jams and jellies.

Louisa leaned against the rough bark of the elm tree. *Home, Lord. Oh, please, I want to go home.*

"Miz Highwood, come quick." The lieutenant's voice propelled her into a decidedly unladylike run.

CHAPTER THIRTEEN

Western Kentucky
September 29, 1862

"He one sick baby." Ophelia frowned in concern over the little tyke they had rescued.

Jesselynn nodded. Ophelia wasn't exaggerating this time. "We've got to get his fever down." The baby twitched in her arms. Thaddeus sat leaning against her, forefinger and thumb both in his mouth. He didn't look too good either at the moment.

It had taken them two days to get all dried out after the rainstorm, but the roads were still too muddy to make decent time, so they decided to stay where they were for another night. Right now she was wishing they didn't have the wagon—or the extra horse that needed to stop for rests. Riding, they could have been long gone and able to cover the country faster. But riding with Thaddeus would be miserable, near to impossible. Besides, they didn't have enough horses to pack all their supplies, meager though they were.

"See if you can get some more milk in him while Thaddy and I go search for some willow bark. A tea of that should help bring his fever down." *If only I'd brought more of Mother's simples.* But now was the time to be out harvesting things like ginseng, Solomon's seal, wood sorrel, and the like. If she didn't have to sleep during the day, she could be searching for them in the afternoon. How much easier it was at home where she knew where the best patches of everything grew.

Here it was hit or miss, although Meshach had brought in a fine mess of cress and dandelion to boil up for dinner. Stewed with the rabbit he'd snared and the wild onion, it tasted mighty fine. That was one good thing about Kentucky—one could live off the land if need be. While Benjamin and Daniel were catching some much needed sleep, Meshach seemed to need little rest. When she asked him about it, he shrugged her off.

"I gets enough, Marse Jesse. Not to worry."

But worry she did in spite of her good intentions. While she knew they were heading west, they'd had to detour so often she wasn't sure where they were or if they were traveling the best way. She rubbed her forehead, the ache behind her eyes getting worse instead of better. *What if that baby has something we can all catch? How do I care for all these people if I get sick? Or Meshach?*

The last time she remembered being sick she had the chicken pox, but Lucinda and her mother had cosseted her back to health in spite of the itchy bumps all over her body. While Louisa and Zachary had gotten off lightly, she and Carrie Mae had had bad cases. Her mother had always said it was amazing she didn't have more scars on her face.

Lucinda had warned her that if she scratched, her skin would all fall off and she'd be nothing but bones.

That picture kept her from digging at the sores.

But what did this baby have? Other than being out in the rain and wind by himself. No wonder he whimpered every time they put him down, poor thing. Too easily the picture of the dead mother came to her mind. She was trying to escape with her babes, and look what it got her. The scars covering her body said she'd gone under the lash more than once. It didn't take too strong an imagination to see the horrors she must have endured.

Jesselynn shuddered. While she'd heard many stories, she'd never seen one human beaten by another, other than the whipping Dunlivey had given one of the field hands. That had been Dunlivey's last act at Twin Oaks. Later on they'd learned that he'd beaten others, but by threatening them with worse, he'd never been caught at it.

What if he is searching for us now? The thought made shivers chase each other up and down her back. The sight of his snarling face made her stomach clench—and her headache worsen.

While she needed to be sleeping herself, she couldn't do that with the baby crying and coughing.

"Jesse, hold me." Thaddeus held up his arms. She wiped his runny nose with a square of cotton she used for a handkerchief and, picking him up, let him wrap his arms around her neck and his legs around her waist. He clung like a baby possum to its mother's back. She kissed his forehead and, sure enough, he felt warm too. Two sick children, muddy roads, and patrols going past not a quarter mile away. How were they to manage?

Now her headache felt like the drum of galloping horses' hooves on a wooden bridge. An entire platoon.

"He won't take no milk." Ophelia carried the baby on her hip, jiggling him gently but without much success. He cried anyway.

"Here, you take Thaddeus." Jesselynn tried to pull the limpet off her neck, but then he stopped whimpering and fell to out-and-out crying.

"Want you, not 'Phelia," he stammered between sobs.

"But the baby needs me." She tried prying again with no success.

"No-o-o-o." He scrubbed his runny nose against her neck.

"Hey, how 'bout we think of a name for the baby?"

"No. Don' like baby." He clung so tightly, he almost cut off her air.

"Thaddeus Joshua Highwood, you stop that this instant." She bounced him with a sharp jerk to get his attention.

"No!" He cried harder, stiffening his body and banging his head against her collarbone.

Wonderful. Now he was working his way up to a full-sized Highwood tantrum. She recognized it well, having thrown a few herself. One time Lucinda had dunked her in cold water. Trying to breathe around the shock made a screaming tantrum pretty near impossible, when she got her breath back, that was. She'd never thrown one again.

She hoped something like that wouldn't be necessary with Thaddeus.

But when he began shrieking and nearly threw himself out of her arms, she started looking for a bucket of water. When none was in sight, she thunked him down on the wagon bed. "Now you just stay there until you can behave. I will not hold a boy who kicks and hits me."

He rolled from side to side, arms thrashing.

Meshach came running from the woods. "What wrong?"

Jesselynn shook her head, disgust narrowing her eyes. "My little brother is throwing a tantrum, that's what. All because he is jealous of our new baby."

The poor baby was also screaming at this point, but stopping to cough brought his cries to a standstill. He coughed until he threw up what little milk Ophelia had gotten down him and then coughed some more. It sounded like he was coughing his lungs right out.

"You stay with him," she said to Meshach, pointing to Thaddy, then ran around the wagon to help Ophelia with the other one. She dunked a cloth in warm water and washed the baby's face and his nappy hair. His cries subsided, his eyes drifting closed and a hiccup jerking his entire body. While they had put one of Thaddy's shirts on him, she could still count every bone in his neck. His fingers looked more like claws than baby hands and his bowed legs didn't have the strength to hold him up yet.

Jesselynn thought back to the fat black babies tumbling around the little house where the babies stayed while their mothers worked in the fields. Twin Oaks had few women working alongside the men in the tobacco and hayfields, having them instead work the acre-sized garden and the orchards, and do the household tasks like spinning and weaving. Providing food and clothing for all the folks on the plantation took many hands and many hours. It seemed they never had enough of either.

She and Ophelia nursed the children through the afternoon and evening, but as the stars poked holes in the heavens, Meshach came to stand beside her. "We best be pullin' out."

"I know, but dare we travel with this one so sick?"

"Got to get away from sojers."

"I know." They'd heard another patrol just before dusk. "All right. You want to drive or ride?" Asking his preference was a real act of grace on her part. All she wanted to do was mount up on Ahab and ride free, gallop through the night far enough ahead so she couldn't hear children crying and coughing. If only she had some of Lucinda's elderberry wine or a hot toddy for the black baby. Her mother mixed honey, lemon, and whisky for sore throats and coughs. Surely there was something in the simples bag to help, but for the life of her, she couldn't remember. Why, oh, why hadn't she brought her mother's housekeeping journal along? It held all the recipes.

"I drive. 'Phelia can take care of both boys in de back of de wagon. They go to sleep and wake up better in de mornin'."

"What makes you think that?"

"I bin prayin' for dem."

Meshach's simple faith smacked her in the face. She had not thought to pray lately, other than a frantic "Oh, God" a few times. And how long since they'd read the Scriptures? She'd seen him reading in the early morning. Why hadn't she?

She squinted her eyes, staring at the fire until the flames seemed to fill her mind. *Because I'm no longer sure that God is listening.* She plundered her mind some more. *Or cares.*

"I'll saddle Ahab, then." Relief flooded her mind. She could get away. "And I hope your God is listenin'."

"He yo' God too, Marse Jesse, and He won't let you forget it."

"Yes, well . . ." She turned to Ophelia. "Let's fill that jug with hot water and wrap it in one of the quilts so you can use it as you need it." She tucked a quilt around Thaddeus, who had finally fallen asleep. When she felt his forehead, he didn't seem any cooler. *So much for God making them better. Maybe if I can find some willow bark by a stream that would help.*

Within minutes they were on the road, heading toward the evening star again. After the deluge the nights before, the air still smelled fresh and clean. A hint of woodsmoke, the tang of a long-departed skunk, ammonia of fresh horse droppings, the smells of forest and fall melded into a rich soup of aromas.

A rising half-moon cleared the treetops and sent their shadows leading them onward.

In spite of herself, Jesselynn dropped back to see how the babies were doing. Ophelia was rocking the black baby, and Thaddeus coughed in his sleep beside her.

"He burnin' up wid fever."

"Unwrap him from the quilt."

"Him get cold." But she did as Jesselynn ordered and loosened the covering. As the cool air touched his skin, the baby set up a howl.

"Here, hand him up here. Maybe the rocking of the horse will settle him down."

"With Ahab?" Meshach joined the conversation.

"Oh, you're right." Jesselynn felt like plugging her ears and riding hard—away. If she'd used her head earlier, they could have harnessed Ahab and she could have ridden the mare. "Up ahead, if he doesn't calm down, we'll switch the team around."

"Should do that anyways. De mud makes for heavy pullin'."

At least we're not hub-deep in it. That alone was something to be grateful for.

The moon floated high above them, silvering the trees and whitening the road. Jesselynn let herself slump in the saddle, riding far enough ahead so the fitful cries of their sick ones sounded more like bird twitterings.

"Halt! Who goes there!"

Her heart hit triple time before she could suck in a breath.

CHAPTER FOURTEEN

Richmond, Virginia

"I'm comin'!" Louisa picked up her skirts and dashed back inside.

"No need to fret yourself." The old black man shook his grizzled head. "I gets de water."

"Sorry, no . . ." Louisa checked her rush up the stairs.

"You go on." He chuckled this time, still shaking his head. "Young ladies don' go runnin' like dat. Just not proper." But he made shooing motions with his hands, sending her on up the second set of stairs.

Louisa didn't need another invitation. She could hear laughter from *her* floor, laughter like she hadn't heard since she started volunteering over a month ago. Whatever could be so hilarious?

But when she burst through the arched doorway, silence fell with laughter choked off so quick it sent one patient into a fit of coughing. A snicker came from the region of the unknown soldier.

What in heaven's name is going on? She glanced over to the window where the lieutenant stood looking out as if he'd never ordered her to come back in with such urgency. Several others refused to look her in the eye, feigning sleep instead.

The low drone of Corporal Shaddock reading to the comatose man picked up again.

"All right, children, fess up. There's something going on here."

A snicker from the corner. She whirled to see who it was, but no one looked guilty even.

A moan came from a new man just returned from surgery. Lopping off limbs seemed the answer to most injuries, but a quick glance at two beds down on her right showed all four appendages in place.

"No more cookies until someone tells me what is goin' on."

Still no response other than a groan, this one forced enough to tell her it wasn't due to pain.

What could have happened? She hadn't been gone more than fifteen minutes, if that. Who could she intimidate the most?

Stopping at Corporal Shaddock's side, she cleared her throat. He stopped reading and sent a quick look her way, then glanced at the man whom she'd been calling the unknown soldier.

Shivers chased up and down her spine. The doc had changed the dressings, so one eye now showed. The dark brow above it arched in an oh-so-familiar way. The man was definitely conscious.

Her heart felt as though it had stopped. The whole world stopped only for an instant. She took four steps forward and sank to her knees, grasping the hand that lay on top of the sheet.

"Zachary?"

"None other." The hand squeezed hers back, weak but no weaker than the voice.

He's alive, my brother is alive. Oh, God, thank you, my brother is alive.

"At least what's left of me." The tinge of bitterness that underlay his words sounded so familiar that she laid her cheek on the back of his hand.

"But you're alive. That's all that matters. You're alive." *My brother who we feared was dead is alive.*

Hand clapping from those able and a cheer from others brought her back to the current place and time.

"How . . . how long have I been unconscious?"

"A week or so. You were muttering when they brought you in, but then we heard nothing more from you." She swiped away the tears that refused to stop. "We've been praying for you so long, never knowing if you were in prison, alive, or dead." She shuddered on the last words. *I can't tell him about Daddy yet. And Jesselynn. Or how they are at home.*

"Where . . . where am I?" He cleared his throat.

"Richmond. I'm visitin' Aunt Sylvania. Carrie Mae too."

"Why?"

"Jesselynn made us come here." She knew that wasn't altogether true. Carrie Mae had pleaded to go when the invitation arrived. And since Jesselynn wouldn't allow the younger sister to travel alone, they had both been sent off. Sometimes she still smarted under the injustice of it all. She thought a moment. "How did they all figure out—?" She stopped, not certain how much he knew.

"When I gave my name and rank, the lieutenant put two and two together."

"Really?" She kept herself from looking at the man still staring out the window.

"And figured out you are my wife. Mrs. Zachary Highwood, right?" At least he had the sense to whisper.

CHAPTER FIFTEEN

Gordonsville, Kentucky
September 30, 1862

Where was Benjamin, and why hadn't he warned them?

"Speak or I'll shoot!"

"Jus' some weary travelers, suh." She deepened her voice, masking the fear.

A man stepped out of the shadows, his uniform light in the moonlight, a rifle held across his chest.

She shot Meshach a look meant to keep him quiet and kept her hands in front of her. Not that she had anything to hide. The rifle lay safe behind the wagon seat. And of no use at all.

"Where y'all goin'?"

"Not far up yondah." She nodded toward the west, keeping her hat low over her face. The urge to tell him more caused her to bite her tongue. Benjamin had reminded them just before starting out tonight that the less said, the better.

"What are ya carrying?" The soldier stepped closer to the wagon, his rifle at the ready.

"Nothin' much." *What do I say?* "Jus' tryin' to gits home." She could tell by his accent he was southern, but a rifle pointed was still a rifle, no matter whose side held it.

"Where's home?" This time he looked at her directly.

She squared her shoulders and sucked in a deep breath trying to conceal the frenzy of her thoughts. Why hadn't she figured for this in advance? What town lay ahead? Where had they been?

The black baby let out a wail that made her spine tingle, it sounded so like a wounded animal.

The soldier stepped back.

An idea sizzled into her frozen mind. "Ah, you might not want to get too close, suh. That baby real sick. You might catch what he got."

"Sick?" The man stepped back again.

"Can you tell the smallpox?"

"S-smallpox?" He took three more steps back, moonlight glistening on the whites of his eyes.

"Well, we ain't sure what it is, but the baby be right sick. You know how to cure the pox, if that be it?"

"No. No, I don't." He waved his rifle. "You git on outa here now." The baby wailed again.

"Right now, you hear me?"

"Yes, suh. Thankee, suh." Jesselynn put her heels to Ahab's ribs as Meshach clucked the team forward. They trotted down the road without looking back, even though for Jesse the temptation was nigh unbearable.

They caught up with Benjamin about a mile or so up the road when he whistled his presence.

"He din't stop me," the young man answered when questioned. "I din't know he was even dere."

"Most likely sleepin' at de post till we come by. Horses and wagon make more noise."

With the wagon moving again, the baby settled back down and fell asleep.

"How are they?" Jesselynn rode up next to Ophelia.

"Both sleepin'." She glanced over her shoulder to the two children in the wagon bed, then up at Jesselynn. "You really think him got de pox?" Her voice carried the same fear heard in the soldier's.

"No, not at all. I've never seen smallpox, but Mother told me what to watch for. You'd most likely be sick too if you spent the night in the rain like he did, naked, hungry. Poor baby."

Daniel rode up beside Jesselynn. "I 'bout wet my britches when dat sojer hollered."

Ophelia snickered. Meshach chuckled. And Jesselynn gave an undeniably feminine giggle before correcting herself with a deeper voice.

" 'Might be smallpox.' " Meshach imitated her comment, even to the hint of fear in her voice. Only the soldier didn't know that the fear had nothing to do with smallpox.

Their laughter rang through the night as they kept the horses.

at a trot to cover the ground they'd missed because of the sick boys.

But as they trotted on through the night, following the moon on its westward descent, thoughts continued to plague Jesselynn. What *was* wrong with the black baby? Had Thaddeus caught something from him so quickly, or was it the rain and traveling that gave him the grippe? By the time they could see individual trees instead of just a dark bank, she'd decided that she was going herself into the next town they came to. They needed supplies, and she needed information. Maybe there'd even be a newspaper to tell her what was going on with the war in general and Kentucky in particular.

As always, she would check the posted list of dead and missing. Never seeing the name of Zachary Highwood helped keep hope alive. Not much but enough.

When Benjamin whistled them off the road and into a clearing, she could finally give up the feeling that she needed to keep looking behind her in case the soldier changed his mind.

"All I seen is a couple of small farms," Benjamin said in answer to her question. "Man always up settin' out to milkin' him cows. You want I should go dere?"

Jesselynn nodded. That was another reason she needed to get to a town. They were about out of small coins. What farmer would be able to change a gold piece? And a young black man carrying a gold piece would be sure to create all kinds of suspicion.

While the others set up camp, Jesselynn took her little brother out behind the bushes and then down to the creek, still swollen from the rains, to wash. When she laid her cheek against his, no longer did the heat meet her. While his nose never ceased to run, and he coughed at times, she could tell he was on the mend.

"Stay here!" He pointed to the side of the creek when she tried to take him back to camp.

Yes, he was definitely feeling better.

"Aren't you hungry?"

"Want hot cakes and syrup."

She groaned inside. "Come, Thaddy. Jesse needs to eat and get some sleep." When his lower lip came out, she swung him up in her arms and tickled his ribs. With giggles floating behind them, they marched back to the fire.

"We need a name for that boy," she said after they'd finished eating and Ophelia went back to walking the baby. While he'd take milk from a spoon, drinking from a cup was not tolerable. And a sugar-tit took too long to make him content either. While she hated to give up one of the leather gloves, they might just have to do that. The leather would hold the milk and a hole in the end of a finger would make a nipple. If he would even suck on that.

"Call him ornery." Meshach dumped another armload of broken branches on the ground by the fire.

Ophelia sat on a log and commenced to spoon milk into the baby's mouth again. "Sho' wish him mama learned him better."

Jesselynn shuddered at the memory of the dead mother. All alone like that and having a baby. Often she'd assisted her mother in caring for a newborn baby and the proud mother down in the slave quarters. Birthing babies was a natural part of life, even to losing some, but to die alone like that, knowing there was nothing to be done for the older child must have terrified the woman.

She snagged Thaddeus, who was digging in the dirt at her feet, and gave him a loud kiss on the cheek.

He pushed back against her shoulder with both hands. "Down, Jesse. Me down."

She set him back on his feet, and he immediately plunked down to dig under the log again. When he had his mind on something, changing it was harder than stopping up a flooding creek.

The sun was well past the center point and the camp eerily quiet when Jesselynn woke again. *Where's everyone? Surely they didn't go off and leave me.* The nicker of a horse nearby made her shake her head at her crazy thoughts. She sat up and looked around, brushing away a persistent fly while straining to hear a voice, any voice, or rather any of the voices that belonged to her people. She scrubbed her face with her fingertips and brushed her hair back. Only two weeks on the road, and already it was falling in her eyes. No wonder men had to have their hair cut so often. Braiding it back would be a dead giveaway.

She smashed her hat onto her head, effectively solving the flopping hair problem, and stood, stretching out her body as she did so. She wasn't sure which was worse, riding all night, sitting on the wagon seat, or sleeping on the hard ground. Glancing around the camp, she saw Daniel sleeping soundly and left him to it.

Following the sound of another nicker, she found the horses hobbled in a small clearing, Ophelia lying asleep under a tree with the two boys curled against her like sleeping puppies, and Benjamin sleeping not far from her. As usual, Meshach was checking the horses' hooves. Still yawning, she wandered over to him and leaned against the mare's shoulder.

"Meshach, don't you *ever* sleep?"

"Sho'nuff. I slept myself plenty right after breakfast. Benjamin, he watch den." He picked up another of the filly's hooves and dug out the packed dirt and rocks. A rock caught between the frog and the inner part of the hoof could lame a horse faster than anything. "Ahab got him a loose shoe. I 'specs I better reset dem before we leave."

"You need the forge?"

"No, I just reset dem. Got plenty wear left."

They had the small hand-cranked forge with them that used to go to the track. While they had plenty of horseshoes, they didn't have much charcoal. One more thing that needed doing.

"What about the mule?"

"He fine."

"Did Benjamin find out if there was a town near here?"

"'Bout five miles. Not much more den a store or two."

"No train station?"

"Didn't ask dat." He moved on to Domino, the younger stallion. "Stand still, you. I gots no time for you actin' up."

"How's Chess doin'?"

"Good. Him chest healin' good. I's thinkin' we might sell him soon as he's able."

Jesselynn nodded. "Good idea." She took hold of Domino's halter. "You just want extra attention, don't you?" She rubbed his ears and let him snuffle her neck. She inhaled the scent of horse. While her sister Carrie Mae might bewail the lack of Paris perfumes, she'd take honest horse aroma any day. That thought brought on another. How were her sisters managing with Aunt Sylvania? Jesselynn had visited Richmond and her aunt once and thought it enough to last for a lifetime—or two.

So then why did you send them back there? The voice in her ear sounded vaguely familiar, like a cross between her mother and Lucinda with a dash of Jesselynn thrown in for reality's sake.

Instead of arguing with herself, she went to saddle up the mule.

"I'll be back as soon as I can. Y'all go on and eat without me if I'm not here."

"You sho' might need one of us."

Jesselynn hesitated. It most likely would be a good idea to have one of them along, but the thought of being alone for a couple of hours was tempting beyond measure. Surely she'd be back before dark. And who would bother a rough-looking boy on an old mule?

Anyone needing a mule, that's who! The thought made her shake her head. "I'll take the pistol. It's not fair waking up one of the boys. And, besides, the horses need rest and time to graze too." She touched two fingers to the brim of her hat. "I'll be fine." She swung aboard the bareback mule and kicked him into a joint-cracking canter.

His trot was worse. By the time they rode the five miles to town, even her teeth hurt from the pounding.

"Grind you up for sausage," she muttered as she slung the reins over his long ears and tied them to the hitching post in front of the store. Several other places of business lined the street, empty but for a brown-and-white dog sniffing horse droppings. She walked around him, more to get her legs moving than to check out her mount, and took the four steps to the shed-roofed front porch in two. Two men, who looked older than the gnarly oak that shaded the west side of the building, nodded to her. *If they have three teeth between them, that would be sayin' some*, she thought.

"Hey, boy, you a stranger here?"

She kept herself from looking over her shoulder to see who the *boy* was they were talking to and nodded. "Yes, suh. Goin' west."

"Where ya from?"

She nodded over her shoulder. "Off thata way." She bobbed her head again. "Good day."

She knew she'd been rude, but the sun was racing for the horizon, and she had to get back so Meshach wouldn't worry. After telling the man behind the counter what she would need, she studied the jars of candy. Perhaps some horehound drops would help Thaddy's cough. Her grandmother used to keep a jarful for that very purpose. She added that to her list.

"They post a newspaper anywheres around here?"

The man nodded. "Only a day late too. Comes in on the train."

"Mind if I go read the casualty list while you get things together?"

"Not a'tall." But he paused, studying her through slightly squinted eyes.

"Don't worry, I kin pay." She pulled the gold piece from her pocket and held it up for him to see.

"Can't be too careful these days. Confederate dollars drop fas-ter'n a pound of lead. Now is there anything else you might be needin'?"

"I'll be back." She strolled out the door like she had a month of Sundays to spend as she wished, greeted the two holding down the rockers and headed for the train station. Strains of "Dixieland" floated out the saloon door as she passed, and the smell of frying chicken from the hotel made her lick her lips and wish for some. The news had to be old already according to the folks around Gor-donsville, since no one else was standing on the dock reading the paper. The name of the town could be found on either end of the station in fading white letters on an equally faded black sign.

She stuck her hands in her pockets and studied the paper tacked to the wall.

"General Buell Liberates Louisville" was one headline, but most of the page was taken up with Lincoln's proposed Emancipation Proclamation. She finally allowed herself to read the dead or miss-ing-in-action lists, not breathing until she was positive Zachary Highwood was not listed. Thinking that the man had her order ready by now, she headed back for the general store.

A burst of laughter from the saloon struck her like a fist in the midsection.

Surely no one else on the entire earth laughed like that. Only Cavendar Dunlivey.

Horror tasted like blood on her tongue.

CHAPTER SIXTEEN

Richmond, Virginia

"I can explain." She dropped her voice.

"I'm sure you can, but let me guess. You got bored at Aunt Sylvania's, and since you've always taken care of the wounded, be it bird, beast, or human, you decided to help out here at the military hospital. Only they would never let a young unmarried girl in the door to visit even, let alone care for the sick and dying, so you figured you needed a husband."

She nodded and looked at him from under her eyelashes. Was that a laugh she heard in his voice?

"But why me?"

"Because they say if you are going to tell a lie, keep as close to the truth as possible. So I just kept my name and added Mrs. Zachary in front of it." Her whisper was meant for his ears alone.

"So they call you Miz Highwood or Miss Louisa, which?"

"Don't you think you should take a nap or somethin'? You're lookin' mighty weary."

"It's wakin' up to find I have a wife that is wearyin'."

"You won't tell anyone, please?"

"Not unless that glowerin' lieutenant over there decides to beat me to death with his crutches."

"Zachary Highwood, why I never . . ." The heat rushed up her neck and over her face so fast it nigh to set her hair on fire.

"I know that, dear Louisa. Now why don't you get me a drink of that fresh water you went for, and I'll go back to sleep like a good boy—er, husband." He clenched her hand for a moment, then groaned. "Never try to yawn with a broken jaw. It hurts like . . ."

She could tell how bad by the way his hand shook. "I'll be right back."

But when she returned with the bucket and dipper, he was sound asleep.

After offering another drink to the men who were awake, Louisa returned to the closet where she kept her things and let the shock of Zachary being here roll over her. Her brother was alive. After the years of prayers and tears, here he was, in her hospital and on her ward, no less. The mercies of the almighty God were far beyond imaginable. If this didn't qualify as a miracle, what would? Now, if only she could let Jesselynn know right today. Since the war began, letters took so long to get anywhere, and she hadn't heard from home in far too long. Up to this last month, her sister had been a faithful correspondent.

But she *could* tell Carrie Mae and Aunt Sylvania, and maybe when Zachary was well enough, they could all go home to Twin Oaks. Well, not Carrie Mae, since she would be living in Richmond with her newly wedded husband.

Her thought flickered to the walking rack of bones with the title of lieutenant. He might be handsome with some meat on his frame and a smile on that dour face. He stumped back and forth in front of the window like a sleek painter she'd seen caged once. All she'd thought of was opening the gate and letting the big tawny cat go free.

If only I could give the lieutenant back his leg and let him go free again.

That thought sent her scurrying back out with her copy of Shakespeare's *A Midsummer Night's Dream*. The tall stool was already set up for her, compliments of the lieutenant, she was sure. Since she'd started reading every afternoon, the men had taken to reminding her of it, just in case she forgot.

She glanced at her brother, who lay sleeping again as though he'd never been awake. *I could leave first to go home to tell the news.* The thought held certain possibilities. But when she looked up from finding her place, the eager looks on the faces of her wounded men drove the idea straight out of her mind.

She began with the words of Oberon:

" 'I know a bank where the wild thyme blows,
Where oxslips and the nodding violet grows . . .' "

A cup of cool water appeared at her side when her voice began to creak. She glanced up to smile at the man who leaned on his crutches. "Thank you."

"You're welcome. At least I didn't spill it all."

The tone of his voice caught in her throat. Despair, disappointment, disillusionment, all words to describe the pain she could hear and see when he let her. Or accidentally when his blackness grew too dark to see or think or do anything but feel. She drank the water and handed the cup back to him, wishing she could do something other than read for him and the others caught in that same black hole.

"Go on, please, can you read longer?"

"Yes, of course." She smiled at the young private who shaved once a week whether he needed it or not. The smile on his face helped her forget that he'd lost one eye and most of the sight in the other.

Louisa continued her reading:

" 'Quite over-canopied with lush woodbine,
With sweet musk-roses, and with eglantine,
There sleeps Titania sometimes of the night . . .' "

When she closed the book, the private pleaded, "One chapter from the Good Book too, please?"

"Surely."

"Good, that comforts me more than about anything." The scars around his eyes puckered with his smile as he leaned his chin on his knees. He always sat on the floor a foot or so from her stool where she could lay her hand on his head when she moved on. One of the men had teased him about being more devoted than the spaniel he had at home until one of the other soldiers had warned him off. Neil had become a favorite around the ward because of his good spirits in spite of his wounds.

Corporal Shaddock handed over her Bible. "First chapter of John, please."

"But we read that yesterday."

"I know, but I'm tryin' to memorize it. My ma said if you memorize the Word and keep it in your heart, God will bring it to yer 'membrance when you need it. So if you read it, and I talk it with you, maybe it'll go faster."

Louisa glanced around the room and, at the shrugs of the others, began. " 'In the beginning was the Word, and the Word was with God, and the Word was God.' "

When she finished, the only sound to be heard was the mutterings of a man trapped in delirium. Ready to stand and go home for the evening, she smiled at each of the men looking her way.

Ask them if they'd mind if you prayed. She cocked her head as if that would help her hear better. *I can't do that, I . . .*

Ask them.

She bit her lip and closed her eyes for a brief moment.

"You all right, Miz Highwood?" Neil touched her hand gently.

"Yes, yes. I'm fine." She took in a breath, hoping it would stop the quivering going on in her chest. It didn't.

She cleared her throat. Then again. "Ah, would y'all mind if we said a prayer?" The words burst from her mouth like Thoroughbreds out of the starting gate.

A snort from a man several beds down caught her attention. "Prayin' don't do no good."

"Does so. I'm alive, aren't I? I prayed for someone to come for me, and they did, and I'm alive." Neil flung his hands wide, bumping her skirt-covered leg in the motion. " 'Scuse me, please." He looked up at her, his one eye pleading for her agreement.

"Of course." How easy it would be to wrap her arms around him and play at being the mother he missed so sorely. "Those of you who want to pray, join with me. The rest of you can put your pillows over your ears."

Several chuckles greeted her reply.

She bowed her head and closed her eyes. Some shufflings, throats being cleared, and then the room again grew silent. "God in heaven, Father of us all, we're all here through no fault of our own. These men fought for what they believed and now bear the scars. Jesus, thou bore our sins and wear our scars. Please, we beg of you, come into this room and lay thy healing hands on each man here. Give them strength to go on with their lives, to seek thy purpose. Father, help us all to know how wide and high and long and deep thy love is for us, for thy Word says we are precious in thy sight, our Rock and our Redeemer. In the name of Jesus, in whom we put our trust, we pray. Amen."

"That was plumb beautiful." Neil ducked his head to wipe a tear. "Thank you."

Other thank-yous came from around the ward as she took her

books back to her closet. She glanced over to the window where the lieutenant kept his vigil. His jaw was clamped so tight the skin shone white over the bone.

"Time to go home, Missy." Reuben stood just inside the doorway.

"Yes, it is." *What can I do to help you?* she silently asked the lieutenant. She tried to smile at the face that had turned, but her lips wouldn't stop quivering. She waved instead, took up her basket with dirty aprons and empty napkins, and slipped out the door.

It took her better than a block to get the memory of his eyes out of her mind. Then remembering her joyful news, she burst out, "Reuben, I have wonderful news."

"What dat?"

"Zachary is alive, and he's in my ward."

"Don't make such jokes wit an old man, Missy. Tain't nice."

"I'm not joking. You know the man I told you about who lay unconscious for the whole week? Why, he woke up, and he's Zachary. My brother is alive!" She felt like whirling around in a circle and shouting for the entire town to hear.

"Praise de Lord for dat."

"Maybe as soon as he can get around good enough, we could go home."

"I wouldn't say dat to Missy Sylvania. She get right upset, she would."

"I know." Louisa took one skip and smiled at her companion. "And to think he's been there all week, and we didn't know." A couple steps later, she added, "But there was something about him. I came home thinking that two times at least. Something that seemed familiar, but all I could see was bandages."

"Miss Sylvania always like dat boy. She be right happy." He held open the door and motioned her through.

"Aunt Sylvania, Carrie Mae, where are you? I have wonderful news."

"She was here when I left." Reuben shook his head, confusion clouding his faded eyes. "Not tell dis ol' darkie she going somewhere."

Motioning Reuben to take her basket back to the kitchen, she climbed the stairs, one hand trailing on the carved walnut banister. *Where could Aunt Sylvania be? Ah, if only I could tell Jesselynn the wonderful news too.*

CHAPTER SEVENTEEN

Gordonsville, Kentucky

It can't be him. It can't be.

Jesselynn took the stairs to the store in a rush, checking herself before bursting through the door. *Don't call attention to yourself. Take it easy. Thank God those two old men are gone.* She pushed the door open to the sound of the bell tinkling above her and crossed the store to stand behind a woman wearing a dark shawl and chatting at the counter with the proprietor.

"Land sakes, you'd think they would know better, don't you think?"

"Yes, ma'am, I agree." He tied a string around her brown paper parcel. "Will there be anything else?"

Jesselynn almost grabbed the packet by the string and the woman by the arm and threw them out the door. What if indeed that man in the saloon was Dunlivey and he walked in here right this minute? What could she do?

She shifted from one foot to the other and cleared her throat.

The woman turned, gave her a dirty look, then shaking her head, picked up her package. "Thank you, Mister Charbonneau, and greet your dear wife for me. I do hope she is feelin' better soon."

Oh, please, just hurry and leave. Jesselynn could feel someone drilling holes in her back. Surely he was right behind her. But she knew no one had come in after her; the bell hung silent. But knowing and feeling had nothing to do with each other right now. Maybe she should have just left the order and headed out.

"I will do that. Thank you, and good day, Missus Levinger. I'll let you know when your order arrives."

Fine, good, now go.

The woman started to turn, checked herself, and leaned back across the counter. "You heard about . . ." Her voice dropped to a whisper that even Jesselynn couldn't hear, not that she wanted to. Sweat drizzled down her back.

The woman was shaking her head again. "Well, I better get on home and get some supper on the table."

Yes, your family is starving and your house is burning.

Missus Levinger gave her a baleful stare as if she'd been listening in on Jesselynn's thoughts, sniffed, and sailed out the doorway.

"Kin I help you? Oh yes, the young man with the order. I surely do hope there was no one on the casualty list that you knew." While he talked, he set her supplies on the counter and motioned to the white tow sack. "I saw that you rode in, so this will be easier for you to carry."

"Thank you." She kept from looking over her shoulder through sheer muscle-cramping determination. Digging her ten-dollar gold piece out of her pocket, she laid it on the counter.

"That'll be one dollar and seventeen cents, please." He took the coin and, turning to the cash register, pulled out Confederate dollars and change.

"Could I have that all in silver or gold, please?"

He looked at her over the tops of his glasses, raised an eyebrow, and went back for the change. "If you want a job, young man, you could come work for me anytime. You've got a head on those young shoulders of yours." He counted the change into her hand.

"Thank you kindly." Jesselynn shoved her money in her front pocket and took up the sack. Peeking inside, she glanced up at him again. "I didn't ask for any peppermint sticks."

"I know, but little ones like peppermint 'bout as good as horehound, and once they're feelin' better, this'll help."

"How'd. . . ?"

He tapped his head. "Just suspicioned. And your face says 'tis so. Call that my gift to you for bringin' me a gold piece."

"Thanks again." She took her sack, waved once on the way to the door, and stepped outside. This time she didn't dare just walk off. What if *he* was standing outside the saloon? But while the piano tune and laughter dressed in alcohol floated out the half door, all the men remained inside.

She didn't run the mule until she was far enough out of town to not be noticed. She didn't want to quit running him until they reached camp, but her father's training soaked through her fear-induced haze, and she tightened her reins enough to bring him to a walk. Once he caught his breath, they could trot again. Checking over her shoulder for about the fiftieth time still revealed only an empty road. Had it really been him? Was Cavendar Dunlivey following her, or did he happen to get stationed farther west? Could God be so cruel as to let that happen?

Ideas and fears tumbled around in her head just as her stomach was doing at the mule's gut-splitting gait. Surely she must have been hearing things. But no one else in the whole world could sound more like a braying jackass than Dunlivey, especially when he was drunk or whipping someone. That's why her father caught him. He could hear the man laughing and went to see what was so funny.

Strange how her mind could flip back to things like that in spite of the jolting trot. She kicked the mule into a canter, which wasn't a whole lot better. When she saw dark patches showing on his neck and shoulders, she pulled him down to a walk again. What could they do? No way on earth would she drive or ride through that town again. Benjamin would have to scout out a way around it, that's all.

When she rode into camp, she still felt like eyes were drilling her back. She flung herself off the mule's back and tossed the reins over his head.

"Where's Meshach?"

Ophelia turned from stirring a pot over the fire. "Gone to water de horses."

"Benjamin?"

"Wid him. Daniel fetchin' wood. Babies sleepin'." Her eyes grew rounder with each word.

Jesselynn plunked down the sack of supplies and swung back aboard the mule. "Thanks."

She trotted down the trail to the creek, ducking under the oak branches to keep from being slapped off.

"Hey, you back sooner den I guessed." Meshach's smile turned to a frown when she drew closer. "What wrong?"

"I think I heard Dunlivey laugh."

At the look of confusion he shot her, she continued. "I was walking from the store to the railroad station to check the casualty lists and had to go by the saloon. I heard men laughing, and one sounded just like Dunlivey. Who else in the entire world would laugh like that?"

"I don' know. He laugh mighty strange."

"I swear it was him." She slid off the mule and leaned against his shoulder. "We can't go through Gordonsville."

Meshach scratched his head. "Might be good idea to make certain." He studied Benjamin, who held the long lines so the horses could graze. "Send him in."

"They wouldn't let him in."

"He can look through de window, hang outside and see him come out."

"You think that's better than just heading out?"

Do I want to know or not? What difference does it make? She caught her breath in shock at the thought that whipped through her mind. *We could wait for him to come out and shoot him.*

"No, let's just get on the way again. Let Benjamin find us a way around town. There must be a back road somewhere." She led the mule down to the stream bank and let him have only a couple of swallows. "Sorry, boy, you'll get more later when you cool off."

Benjamin left shortly thereafter and returned later than she had hoped. All the while her mind played out scenes involving Dunlivey—his finding them, or getting killed in a skirmish, or baying on their trail like an old coonhound.

"Jesse?" Thaddy leaned against her knee when she sat by the fire.

"What?"

He climbed up in her lap with her belated help. Turning, he put his palms on either side of her face and looked deep into her eyes. "You mad?"

She shook her head.

" 'Phelia been cryin'."

"Oh."

He patted her cheeks. "Joshwa good boy."

"Umm." *Where was Benjamin? He should have been back by now.*

"Jesse!" He clapped his hands on her cheeks.

"Ouch!" She sat him on the ground with more than a gentle thump. "Thaddeus Joshua Highwood, you don't do things like that." Her cheeks smarted from the blows. "Whatever got into you?" Wagging her finger in front of his nose, she added, "Naughty boy."

"I not naughty." Hands on his hips, he met her glare with one of his own. "Me talkin' to you."

Jerked out of her stewing, Jesselynn swung between the desire to give him a swat on the rear or grab him and squeeze him tight. A little fighting rooster. That's what he was. And it was her job to protect him better than she had before. She had almost lost him. She snagged one arm around him and snugged him up between her knees, the better to give him smacking kisses on both cheeks and a tickle on his belly.

"More," he insisted in between giggles.

Jesselynn did as he asked, trying to keep one ear clear for a returning horseman. *Oh, Lord, what if I sent him out to get caught? By Dunlivey?*

"We got to give dis baby a name." Ophelia stopped walking the sick child.

"I guess."

Thaddeus leaned back in Jesselynn's arms. "He Sammy."

"Sammy? How do you know?" Jesselynn stared at her baby brother.

Thaddeus shrugged. "Don't know."

"Why call him Sammy?"

"Dat's his name."

"He's too little to talk."

"He Sammy." This was said with the utmost assurance that he was correct and why on earth was his sister disputing his word?

You are so much like your father, I can't begin to believe it. "Sammy it is, then," Jesselynn agreed.

"Sammy is a fine name," said Meshach, flicking another curl of wood from his whittling into the fire.

All right, so you have a wait ahead. Get busy with your knitting. Wanting to argue with the voice in her head but knowing it was useless, she got to her feet and strolled over to the wagon. Digging down into a carpetbag of her own things, she retrieved her ball of yarn stuck on two knitting needles. When she got back to the fire, Ophelia sat on the log rocking Sammy, and Thaddy had climbed up in Meshach's lap.

"Tell me a story."

"Please." Jesselynn added without really thinking about it. No matter if they lived in the wilds of whatever, he needed to learn good manners. Every southern gentleman had good manners, and if he was to be the patriarch of Twin Oaks someday, he needed to know how to behave.

Zachary, where are you? You need to come teach your little brother how to be a man.

"All right," Meshach said to Thaddy, hugging him close. "Long time ago der lived a boy by name of David. David took care of his father's sheep way out in de fields. He kep' dem safe from de wolf—"

"What's a wolf?" Thaddeus asked the question around the thumb and forefinger triangle that fit so perfectly in his mouth.

"Like a big ol' hound dog, only gray and lives wild in de woods."

"Like the woods here?"

"No, far away in Bible lands."

Jesselynn put down her knitting, the better to listen. Surely that was a horse she heard. Or was it more than one? She tried to block out Meshach's voice so she could hear better. One of the horses whinnied.

Another answered from not too far off.

Meshach stopped his storytelling. "Shush, listen," he whispered.

"Hey, is Benjamin."

Jesselynn let out a breath she had no idea she'd been holding. When she stood, she took a step forward to help settle her head, which felt as if it were floating off into the clouds. "What took you so long?"

Benjamin kicked his feet free of the stirrups and swung to the ground. "I found a way."

"Good."

"An' . . ."

Her breath caught in her throat. "And?"

"An' it be him. Cavendar Dunlivey be playin cards in de saloon."

Chapter Eighteen

Richmond, Virginia

"Aunt Sylvania?" Louisa stuck her head into the sewing room. No one there, but she could tell they'd been busy sewing the wedding finery. Laces and ivory satin pieces draped the chair and hung over the three-paneled screen. A bodice fit perfectly on the dress form with a swath of lace pinned to one shoulder. Bits of thread and scraps of fabric littered the floor like the leaves that were falling from the trees in the yard.

She carefully shut the door and walked down the hall to her aunt's room. As usual the door was closed. She tapped once and waited. Nothing. Turning the handle gently in case her aunt was napping, she pushed the door open enough to peek in. The bed was made up with every pillow and bolster in place.

She pushed the door open a bit more and scanned the remainder of the room. Everything appeared neatly in place, including her aunt's wire-rimmed glasses sitting atop her Bible that lay in its usual place on the whatnot table beside the rocking chair.

She closed the door again and went into her own room to hang up her shawl and wash her hands. After tucking stray locks of hair back in the bun at the base of her head, she rubbed rose water and glycerin lotion into her hands and left the sanctuary of her room behind. How good it would feel to lie back on the chaise lounge and let the knots relax out of her lower back and shoulders. To pick up her book of poems by Henry Wadsworth Longfellow and dream of the love she knew God had waiting for her somewhere. While she refused to be paraded on the marriage block like Carrie Mae, she knew that someday her prince would come.

He didn't need any armor or a snowy white horse. Or a crown either. The thought of a tall, terribly thin man galloped through her mind and kept on going, crutches tied behind his saddle. That thought reminded her of her brother.

She *had* to share the good news.

"She out in de garden," Reuben said when he met her descending the stairs. "I was comin' fo' you."

"Thank you. Have Abby bring out some lemonade, would you, please?"

"Surely will do dat." He motioned her to go down the hallway first and followed close behind. "She lookin' a mite peaked. Dis cheer her."

But when Louisa opened the French doors and stepped out onto the slate patio, her aunt didn't look sad. She was sound asleep. *Something must be wrong, this is so unlike her.* She hesitated, taking her aunt's wrist and counting her pulse, something she'd learned from one of the assistants at the hospital. If Aunt Sylvania was coming down with something, perhaps she should just call the doctor, not that he had much time for house calls with all the wounded he tended at his house too. The military weren't the only ones wounded in this war.

Come to think of it, Aunt had been a bit pale lately. Was she moving more slowly too? Louisa tried to think back over the last weeks. When did she first notice a difference? Or maybe it was just the unseasonably warm weather.

So instead of saying anything, she sat down on the other chaise lounge, just as she'd wished to do upstairs, only now she could look over the garden. The roses still bloomed, scenting the air with a perfume all their own, from sweet to spicy and layers in between.

A fat bumblebee trundled from blossom to blossom, tasting the chrysanthemums and the fading petunias, then arising with pollen yellowing his legs. A pot of gardenias lent their heavy scent and glowed in the dimming light like pure beeswax candles. She stroked one of the blossoms, then leaned over to inhale their perfume. The creamy flowers against their dark glossy leaves always showed their best at this time of day.

When Abby brought out the tray, Louisa pointed to the table and touched her finger to her lips, glancing at the sleeping woman to signify silence.

Abby nodded, set the tray down with barely a tinkle of the filled glasses, and tiptoed back into the summer kitchen set off from the house. The peace of the garden seeped into Louisa's bones and calmed her as nothing else ever did. Doves cooing in the magnolia branches above the brick wall added one more layer to the contentment. No wonder God created a garden to wander in of an evening.

When she first came to Richmond, she had spent hours digging in the garden, transplanting daisies and irises, trimming the spent roses and tying up the honeysuckle that did all in its power to disguise the fence and overrun the plum tree. Taming the honeysuckle had helped keep the tears of homesickness at bay. Or else the salt of her tears had dampened its rampant growth. Either way, the garden had been her salvation until she answered the call to service at the hospital.

The irony of one of her aunt's friends helping her get on there had been lost on Aunt Sylvania. After hours of hand wringing, feigned sick headaches, and outright threats, she had finally given in. However, she had no idea what Louisa really did there, and the less said of it the better.

Studying the garden gave her mind a bit of an itch. If working in this one had helped *her* so much, what could it do for her broken soldier, Private Rumford? His body was gaining health by the day, but his mind—who knew where it wandered? There were gardens out behind the hospital in terrible disrepair. What if she took him and others like him out to restore the garden? Her gaze narrowed on the garden shed. There were enough tools in there to equip a platoon of garden lovers, and if they weren't that when they began, the garden itself would bring them to that feeling with time. And maybe, just maybe, would take them out of the shadowland that kept them prisoner.

She started to rise to check on the contents of the garden shed when her aunt harrumphed and sat up.

"Land sakes, child, what are you doing sneaking up on me like that? I just closed my eyes for a moment and—"

"Now, Aunt Sylvania, I just sat down here to enjoy the garden with you. And see, Abby brought us some lemonade." She got up and carried the tray over. "Here, have a sip while I tell you our most wonderful news." She carefully kept from looking at her aunt's face, so flushed now that perhaps she was running a fever. Instead, she set the tray down and took her own glass, holding it against her cheek as she sat back down. "My, doesn't that feel wonderfully cooling. Is it always this warm even when almost October?" She refrained from saying Kentucky would be cooler, because the last time she'd mentioned home, she'd received one of *those* looks.

"News? What news?" Sylvania took a sip of her lemonade and settled her glasses back on her nose, the better to stare over them at her niece.

"Well . . ." Louisa tipped her head to the side and shrugged just a bit, keeping the smile from bursting forth only with great effort. "Remember I mentioned the soldier who was so bandaged up we couldn't see what he looked like and had not regained consciousness since they brought him in?"

"Now, Louisa, you know that—"

Louisa did the unforgivable. She interrupted. "I know, Aunt, but listen. That man is Zachary. I knew there was something—"

"Our Zachary?" Some of the lemonade splashed out of the glass when Sylvania jerked upright so quickly. While dabbing at the front of her dress, she asked again, "Not *our* Zachary?" Her chin quivered on the name.

"Yes, Aunt. My brother Zachary is alive." She set her lemonade down on the slate at her feet and, rising, crossed to take her aunt's hands in her own and kneel in front of her. "Zachary is badly wounded, missing one leg below the knee, and I'm not sure what else, but he is alive."

"Hello, y'all. Sorry I'm late." Carrie Mae breezed through the French doors, stopping at the look on her aunt's face. "What's wrong? Aunt, are you all right? You're flushed as if you've been runnin' 'round the garden."

"You're just in time to hear the news." Louisa rose and turned to take her sister's hands. "Maybe you'd better sit down first."

"Stop teasing her." Aunt Sylvania harrumphed again but dabbed at her eye at the same time. "Our boy is here in the hospital, and he's comin' home soon."

"Zachary?" Carrie Mae took her sister's advice and sank down on the lounge. "You're not teasing?"

"No, he's the man who's been all bandaged and unconscious."

Carrie Mae shuddered when Louisa listed her brother's injuries. "But he's alive, oh, thank you, heavenly Father." She clasped her hands to her chest. "Ah, if only we could tell Jesselynn. I'll write to her tonight."

"I think we'd better bring Zachary home as soon as possible. We can take much better care of him here than they do in that pest hole." Sylvania clasped her hands in her lap and looked skyward. "Oh, thank the good Lord, at least one of the men in our family has made it through the war. I haven't heard from Hiram in months, and with Joshua still fighting, God only knows where." She took a bit of cambric from her pocket and dabbed her eyes, then straightened. "And why, Missy, did you not bring that news home to me as soon as you knew?"

Louisa sat back on her heels, shaking her head. *So much for that brief moment of shared joy.* She returned to her own lounge and sitting down, picked up her glass and took a long swallow. When she set it down, she met the hard line frequently seen on her aunt's face when directed at her.

While Carrie Mae could do nothing wrong, sometimes it seemed that Louisa could do nothing right.

Guilt sneaked up behind her and grabbed her around the throat. She should have come right home. She had thought of it at the time. But all the injured men needed her so much worse. Should she tell Carrie Mae about her concerns about Aunt Sylvania? What should she do?

CHAPTER NINETEEN

Gordonsville, Kentucky

Wish I had shot him when I had the chance, Jesselynn thought, but knew deep down she couldn't kill the man, no matter how evil he was.

"You want we go take care of him?" Meshach spoke softly enough that none of the others could hear.

The temptation to say yes was so strong she had to bite her lower lip to keep the words from rushing forth. "No, we will just get on around that town. Dunlivey has no idea we are here. He can't know that." She turned to Benjamin. "Were any other soldiers there with him?"

"Not dat I could see. Least no uniforms."

"Was he wearin' a Confederate uniform?"

"Had gray pants and s'penders. He din't have no jacket on."

Jesselynn thought back to the last meeting with Dunlivey at Twin Oaks. He'd worn an officer's jacket then, looking right resplendent. Was he still in the army, or had he deserted? She had a hard time believing that the Cavendar Dunlivey she knew would tolerate military discipline for long. But being in the army gave him permission to kill and maim, and that part he would love, along with taking advantage of the soldiers under him. The snake loved to hurt living things and especially people.

The thought that he'd been riding a Twin Oaks horse made her want to . . . to . . . she didn't dare contemplate the things that came to mind. She wondered what officer he had stolen the horse from. Why did God let scum like him live while fine men like her father and brothers died?

If anyone ever thought this life was fair, the war would surely prove them misguided.

Ahab nudged her shoulder.

"We best be goin' on, Marse Jesse." Meshach's soft voice brought her back from her wandering thoughts. She pried her clenched fingers loose from the reins and flexed them to get the blood flowing again.

"Yes, you're right. Let's move on." *And not stop until we're clear across the Mississippi.*

By the time they'd detoured around Gordonsville and picked up the road again some miles west, her ears and eyes ached from the strain of watching shadows and hearing night noises. When an owl hooted not far above her head, she jerked the reins so hard that Ahab reared. Calling herself all manner of uncomplimentary names, she stroked his shoulder and leaned forward to rub his ears. "Sorry, old son. That was uncalled for. I'm just lucky you're gentleman enough to not dump me on the ground."

When she finally got her middle settled back down, her thoughts kept returning to Twin Oaks. How had the tobacco harvest been? Had Joseph insisted on payment in gold as she'd instructed him? That would give those on the plantation something to live on in the months ahead and perhaps even send some money to her sisters. There would be enough to plant again in the spring, and when Zachary came home—she had to believe he was still alive—she could hand a thriving plantation over to him, in spite of the war.

If he comes home. That thought warred with the others.

She turned around, trotted back to the wagon, and rode alongside it for a while. At times Sammy still coughed until he threw up, making her wish she had bought some whisky in town. That and honey would surely help this poor baby. She heard Ophelia singing to the little one, a song that sang of glory in the by-and-by.

How can she really believe that glory by-and-by? With all the death and filth we've seen! Jesselynn scratched a mosquito bite on her neck. Sammy's crying brought back the horror of finding his dead mother. What terrible things had that woman endured to try to save her babies? And now Jesselynn had her people depending on her for their safety. She caught herself shaking her head. Riding in the dark, where even the scenery couldn't be a distraction, gave her too much time to think.

"Nudder river comin' up." Benjamin dropped back to ride beside her as dawn played hide-and-seek with the dark.

Jesselynn sighed and shook her head. "We just get dried out and there's another creek or river to cross. How big is this one?"

"Big."

"The Mississippi?" Hope leaped into her voice.

"Maybe."

But it wasn't. They crossed the Cumberland and then the Tennessee at Jenkins Ferry and kept on following the sun west.

A day later she rode the mule into a town crawling with blue uniforms. After tying her mount to a hitching post behind one of the stores, she strolled back and leaned against the wall of the local hotel.

Half the people in the streets wore blue uniforms. The other half swished their full skirts and simpered at the officers, twirling their parasols and giggling.

She ambled on down to where they had corrals for the army horses. A cloud of dust rose that made her sneeze as she climbed up on the corral posts to get a better look at the horses now cavorting around the corral, bucking and kicking, getting the kinks out. One trotted past that she was sure she recognized because of a twist of white hair on an otherwise deep red chest.

"Hey boy, get down from there." A heavy hand grabbed her shoulder, tore her off the rails, and thrust her down.

Her rear smacked the hard ground first with such a jolt her tongue got caught between her teeth. The metallic taste of blood filled her mouth and rage clouded her eyes. "Why you . . ." Just in time she caught herself from saying anything to draw unwanted attention. She stared at the shiny black boots planted beside her.

The hand reached down this time and, grabbing her shoulder, picked her up and slammed her against the corral bars. "Now you git yer carcass on outa here and don't be bothering our horses."

"Can't hurt lookin' at 'em." She remembered to lower her voice and spat a chunk of dirt at the ground. Good thing her brothers had taught her how to spit, another skill of hers that hadn't pleased her mother.

"Don't want no Johnny Reb hurtin' our horses."

"I ain't never hurt a horse, you—" At the memory of his giant hand on her shoulder, she thought better of calling him a bluebelly bushwhacker. He could pick her up and shake her like a dog with a rat. And he nearly had. Her head hurt from the slam against the corral bar, and her posterior still protested the abrupt contact with the ground.

He waved his hands as if shooing a fly. "Git on with ye now."

Jesselynn *got*, but her estimation of Union soldiers sank another notch. She made her way back up the street to the front of the newspaper office to study the lists of casualties. "Lee Defeated At Antietam" read one headline, "Lincoln Declares Slaves Will Go Free," another. Her heart nearly stopped when she read the name Zachary on the dead list but started again when the last name was Arches.

She continued her stroll through the town, past the stores, looking in the windows at the ladies' apparel shop, then hurrying on. No boy her size would be caught dead looking at ladies' garments. When she passed a saloon the temptation to go on in and look for Dunlivey slowed her steps. *What if he's here?*

"Hey you, boy!" She glanced around to see whom the soldier was talking to and started to walk on when he yelled again. She flinched. *Is he yelling at me?*

She turned, keeping her chin low. "Yes, suh?"

"How old are you? I kin sign you up for the army."

"S-sixteen, suh."

"Ah, the rebels might take boys like you, but you have to be a man to join the Union army."

"Yes, suh." *Like there's any chance I'd join either army, least of all yours.* She bobbed her head, backing away at the same time. About the time she could turn and walk away, she bumped into something soft that emitted a feminine "oof."

"Young man, where in the world did you leave your manners?" The matron staring at her looked so much like her Aunt Sylvania that she almost blurted out the name.

"Ah, sorry, ma'am. Please, I'm sorry." She backed away, touching the brim of her cap and half bowing at the same time.

"You might look where you are goin' next time."

"I will. I surely am sorry." At the corner she turned and jogged down the alley. No way was she staying in this town another minute. But when she rounded the next corner, Union soldiers marched three abreast down the street, gold buttons flashing in the sun, sabers clanking all in perfect cadence. The line appeared to go on forever.

No wonder we're losing the war. They even all have rifles. Her father had been right, the Union army would be much better supplied, and no matter how dashing and chivalrous the southern soldier might be, guns were superior to sabers and rebel yells any day.

Instead of turning around and going the other way, she leaned against the wall, hands in her pockets as if she had all the time in the world. Overhearing the word "bluebellies," she stepped closer to the corner of the building to listen. Maybe she could learn where the fighting was so they could go around it.

"With Grant at Cairo, we got them all over the place."

"If we could get Shelby over here, we might see some changes made."

Shelby? Who's Shelby? Jesselynn tried to appear totally uninterested, taking out her knife to dig under her fingernails. She'd seen her brothers use the tactic all the time. In the same instant, she took one step closer.

"He's too busy in Missouri, and ferrying all those troops across ol' Miss, Grant would have 'em before the hounds could howl."

"I know. If'n only General Lee would send someone here to help out. 'Course they got him all tied up in Virginia."

The bugler passed, along with three drummers, and a platoon of prancing horses kept pace behind them.

Someone shouted an obscenity that brought a laugh from the crowd. The marching soldiers kept their faces straight ahead.

"God protect us," a woman's voice murmured.

God doesn't seem to care much. I think He's ashamed of this whole mess. Young men, old men, all killing each other for what? Sometimes even brother against brother. While she hadn't agreed with her brothers, believing her father might be more right, she was grateful they hadn't been fighting each other. Two brothers of one of the neighbors back home about broke their mother's heart when one went to fight for the North.

Jesselynn snagged her wandering attention and brought it back to the scene before her. And listened to the gossip.

When nothing more was forthcoming, she peeked around the corner to find the bench vacant, the two men gone.

Two young women were taking over the bench. "Ain't he just the handsomest man you ever saw?" They settled their skirts around them and tipped back their parasols.

Jesselynn looked out to see an officer riding by. Not that any man wearing blue could be handsome as far as she was concerned, but he did cut a fine figure. So did his horse. Must be one of the Thoroughbreds from Kentucky—not a Twin Oaks animal but a fine Thoroughbred nevertheless.

When he tipped his hat to the two women on the bench, they both giggled and tittered.

Jesselynn wanted to whack them with their parasols. Instead she pushed off from the wall and strolled on back to where her mule was tied. Slipping the knot on the reins, she swung aboard and turned him toward the back streets. She'd learned what she needed. The Union army was everywhere.

When she told her people the news, Ophelia whimpered, Meshach frowned at her, and the others simply shrugged.

"How we keep away from dem bluebellies if dey's so many of dem?" Ophelia finally asked what everyone was thinking.

"Go further south. They can't control the entire river." Jesselynn spoke with far more certainty than she felt.

They spent the next two nights threading their way between Union camps and scouts. By the time they reached a ferry without a cordon of blue-uniformed guards, they'd about been caught three times. Sometimes Jesselynn thought it might be easier to just head on home and only have the horses to hide. They hadn't had any hot food for three days, not taking a chance on building a fire.

They drove on down south of the ferry and stood looking across the muddy, roiling river.

"I cain't cross over dat." Ophelia sniffed back the tears and clung to Meshach's arm. "Please don' make me go dere."

"Oh hush, 'Phelia. 'Course you can. We all be on a ferryboat just like before. It's not like you have to swim."

"I cain't swim." Now she really was crying. Sammy picked up on her fear and began to wail. Thaddeus clung to Jesselynn's arm, his chin quivering and a whimper in his voice.

"We go home, Jesselynn. Please, we go home."

"Thaddeus Joshua Highwood, my name is Jesse! Jesse, remember that!" She wanted to shake Ophelia but knew it would do no good.

Surely after all we've been through, we won't be stopped now. She looked up at Meshach for reassurance, only to see stark fear on his strong features too.

CHAPTER TWENTY

General surgeon's office
Richmond, Virginia

Louisa felt like saluting.

"So, Miz Highwood, what is it I can do for you today?" The general in charge of the hospital folded his hands on his walnut desk top and gazed at her through eyes that seemed to have forgotten how to smile. His clipped voice made her sit straighter, wishing she had remained standing in spite of his invitation to sit. If she sat any closer to the edge of the chair, she'd be on the floor.

"Ah, well, General, sir, I . . ." *Oh, Lord, please give me the right words to say. I feel like a featherbrain whose feathers were blown away on the wind.* She took in a deep breath, locked her questing fingers together, and started again. "You know that I help out on Ward B." Was that a twinkle she saw peeking out of the wintry blue?

"Ma'am, from what I hear, your *helpin' out* is savin' some of our men's lives. They call you the 'angel in aprons.' Did you know that?"

She shook her head, the heat racing to her cheekbones and above. "I-I'm glad to be of service."

"And to find your husband wrapped in bandages. Now that is a true miracle."

The heat turned from flaming to full-fledged roaring.

Oh, God, I hate this deceit. How long will this have to continue? If I tell the truth, will he throw me out? Her inner battle must have shown on her face.

"Is there something wrong, ma'am?"

"N-no, of course not. I . . ." She kept her eyes on his and forced a smile to lips that would rather tremble. "My . . . my h-husband, um, will it be possible for him to leave the hospital soon and join us at my aunt's house? We can take good care of him there, and that will free up another bed—on the ward, that is." *You ninny, any fool could tell you are lyin', and this man is about as far from being a fool as . . . as . . .* She wished she could just sink through the floor.

"Why, as soon as the doctor says he can be moved, I reckon he would be much more comfortable there. So good to have a chance to see firsthand a husband and wife reunited." He shuffled a paper in front of him, then looked right at her again. "Is there somethin' else you needed to ask me?"

"Why, yes, sir, there is. You know of Private Rumford, one of the men on my . . . ah, Ward B, sir. He's the one who seems to have lost his grip on reality."

"Like many others, I'm afraid, but yes, I know to whom you are referrin'." The general clasped his hands on the desk in front of him and leaned forward. "What about the private?"

"Well, I thought, I mean, the garden at my aunt's house helped me so much when I first came to Richmond."

He nodded, but one raised eyebrow let her know he wondered what she could be leading up to now.

She rushed full tilt into her request. "You know the gardens out behind the hospital—they've gone to terrible wrack and ruin, and I . . ."

The other eyebrow joined the first.

Oh, now I've offended him. Mama, you told me to always watch my tongue, and now it is giving me nothing but difficulty. "Sorry, sir, I don't mean to be critical but . . ." She took in a deep breath to try to forestall the feeling of a featherbrain bereft of feathers. "Oh, bother!" She scooted forward and leaned against her hands on the edge of his desk. "I believe workin' in the garden would help bring Private Rumford back to reality and perhaps give some of the others who have lost so much a place to heal. Diggin' in the dirt is good for the soul, my mama always said, and I know firsthand that she was right. Helpin' things grow reminds us how God grows us, you see, I mean . . ." She shook her head. She should have stopped while she was ahead, whenever that was.

The general nodded. "I see." He steepled his fingers and studied her over the tips. "And who will oversee this project of yours?"

Up to that point, flummoxed had been just a word in the dictionary. Now she knew how it felt. Featherbrained and flummoxed. She sucked in a deep breath and let it out, praying for any kind of inspiration to answer his question. Would he let *her* supervise? She gave an inward shake of her head. Reuben could do so very handily, but some of the soldiers might resent being governed by a black man, no matter how gentle his orders.

The sun sprang from the horizon, in her mind, that is. "Why, Lieutenant Lessling could do that. Though he can't get down on his knees yet to dig and plant, he could supervise." She nodded and clasped her bottom lip between her teeth. "Why, yes, that's the perfect answer. It might help him with his moroseness too, just like the private."

"Are you suggesting that Lieutenant Lessling is out of his mind?"

"No, sir, of course not. I just thought that . . ." She looked up in time to be sure there was a twinkle in his blue eyes, which were no longer frosty.

"Miz Highwood, forgive me. I couldn't resist teasin' you. It's been far too long since I saw a comely young woman blush. I will give the order for the beds to be dug up this afternoon, and by tomorrow you can have your garden brigade busy out back. Do you have any seeds?"

"I'll find some." Louisa got to her feet. "Thank you, sir. Reuben will bring some extra tools with him in the morning."

"Thank you, ma'am. I'm sure the men will be fightin' over who gets to help you first."

"Sir!" It would be a miracle if her bonnet didn't catch fire from the heat flaming up her face.

"Let me know if there is anything else I can do to be of service. Aide, show Miz Highwood out."

Louisa nodded once more and turned to follow the stiff-backed aide from the room. At the door she paused and looked back. "God bless you, General."

"And you." He cleared his throat and nodded one more time before taking his seat again. The picture she carried with her up to the ward was of a man so burdened he could barely keep his head up. *Think I'll ask the ladies to pray for this man especially,* she thought as she mounted the steps. *Sometimes prayers mean more when there is a face attached to the prayer.*

Keeping her wonderful news to herself took more skill than she imagined. Every time she passed a window, she glanced back at the decrepit roses and the overgrown vines. An arbor sagged to one side, a victim of decay more insidious than the battle wounds suffered by her men.

Zachary lay sleeping again, but one look at the unbandaged side of his face let her know it was the sleep of healing. The man two beds over was a different matter. He flayed at the mattress with both hands and feet until one of the nurses came with strips of old sheet and tied his limbs down so that he wouldn't reopen the wounds so recently stitched closed.

Louisa pulled a chair over beside him and, with a cloth and basin of cool water, began bathing his face. Ever present at her side when she was on the ward, Rumford stared at her hands as if fascinated. But when she turned to say something to him, he wore the same vacant stare as ever.

"Would you like to help me?" She kept her voice gentle and soft so as to let the man in the bed behind her sleep. She extended the dampened cloth to the hovering man, but he never said a word nor showed that he heard her.

But he has to be aware. Why else would he follow me around so? This question, like many of her others, had no answer.

"W-will you read today?" one of the men asked from across the aisle.

"Yes, of course." She flashed him a smile and caught some movement from the corner of her eye. The *shuffle-clunk* of a man on crutches let her know who it was before her eyes did. The lieutenant stopped at the foot of the bed.

"You want I should get the books?"

"Yes, please." *What I really want you to do is read in my place.* But she kept the words inside, not wanting to embarrass him. After all, not everyone loved reading aloud as she did. She took the basin over to her brother's bed and set it on the floor underneath, out of the way of anyone's feet. She'd help him wash as soon as he woke up. Glancing up, she saw her stool set in place and the two books on top of it, her Bible and Shakespeare. She'd thought of bringing Dickens but knew she'd get in trouble if she didn't finish *The Taming of the Shrew*. By sticking to the comedies, she could bring a smile to some of the men and even raise laughter from some of the others. She'd already finished *A Midsummer Night's Dream* and *The Merchant of Venice*.

There was far too little laughter on the ward.

She smiled her thanks to the lieutenant and settled herself on the high stool. "Today we will begin with Psalm 91, for I think we all need to be reminded how closely God holds us." She found her place and began. " 'He that dwelleth in the secret place of the most High shall abide under the shadow of the Almighty. I will say of the Lord, he is my refuge and my fortress: my God; in him will I trust.' " Louisa continued reading to the end of the psalm. From there she went on to Psalm 139, and then to Paul's prayer to the Ephesians: " 'That he would grant you, according to the riches of his glory, to be strengthened with might by his Spirit in the inner man; that Christ may dwell in your hearts by faith; that ye, being rooted and grounded in love, may be able to comprehend with all saints what is the breadth, and length, and depth, and height.'

"And that is my prayer for each of you." She kept her finger in the place and read the passage again, finishing with, " 'And to know the love of Christ, which passeth knowledge, that ye might be filled with all the fulness of God.' "

"Amen." Another man echoed the first.

"You read so purty."

"Thank you. God's words make me want to keep reading them over and over. We need to hear again and again how much He loves us." She glanced around at all her men. "In spite of all this."

The lieutenant had returned to his window vigil while she read and now kept his back to her. The urge to go to him almost made her slide off the stool, but she righted herself and set her Bible on the bed nearest her.

"Read some more—please."

"Which, the Bible or Shakespeare?"

"Don't matter. I jus' like to hear the words."

"Shakespeare."

The men called their preferences in voices tired and hoarse and pleading.

She found her place and began again, sneaking occasional peeks to the still, lean form propped on crutches. He never turned when she finished, not even when she gathered her things to leave a while later.

"Good-bye, dear wife," her brother whispered, holding her hand for a long moment.

"The general says we can bring you home as soon as the doctor releases you."

"Is Aunt Sylvania in agreement?"

"Of course, dear boy."

"You sound just like her."

"I meant to."

He flinched as he shifted on the bed. "I'll see you tomorrow, then?"

"Yes. But I won't wake you." He'd already scolded her for letting him sleep so long.

"As you wish." He paused for a moment. "Are the peaches ripe?"

"All gone, I'm afraid. I'll bring some preserves tomorrow." Her gaze strayed back to the form at the window.

"Well, will ya lookee that." One of the other men who watched out a window turned to the others. "There's someone diggin' up the rose bed."

"You promise." Zachary still clutched her fingers. "Maybe tomorrow I'll be able to see better if they take some of the bandages off."

Please, God, that he'll be able to see out of both eyes. She gently withdrew her fingers and stepped back. "Peach preserves, I promise. And biscuits."

As she and Reuben walked the streets to home, she could hear a train whistle in the distance. That meant new wounded in the morning. Perhaps Zach would be released sooner than they expected.

"Louisa, it came." Carrie Mae waved an envelope in the air when Louisa reached the front portico.

"Who is it from?"

"Jesselynn—our sister—you won't believe it. She left Twin Oaks to go to Uncle Hiram's in Missouri."

Louisa snatched the letter and sank down on the wooden glider, barely able to open the envelope her fingers shook so badly. She withdrew the paper, tears burning at the sight of the dear handwriting. She read it once, glanced up at some children running by, laughing and calling as they went, and then read the letter again. Jesselynn was somewhere between Midway, Kentucky, and Springfield, Missouri, with horses, and no one was taking care of Twin Oaks.

"She had to keep her promise."

"I know." Carrie Mae studied the toe of her black slipper. "Daddy wasn't in his right mind, or he would never have asked that of her."

"But without the horses . . ."

"The land will always be there. Zachary can go home and plant the land."

Louisa set the glider to moving, the squeak of it comforting in the twilight.

"At least we know God is watching out for her when we can't."

"Thank the Lord for that." Carrie Mae let her head fall against the glider back. "Wait until I tell Jefferson this latest news. He won't believe it."

"Won't believe what?" Louisa recognized a look of concern when she saw it.

"That a woman of our family would do such a crazy thing."

"Then he doesn't understand the value of Twin Oaks horseflesh and the burden of a vow." Louisa rose and headed for the door. "I need to wash up before supper." She opened the door and turned back to her sister. "How does Aunt Sylvania seem today?"

"Better. I think the good news helped. She worries more than she lets on—the wedding and all."

"Really." Mounting the stairs to her room, Louisa trailed a hand on the banister. *Glad it's her marryin' Jefferson and not me.*

———

The lieutenant met her at the door in the morning, his jaw clenched so tight the outline of the bone showed through his skin. "And just what is it you think you're doin', Miz Highwood?"

Chapter Twenty-One

On the banks of the Mississippi River
October 2, 1862

"Hush now!" Jesselynn knew her voice sounded sharp, but she was past caring.

"Big river," Meshach said from slightly behind her.

"It's not like we have to swim it. Back aways they said there were ferries, depending on where we want to cross. They say General Grant owns this stretch, so we're safe from the Confederates."

"Bluebellies want horses worse."

She wished he wouldn't say such things. She'd just about get her confidence up, and he'd douse it with a few words of common sense. "So we stay away from Grant too. Let's find us a hiding place, and I'll go looking for ferry owners in the morning." She didn't mention the possibility of a guard on the ferry, nor the fact that she was hoping to get them ferried over after dark. Once on the other side, they could disappear into the Missouri woods and rest a bit. She studied the river, the currents changing the face of the water even in the starlight. With only a sliver moon, they would be even less visible.

Ignoring the whimpering of Ophelia and the little boys, she fingered the dwindling supply of coins in her pocket. She *had* to save what she could to get them to Springfield and Uncle Hiram's. At their last stop she'd heard of fighting going on in Missouri too, fierce fighting. Only by refusing to let herself think about what lay ahead could she keep from turning tail and heading back to Twin Oaks. If her father had known what the trip would entail, would he have exacted her promise anyway?

For one brief moment she allowed herself to remember life as it had been before the war. Twin Oaks had sheltered them through all the seasons. She could picture winter and the mares dropping their foals; sowing tobacco seed in special beds; starting other plants; then pegging tobacco; setting out tomatoes and petunias, grateful for the rains that came when needed. She closed her eyes to see the kitchen, separate from the house, but full of harvest smells.

Her stomach grumbled her back to the present. Would they be able to be home in time to plant tobacco seeds? She'd instructed Joseph to save seed from the best plants in case there were none available to purchase, or they had no money. Since there'd be no yearlings to sell this year, the tobacco had to do well. Surely by now all the stalks were hanging in the drying barn, each hooked over the rods and spread apart just enough to allow air to circulate freely. Drying tobacco had its own pungent aroma, nothing like that of pipe or smoke. To her it smelled like hard money. How many hogsheads could they fill?

"Marse Jesse." Benjamin's soft voice interrupted her reverie, cutting off the ache to be at home tending to the tobacco and putting food by for the winter. "I found us a place."

"Good." The sigh caught her by surprise. "Let's go." *You better toughen up, or you'll be squalling like Ophelia and the babies. If you're going to wear the britches of a man, you'd better act like one.* She spun on her heel, then back at the wagon untied Sunshine's reins and swung aboard.

She woke to the sun warming her and two yellow butterflies dancing above her pallet. She lay and watched as they came together and fluttered apart again, one leading up a sunbeam toward the oak tree and the other first following, then tagging and flitting away. They were playing hide-and-seek in the oak leaves when she threw back the quilt and dug under the pallet for her boots. The smell of boiling coffee drove everything but food from her mind.

An hour later, hat pulled low on her forehead, she rode the mule back toward the shoreline. Belatedly, she realized it was market day. Teams of horses, oxen, and mules with their wagons lined the streets in front of brick stores and businesses. Laughter drifted from the saloon, and a dog barked at a cat that ran under the porch of the millinery store. Farmers leaned against posts to discuss their crops and the latest war news while their wives chatted on the benches. Small children played under the benches and around their mothers' feet.

Jesselynn noted several blue-clad soldiers, but they were busy shopping, not guarding or searching for anything—or anyone. At least it appeared that way.

She nudged the mule off Main Street and rode down an alley where a man was chopping firewood. He nodded as she passed by and, wiping the sweat from his brow, set another chunk of wood up on the chopping block. A boy called "hey" to her from where he was swatting a rug with a rug beater and sneezing at the dust he raised.

"Hey, yourself." Jesselynn kept her voice in the low register and nudged the mule to keep on going no matter how inviting a hank of grass appeared.

When she reached the shoreline, she could see the ferry halfway out in the river taking a cargo across. She watched as the three oarsmen on either side pulled to keep the bow straight and the boat on course. A man with a long oar guided from the stern, if the flat ends could be called that. From what Jesselynn could see, they would load and unload from either end. The ferry didn't look big enough to hold a wagon, let alone the team and the others, but the team aboard stayed hitched to their wagon. When the ferry grounded itself on the slope of the bank, planks slid off, and the team pulled the wagon off the ferry and up to the road.

It looked easy.

But would it be so simple at night?

Several horses and riders walked up the planks and the return trip began. As they neared the shore, one of the horses shifted restlessly and the rider standing holding the bridle flipped off his handkerchief and drew it over his quivering mount's eyes.

Jesselynn resolved to take enough handkerchiefs for all the horses. *And maybe my hands too.* If the hands of her men shook as bad holding the horses as they had looking at the river, she knew they were in for a rough crossing. The men knew how to swim, but Ophelia's shrieking was enough to scare Saint Peter. She'd just have to tell Meshach to keep her quiet. Ophelia listened to him as if he were Moses coming down from Mount Sinai.

Dismounting, she tied the mule to a tree and, hands in her pockets, ambled on over to the road when the ferry was still a few yards offshore. Another wagon waited with a farm family, heading home after a day in town, empty tow sacks folded in the back of the wagon bed and held in place by full ones that appeared to hold flour and beans and such. One of the barefooted boys sucked on a red-and-white peppermint stick, and a little girl perched on her mother's hip, arms clasped around her neck.

Jesselynn stopped near the whiskered man. "You use the ferry often?" she asked after exchanging greetings.

"Mostly on market day. We bring over some and take some home."

"Umm. Always this busy?"

"Nope, only market days or when the troops are movin'." He laid his hand on his son's head, and the boy stilled.

"How much for one way?"

"Depends. Jed charges more for someone he don't like or if'n he's in a foul mood. Drink'll do that to a man."

"Ah." *Does he ever run at night?* She knew she'd better keep that question between her and Jed. When the horses and riders walked off the ramp, she saw the broad-shouldered man who manned the sweep oar used as a tiller pull a flat bottle from his back pocket and take a long swallow. Wiping his mouth with the back of his hand, he hollered something at one of his oarsmen, then stepped ashore and climbed the slope with long strides.

"Be back soon." He waved to those waiting and strode on up the street.

Jesselynn watched him push open the doors to the saloon and disappear inside.

Did she dare go in after him? The family pulled their mules over to the shade of an ancient oak tree, and they all sat down, the boy pillowing his head in his mother's lap.

"Might just as well make yourself comfortable." The man indicated the cool of the shade with a sweep of his hand. "Might be a while. They's no hurryin' Jed."

Jesselynn debated. If she waited by the saloon door, perhaps she could talk with Jed alone on his way back to the ferry. She glanced at the six black men over on the plank ferry, which was built on floating logs. Several had curled up by their benches and fallen asleep. One, who appeared to be the leader, paced on the shore, carefully inspecting the rigging of the logs. Another played a Jew's harp, its plaintive notes drifting on the still air.

Laughter floated down the street from a group of children playing tag.

Jesselynn glanced again at the waiting family. All appeared to be asleep except the mother, who sat knitting. In between stitches, she brushed the flies from the faces of her children.

A memory of her mother doing much the same flashed into Jesselynn's mind. They'd been on a picnic by the river and Louisa had fallen asleep just like the boy. *Ah, Louisa, if only I dared write and tell you where I am.* Surely Dunlivey wouldn't go all the way to Richmond to ask his questions. How could he? He was in the army, wasn't he? No longer free to go where he willed?

She tried to bring up a picture of her two sisters sitting in the garden at Aunt Sylvania's house and sipping afternoon lemonade under the magnolia tree. And what of Zachary? Had anyone heard anything of him?

Nodding to the knitting woman, Jesselynn strode up the street in search of Jed. They *had* to cross tonight. She'd just reached the steps to the saloon when the swinging doors blew open, and Jed, another flat bottle in his hand, roared in laughter at something someone behind him called. If Jesselynn hadn't stepped back, he would have barreled right over her.

"Ah, sir. Mister Jed."

"Who's callin' me?"

"I am." Jesselynn stepped in front of him, her gaze traveling up an unbuttoned dirty shirt worn over a filthier woolen union suit. A small stick lodged in his beard, and dark eyes flashed under bushy caterpillar brows. She swallowed, then cocked her head at an angle and started again. "Ma daddy sent me to ask how much you'd charge to take over a wagon and team, along with a couple other horses."

"How many folk?"

"Five grown and two little'uns." She spat off to the side of her boot after he did it first.

"When?"

"After dark."

"You runnin' from the law?"

"No, sir."

"The army?"

"No, sir. Just got to get to a funeral. Grandpappy died unexpected like." The story came out before she even had time to think on it.

"You wouldn't lie to ol' Jed, now, wouldja?" He took another slug from the bottle and held it out to Jesselynn, who shook her head.

"Ma daddy would tan me good if'n I came home with liquor on my breath."

Jed nodded and swigged again. He named his price.

Jesselynn kept herself from flinching with the most supreme effort. After talking with the man at the ferry, she knew the price was doubled. But there would be more dangers at night, so she nodded. "I'll tell him. You need to know what time f'sure?"

"Jus' come." Jed clapped her on the shoulder and strode off down to the ferry, leaving her with both a smarting shoulder and the desire to jig her way back to the camp. She had found a way across the river. Now to get her people ready for it.

Back in camp, the boys, both big and little, were sleeping soundly. Meshach sat under a tree with his Bible on his knees reading to Ophelia, who still rocked back and forth in her distress. Jesselynn stripped the saddle from the mule and, tying him to the long line, took off the bridle as well. She studied the horses grazing so peacefully. They looked too good, even though they had matted manes and tails and hadn't seen a grooming brush since they left home.

"Is there some way you can make Ahab limp?" she asked after sitting down by Meshach.

"I 'spects so. Why?"

"I don't know, just got me a feelin'." Jesselynn turned to study the horses. Domino, the younger stallion, stood looking off to the west, ears pricked, the breeze blowing his tail. No matter how filthy, he showed Thoroughbred through and through.

"We're takin' the ferry tonight and ... and if he was limping with head down, maybe ... maybe he wouldn't be so ..."

"I kin make 'im limp."

"But it won't hurt him permanently?" She could hear the anxiousness in her own voice. She sucked in a breath. "What about the others?"

"If we harness the mare with the mule, get ol' Ahab to limpin' so I'm leadin' 'im and Chess ..." He thought a long moment. "I got some stuff to set Domino to coughing, so Benjamin can lead him.

Then you drive the wagon, and Daniel can ride Sunshine and lead the filly. Shouldn't nobody look twice at 'em dat away."

"Don' wanna go over dat der river." Ophelia's hoarse whisper made Jesselynn flinch.

"Won't be any different than crossing the Tennessee. We took the ferry there too, remember? And others before that."

"I 'member." She shook her head slowly. "Not big like dis here one."

"Okay, you stay in the back of the wagon with the babies, and all of you can cry all you want. I'll tell the man you got the vapors or something. But we are crossing the Mississippi River tonight, and that's that!" Jesselynn stood and glared down at the wide-eyed woman. "I told him we are goin' to a funeral, so your weepin' and wailin' should be right appropriate."

"Now, 'Phelia, God done took care of us till now. He can float us 'cross dat river jus' like de Jordan."

A sniffle was her only answer, but Jesselynn could tell the woman was calmer. Meshach's gentle words put her in mind of the song she'd heard sung so often from the slave quarters. "*. . . my home is over Jordan. Deep river, Lord, I want to cross over into campground.*" She sighed. "Let's get on with it. Meshach, you better say an extra prayer or two for all of us." Turning away, she headed for the wagon. Sometimes the burden seemed beyond her strength to bear. Maybe letting the army have the horses so she could head on back home would be the best choice after all.

———

Stars provided enough light for them to make their way through the town and down to the ferry. The water lapping against the bulky craft sent the timbers to creaking and, along with the creak of the wagon, sounded loud in the stillness.

"Marse Jed?" Jesselynn kept her voice low but insistent. She waited, hearing a scuffling on the boat.

A light flared and lit the lantern. Jed seemed even bigger, if that were possible, in the glow of the lamp as he staggered down the plank to the riverbank. "You ready?"

"Yes, suh."

"You got the money?" Jed swung the lamp up to look her in the face.

"Yes, suh." Jesselynn ducked her head and dug in her pocket for the coins needed. She counted them into the shovel-sized palm. "That's what you said."

"I know." He spun around and picking up the end of the plank, thudded it against the ferry planking. "Let's go, boys. We got us a load."

Men scrambled up from where they slept and took their oars. Several more planks were slid into place, and Jed gave orders from the ferry.

"Lead your horse on up here real easylike. They ever been ferried before?"

"Yes, suh." Jesselynn climbed down from the wagon, hearing Ophelia moaning "Jesus" over and over. She took the mule's reins under his chin and, clucking him forward, led the team up the ramp and forward on the low craft. With horses on either side, all facing forward, the men pulled in the planks, and Jed pushed off with his long pole. The stroke of six oars slicing the water in tandem and the sweep of the stern oar brought them out into the current. The prow of the ferry swung downstream with the current before righting and plowing forward.

Jesselynn felt the planking shuddering under her feet. The mule laid back his ears and stamped one front foot. Domino coughed until he broke wind, and the sailor nearest him made a rude remark that brought laughter from another.

Short chop broke over the prow, soaking Jesselynn's boots. Ophelia moaned again, and Sammy set up a wail.

"Ohh." Even Meshach groaned.

"Enough!" Jesselynn forced out the word in spite of the shaking that she attributed to the creaking craft. The far shore seemed to get farther away instead of closer.

Was the current carrying them downriver? She turned to look at Jed, who appeared more shadow than man at the stern. Was crossing at night against the law? Why had he blown out the lamp?

"Heave on, boys," the order came, calm as a summer day.

"Oh, Jesus, sweet Jesus, we comin' home," Ophelia sobbed.

Jesselynn wished she had put a rag in Ophelia's mouth before they'd left camp. Sammy hiccuped after crying. Must be hours that passed, the ferry held prisoner by the river.

"Pull, you worthless scum. You want a glug of rotgut at the shore, you pull now."

"Oh, Lord, bring us safe to shore, please, precious Jesus." Like

Ophelia, Meshach murmured his prayer over and over.

The young stallion coughed again, pounding his front hooves on the planks.

"Whoa, son." Benjamin could be heard above the creaking.

An expletive choked.

The raft shuddered from the impact and spun to face down-river.

"Easy! No!" A mighty splash drenched those nearest and then another.

CHAPTER TWENTY-TWO

Richmond, Virginia

If looks were spears, she'd have been run through more times than she could count.

Louisa focused her attention on the men kneeling in the dirt and those missing a limb who were learning to use shovels and rakes to clear out the dead wood of the rosebushes and encroaching vines. In spite of herself, her gaze repeatedly drifted toward the lieutenant. His orders had been to supervise, as if leaning on his crutches and glaring provided good supervision.

As the hours passed, she surreptitiously wiped the perspiration from her forehead and neck. When she caught him staring at her, she dropped the corner of her apron at the same instant she raised her chin. After all, she'd suggested working in the garden for the good of *his* men. As if all these were under *his* orders, anyway. They were from all different regiments, not just *his*. She nodded an answer to a question from one of the others.

As she was just about to stalk over and confront her nemesis, a shadow gave her shade. She turned enough to realize he stood right behind her, so close that if she took in a deep breath, she might touch him. While taking a step back might indicate defeat, she did so anyway. Sometimes retreating was the better part of valor.

At least she could breathe then.

"Goodness, do you always sneak up on a body that way?" She clenched her fists to keep them from offering calming pats to her tripping heart.

"I *was not* sneaking." His lips barely moved, his jaw clamped so tight. Even so, he kept his voice low so that the others might not hear.

Feeling loomed over, she took another step back. "Well, *sir*, since I am not one of *your* soldiers, I would appreciate a more civil tone." *Oh, fine, now you've gone and done it. He finally talks to you, and you scold like his mother.*

She watched as he forcibly gathered himself together, stood straighter, and adopted a polite expression that wouldn't fool a year-old baby.

"Pardon me, ma'am. I believe I have a right to know why you asked the surgeon to assign me to garden duty."

She straightened as he had, if it were possible for her to get any taller and straighter. Totally ignoring the memory she had of suggesting to the surgeon general that garden duty might be good for the lieutenant, she matched him glare for glare. "I asked if I could bring Private Rumford and some of the others out here because I thought that working in the soil might help them. My aunt says gardening is one of the best medicines God has given us, and I concur." She didn't add that such had been her salvation when her sister exiled her from Twin Oaks to Richmond. Before she took time to think, she stepped forward and pointed a soil-crusted finger at his chest. "And if *you*, Lieutenant Lessling, would unbend even a smidgen, it might help you too."

She caught her breath at the narrowing of his eyes. For sure she had gone too far. *Oh, Lord, why can I no longer control my tongue? What is happening with me? My mother would turn over in her grave to hear her daughter attacking any person, let alone a young man like this.* And a wounded man, at that.

"I . . . I'm sorry. That was unbelievably rude of me. Please . . ." She looked down at her dirt-crusted hands and even dirtier apron. Shame can cause as much heat as pure embarrassment. She felt it flaming her face. "Please forgive me?" She glanced up from under her eyelashes in time to catch a hint of something in his eyes. Was it compassion she saw? By the time she named it, the look had fled, and one of such bleakness that it made her heart cry out for him took up residence instead.

"Forgiveness needs to go both ways, Mrs. Highwood. I'm sorry for the way I've been actin'. Such conduct befits neither an officer nor a gentleman."

Could one drown in eyes so sad?

She gathered her ruffled feelings around her like a hen gathering chicks and allowed her lips to smile in what she hoped was a motherly fashion. Why could she treat all the other men like her brothers or cousins, but this man refused to be treated as such?

"Then may we be friends?" The words crept out before she had time to cut them off.

"Friends, yes." He touched one finger to the fading scar on his forehead. "If your husband won't mind."

"But I—" This time she caught herself. "No, I reckon he won't mind at all."

"Miz Highwood, you think this here is dug deep enough?" one of her workers called out.

She turned to answer the soldier's question and, throwing a smile over her shoulder to the lieutenant, made her way to inspect the holes being dug to transplant some of the overcrowded rose-bushes.

"That will be fine." She glanced over to where Rumford and Reuben had dug around the well-watered bushes to prepare them for lifting. As long as Reuben indicated exactly where to place the shovel and when to step on it, the young man leaning on the handle and staring into the distance was able to dig.

At further instructions he lifted the roses out of their holes as carefully as if he were lifting a baby. By the time they'd moved four bushes, watered them in, and pruned off a couple of broken branches, the orderly announced the noon meal.

"Now, doesn't that look much better?" She stood with her crew gathered around her and surveyed the results of their labors. While there was still a lot to do, the newly planted roses gleamed against the rich soil, and the weeds were now piled off to the side instead of choking life from the bushes. A mass of tangled vines topped the weed pile.

"As my mother always said, 'Termorrer is another day.'" Corporal Shaddock wiped sweat from his brow with the back of his good hand.

"So true, and thank y'all for helpin' me out here."

The snort from behind her could have come from only one voice. She ignored him, and together she and her crew made their way back to the ward, those on crutches hopping up the marble stairs, the seat of their pants mute evidence as to how they'd managed to work in the garden. Only the lieutenant bore no badges of honorable work, but he had been there, and he had asked her forgiveness. He'd even smiled at a joke one of the men made.

When she brought around the bowls of stew, she nearly dropped one when she reached her brother's bed.

"You're sitting up, and I can see part of your face."

"Now, aren't you the observant one?" His drawl sounded more familiar now that more bandages had been removed, and the teasing sparkle in his eye had not dimmed. "Looks like they'll be calling me One-Eyed Jack, though." He touched the bandaged side of his face with his fingertips. "Guess my right side took quite a beatin'." Talking was still difficult with the jaw healing.

His teasing tone dropped on the last words as the sparkle flickered from his eye.

"But you're alive."

"Half of me anyway."

"Soon as we get you out of here, I reckon you'll be feelin' some better with Aunt Sylvania fussin' over you."

He studied the bowl of stew she set beside him. "The food'll be better. That I know." He took the spoon she handed him and dug in, slopping some of the colorless liquid over the edge. "Shame I didn't work on becoming ambidextrous like Adam did."

"Learnin' to use the other hand is never easy." She kept herself from reminding him he was fortunate to have one good hand. Some didn't.

———

"I think you should be able to take him home in two or three days," the doctor said when he made his late afternoon rounds. "Unless we get another battery of wounded, that is, and need his bed. How did"—he nodded toward Rumford—"do outside?"

"I set him to working with Reuben, my aunt's gardener, and he followed all Reuben's orders without a grumble."

"With no visible response, you mean?"

"Well, he *did* do as asked."

The doctor nodded. "You're right. Thank you, my dear, for all your efforts on behalf of these men. If I had ten more like you, the care here would improve dramatically."

"Doctor?" one of the orderlies called from the door.

"Yes?"

"Train just pulled in full of wounded."

"So much for two or three days. I hate to ask this, but can your aunt or anyone else take in some of these men?"

"I'm sure, but I'll ask." Louisa untied her apron as she headed for the doorway. "We'll be back with a wagon as soon as we can."

She nearly tripped over her skirts in the rush up the front steps to Aunt Sylvania's house. She paused only long enough to catch her breath, knowing that a scolding about propriety would set her aunt in a less-than-generous fashion. But then, she *had* asked what more she could do for the "dear boys," as she referred to the soldiers. Only, up until now, the dear boys had not been needing one of her lovely rooms.

"Aunt, where are you?" Louisa paused for a moment to know where to search.

"In here." The answer came from the back of the house.

Louisa found her aunt watching Abby arrange flowers in the pantry.

"You're home early." Weariness rode Sylvania's face and left her hands shaking.

"I know. I need to get back. The doctor said we could bring Zachary home if we had a place for him." Louisa breathed another calming breath. "But we couldn't take him upstairs very easily."

"Then we will have to move a bed into the parlor." Sylvania rose from her chair. "Come, Abby, call Prissy to help you."

"Ah, while we are moving one bed, could we do two—or maybe three?"

Sylvania studied her niece over her glasses rims. "What did you have in mind? Bringing in the whole hospital?"

Louisa ignored the sarcasm and shook her head. "A train pulled in with a load of wounded. The doctor asked if I knew anyone who would be willing to help with the men who are so much better, that's all." *Please, God, let her decide to help.*

"I see." Sylvania turned to Reuben. "Go next door and ask for Miss Julie's Sady. She can run notes around while you and the girls get the parlor ready. We can lay a pallet or two in the dining room if need be."

Louisa breathed a sigh of relief. Why had she been so afraid to ask this of her aunt? It wasn't as if she hadn't been knitting socks and sewing uniforms for their soldiers like the rest of the women. She just hadn't approved of her niece working at the hospital. After all, women nurses were considered little above the prostitutes, of whose existence Louisa was not supposed to even know. Her brothers had called them various other names, but she had eavesdropped often enough to learn things not discussed around womenfolk.

Thanks to her brothers, both she and Jesselynn knew many things young women were not supposed to know. Carrie Mae, however, had never cared to follow her sisters. Instead, she had become an expert musician, and her singing, as well as her piano playing, had entertained them all, including the surrounding neighbors.

Suddenly, homesickness for Twin Oaks bathed her like a pouring rain. *Please, God, let the war end soon. I want to go home.* Taking time to count the numerous pleas of this sort she'd sent heavenward would be a waste of precious seconds.

They had two beds set up by the time Sylvania's notes were ready to be carried around. Reuben listened to his instructions, nodded, and slipped out the door as Abby and Louisa smoothed the clean sheets into place and folded a blanket at the end of each bed. The weather was still far too warm to put two blankets on, let alone winter quilts. By the time they'd folded the quilts up for pallets and made up two in the parlor, Reuben returned.

"We's got two yeses, two maybes, and one not to home." He handed the papers back to Sylvania. "Asked Widow Penrod if we could borry her horse and wagon, so soon's I git dat, we be off." He smiled at Louisa. "Dat brudder of yours be home before supper."

"I already told Cook to make enough supper for four more." Aunt Sylvania sat in her chair and picked up her fan. "Lawsy, this is unseasonable weather. No wonder those men in the hospital are so miserable."

Louisa didn't tell her about the garden efforts, figuring that the borrowed garden tools would be back before they were missed. At the same time she wondered who their guests would be. The thought of the lieutenant flitted through her mind, but as if it were a yellow jacket, she brushed the thought away.

She'd just started out the door toward the wagon when another thought buzzed by her. This one made her stop and blink. How would she keep these men from realizing she was not the wife of Zachary Highwood but his little sister instead?

Oh, Lord, now what have I gotten myself into?

CHAPTER TWENTY-THREE

On the Mississippi River

"Benjamin and Domino fell in!"

The oars stopped. Shouts filled the air. Ahab whinnied, just about breaking Jesselynn's eardrums. The ferry drifted downriver.

"Can you see him?" Jesselynn didn't dare leave her post at Ahab's head to go see for herself, or everything might end up in the river.

"Lawd, Lawd, we's comin' home," Ophelia added to the din. The boys' cries could be heard from the back of the wagon.

A string of expletives came from the ferry owner at the rear. "Pull, you fools, or we'll end up on a sandbar. Row!"

Oh, God, not Benjamin. Let him live. The shore isn't that far, Jesselynn pleaded over and over in her mind while she kept up a steady murmur that calmed both herself and the horses.

" 'Phelia, enough!" Meshach's command cut off the blubbering like blowin' out a candle. "Good. Now take care of de boys."

"I is."

Benjamin, where are you, Benjamin? Jesselynn and Benjamin had grown up together, playing games in the orchard and snitching cookies from Lucinda's baking only to run off laughing when scolded. He couldn't be gone, not after living through the war and bringing her daddy home to die. He'd saved her father, and right now she could do nothing to save him.

The ferry moved ahead again and within minutes bumped into the packed sand of the shoreline.

Ahab shifted at the jolt, and Jesselynn clamped the reins under his bit even tighter. "Easy, son." She resumed her reassuring murmur as two of the oarsmen slid planks in place for them to disembark. Meshach led his horses off first, then Sunshine, before coming back to lead the team down the incline. Once they were all on the ground, Ahab shook himself, setting harness and chains to rattling.

"Sorry as I kin be 'bout that other horse and your boy. I wouldn't give up hope, though. They mighta swum in." Mister Jed shook Jesselynn's hand and motioned his hands to ready the ferry for the return. "Floatin' logs and such are the hazards of night crossin'."

"I understand. Thank you for the service." Jesselynn climbed up on the wagon seat and clucked the team forward. "Meshach, you go look that way, and Daniel, you go downriver." When the two riders took off, she turned to the woman still whimpering in the back of the wagon. "Ophelia, if you don't stop that, I'll send you back across the river."

"There's a road back up thata way," Jed called as he poled the ferry back out into the current.

Once on firmer ground, Jesselynn stopped the wagon and got out again, this time to remove the stone that Meshach had wedged in Ahab's hoof to make him limp. Last thing they needed now was a truly lame horse. Once moving again, the horse and mule leaned into their collars as the wheels rolled through shallow sand. She slapped the reins to keep them pulling forward, sure that if they stopped, the wheels would sink. Between Ophelia's continued sniffling, the boys' whimpering, Benjamin's getting lost, and not knowing where the road was, Jesselynn wanted to do nothing more than run screaming down the road or hide her head under a blanket and sleep until life improved.

Where was the road? Surely they hadn't drifted that far off course.

Just as she recognized a lighter spot in the woods as the break for the road, she heard a horse cough, the kind of cough induced by the herb that Meshach had given Domino.

"Benjamin?" She raised her voice and called again. "Benjamin?"

Ahab nickered, and a horse answered, then trotted out of the darkness to meet them. The filly tied to the tailgate joined in the welcome, and Jesselynn tightened the reins enough to stop the team. Flipping the reins around the brake pole, she vaulted to the ground and dashed to the end of the wagon before slowing and picking up the cadence of her soothing murmur. Domino flung his head up, then at her familiar song, nosed her outstretched hand and let her grab his reins.

"Oh, Lawd, you took Benjamin down to de depths of de river, and now he's home wid you. Lawsy, lawsy." Ophelia's crying and moaning renewed the wailing of the two boys, who might have dozed off again had she not started anew.

Jesselynn felt around in the wagon bed until she located a lead shank. She snapped it to the horse's halter, then removed the water-soaked bridle. As long as her hands kept busy, she could keep at bay the thought of Benjamin drowning.

If Ophelia didn't shut up, she was going to scream.

"Ophelia, stop! I can't hear myself think." In the ensuing quiet, she listened hard. Was that a horse she heard coming from the river? Scant seconds later, she heard Meshach call her name.

"Marse Jesse, I found 'im. Benjamin be alive."

"Oh, thank you, blessed Lawd."

This time Jesselynn didn't try to quiet Ophelia; rather she wanted to join in, but instead, she ran back on the road to meet Meshach.

"Praise de Lawd, Marse Jesse, our boy done be saved."

Benjamin slid off the back of the horse and right into her arms.

He raised his head enough to ask, "Is . . . D-Domino all right?"

"Yes."

At her answer he straightened, then bent over coughing until he vomited up half the river.

Jesselynn put her arm around his waist and half dragged him back to the wagon, where Meshach had his horse tied by this time. The big man lifted the smaller and, gentle as a mother with her baby, laid him on the quilts Ophelia spread out.

"I get dem wet." Benjamin tried to rise, but Jesselynn put her hands on his shoulders and pushed him back down. "Just rest for now. Soon as Daniel catches up, we'll see where this road goes."

Meshach dried off the younger stallion while Ophelia and Jesselynn rubbed Benjamin until he no longer shook from cold and exhaustion. With him and the boys asleep in the wagon bed, Jesselynn leaned against a wheel, growing more restless by the moment. They were right out in the middle of a road with land flatter than Lucinda's hot cakes stretching on either side of them. While the moon didn't show much light, other than the willows and cottonwoods along the river, the land looked bare.

Ahab whinnied, and a horse answered. At the same moment, she heard a horse trotting toward them from the river. Ahab whinnied again.

"You're better'n a watchdog." Jesselynn joined Meshach at the back of the wagon. "Think it's him?"

"A'course. Ahab done say so."

"Sorry, Marse, I din't find nary horse nor—"

"I found 'im," Meshach interrupted the rush of words.

"Thank de Lawd."

"Benjamin's sleepin' in the wagon. Domino here is all right too. We're glad you're back. Now we can go on." Jesselynn patted Daniel on the knee and swung up onto the wagon seat. "Now, let's find us a place to camp."

———

Jesselynn woke that afternoon when the sun had crept past the high point. The willow branches had shielded her up to then, but the sun in her eyes made further sleep impossible. She stretched and tossed her quilt aside. Today she would write home and tell them that she and her band were now safe in Missouri. Surely Dunlivey would not track them there, and even if he could, they would soon disappear in the oak and hickory forests her uncle had written about those years ago. He'd passed through them and broke land on the prairie for his horse farm. She'd read his letters before she left home, not that there were too many of them.

Taking paper and the ink bottle, then sharpening a quill, she accepted the coffee Ophelia brought her and began to write. She covered two sheets before signing Jesse Highwood and blowing on the still-damp signature. She stared at it, shaking her head. Seemed like she'd been a male now for longer than three weeks, as if her life had begun the night they fled Twin Oaks. While folding the letter, her thoughts roamed to the homeplace. Surely all the Burley was cut by now and hanging to dry in the barn. It shouldn't be long before it could be stripped and packed in the hogsheads for transporting to Frankfort.

They'd always held a celebration when the tobacco was sold. All the neighbors joined in too. There was dancing and tables groaning with delicious food. Her stomach rumbled at the thought of all the spicy boiled shrimp, the sweet potato pie that Lucinda was known for, biscuits lighter than a cloud. Her stomach rumbled louder.

She finished addressing the envelope and went in search of a dab of flour and water to paste the flap shut. While she'd brought her father's sealing ring, she'd neglected to bring the sealing wax.

"You want to go into Charleston with me?" She paused by where Meshach was cleaning the harnesses and bridles.

He shook his head. "I needs to grease de axles and tighten up de shaft. 'Sides, no one recognize Daniel."

"You don't think . . ."

"No sense takin' chances. We come too far for dat."

The hairs up the back of her neck stood at attention. And here she'd just been congratulating herself on getting away and was beginning to feel safe.

"Take de mule. De horses need more grazin' time and a rest."

Jesselynn sighed. When would they really be free?

A short time later they trotted into town double mounted, both of them leaning back to keep from being jostled to bits by the mule's sledgehammer trot. The bony ridge of his back didn't help either. They both sighed when they slid off behind some buildings.

Daniel rubbed his seat. "I think he do dat on purpose."

"What? Trot harder?" Jesselynn grinned. "Might be. You go that way, and I'll try this way. Just stop and listen to people talkin'. Like you used to do at home."

Daniel tried to look affronted but laughed instead. "Don' you go leavin' me behind now."

"Then be back when the sun goes behind that willow tree over there." She nodded to a tree that had obviously outlived many a flood.

Jesselynn located the post office first thing, mailed her letter, then strolled across the dirt street to the store where several men had gathered.

She dug in her pocket and pulled out a jackknife to begin cleaning the dirt from under her fingernails. With her rear tight against the porch floor, she hoped she was as invisible as she felt.

The more they talked, the more her stomach churned. There were more skirmishes going on in Missouri than in Kentucky, and the fighting had started earlier. Why hadn't she known that? She could answer that question before thinking. They'd been so isolated at Twin Oaks that until the army took the horses away they'd not been much bothered by the war.

One thing for sure, they'd not be going north to try to hook up with the Wire Road. Whyever they called it that was beyond her. When the talk turned to the bands of deserters who were terrorizing the countryside under the guise of Confederate soldiers, her throat went dry. She'd heard about Quantrill's Raiders in the last town, but they were said to be more in the Kansas City area. Springfield was a far cry from Kansas City.

At least Dunlivey was on the other side of the river. If she'd reminded herself of that once, it had been ten times. It wasn't hard to picture him as the head of a band of raiders. But he'd been an officer in the Confederate army the last time she'd seen him. Then what had he been doing in that tavern? Of course the army did move their forces around.

The argument kept up in her mind apace with the cussing and discussing on the porch. When they began in on "that nigger lover in the White House," she sidled away. Her father had a great deal of respect for President Lincoln, and therefore she did too. *"One nation under God, the way the United States had been founded, and the way it should stay."* She could hear her father's words as plainly as if he were walking beside her.

Checking the angle of the sun, she moseyed back to where they'd tied the mule. Daniel sat with his back against the wall, chewing on the end of a stalk of grass. Jesselynn swung aboard and braced her foot for him to use as a step to swing up. Once he'd settled behind her, she turned the mule back the way they'd come and headed out.

"What'd you hear?" she asked when they were out in the country again.

"Dem folks sure don' like Marse Lincum."

"I heard that too. What else?"

"Bad sojers about. Man in tavern laughin' him head off 'bout dem hangin' a runaway slave."

"Where?"

"Don' know."

"This side of the river?"

"I guess. Dey talkin' 'bout Missouri."

Jesselynn looked up to see if the despair settling over her wasn't a cloud in the sky instead, but the sun still shone as it sank closer to the horizon.

What if someone found their camp and wouldn't believe Meshach when he said they were free blacks?

CHAPTER TWENTY-FOUR

Richmond, Virginia

"I can't believe I'm in a *real* house."

Louisa folded back the sheet over her brother and smoothed it into place. Her eyes burned at the relief she heard in his voice and the way his hand repeatedly smoothed the sheets.

"Where's Aunt Sylvania?"

"Helpin' the neighbors get their boys settled in. She'll be home soon for supper." She turned to see Private Rumford, dark hair falling in his eyes, sitting in the chair by the window where they had put him. Not looking out—just not looking. *Tomorrow,* she promised herself, *tomorrow he will be out in the garden here, and I know that will make a difference.* The thought of the lieutenant living in the house next door set her pulse to tripping.

"And Carrie Mae, where is she?"

"Off with her betrothed, I believe." *As if she were ever anywhere else. You'd think they were already married.*

"When's the wedding to be?"

Louisa thought for a moment. "Why, it's only two weeks away. Where has the time gone?"

Zach studied her for a long moment.

She could feel it even though she resisted looking into his one good eye. Somehow she knew he was going to ask a question that either she wouldn't like or would have no idea how to answer. She heard the front door opening and gave a sigh of relief. Saved by Aunt Sylvania. When she started to rise, Zach laid his hand on hers.

"What are you going to do about tomorrow?"

"Tomorrow?"

"The hospital. I don't like the idea of you workin' there."

"I don't *work* there. I volunteer there." She could feel her face begin to heat up, let alone her temper. "What difference does it make to you?"

"Well, you . . ." He glanced over at the corporal and shook his head. "We'll talk about this later." Like hers, his accent broadened when he grew agitated.

"Private, would you like to join us at the supper table?" Aunt Sylvania appeared in the doorway, smiling her welcome to their guest. "Cook is fixin' plates for the others." She crossed to Zachary's bed. "Do you need help, nephew, or can you manage on your own?"

"He needs . . ."

"I can manage." Zachary and Louisa spoke at the same time.

"Well, which is it?"

"If someone will help prop me up, I imagine it is time I continue learning to use my other hand." He lifted his left hand. "Shame I didn't learn to shoot with either hand like Adam did."

"Lot of good it did him." Louisa was as surprised at her comment as the other two. Surely shooting with either or both hands hadn't been instrumental in getting her older brother killed in action, but then it hadn't saved him either. To carry the thought to a logical conclusion, cannonballs and artillery shells didn't discriminate. She spun on her heel, her skirts swishing in the speed with which she left the room.

More and more she was learning how much she resented the war—and the men who'd been so vainglorious about whipping the Yankees in two weeks. No wonder Jesselynn had taken the horses away from home. They'd need something to rebuild with when this massacre was over.

Maybe she'd read the letters to Zachary after supper so he could know what all had transpired since he'd left home. Come to think of it, strange that he'd not questioned her about Twin Oaks. Of course, she'd told him about their daddy dying, so maybe that was all he wanted to know for now.

Soon though, soon they could go home. Even if Zachary was badly crippled, he would find things to do at Twin Oaks. Surely he'd be able to manage getting around with crutches or maybe just one. And anyone could learn to use the opposite hand.

Curious, she assigned herself the task at the supper table.

"Whatever is the matter, child?" Aunt Sylvania stared at the gravy blob staining the white linen tablecloth.

"I . . . I was trying to cut my meat with my left hand. The knife slipped." Using her napkin, Louisa dabbed at the spreading blob.

"Whyever for?" Sylvania sent Private Rumford a questioning glance, but he never looked her way. He did clean up his plate, however, without anyone prompting him. Since sometimes at the hospital she'd hand-fed him when he paid no attention to his food, Louisa felt a stir of pleasure.

"Well, since Zach will have to learn to use his other hand, I . . . I wanted to see how difficult it would be. But I have two hands, so really it isn't the same after all." Her words came in a rush.

Her aunt's "tsk-tsk" sent a shot of stiffener up Louisa's spine.

"We can't wait on him forever. Like he said, it's time he began to try things on his own."

"We shall see."

Louisa studied her aunt. Instead of looking worn-out as she'd been the few days before, the new responsibility seemed to be bringing the older woman back to her earlier energy. She, too, had cleaned up her plate, rather than picking at her food, which had become the norm. Pink had reclaimed its place on her cheeks, and the pallor of the past weeks seemed in retreat.

"Perhaps you would like to read to the men tonight? They missed out on their chapters of Shakespeare since we were moving them at the time I usually read. I always read a psalm or two and a chapter from one of Paul's letters."

"Why, I reckon I might just do that." Sylvania nodded her approval at the tray of desserts Abby showed her. "See how my nephew is doing too, will you, please? Peach cobbler has always been his favorite dessert."

"I thought the peaches were gone." Louisa shrugged at her aunt's innocent look. Life had always been like that. Her brothers were treated like royalty by Aunt Sylvania, and the girls were made to mind. Surely that wasn't fair, but then, as her mother had always said, *"God didn't promise life would be fair."*

After supper, when she had Sylvania set up in the hallway to read so she could be heard in both rooms, Louisa wandered out on the front porch to catch any breeze that had come up. Not sure why she didn't head for the garden as was her wont, she settled into the rocker, setting it into motion with the push of her foot.

A young boy and a girl ran by laughing, the pong of their sticks on the hoops rolling in front of them adding to their merriment. A flycatcher called from swooping about the trees. A squirrel chattered in the elm directly in front of the house. She caught sight of him descending the tree in quick bursts of speed.

The chair creaked its own song. Louisa sighed and leaned her head back against the cushion, remembering home ... the slaves singing down in the quarters, and Jesselynn sitting on the veranda, busy with some kind of needlework.

As you should be doing.

The thought brought her foot to the floor. Wasting time like this! What in the world was the matter with her? And how come she kept thinking of home so much today anyway? But with Jesselynn gone, someone should be there to keep things running. After all, could the slaves—she had to remind herself that their people weren't slaves any longer, thanks to the papers Jesselynn had given them—could their *workers* keep the place running without someone overseeing them?

"Good evenin'."

The male voice so near brought her hand to her throat.

"Why, land sakes, you need to sneak up on a body that way?"

"I didn't sneak up on you. I came to check on my men." The lieutenant straightened his shoulders in spite of the crutches.

"Oh." Bringing her mind back from Twin Oaks took some doing. Now, if a man like this came calling there, he would be treated—Louisa cut off her thought. She was getting tired of her face flaming at the slightest provocation. The man in front of her was the lieutenant, coming to check on his men, not a potential suitor.

A buggy pulled up at the street and the two laughing occupants stepped down, or rather, her sister was handed down by her adoring fiancé, who had learned to use his one arm to an advantage. No morose scarecrow he. As the two of them came up the walk, the lieutenant glanced their way, then gave Louisa one of his formal stares.

"My men?"

"Ah yes." Louisa started for the door when Carrie Mae, who had taken her eyes off her escort long enough to see her sister and the lieutenant, spoke.

"Why, Louisa, I see you have comp'ny." Carrie Mae's soft Kentucky accent had turned entirely Virginian since their arrival.

"Ah, n-no. The lieutenant is j-just here on business." Since when had she taken up stuttering?

Carrie Mae paused at the bottom of the steps. "Are you not going to introduce us?"

Oh, sugarcane and cotton combined. Louisa thought two of her most vitriolic incantations, all the while keeping what she hoped was a smile on her face. She turned to Jefferson Steadly, Carrie Mae's fiancé. "Pardon my manners, Mr. Steadly."

"Since we are about to become related, surely you could call me by my given name by now."

"All right." *Let's just get this over with.* "Jefferson, this is Lieutenant . . ." For the life of her, she couldn't remember his last name. Had she ever heard him called anything but the lieutenant?

The lieutenant straightened and extended his right hand. "I'm Gilbert Lessling, First Lieutenant of the Second North Carolina Rifles." He nodded. "Pleased to meet you, Miss Highwood. Miz Highwood here has spoken of you often."

The floor couldn't open and swallow her soon enough.

CHAPTER TWENTY-FIVE

Southeastern Missouri
October 6, 1862

So far, so good.

Jesselynn looked back over the marshy river delta and shook her head. Thanks to Benjamin's careful scouting, they'd missed burying the wagon in swamps and ponds more than once. The one digging-out they'd had to do was bad enough. But they were still safe, and considering the possibilities, that was a miracle in itself.

"Found de Indian trace dat man tol' me 'bout." Meshach rode beside her as she guided the horses up the faint road.

"Where?"

"South of here. Not better'n dis but no worse."

"If only we dared go on up to the Wire Road. Heard tell there are even bridges across some creeks." Jesselynn rubbed her forehead with one hand, wishing the headache that came with her monthlies would disappear, the cramps too. Maybe she should let Ophelia drive the wagon and she could sleep in the back with the boys.

Thoughts of her mother handing her a hot brick wrapped in flannel and tucking her back in bed for a nap crossed her mind. A breeze fluttering the curtains at the window, clean crisp white sheets, a pillow, and when she woke up, she could curl up with a book if she wanted. The work of the plantation would go on around her, and . . .

"Marse Jesse, you all right?"

Jesselynn sighed. "I reckon. Show us the way to the trace. I can't wait to get to Uncle Hiram's, and if that way is faster and safer than this, I'm all for it."

Since they hadn't seen any sign of habitation for the last two days, they had decided to travel in the daylight, hoping to make better time. With Meshach clearing brush with his machete at times, they still were able to keep moving. A campfire at the end of the day, hot food and coffee, and the dreams of home didn't cause quite so much pain. She sat on a log and opened her journal, using the light from the fire to guide her.

> We made a good twenty miles today, the best in some time, but now the trail is thickening in again, the brush trying to reclaim the space. Finally Sammy is feeling good and he and Thaddy, or Joshwa, as he insists on being called, are near close as brothers. To think I even considered leaving him. If Mama knew the thoughts I've had, she would be so disappointed in me that I couldn't bear the sorrow in her eyes. She would tell me to get down on my knees and ask the Lord's forgiveness, but I cannot tell her that I have begun to wonder if there really is a God who would allow such terrible things to go on. She would say "God is love," but all I seem to see and hear lately is pure hatred.

She glanced up to see Ophelia scoop the two boys up and whirl them around, making their giggles bring a smile to her face. No, not all was hatred, at least not here in the safety of their camp.

Ahab stopped grazing and, lifting his head, nickered, his ears pointing into the scrub oak. Meshach slapped his Bible closed and in one smooth motion stood with his rifle in hand. Jesselynn reached for the pistol she kept at her side.

"Don't shoot." The voice sounded like a child's cry.

Jesselynn capped her ink bottle and set her journal down on the log, easing to her feet at the same time.

"Come, show yo'self." Meshach held the rifle at the ready.

"We'uns was jus' hopin' fer some supper." Only her tattered skirts let them know she was a girl. She clutched the hand of a stick-figure boy. They were both barefoot and shivering in the evening chill. While the days had stayed warm, the nights were a different matter.

Ophelia set the boys down and swung the kettle back over the low flames. "Come on over here and git warmed up."

The two moved toward the fire as if walking on coals, so hesitant were they.

"We don' mean no harm." The girl held out her empty hands.

"Don' got no gun nor nothin'." The boy clung to her skirt, staring at the kettle as if he'd never seen anything so fine in his life.

"My name is Jane Ellen, and this here is John Mark."

"Where are your folks?"

"Daid. Shot by some soldiers in butternut uniforms. We was hidin' in de cave where Mama kept food cool. We'uns went back too fur for anyone to find us. They took all our food and the cows and chickens."

Ophelia handed them each a bowl and spoon and stepped back. Before she could turn around, they'd scraped the bowls clean.

"Dey need more." Meshach filled the bowls again. "Y'all better slow down or you be sick." He glanced over his shoulder. "Dey might like hot water to wash."

Benjamin threw more wood on the fire, poured water into another pan, and set it in the coals. "I git some more."

"We ain't had hot food for I don' know how long. I caught us a squirrel in a snare, but it weren't easy to eat without cookin'." When Ophelia handed her a cup of hot coffee, the girl cupped her hands around the heat and sniffed the aroma, her eyes closed in delight.

Sammy and Thaddeus edged closer to the boy, who used his fingers to scrape the bowl clean. They stared at each other, then back at the boy.

John Mark looked up at them, then edged closer to his sister, if that were possible, clutching the bowl to his chest as if they would snatch it away. Just as Ophelia reached for the two little boys, the shivering boy on the ground vomited his supper all over both himself and his sister.

"Pew." Thaddeus stepped back, Sammy with him. "Stinky."

"Don't you no nevermind," Jane Ellen said, comforting her little brother, while trying to shake the gluey mess off her already filthy skirt. "You got any bread or biscuit he might have?"

Ophelia dug in the box where she kept leftovers and handed a biscuit to the boy. "Now you eat dat nice an' slow, you hear?"

At the same time, Meshach poured a cup of warm water and gave that to the child. "Here you go, easy now. Maybe soak yo' biscuit in de water and chew real slow."

The boy flinched away when Meshach extended a hand to help brush him off. " 'Phelia, surely you got some soap and water fo' dese two young'uns." His gentle voice and warm smile did more to stop the two from shivering than anything else.

"We don' gots no other clothes." Jane Ellen stiffened her back and raised her chin, daring them to clean her up.

"No, I 'spose not. But we do." Meshach rocked back on his heels. "Y'all go behind de wagon and strip off dem things, and 'Phelia bring you hot water and soap to wash in. You feel better den."

"I'll get them something to wear." Jesselynn tucked her pistol in the back of her pants and headed for the wagon. Sure enough, here they hardly had enough to keep body and soul together for those she had with her and now they had two more. Three more mouths to feed than she had counted on, plus one more horse. And only one five-dollar gold piece left along with two nickels. How could they earn some money to augment what they had?

How long would it take them to get to Uncle Hiram's anyway?

She paused with one foot in the wagon. Was that gunfire?

"Douse the fire! Now!"

But Meshach was ahead of her. Steam billowed up from the soaking ashes.

Within moments, the men brought in the horses and hid them in a thicket with the others standing to clamp a hand over a horse's muzzle in case they started to whinny. Ophelia had the boys tucked down in the wagon, the two guests hunkering under the wagon bed.

Jesselynn stroked Ahab's shoulder and kept a hand on his muzzle. "Easy, old son," she whispered. "You gotta keep quiet. Easy." All the while she strained to hear anything else. Surely there hadn't been enough shots fired to show an ambush or an attack. Wouldn't they have heard something earlier if there was a military patrol around?

But they had gotten lax. No one had been on guard or scouting. *Never again*, she promised herself. *No matter how safe we feel, someone stands guard.*

Rifle fire crackled again, sounding farther away. How many shots? She tried to count them so she'd know how many men. Were they regular troops or the marauder they'd been hearing about?

But according to what I heard in town, there are no regular troops this far south. Unless the Confederates have come up from Arkansas.

But no matter how hard they listened, they heard only the night sounds that had come up again in the forest around them. An owl hooted. A coyote yipped and was answered by another. If the wild animals felt safe enough to resume their hunting and foraging, there could be no better alarm system.

She let out the breath she didn't realize she'd been holding and led Ahab out of the thicket. Moonlight washed the wagon in silver and glistened white on the pairs of eyes peeking over the wagon sides.

"Dey's gone?" Ophelia's whisper carried on the gentle breeze.

"I guess." Ahab nudged her in the back, so Jesselynn handed his lead rope to Meshach to tie them out again. "I'll take first watch. The rest of you get to sleep."

With the two guests cleaned up and their clothes washed in water from the stream, Ophelia tucked them into the blankets with the boys in the wagon bed and crawled in beside them all. The men rolled in quilts under the wagon, and the only sound was the horses grazing.

Jesselynn hunkered against the base of a tree overlooking the trail back the way they'd come. Because of the moonlight, the shadows seemed even deeper and darker. But the forest critters went about their business, so she felt about as secure as possible in spite of the shots fired.

In the morning she'd send Benjamin out to scout, but for now they all needed their rest.

She stretched and hunkered down again several times, yawning to keep awake, even resorting to pinching herself. While walking around helped, the forest noises quit at her movements, and she would feel the hair stand up on the back of her neck. Surely there was someone behind that big oak, the hickory, in the brush.

When Meshach spoke her name, she bit off a shriek, leaving the taste of blood in her mouth.

"Sorry, thought you heard me comin'."

"How could I when you don't make a sound?" Jesselynn whispered back, her heart still racing as if she'd been jumping logs.

"Heard anythin'?"

"Nope. One of the horses grunted and rolled—that 'bout gave me the shakes—but other than wild critters, nothing."

"I'm goin' take a look around. You stay here."

"Good." How could she tell him that the thought of tramping around in the dark like that scared her spitless? Maybe because her brothers used to jump out at her from dark places and scare her witless, she'd never been comfortable without a lantern or candle in the dark. Now driving the wagon, or riding, that wasn't so bad, but walking? Uh-uh. She settled back against the tree trunk, every sense on full alert.

When Meshach returned, he cleared his throat a distance away, then whistled a whippoorwill's song to let her know it was he. "All's good."

"I thought so." Jesselynn stretched and handed him the rifle. "Call me if you need me."

"I will."

She was asleep before she had the quilt wrapped clear around her.

———

She opened her eyes when Benjamin rode back into camp. Throwing back the quilt and pulling on her boots all in one motion, she dug her jacket out from under the quilt where she kept it so the dew wouldn't be able to soak it in the dark hours before dawn. By now she'd learned to never stand up until she crawled out from under the wagon. One crack on the head had taught her the lesson well.

She headed to where the two men stood talking. "What did you see?"

"Nothin' much. Someone camped but left in a hurry." He handed her a tow sack. "Couple men, I think."

She opened the mouth of the sack and saw dried beans, a side of bacon, and two small bags she assumed to be salt and coffee. "But what if they come back for their supplies?"

Benjamin shrugged. "One never come back. He daid. Confederate sojer. Found 'im in de woods some ways from camp."

Sure, nothin' much. Has death gotten so normal we think nothing of it? She kept the thought to herself. "See any tracks?"

"Spent shells. Horses leave fast."

"How many?" Getting information from Benjamin was like pulling pokeweed.

He shrugged. "Din' count but dey gone."

"Which direction?" Meshach looked up to study the clouds coming in from the west.

"Dat way." Benjamin pointed south.

"And we're going west." She looked up at the man beside her. "Stay or go?"

"We go, but dere's rain in dose clouds. Rain soon."

The man could be a prophet. Jesselynn hunkered under her canvas, the pouring rain splattering on the rumps of the team. They were climbing again, the horses straining against their collars. Wet leaves plastered their hides, yellowed by an earlier frost now that they were climbing higher. She braced her feet against the floor of the wagon and tried to keep the tent over her head from slipping.

They breached the crest and let the horses stop under a tree to catch their breath. Jesselynn rubbed her wet hands together and studied the sodden world. Nothing looked drearier than oak trees losing their leaves to a pounding rain and horses hanging their heads, rivulets running down their manes.

After a short rest Meshach waved, signaling it was time to move forward.

Jesselynn slapped the reins and clucked to the team. They leaned into their collars, and the wagon groaned but began to move. The sound of a galloping horse could be heard above the rain.

"Hey, I found us a cave." Benjamin pulled the mare to a stop. "Right near."

Jesselynn didn't wait for her heart to stop pounding, she just turned the horses in the direction he pointed. Within minutes she saw the hole in the limestone cliff face. While it wasn't big enough to drive the wagon in, the horses would make it. And they could build a fire.

"Get inside," she ordered the passengers in her wagon as she leaped to the ground to unharness the team. "Take what you can with you."

Benjamin came out of the cave, his hands raised to stop them. "Someone in dere."

"Someone who?" Meshach strode into the opening.

Jesselynn finished unhooking the traces and hooked the ends up on the rump pad. She was already soaked from the driving rain. Who cared if there was someone else there? Surely there was room for all. Unless of course that somebody didn't want to share or would steal some of their precious supplies.

Meshach waved her in. "Leave de horses for now."

Jesselynn knotted a tie rope around a tree trunk and entered the cave. A man lay on the cave floor; another was propped against the wall. Dressed in the butternut uniform of the Confederacy, both wore the bloodstains of terrible wounds.

"Dey alive?" Benjamin squatted down to check.

"They won't be arguing over the cave, the condition they're in." Jesselynn couldn't believe she'd said anything so uncaring. Whatever happened to her mother's training? She froze. Was that a gun cocking she heard?

CHAPTER TWENTY-SIX

Richmond, Virginia

"Miz Highwood? What kind of game are you playin'?" the lieutenant asked.

Louisa shot her sister a look that should have fried the flowers on her bonnet. *Please, Carrie Mae, don't say anything more.*

"Oh, did I say somethin' I shouldn't?"

If she'd been closer, she would have stamped on her blabbermouth sister's foot. Instead Louisa made the mistake of looking up at the lieutenant. If he'd looked sober before, he did so no longer. Thunderclouds now rode his brow like a cavalry unit set to charge.

Jefferson Steadly gave Louisa a pitying look, took his betrothed's hand, and tucked it back under his arm. "Come, my dear, let us go in and speak with your aunt as we had planned." The wink he sent Louisa as he passed her made her face flame anew.

"Would you like to tell me what is going on?" The lieutenant's tone had softened but only enough that an ear tuned to his voice would pick it up.

Louisa had learned it well, even with the few words he spoke so seldom. Could she brazen it out? She felt her shoulders sag. Now, if it had been Jesselynn caught in a lie of this magnitude, she might have breezed right through it, but not Louisa. Living this lie had been one of the hardest things she had ever done in her life.

"Would you like to sit down?" She motioned toward the chairs on the portico. "This will take a bit of time."

"Seems I have all the time in the world at this point." The lieutenant put both crutches under one arm and, using the handrail to pull on, hopped one-legged up the three steps. When he took the chair she indicated, he sat down with a sigh.

Louisa sat in the other chair. "Does your leg still hurt awfully?"

"Not always. But I banged it in the move, and now I'll pay for that for a time."

Louisa leaned forward and pushed the hassock next to him. "Put it up on that."

"Thank you." The lieutenant settled his leg and tried to cover the sigh. He leaned his head against the high back of the rocker and closed his eyes.

Louisa studied his profile in the dimming light. Surely the bones in his face were no longer so prominent, and his color had most definitely improved. The scar on his forehead had receded until now it only made him look more interesting. When he went home, the girls would comment that it made him look more dashing.

Why did that thought not make her chuckle as she'd hoped?

A whippoorwill called, his song gentle on the ears, almost melancholy in tone.

The lieutenant would be going home—soon. All he needed was a mode of travel.

"So, Miz Highwood." His accent on the *Miz* told her what he thought about the whole thing. "Maybe you'd like to explain now."

"No, I would not *like* to explain, but if you can keep from informing the surgeon general, I might *choose* to explain. You see, I am not one of your men to be ordered around, and . . ." Her words came faster as she got up a head of steam, much like a locomotive leaving the station.

"I'm aware of that. Let me rephrase my question. Would you *please* explain? And I cannot promise not to tell the surgeon general. I will have to do what I believe best."

Louisa nodded. And sighed. This seemed to be an evening for sighing. "I have to go back a ways."

It was his turn to nod.

"When my sister Jesselynn decided it was no longer safe for us at Twin Oaks, she took it upon herself to send her two younger sisters here to Aunt Sylvania's. Since her fiancé had been killed in battle, I think she was hoping we would find—" Louisa clapped a hand over her mouth. *Oh, Lord, what am I saying?* She took in a deep breath and began again. "Safety. Yes, she hoped we would find safety here in Richmond. Right from the first we attended the meetings with Aunt Sylvania where the women knitted, sewed uniforms, and wound bandages for our men in the war. But I wanted to do something more. It was like ... like all our fine men were without faces, and while I stitched the best and fastest that I could, I ... I wanted to be where it mattered."

"You think socks and uniforms and bandages don't matter?" One eyebrow arched.

"No. No, that isn't what I meant at all." Louisa stopped her hands from wringing together. What kind of a ninny was she becoming? Sighing, hand wringing? She let out a huff of air and gritted her teeth.

"You are deliberately misunderstanding me, sir, and I resent that. You asked for my explanation, and I am doing the very best that I can."

"Yes, forgive me. I'm sorry."

Her eyes flew wide open, and she closed her mouth before it gapped. He, Lieutenant Lessling, had asked for her forgiveness.

"You're forgiven." She clasped her hands primly in her lap, but even so, one forefinger insisted on smoothing the one beneath. "One day I heard one of the women talking about volunteering at the hospital. She said they needed widows to come in and help on the wards, but that young unmarried women would not do since we, since ... ah ..."

She knew they would need no lamp on the veranda. Her face would light them better than ten lamps—with reflectors.

"So I appropriated my mother's ring and introduced myself as Widow Highwood, telling everyone my husband Zachary had died in battle. We were so afraid he had, you see."

"And no one questioned you?"

"Some." She remembered how she had feigned tears when they did, wiping her eyes with a handkerchief she kept in her sleeve. The interrogator then had gotten flustered and withdrew. Worked every time. *That* she would not tell the lieutenant.

"And?"

"And so I began working in the ward, bringing water, reading, writing letters. I've never done any nursing chores. I'm not trained for that." When she thought about it, that was not entirely true. Her mother had trained all three of her daughters in the healing arts, how to use herbs and unguents she'd created, how to apply poultices, dress wounds, even set broken bones. All manner of accidents happened on a plantation like Twin Oaks.

She sighed. Lying was so difficult. Why had they forced her into it?

"I know I have been a help." The silence lay between them, soft like the air that kissed one's skin like a lover. "You'll keep my secret, won't you?"

It was the lieutenant's turn to sigh. "You put me in a difficult position."

"But isn't your job to look out for the good of your men? And I have been part of that good. I know their lives in the hospital are easier when I am there."

"Granted, but there are rules."

"I'm not hurting anyone."

"Does your brother have anything to say on this?" The question came after another companionable silence.

Oh, cotton bolls. She straightened and lifted her chin a fraction. "He said he doesn't want me going back there."

"And you would defy him?"

"He is being well cared for. Why would he deny that care to others? If I were not his sister . . ."

"Ah, but you are."

"I can run faster than he can."

For a minute she thought he was choking, then realized he was laughing, a rusty sound as if it hadn't been used in far too long. She'd actually made the dour lieutenant laugh.

"Could when we were younger too, but don't you dare tell him that. Then he'd have to tell a lie."

The man beside her snorted again.

"Won't you have enough to do caring for the men at your aunt's house?"

"Her servants can do most of the work here, and I will read to them as I do at the hospital, unless Aunt wants to do that. I plan to set Private Rumford to work in the garden with Reuben overseeing him." She grabbed her audacity with both hands. "You could help if you'd like."

"I will if you are there."

Oh, cotton and tarnation tripled. He had her there. How could she be in both places at once?

"Is it a bargain?" He extended his hand, obviously expecting her to shake on an agreement.

"For the mornings." She put her hand in his. Heat shot up her arm and suffused her neck, flaming up her face. "I . . . I think I hear someone calling me." She leaped to her feet and disappeared into the house as if an entire cavalry unit were charging behind her.

"Oh, Lord, help!"

CHAPTER TWENTY-SEVEN

A Missouri cave

"How bad is he?"

"Alive, but not for long 'less we help 'im." Meshach looked up at her from his kneeling position by the wounded soldier. As he spoke he removed his handkerchief and tied it above the man's knee, then examined the wound in his side. "He in bad shape."

"Put the horses back there." Jesselynn pointed to the rear of the cave before it shrank down to a small tunnel. "Get wood and let's get a fire going. Get him warmed up and us dried out. Thaddeus, you and Sammy sit over there and don't you move. Jane Ellen, keep your brother close beside you."

"I kin git wood."

"I know you can. Thank you, but I think your brother needs you more right now."

John Mark shuddered and coughed, a deep, gagging cough that made Jesselynn shiver. She'd heard that kind of coughing before, and a damp cave with wet clothes was not a place to start coughing like that.

"Don' worry, Marse, John Mark cough like that alla time." Jane Ellen patted her brother's shoulder, clutching him close in front of her. "He been puny since the day he was borned." Her declaration seemed a banner of pride. "I allus takes keer of 'im."

Jesselynn nodded and headed back out in the rain to help find wood. Wet as she was already, what could a few drips more matter? Finding dry wood in the downpour was no easy task. She broke dead branches off the underside of pine trees and, carrying an armload, dragged a larger branch behind her. She hoped the men would fare better. How far away was water? They needed plenty of hot water to clean the soldier up. What could they use for a poultice? If those wounds were infected . . . She shook her head. *Mother, what would you do?*

No sense in waiting for an answer. If there were to be any answers, they would have to come from her, and right now she felt cold, wet, and long out of answers. She stumbled over a rock just inside the cave entrance and tossed the wood into a pile before stopping to rub her toe. Felt like a horse just stepped on it. No, stood on it.

She headed back out to the wagon for an ax to chop the bigger pieces. Where were the men?

By the time she returned, Ophelia had shaved off curls of wood to lay over the smoldering coals they kept in a lidded pan for fire starter. Within moments tendrils of smoke arose and then flames as soon as she blew on it. Thaddeus squatted beside her, breaking twigs into smaller pieces to add a bit at a time. Sammy sat in the dirt behind them, picking up handfuls of sand and watching them drizzle back to the floor.

"Jane Ellen, take one of those quilts and wrap it around your brother. Then you can help with the fire while Ophelia and I get a pallet made for the wounded man." Talking was difficult with your teeth chattering.

Benjamin and Daniel dragged in a tree trunk that would burn for long hours, but no one had seen Meshach.

Once a canvas had been folded into a pallet, they each took a limb and hoisted the still-unconscious man into place next to the fire. As soon as a bucket of water from their barrel on the wagon was hot, she knelt down to inspect the wounds. The hole in his side had both an entrance and an exit, so she knew there was no bullet to dig out. Dirt mixed with blood crusted the wound, setting her to shaking her head. How could she clean it?

She rocked back on her heels, wishing she were anywhere but in a cave—in Missouri—tending an injured man she'd never before laid eyes on. She glanced up and caught sight of the dead man propped against the cave wall. If she dragged him outside, the wild animals would get the body during the night. There was no way she was sending her people out in the pouring rain to bury a man. So he had to stay, gruesome or not.

Where was Meshach?

She shifted her inspection to the leg. Cutting away the remains of the man's pant leg, she kept herself from gagging only with the greatest effort. She closed her eyes and took several deep breaths to calm the need to faint. If there was to be any chance for the man to live, the leg would have to go. With all the dirt and shredded flesh and bone, the wound would putrefy before morning.

Whatever had kept this man alive this long?

"Well, sir, if you want to live this bad, we'll sure do all we can to help you." She got to her feet. "Benjamin, bring in our saw. Ophelia, get your sewing kit. We got work to do."

"My ma allus said, you cut off a limb, you gotta burn it with a knife or somethin'." Jane Ellen had the three boys huddled under a quilt with her, so only their faces showed in the flickering firelight. "Might help that hole in his side too."

"Thank you. My daddy said pouring enough whisky over any wound would clean it right up, but we don't have any whisky, and we do have a big knife or two." Jesselynn dug into her box of simples that was becoming sadly in need of replenishing. What could she use to help keep away the poison? If only she had some onions, or mustard, or even bread and milk—all things they had taken for granted at Twin Oaks. And whisky . . . there had been plenty of that too.

Where was Meshach? Good thing the soldier had yet to regain consciousness, but even so, she wanted Meshach there not only to help hold him down but to saw off the leg. Should they try to save the knee?

She took soap and water and started scrubbing, then rinsed and went back to studying the wound. Looked like good bone below the knee for a couple of inches anyway. Unless the infection had already set in and traveled upward. She sniffed the wound. Nope, it didn't smell like the one that killed her daddy. Putridity had a stench all its own.

"Any of you know where Meshach went?"

Benjamin and Daniel shook their heads.

Ophelia said, "He took the rifle."

So that was the rifle cocking she heard. He must have gone hunting, whether for man or beast she wasn't sure.

One of the horses stamped and snorted. Firelight flickered on the walls, setting shadows to moving in a macabre dance that sent shivers up and down Jesselynn's back. She glanced over at the children and saw they were all asleep, piled like puppies in a heap.

Dumping the bloody water, she poured more from the kettle and went back to work, not even bothering to clean the lower leg. His foot was cold to the touch, as if it had already died. The wound in his side started to bleed again as she cleaned out bits of shirt fabric and removed the handkerchief he must have packed in the wound to staunch the bleeding.

She listened to his breathing. Sounded pretty strong for a man in his condition. Could she touch the hot knife to his flesh and hold it there long enough to do its job? She eyed the broad-bladed knife that Ophelia had set in the flames. Meshach could do this better than she, but since he wasn't here, she'd better do it.

She called Benjamin and Daniel to help. "All right, hold him down," she ordered. The eyes of the two men and Ophelia glistened in the firelight, but they took their places and leaned on the still form. Jesselynn closed her eyes for a moment, then taking the bone handle of the knife, she applied the blade to the front of the wound.

The man bucked and groaned. The stench of burning flesh made Jesselynn gag. None of her helpers watched the knife, but Benjamin threw his body across the man's upper legs to hold him down.

Jesselynn put the knife back in the fire. "We got the back to do too. Roll him over real careful-like, so the bleeding doesn't commence again."

By the time they were finished, sweat ran down their faces, but the wounds were clean. The leg would have to wait for Meshach. Jesselynn could hardly grip the handle of the knife she was shaking so. Sammy and Thaddeus now whimpered from under their quilt, but Jane Ellen held her ground, her arms securely around all three boys, murmuring a soft singsong, trying to calm them.

"What do we have for bandages?" Jesselynn asked.

"I gits dem." Ophelia dug in her box and came up with several rolls of old sheeting. "Lucinda packed dis. Thought we might need 'em."

"Looks like we do." Jesselynn took the rolls and folded some into pads to apply back and front, then wound more around the man's midsection to hold the pads in place. They'd just have to wash the bandages in between. There were not enough to throw away. "We'll let him sleep now. Ophelia, we need to make a tea of this willow bark. Get him to drink it soon as he wakes up. If only we had some meat to make a broth. Mother always said to give a wounded man beef broth to build the blood back up."

"Will venison do?" Meshach and the deer he had tied over his shoulders filled the mouth of the cave.

No need to ask where he'd been. He laid the carcass down on the other side of the fire and untied three rabbits from his belt to hand to Ophelia. "We can skin dese de quickest and get dem to boilin'. I spotted some wild onion and Jerusalem artichoke for diggin'. I gits dem next." He stepped around the fire and knelt down by their patient. Nodding, he smiled up at Jesselynn.

"You done fine, Marse Jesse."

"I thought to wait a bit on the leg, let him gain some strength." *Liar. You just couldn't bring yourself to do it.*

"No, poison get 'im. We do it now. Got to come off?"

Jesselynn nodded. "All I can see. Good flesh and bone just below the knee, so maybe we can save that."

"We try."

Within minutes, they were ready. Even with four of them holding the man down, he bucked at the first bite of the saw. Jesselynn nearly screamed herself. Instead she hummed a song under her breath, anything to blot out the horrible noise.

"Done. Hand me de knife." Again the stench of burning flesh filled the cave.

Jesselynn sewed the flap of flesh over the stump and applied the bandages. Very carefully, she released the knot on the tourniquet above the knee and watched to see if blood would soak the white cloth. When it didn't, she finally let out the breath she'd been holding, surged to her feet, and dashed outside. After throwing up in the bushes, she tilted her face to the sky to let the rain wash her clean again.

She looked heavenward and raised her fist in the air. "God, if you are indeed God, how can you let this war go on? I don't want any part of you ever again. You hear me?" Tears and rain flowed over her cheeks and down her neck.

Shuddering both from cold and wet, she strode back into the cave to find the soldier covered, the dead man gone, and the rest of the group eating warmed-up beans and biscuits. One rabbit simmered in the cooking pot, and cut-up pieces of another sizzled in the frying pan. The stench of blood and burnt flesh had been replaced by supper cooking, and the cave now seemed more like a home than a hospital.

"Jesse, sit here." Thaddeus patted the empty space on the log beside him.

Ophelia handed her a steaming bowl and, while Jesselynn had thought it would be a long while before she could force food down, she shoveled the beans and biscuits in, grateful for the warmth and the flavor.

"I'll be gettin' the onion and chokes," Meshah said. "Benjamin, you rope up de horses, and I show you a clearin' I found. Wet or not, dey need grazin'. We can skin de deer after dark, dry some of it all night. Ophelia, you kin scrape de hide."

"I knows how to do that," Jane Ellen volunteered.

"When de sun come out, de hide kin dry on de wagon."

"My ma used de brains, lye from fire ashes, and water fer tannin' de hide."

"Good. That be your job den, girl."

"No rush, we won't be leavin' here anytime soon," Jesselynn said, shaking her head. "Can't leave him and can't take him with us yet, so looks like here we stay." She glanced over at John Mark, who was doubled over with coughing. Another reason they wouldn't be going anywhere fast. Her mother always made cough syrup out of honey, whisky, and lemon juice in hot water. What could she use instead?

By the time they settled into their quilts that night, thin strips of deer meat draped on racks of green sticks hung over a low fire. They'd gotten some broth down the wounded man, and the deer hide was scraped and ready for tanning in the morning. Best of all, Daniel had found a bee tree, so they had honey on the biscuits that went along with fried rabbit, boiled artichoke roots with wild onion, and carrots. Quite a feast, and to top that off, they were warm and dry.

Stars shone overhead when Jesselynn made her final trip outside. Snuggling down in her quilt later, she listened for their patient's steady breathing. The odor of fresh horse manure overlaid the sizzle of drying deer meat. Things seemed as right as possible, but she'd closed her ears when Meshach read the nightly Scripture. While she wasn't about to tell him to quit reading, she knew she'd been living a lie. No longer did she believe there was a God, let alone a good one.

Somewhere in the wee hours, she got the soldier to take some more broth, and while his mumbling didn't make sense, the fever seemed only mild, so far.

She fell back asleep without waking anyone else. They needed their rest as much as she.

Screams brought her straight up and out of sleep. Tiny furry feet crawling all over her made her scream too. She flung one of the creatures off and saw an arched tail in the dim firelight.

Only one critter looked like that! Scorpions!

CHAPTER TWENTY-EIGHT

Richmond, Virginia

The dour look returned with the lieutenant in the morning.

"I'm happy to see you decided to join us." Louisa, resolving to ignore the dark cloud on his countenance, gave him the same smile she gave the others. Last night was as though it had never been. She hid the sigh behind a flurry of pointing, assigning jobs, and identifying plants for Corporal Shaddock so he would know which were weeds and which were perennials gone dormant. She hoped to divide the irises today and the butter lilies.

"If we dig up the clumps, do you suppose you could stand at the bench, or sit if you prefer, and divide them?" She motioned toward the potting bench along the brick wall, glancing up at the lieutenant at the same time.

"I reckon."

So much for conversation.

"Have you ever divided irises before?"

"No, can't say that I have."

"Fine, I'll be right with you, then." She trotted over to where one of the other men was digging with a fork. "Sergeant Andrews, over here, please." Within moments she had several washtub-sized clumps of iris covering the potting bench and Andrews back to digging up the iris bed. "We need to dig in manure and compost. That's behind the shed."

While Sergeant Andrews had only one eye and still wore a bandage around one thigh, the smile he gave her lacked for nothing in the male-appeal department. "I'll get right to it, ma'am."

Louisa could feel her face heat up in spite of the broad-brimmed straw hat she wore. Maybe it was more important to get these men back out in society than to improve their attitudes through digging in the dirt. If only she could discuss such things with the lieutenant.

She checked on Private Rumford and, laying a hand on his shoulder to get his attention, smiled and nodded. "Very good. It looks so much better." Was that life she saw in his eyes or a trick of the shadow? But when she smiled again, the corner of his mouth lifted ever so little. He had responded. Her heart sent joy spiraling upward and blooming on her face, such joy she could scarcely contain it. If she ran and danced as she ached to, all the men would be appalled. One just didn't do such things. "Thank you, Private. Thank you so very much."

He returned to his digging and she to the lieutenant.

"Did you see?" she whispered.

"See what?" The man stared from the knife in his hands to the tangle of rhizomes, roots, soil, and long slender leaves.

"Private Rumford started to smile, barely, but it's a step in the right direction. Now." She rolled the clump over so the leaves and rhizomes were on top. Pointing as she talked, she identified the old wood for him, the new growth, and where to cut. "Now, iris are really hardy, so you needn't be too careful, but keep the new plants from each clump together and separate from the others, as they are of different colors." She glanced up to see that he was following her instructions but caught him staring at her instead.

"What? Do I have dirt on my nose or something?"

He shook his head and transferred his attention to the iris. "I cut here and here and—"

She leaned forward and her shoulder accidentally bumped his. They both leaped back as if they'd been burnt.

"Sorry." Their apologies even came at the same instant.

Why had she never noticed how long and fine his eyelashes were? And the gold that flecked his eyes. *Louisa Marie Highwood, quit acting like a . . . like a—*

"Miz Highwood, this somethin' you want dug out or left?" Andrews called out, breaking the spell of the moment.

"I . . . ah . . . I'll be right there." She drew back, wishing she had a fan. A big fan that would create a big breeze and hide her face.

Lord, I feel like I can drown in his eyes. I want to smooth that frown from his forehead, and . . . and . . . I've never felt like this. Do you think he feels the same way? Is this the beginning of love? And if so, what do I do next? She hustled over to Andrews and bent down to study the clump of leaves. "No, that stays, but you can dig around it. I forget what Aunt called it, though."

On her way to fetch the wheelbarrow, the thought hit her. *What if he doesn't feel the same way?* Trundling the wheelbarrow back, she let the posts down with a thunk. Tonight she'd ask Carrie Mae about it. Surely she would know.

By the time Abby came out with glasses of lemonade and fresh lemon cookies, the iris were all replanted in the re-dug bed with a thick layer of compost on top, the peonies were weeded, and another bed was prepared for winter vegetables. The men were wiping sweat from their brows in the full heat of the sun, and Louisa's nose felt pink, since she'd given up trying to keep her hat on hours ago.

"Dinner be ready 'bout an hour." The slender woman with skin like creamed coffee handed 'round the glasses. "Looks like you been diggin' up a storm."

"Miz Highwood here, she keeps us right busy." Corporal Shaddock grinned up at the serving woman from his seat on the grass. "But we make her pay back by readin' to us. Out here would be a fine place to lay back and be read to. Right after dinner."

"But I . . ." One look from the lieutenant and she clamped her lips shut. "What about the others?"

"We bring 'em out too. Be better out here in the sun and breeze than inside."

Louisa stared at the young man in astonishment. He'd never said so much at one time since she handed him his first drink of water three weeks earlier.

"Bring 'em out here to eat, right, Lieutenant?"

Louisa looked at the man leaning back in the recliner with his eyes closed.

"Now, how you goin' to bring them out? Gettin' 'em here yesterday was hard enough." He brushed at a fly that insisted on buzzing around him.

Abby had the answer to that. "Reuben fix dat last night. He make up a two-wheel chair. We bring dem out."

Abby was as good as her word. Zachary came out first and settled onto the lounger the lieutenant vacated. The two young men from the parlor followed.

"Now if we could fashion a gate through that wall." Louisa

stared at the brick wall, daring it to form a gate so the men in the other house could join them.

"Gettin' over here will be a good incentive for those two to walk again," the lieutenant said from beside her.

"Gardens have a way like that."

"It's not the garden, Miz Highwood, it's you." He spoke so only she could hear, but she jumped anyway.

"What a thing to say," she hissed. "I never—"

"Dinner is served."

She spent her time helping the men eat, cutting meat for those missing a hand and adjusting pillows so they could sit straight enough. When she sat down to her own meal, she found herself between Zachary and the lieutenant. Her brother started the story-telling, and soon the others took part, stories of home and growing up and families that wrote more often now that they knew where their boys were.

Surely she could go over to the hospital while everyone napped in the afternoon.

As soon as silence fell, she left her place and sneaked back in the house. Aunt Sylvania had returned from her morning with the sewing group, and now she too was taking a lie-down.

"I'll be back in an hour or two," she whispered to Reuben as she packed some leftover biscuits and honey in her basket. She added cookies and contemplated the jug of lemonade.

"I carries dat for you." Reuben hoisted the gallon jug, sweating in the warm kitchen.

"Surgeon general wants to see you," the orderly said when she walked into the ward a few minutes later.

"Oh." Her heart set to triple timing. Had the lieutenant broken his word, then? The thought made her stand two inches taller and march out of the room and down the hall to his office. The sub-altern showed her in.

"Why, Miz Highwood, I'm surprised to see you here." The surgeon general rose from behind his desk and motioned her to the chair.

"And why is that, sir? I am sorry to be late, but—"

"But you have men to care for over home, and your husband sent me a message saying you would no longer be helping us here."

"He . . . he what?" She felt like scrubbing at her ears. Surely she had heard wrong.

"So I want to thank you for all you've done for our men and for taking soldiers into your home."

"General, sir, more wounded coming in." The young officer made the announcement from the doorway.

"I'll be right there." The surgeon general came around the desk and extended his hand. "Thank you, indeed, Miz Highwood."

Rising, she placed hers in his and nodded. "I will go back home then and care for my own men." She fought to keep a smile on her face when all she wanted to do was scream.

CHAPTER TWENTY-NINE

A Missouri cave
October 10, 1862

"Get 'em off! Get outside."

"Oh, Lawdy, save us!"

"Come on, run!"

"It's in my hair!"

Screams echoed around the cave. The horses snorted and shifted restlessly. People ran for the cave mouth, brushing at the crawling things and screaming all the while.

"Thaddy, are you stung?" Jesselynn scooped her baby brother up in her arms, checking for the telltale red spot of a bite.

"No." He reached up and brushed one off her hair. "Gone now."

Ophelia shook out her clothes, her eyes rolling white, gibbering and crying all the while, screaming again when she saw one of the black bugs on Meshach's shoulder.

"Stop!" Meshach caught one of the bugs that was trying to burrow under the leaves. He knelt down and studied the insect, then began to chuckle. His great belly laugh grew while the others stared at him. Surely the big black man had lost his senses.

"Dey's no scorpions. Dey's vinegaroons. Lookee here, dey no hurt no one. De fire musta brung 'em out."

Ophelia shuddered, and it was all Jesselynn could do to keep from it. Jane Ellen tittered, the first smile to decorate her face since her arrival.

Benjamin slapped his knee and joined in the guffaws.

"Hey?" The voice came from the cave, and if Jesselynn hadn't been leaning against the entrance wall, she'd not have heard it. She

221

returned and crossed to the sick man's pallet. Kneeling, she studied his gray face.

"Good mornin'. I reckon you might be thirsty about now."

"I didn't die, then?" His voice rasped like a file on wood.

"Not yet, and if we can help it, you won't." She didn't add, *You might wish you had*, but she thought it awful hard. "I'll get you some water. Broth'll be hot as soon as we get the fire goin' again." She brushed a vinegaroon off his shoulder. "Don't worry 'bout these bugs bein' scorpions. They aren't. Meshach says they're vinegaroons."

"Oh." His eyes drifted shut. She laid a hand on his forehead. Hot but not blazing. He might not be minding the cold like the rest of them. But then she wouldn't ask for a fever to keep warm by.

The others wandered back in the cave, and while Jesselynn and Ophelia started the fire, the men took the horses out to water and graze.

"You want I should git some wood?" Jane Ellen offered.

"Would be a right good help. Thanks." Jesselynn blew again on the curls of wood and small twigs she had laid over the coals left from the night. They had almost let it go out. Whose watch had it been? Daniel, that's who. She'd have to have a talk with him when he came back. Just because they were relatively safe in the cave, they still needed a lookout, at least to keep the fire going.

Sure, and a good fire will bring out our marauding insects again. The thought made her chuckle. What a sight they must have been running around and screaming like that. Scare any self-respecting critter back into its hiding place. No wonder the poor things were scurrying so fast under leaves and whatever they could find for cover. One crawled out from under the wood stack when she took off a larger piece for the fire, then scuttled away, tail raised, mimicking the dangerous scorpion. All their patient needed was a few scorpion bites to push him right over the edge.

She glanced over at the man on the pallet. Between the now flickering flames and the fever, he had some color in his face, what you could see above the beard.

Meshach came back into the cave and retrieved his Bible. "Buried de other man. Got to read over 'im."

Jesselynn set the stew kettle over the flames. "If you want." She could feel the look he gave her but kept her attention on the fixings.

He wanted to believe in the God that wasn't, fine, but no more for her. Not until she heard him leave did she look up to find Ophelia giving her a quizzical stare. Thaddeus came and leaned against her shoulder.

"Hungry, Jesse."

"I know. This will be hot pretty soon." She put her arm around him and hugged him close. So much to endure for such a little guy. He should be home safe in the kitchen of Twin Oaks, chewing a piece of bacon and giggling with the slave children. They would be chasing each other around the room and out the door and back in until Lucinda would shake her spoon at them and threaten their eternal banishment if they didn't stay out of her way. There would be corn bread hot from the oven, eggs splattering in the frying pan, and redeye gravy set off to the side.

She could almost smell the ham slices and the rich aroma of good coffee, along with the corn bread.

Instead, she stirred the rabbit stew, making certain it was heated through and didn't burn. If it hadn't been for the lid on the three-legged pot, they'd most likely been having stewed vinegaroons for breakfast.

Ophelia set the biscuits to baking in the frying pan, the tight lid almost making an oven. After they ate, they'd bake up a bunch more and let them dry hard. That way they would travel well.

As if they needed to worry about that for the next few days. Moving this man would kill him for sure. When he woke, she planned to ask him his name. Going through his pockets hadn't been even a thought yesterday. Just keeping him alive was enough.

Jesselynn checked the strips of venison. They needed longer for drying too. That lazy Daniel. She'd tear a strip off his hide if he didn't watch out.

Jane Ellen, along with the help of Thaddeus and her brother, dragged in more branches and began breaking up the ones small enough. With the cracking of the branches and the ensuing giggles, the cave took on an even cozier feeling.

Only Daniel didn't come in to eat with the rest of them.

"He with de horses," Meshach said. He nodded to the again-drying venison. "He let de fire go out."

Jesselynn breathed a small sigh of relief. Thanks to Meshach, she wouldn't have to get after the boy, for that's what he was at sixteen, no matter how hard he tried to be a man.

In wartime, we all grow up fast. Jesselynn's mind flicked back to Twin Oaks, back to the games she played with her sisters and brothers on the lawn. Croquet had been their favorite even after the boys thought they were men and went away to school at Transylvania College in Lexington. How often she'd made Carrie Mae angry for whacking her ball off into the rose garden, and once into the pond. Now *that* had brought a shout of laughter from the boys and reprimands from their mother.

Had the letters she'd written gotten to them, so they knew where she was? If only she could hear from home or from Richmond, this journey might not seem so . . . so arduous. How long it had been since she'd learned a new word and found ways to use it that day. It seemed like centuries, like another lifetime that happened to someone else.

"Water." Their patient was awake.

Jesselynn spooned broth into a cup and, lifting his head with one hand, held the cup to his lips with the other. After only a few swallows, he gagged and shook his head, his groan rising to a near shriek. "God, it hurts."

"Would a spoon work better?" At his nod, she spooned the liquid to his mouth and watched him swallow. By the time the cup was empty, he'd drifted off again, but even in sleep, his moans persisted.

He has nice eyes, gray, I think, but it's hard to tell in here. If only they had more bandages. She glanced around the cave. What could they tear up? Short of Ophelia's spare skirt, nothing had the length. She studied the bandages around the stump of his leg. No blood had seeped through there. Perhaps the stitching was enough to hold it as long as he didn't move around, then she could wash those and change the ones around his belly. How the bullet had gone clean through like that and not hit any organs was nothing short of a miracle.

But it had seemed only a flesh wound. She felt his forehead again. Cooling. Maybe they'd be able to travel sooner than she thought.

Meshach stopped right behind her, studying the sleeping man. "He lookin' better."

"I know. Yesterday I wouldn't have given two bits for his chances, but today . . ." She paused and looked up. "He might just make it."

Meshach nodded. "We been prayin' for him too."

Jesselynn had no answer to that.

Jane Ellen stumbled into the cave carrying her brother. "He coughed so bad, blood came." The terror in her eyes told Jesselynn that had never happened before.

"Quick, put him down." Jesselynn saw the trickle of blood from John Mark's mouth streaking down his chin. His skin looked clear enough to see right through.

Jane Ellen mopped at the trickle of blood. "What we gonna do?"

Jesselynn tried to think back to what her mother had taught her. Coughing like that meant lung sickness. And most people didn't get better from it, especially those who'd gone without good food and lived in the cold and damp. She chafed his cold hands and watched his chest rise so slightly that each breath could be his last.

"Did he fall or anything, hurt himself?"

"No, just coughed till I thought his insides come out." Jane Ellen stroked the stringy hair back from his forehead. "Come on, John Mark, wake up. Please wake up."

His eyelids fluttered. Jane Ellen pulled him close and rocked him in her arms, crooning a song only she knew.

Jesselynn stood up and walked to the front of the cave, her eyes burning and her nose running, but not from any smoke coming from the fire.

The coughing sounded more like a retch.

Jane Ellen squeaked like a mouse caught by a cat, then resumed her crooning and rocking.

Jesselynn returned to see a froth of pink bubbling from the side of the boy's mouth.

"Here, chile." Meshach knelt and tried to take the boy, but Jane Ellen hung on with a fierceness stoked by terror.

"I takes keer o' him."

"Let us help you." Jesselynn took one of the quilts and laid it in front of the log for a pallet. "You sit here where you can hold him more easily, and the quilt will help keep him warm." Together Meshach and Jesselynn moved the two and added another quilt to cover John Mark.

Jesselynn and Ophelia cut more strips of the venison and hung it in places where the others had dried. They rubbed salt into a haunch and hung it above the fire to absorb the smoke. Thaddy and Sammy eventually quit playing in the dirt and fell asleep. Benjamin took one of the horses and went off scouting while Meshach chopped the deer brains, mixing them with ashes and water and working them into the inside of the stretched-out hide.

The afternoon passed to the rhythm of breathing, coughing, and moaning from the man and the boy. And while the man accepted the offers of water and broth, the boy refused everything.

"Help him, Marse Jesse." Jane Ellen raised eyes so darkened by fear they looked black.

"Here, see if you can spoon some of this into him." She took Jane Ellen a cup of broth and held it for the girl to dip from. Every drop drained out the side of his mouth. "Stroke his throat while I try."

Jane Ellen stroked her brother's throat with fingers of pure love, her eyes never leaving his face.

Jesselynn tipped a spoonful of broth between the boy's lips, and this time they watched as, with a convulsive swallow, the liquid went down.

"Oh, another." Jane Ellen resumed the stroking, and Jesselynn tipped the spoon again.

A swallow, a gag, a retching cough, and blood drenched the front of his shirt.

"Oh, John Mark. John Mark. Please, please." The girl rocked and hugged, her hands gripping the skinny child as though someone were pulling him away.

"He's bad, isn't he?"

Jesselynn looked over her shoulder to see their soldier gazing at her with eyes clear and as full of sadness as she knew her own must be. All she could do was nod.

"If you could . . . find my pack." He paused to catch a breath. "I had some . . . laudanum in it."

"Any idea where it might be?"

"Find where we were . . . ambushed. Could be . . . there. Black leather."

"You know how you got here?"

"Partner . . . carried me. How is he?"

"Gone. Meshach buried him this morning. He was sittin' against that wall there, with you lyin' on the floor."

The man closed his eyes. "How come . . . I'm alive and he's dead?" A pause stretched. "Makes no sense."

"I know." Jesselynn glanced at the girl still rocking her brother. "Makes no sense a'tall."

She added more wood to the fire, keeping it low so the strips of venison wouldn't burn.

"How bad is my leg? Hurts like fire."

How to tell him. "Ah, we . . ." Jesselynn sighed. No sense beating around the tree. "We had to take it off below your knee. Wasn't much left of it, and the gangrene would've set in and killed you for sure."

He closed his eyes tighter and swallowed hard enough for her to see the reflex in the firelight.

"I'm sorry." Such a meager word for such a loss as his. But at least he was getting stronger. Her gaze strayed back to Jane Ellen. While she kept wiping her tears away, sometimes she had to wipe them from her brother's face too.

Her brother was all she had. She said so. She hugged him as if her very strength could heal his chest, could stop the trickle of blood from every cough. Coughs that had grown weaker.

"I'll send Meshach lookin' for your pack." Jesselynn got to her feet, her knees creaking, stiff from sitting so long. She stepped outside the cave into sunshine a mite watery but still offering heat and light. From inside the cave, it had seemed dark outside, as if it still must be pouring rain like the day before.

When she told Meshach, he nodded. "Me an' de boys all go look." He got to his feet, laying a hand on Ophelia's shoulder and squeezing gently. "You go on in der. I be back."

Dusk dimmed the trees by the time the horsemen rode back to the cave. Daniel swung the pack down into Jesselynn's arms.

"I found it."

Jesselynn nodded. "Thank you." She knew he'd offered the pack as penance for letting the fire go out. She also knew he'd be more alert the next time he stood watch—Meshach would make sure of it. Now if only the laudanum could help relieve the pain for *both* of the sick ones.

CHAPTER THIRTY

Richmond, Virginia

"Men!"

"What dat, Missy Louisa?" Reuben hurried to keep up with her.

"I said *men* and my brother in particular!"

"Oh." He wisely let a pace or two widen between them.

"If he thinks he can waltz right in here and mess up my life, he has another think coming." She flung open the gate before the older man could get there and stomped her way up the walk, her thudding steps echoing on the stairs. She let wisdom and caution gain a mite of control so she didn't slam the door open or closed.

"Where is he?" Her words came more as growl than question. But her glances into the sickrooms yielded only more frustration. No one was in bed.

She stopped at the open French doors leading to the gardens. Aunt Sylvania sat like a queen in the middle of the group, holding the book up to get the best light. Reading from *The Taming of the Shrew*, she went on, "And Petruchio says,

" 'I pray you do; and I will attend her here,—
and woo her with some spirit when she comes.
Say that she rail; why, then, I'll tell her plain,
She sings as sweetly as a nightingale.' "

"Here, here," applauded Andrews. "You read right well, Miss S."

Miss S.? What is this world coming to? Her aunt was actually smiling and batting her eyelashes at the compliment. Louisa located her brother and shot daggers his way at twenty paces. The volley didn't phase him. In fact, he spoke the next lines from memory.

" 'Say that she frown; I'll say, she looks as clear
As morning roses early washt with dew.' "

They don't need me here, but the men at the hospital do. Why is he being such a selfish prig when I can be doing some good? She started to step back into the house, but the lieutenant turned and beckoned her with a smile.

Even he is smiling. What magic does Aunt Sylvania possess?

Louisa walked forward as if she were dragging a heavy chain. She couldn't talk to her brother now, and when she saw the devil dancing in his one good eye, she knew he realized he was safe. *Cotton and conniptions, I swear I'm going to get even with him if it's the last thing I do. Two can play at this game.* She dredged a smile up from somewhere and sprinkled it with sugar.

"The surgeon general sends his greetings, Mister Highwood, and hopes that all of you are settled in and on the fast road to recovery." She took the seat vacated by the lieutenant and leaned forward. "Keep reading, Aunt. That is most entertaining."

Zachary rolled his eyes.

Good! He knows he's in for it in a big way.

The lieutenant had taken Private Rumford for a walk, so they had the room to themselves. With both doors closed, Louisa felt reasonably certain they wouldn't be interrupted.

"Why did you do that?"

"I told you, I don't want you working over there." He held up a hand. "Yes, I understand the difference between paid work and volunteering, but that ward is no place for a young woman of your sensibilities."

"Meaning I'm too good to give the cup of water our Savior spoke of or to help a suffering neighbor?"

"Louisa, don't go twisting my words."

"I am not twisting your words, brother dear, I am merely trying to understand your motives."

"I have no *motives*, as you say. I just want you safe."

"Safe? Safe? As if anyone would harm me there!" She leaped to her feet, her needlework going one way, her scissors another, and paced the room from one end to the other. "I brought succor to the dying and comfort to the living. Now what on God's earth can be wrong with that? Mother and I did so at Twin Oaks, and I feel called to do so now."

"As the oldest Highwood man, I forbid you to work in the hospital." His eye narrowed and his words lashed.

A soft word turneth away wrath. Her mother's voice floated in her mind so clearly she was sure Zachary could hear it too.

Soft word, my right foot. She took in a deep breath and sniffed back any inclination to tears. Never in her life had she been so close to bludgeoning someone with her soft shoe or whatever else she could pick up.

"Zachary Highwood, you are being utterly cruel, both to me and those I can help."

Zachary shook his head and slumped against his pillows. "Ah, Louisa, I have seen such carnage and waste of good men that I cannot and will not ever try to tell you, but please, I just want to keep you from experiencing even a small part of that. Is it so wrong to try to keep the ones you love from harm?"

Louisa felt the starch go out of her spine. She knelt on the floor and took his hand in hers. "Wrong, my dear brother, no, I suppose not, but perhaps more than a bit selfish." She laid her cheek on his shoulder, where she could hear his heart beat. It would have been so easy for him to have died on the field and never returned to them.

Silence, but for their beating hearts, quieted the striving in the room and let peace tiptoe in and make itself comfortable.

"When we go home, things will be all right again." She whispered the words she prayed so fervently. "Soon, soon we'll go home, home to Twin Oaks."

A harsh sound, more groan or laugh she wasn't sure, ripped from his chest. "Home to Twin Oaks! Don't you know I cannot go home until the war is over?"

She raised her head and looked at him, his face suffused with red heat. "Whyever not? Look at you. You cannot fight again."

"If a Confederate soldier crosses into Kentucky, no matter

how severely wounded, he will be shot or hung as a spy. On sight."

Oh no, God, please, I want to go home, please. Her tears dripped silently down on the back of his hand.

CHAPTER THIRTY-ONE

A Missouri cave
October 11, 1862

Back and forth Jane Ellen rocked as dawn sent tentative fingers trembling into the cave.

Jesselynn heard her crooning the same song she'd fallen asleep to, only now the girl's voice was so hoarse the words were nearly unintelligible. All she wanted to do was pull the quilt over her head and go back to sleep, but something made her look over to Meshach as he stoked the fire. Sparks lit the air above him and the snapping wood sounded friendly. But the sorrow on his face and the way he looked at Jane Ellen answered questions before they were asked.

"Ah no." Jesselynn's eyes and nose ran at the same time, and her heart felt like a giant hand was squeezing the life out of it. She glanced over at Ophelia to see her wiping her eyes with the corner of her apron. The cave vibrated with the absence of coughing or gurgling, the last sounds she'd heard before she finally fell asleep.

Ophelia took a gourd of water to Barnabas White, as they'd learned was the soldier's name. Sergeant Barnabas White of Pine Bluff, Arkansas, serving in the Sixteenth Arkansas. He'd said the words with pride, whatever pride one can have flat on his back with a hole in his side and missing part of a leg.

Both wounds were still clear of putridity, and that alone made Jesselynn hopeful. They all needed a big dose of hope with the girl rocking her dead brother. How could they help her?

But the question deviling Jesselynn as she threw back the quilt and pulled on her boots was more basic than that. *Why do I keep gettin' more people to take care of? First Sammy, then Jane Ellen and John*

Mark, now the sergeant. Here we are somewhere in Missouri, where the fightin' is worse than at home, and I get more people and a Union horse to feed and keep safe. She slammed her booted heel against the sand-covered rock beneath her and pulled on the other. Clapping her hat on her head, she headed for the cave entrance. At least she could be alone when nature called.

"Jesse, I got to go."

When she looked over her shoulder, Thaddeus was sitting up, rubbing his eyes. As always, he had to go first thing. She wished she'd gotten away sooner; the crooning was digging into her like a drill into wood. And she didn't want to wait a moment longer. That meant she'd have to carry her baby brother.

Well, why not? She was carrying everyone else. She stomped across the cave, swung him up to sit on her hip, and again headed for the outside. *Death and tarnation.* Only her mother's training kept her from using some of the words her brothers had taught her. They'd had their mouths washed out with soap for using such language.

"You mad?" Thaddeus patted her cheek.

Jesselynn stopped in midstride. Mad? No, yes. Disappointed? For certain sure. Scared? More so than she wanted to admit. She looked at her little brother only to see a tear trickle down his cheek.

"Ah, Thaddeus, it's not your fault." She hugged him and nuzzled his soft cheek, kissing away the tear at the same time. "Come on, Joshwa, let's get this over with so we can eat, all right?"

His smile beamed in spite of wet eyelashes. Throwing both arms around her neck, he whispered in her ear, "Joshwa loves Jesse."

Frost stenciled a spider's web across their path and glittered the grasses. Jesselynn sucked in lungfuls of crisp air. For right now she could ignore the ordeal ahead in the cave and make her little brother laugh. The tears would come soon enough. How would she be acting if the dead boy were Thaddeus?

Tears choked her throat and made her stumble. She swung him to the ground, but only after another hard squeeze. As soon as he finished, she pointed him back toward the cave.

When she returned, Jane Ellen was still crooning and rocking. Jesselynn glanced at their patient, only to catch his gaze, as sorrowful as she knew was her own. Meshach and the others had taken the horses out to graze and water, and Ophelia moved like a puppet with tangled strings, trying so hard not to look at the misery to come.

Meshach, you take care of this. You'll have the right words. I have none. I'll take care of the horses.

Sammy fussed and demanded to be carried, so Ophelia held him on her hip while she stirred the pot of cornmeal mush. Thaddeus clutched his sister's pant leg, his thumb in his mouth, sending surreptitious glances over at Jane Ellen.

Jesselynn mixed some of the cornmeal into a gruel with the broth from the stewing venison and took it to Barnabas, as she referred to him in her mind. Sergeant White seemed so formal when caring for him.

"You up for some real food?"

"I think so." He flinched when he moved, and sweat broke out on his forehead. "If you'd help me sit up a bit?"

"You sure? Why don't I just prop a saddle behind you or another quilt? The less you move around, the less chance you'll start bleeding again."

"All right." Taking a deep breath brought his hand to his side. "Whew, guess I dreamed I was all better or somethin'."

"You want a dose of that laudanum first?"

"A bit in water I guess." He held out a hand, shaking as though he had the palsy. "Sorry to be so helpless like this."

Jesselynn didn't answer, just prepared the drink for him and held his head up so he could drink it. She too took great care to not look at Jane Ellen. *Meshach, get on back here.*

After about half a cup of the gruel, the sergeant shook his head and collapsed back against the padded saddle Jesselynn had fixed and propped behind him. "Thank you." His soft drawl made "you" into two syllables. Before she could turn around, he was asleep again.

She studied the flat glass bottle she'd corked again so carefully. Maybe a swig of that would let her sleep through the hours ahead, and when she woke, everything would be fine again. Instead, she nestled the precious stuff down into Ophelia's cooking box, where it was well padded.

Who knew when they might need it once more?

Jane Ellen coughed once, then picked up her singsong again, eyes closed, rocking and rocking.

When they'd finished eating, Meshach looked at Jesselynn with one raised eyebrow and a glance at the rocking girl. Jesselynn shrugged and nodded in that same direction.

Meshach closed his eyes.

She knew he was praying, and the thought sent a bolt of anger from head to foot. *Don't you know, man, that you're wasting your time praying? There is no God!* She clamped her fingers so tight her nails bit into her palms. She looked down and opened her hands to see red crescents where her nails had been. *Or if there is, He doesn't care. He lied.*

Then why did you wait for Meshach to come? The thought sent her on a headlong flight out of the cave. She ran through the brush with hands in front of her face, shoving away the branches that snagged at her clothing, tried to trip her, and ripped off her hat. Then, breath heaving, the cold air burning her lungs, she finally leaned against the trunk of an ancient oak. "I will not cry!" She shouted the vow to the few dried leaves that clung to the branches, stark fingers pointing to a sky feathered with strings of clouds. It should be raining.

They had to bury the body. Would Meshach be able to take the boy from his sister's arms?

The unearthly scream that rent the air sent the chills racing from her heels to her hair and raising those on the back of her neck. Taking in a deep breath she started back the way she had come.

Her hat waited for her, still snagged on the branch that had poked a hole in the crown. She crammed it back on her head, using it to push the hair back out of her eyes. She needed to cut her hair again. Concentrating on putting one foot in front of the other, on brushing the branches from her face, on wiping the tears from her cheeks kept her from thinking about the cave and what was happening there.

Meshach met her at the entrance. "De boys diggin' de grave."

Don't think. Don't feel. She nodded.

Thaddeus ran out of the cave and threw himself against her legs. "John Mark dead." He raised a tearstained face to look at her. "No play no more." He raised his arms to be picked up.

Jesselynn started to tell him no but instead reached down and hoisted him to her hip. "I know." *Get in there and hold Jane Ellen.* But no matter how hard she told herself to go, she could not take one step inside the cave. She could not look upon that poor girl, see that still face.

"We's done." Benjamin joined them in the sunshine.

"You want to read?" Meshach held the Bible out to her.

Jesselynn shook her head. "You do it."

Meshach studied her face for a long moment; she could feel it without looking up.

"Yessuh."

Ophelia brought Sammy out first and handed him to Benjamin, then went back in the cave to return with the body, now wrapped in one of their quilts.

Don't throw away the quilt like that, we're going to be needing it worse than he.

Ophelia handed the bundle to Meshach and returned to the cave, this time leading out Jane Ellen. The girl walked stifflike, as if she'd been dunked in a vat of heavy starch and it froze up her joints. Her blue eyes were washed of all life and feeling.

All through the simple service, she never said a word nor wept a tear.

Jesselynn studied the tree branches that shaded the grave. When Meshach finished his prayer, the final leaf broke off and drifted down to settle on the quilt. Even the birds kept silence. Ophelia took Jane Ellen by the hand and led her back to the cave, Sammy resting on her hip. Jesselynn set Thaddeus down.

"You walk now. You're gettin' too heavy to carry."

He clutched her hand and, instead of walking with his sister, turned back. " 'Bye, John Mark."

Jesselynn rolled her eyes upward to give the tears no place to form. She sniffed once and tugged on her brother's hand. Thaddeus walked with her as far as the cave entrance, then plunked himself down.

"Play here. Bring Sammy."

"You stay right here, then."

He nodded, searching for a stick to dig with, crackling the leaves as he dug around.

Jesselynn knew she should go in and help care for Barnabas. She could hear the plunk of dirt clods back at the grave. From inside the cave, the only sound was Sammy telling Ophelia something only he could understand.

"I'm goin' ridin'."

Thaddeus looked up at that. "Me go?"

"No, you stay here." She caught a glimpse of the hurt in his eyes as she swung away. "Benjamin, when you're done there, make sure Thaddeus stays put. You can help work that hide, and Daniel, slice off more of that venison so we can get it all dried before it spoils." She knew she sounded gruff. At the moment she didn't care. If she didn't get out of there, she was afraid she'd be wailing against the tree.

She reentered the cave only long enough to get a bridle and dashed out before Ophelia's song could bring her down. Deep river all right and there was nothing on the other side, no matter what the song said. No home, no Father God waiting, no joyous day.

She bridled and swung aboard Ahab, setting him into an even canter in spite of the trees. Only some small semblance of good sense kept her from urging him to a dead run, as she could have on the track at home.

Each day they stayed at the cave made life together worse. Jane Ellen crumbled into the corner, never speaking, never eating unless someone fed her. If she slept, it was with her eyes open, for every time Jesselynn looked at her, she was staring into nothing.

"Give her time," Meshach said.

Sammy burned his finger on a stick in the fire. Thaddeus whined from morning until he fell asleep at night. He even whimpered in his dreams, setting Jesselynn's teeth on edge even more than they already were.

The only good thing was that Sergeant White grew stronger each day.

"Thanks to all of you," he said in response to her morning question of "How you doin'?"

Meshach brought him a crutch carved out of a slender maple trunk and padded with part of the deer hide. "You wants another?"

"No, thank you." Barnabas sat leaning against the quilt-padded log. He fingered the stout piece of wood. "One of these days I'll carve me a peg, when the stump is all healed. Saw one one day attached with a leather harness. Maybe if I start on it now, I'll have it ready."

"Den I'll find you a good piece of hickory. Coulda made the crutch outa hickory too, but dis little tree looked so perfect-like."

"It is perfect, and I thank you. Perhaps we can get me standing up tomorrow and see how I do."

Two days later he hobbled out to the already loaded wagon,

Meshach and Jesselynn on either side of him ready to grab him if he started to fall. When they boosted him up in the wagon bed, he fell back against the box they'd padded for his backrest. Sweat dripped down his cheeks and ran off the end of his nose. Two red spots stood out like brush fires on his face gone stark white at the effort.

Lastly they led out Jane Ellen and settled her in beside the sergeant. If they stood her up, she stood. If they set her down, she sat. Even the two boys tumbling about her lap brought no reaction.

Two weeks later they arrived in the Springfield area. Leaving the rest of them down in a hollow, Jesselynn rode the mule into town and up to a store. Fingering her remaining coins, she approached the counter.

"Help you, son?" The aproned man behind the counter turned from filling a bag with coffee beans.

"Yes, suh, I's lookin' for the farm of Hiram Highwood. He's my uncle."

"Oh, that's too bad." The man shook his head. "I knowed Hiram for a long time. Good man. Hope you ain't come too far. Hiram was one of the early casualties of the war."

Jesselynn kept from stepping back with a superhuman effort. "And Aunt Agatha?"

"Not sure where she went to. Farm got burnt to the ground, long about a year ago now." He leaned forward.

"You all right, young man? You look whiter'n a sheet on washday."

CHAPTER THIRTY-TWO

Richmond, Virginia

Her sister's wedding day dawned, and all she wanted to do was stay in bed.

"Louisa, are you up yet?" The knock came softly on her door.

"No, and neither are the birds."

"I couldn't sleep any longer." Carrie Mae peeked around the slowly opening door. "Can I come in?"

"Of course." Louisa patted the bed beside her. "Just don't expect any brilliant conversation." When Carrie Mae drew closer, Louisa sat up. "You've been crying."

Carrie Mae sniffed. "I know. All I can think is that I want Mama and Daddy here for my wedding. It's not fair." She flung herself on the covers and great sobs heaved her shoulders. "And . . . and it . . . sh-should be at . . . at T-Twin Oaks."

"I know." Louisa patted her sister's shoulder, tears now streaming down her own face. And here she'd wondered at times if Carrie Mae even thought of home. "We can be grateful that Aunt Sylvania didn't say you had to wait a whole year for proper mourning."

"I . . . I know." Carrie Mae used the bed sheet to mop her eyes. "I don't think I could have borne it."

The silence stretched, punctuated by occasional sniffs on both their parts.

This is the last time we share a bed like this, the last time for all the girl talks we've had through the years. Since the two of them were closer in age than the others, only a year apart, often they had banded together, playing tricks on Jesselynn and tormenting their older brothers. Until the brothers grew up and went away to school and the tutor remained for the girls. Until the war.

Louisa sighed. Should she? "I have a question to ask you."

Carrie Mae rolled up on her side, head propped on one hand. "What?"

"Well, this is kind of personal."

"So?"

"How . . . how did you know when you were in love with Jefferson?" She couldn't look her sister in the eyes.

Carrie Mae flopped onto her back. "Ah, Louisa, when love strikes, you know. I wanted to be with him all the time. When he came near, sparks seemed to fly—even off our clothing." She propped her head up again. "You know how I love chocolate mints?"

"Of course, how many times did I have to beat you away from mine."

"I gave mine to Jefferson because he said he really likes them."

"You didn't."

"Did so. And that isn't all. You know how we prayed for the perfect men to be our mates, how mother had prayed for us that way for years?" Louisa nodded. "Jefferson is that man. He is kind, intelligent, works hard—Daddy would want those traits—makes me laugh—and you know how I love to laugh—will be able to support a family, and"—she paused and her eyes grew dreamy—"he thinks I am the most wonderful woman God ever created, and I plan to make sure he keeps on thinking that. We believe the same and come from the same backgrounds."

"Sounds like a marriage made in heaven. Surely there is something you want to change."

"I wish . . . I wish I could give him his arm back." Tears cushioned the simple words.

"Anythin' else?" Louisa forced her words past the tears clogging her throat.

"Would that we could live at, or at least near, Twin Oaks."

"You'll have to visit often. There's plenty of room, you know." Louisa closed her eyes and pictured the stately columns, the front portico, brick walls warmed by the Kentucky sun, green lawns, and honeysuckle growing up past some of the bedroom windows.

A cardinal sang and another echoed.

"We better get to movin' if you're to be at the church at eleven."

"I know." Carrie Mae turned on her side again. "It's the lieutenant, isn't it?"

"Um-hm." Louisa lay on her side facing her sister. "But . . . but I have no idea if he . . . he . . ." She drew circles on the sheet with her fingertip.

"If he cares for you like you do him?" Carrie Mae sounded older and wiser instead of like the younger sister.

"But I'm not really sure how I feel. I mean like . . ." Louisa drew circles on the bedspread with her finger. "Guess I just better keep on praying, right?"

"And I will too. Oh, Louisa, I want you and Jesselynn to be as happy as I am right now. And Zachary too, though I'm not sure men always know when they are happy."

Louisa nodded again. How seldom she had seen a glimmer of laughter or joy in the lieutenant, but then his situation wasn't of the kind to be laughing a lot over.

But other men find things to laugh about, even in the hospital. Joy is everywhere. You just have to recognize it.

She reached over and hugged her sister. "You grab all the joy you can and spread it around. 'Cause sometimes it's shy and needs invitin' in. Mama and Daddy had it, and I wish it for you. Lord, bless my sister with joy unending, no matter what happens in her life."

Carrie Mae wiped her eyes again, this time with the tips of her fingers. "Thank you. I'll ring for coffee, and we can begin getting ready."

Hours later, standing beside Carrie Mae in front of the altar, Louisa looked up at the Shepherd in the window above them. It seemed He looked right down and smiled at her, a smile so full of love and warmth that she wanted to squeeze her sister's hand and point upward. *Thank you for the blessing. Oh, Lord, fill this marriage with such love that everyone sees it and knows where it comes from.*

"I do." Carrie Mae responded in a clear voice that left no doubt as to her commitment.

"Therefore what God has joined together, let no man put asunder. I now pronounce you husband and wife."

The minister gave the benediction and the organ swelled in a song of joy as the newlyweds made their way up the aisle. When

Louisa took the arm of Jefferson's brother, she glanced up to catch the gaze of a tall, no longer quite so thin, man who seemed to have eyes only for her.

She smiled at him as she passed and waited in the vestibule until he could join her. "You will be coming back to Aunt Sylvania's for cake and punch?"

"An army couldn't keep me away."

Shivers ran up and down her back. Did this mean what she hoped it meant?

Though the wedding had been small due to the recent losses of so many, still the house and garden thronged with people. Louisa helped with the serving since they had such a small staff and wished she could have time to talk with the lieutenant—alone. Once she had even slipped and thought *my* lieutenant. When she passed him a cup of punch, their fingers brushed, and she nearly dropped the cup.

"Can we talk a bit after..." He sidestepped as a young boy chased after another and nearly took out his crutches.

Louisa smiled, fighting to keep from breaking out in song. "Of course."

She helped her sister change into a gray silk traveling dress, since the two would be going to Williamsburg for a week before they returned to Richmond and he to his law practice. They would be living in a little house not far from his office.

"Well, Mrs. Jefferson Steadly, you behave yourself now, you hear?" Louisa tried to sound like their mother at her sternest.

"Oh, I will." Carrie Mae adjusted the brim of her hat and tucked a strand of hair back into her chignon. "There, now, how do I look?"

"Blissfully happy and enchantingly lovely." Louisa dabbed at the corner of her eye and sniffed. "God be with you, my dear sweet sister." The two wrapped their arms around each other and hugged as if they were saying final good-byes.

"Now, off with you. I heard Jefferson is waiting at the bottom of the stairs."

Louisa watched as her baby sister descended the stairs, the plume on her hat bobbing gaily. *Lord bless them, take care of them, and please bring them back home safely.*

Carrie Mae turned at the door and blew her a kiss. Louisa caught it like a treasure.

The company couldn't leave quickly enough. Dusk came and

still some lingered on the veranda. Short of pushing them out the door, Louisa joined in the conversation, making sure her brother and the other invalids were comfortable. When finally the last guest wandered down the front walk, she turned to find the lieutenant sitting in the glider, his crutches balanced against the front railing. He patted the seat beside him.

Louisa sat as close to her end of the swing as her skirts permitted, but still she could feel the heat from his body. "Ah, such a lovely wedding, don't you agree, sir?" She glanced over at him. Where had the smile gone? "Is something wrong, Lieutenant?"

"Do you think you could call me Gilbert?"

The deep timbre of his voice sent a tingle clear to the end of her fingertips.

"All right, Gilbert." She whispered his name as if they were sitting in church.

"And I may call you Louisa?"

Why did her name sing when he said it?

"Yes." The glider moved back and forth just enough to stir the stillness of the surrounding dusk.

"Miss Louisa, I . . . I'm so grateful you aren't married." His words came out in a rush, as if he'd been choking them back for some time.

"Really? Me too. I mean . . ." Oh, gingersnap, was she going to mess things up again?

"I . . ."

He hardly seemed to notice what she had said, concentrating on something he needed to say. Her heart settled into a deeper beat.

"I find I am coming to care for you." He turned and took her hand in his. "Do you . . . I mean . . . is there, I'm . . ."

"Yes."

"Yes, what?" He blinked and rubbed his thumb over the back of her hand.

"Yes, I too think I am coming to care, for you, I mean."

"Ah." He closed his eyes. "The foot, it doesn't matter?"

"Why should it?"

"I'll never walk properly, and riding a horse will be difficult. At least that's what they tell me."

Louisa longed to lay her hand along his cheek, to smooth the lines from his eyes and the deep gashes from the sides of his well-etched lips. "I pray there will be no lingering pain, that is all."

"I . . . I would like to court you. I've already talked with your brother."

Leave it to the lieutenant, right to the point. "I'd like that."

"But I have a bit of a problem."

"Oh?"

"I have to leave for my home in North Carolina tomorrow, and I'm not sure when I will be back. The army discharged me this morning."

"But you *will* be back?" Where did the tears come from so quickly?

"Ah yes, I will be back, and in the meantime we can write?"

"Of course." *At least he isn't going off to war again.*

CHAPTER THIRTY-THREE

Springfield, Missouri
Late October 1862

Where can we go?

Jesselynn slumped against the counter, the edge of it cutting into her hip. The candy jars in front of her grew smaller, then larger. Her head felt as if it would float right off. She blinked and sucked in a deep breath.

"I say, boy, are you all right?" The man reached a hand across the counter and clamped on Jesselynn's wrist. "Lizzie, come here and help me." His raised voice penetrated the buzzing in her ears.

If this was what fainting felt like, Jesselynn knew she was right close to the edge. She bit down on her tongue until she wanted to yelp and blinked again. This time the jars settled back into place, their red-and-white-striped sticks no longer dancing.

"What?" She shook her head. "Did you say something?"

"I asked if you was all right. You looked some dreadful."

"What is it, Lawrence?" A woman slender as her man was portly bustled into the room, took one look at Jesselynn, and changed direction. She pulled a chair from near the potbellied stove that reigned in the middle of the room and, setting it behind Jesselynn, pushed her down onto it. "Now put your head down, young man, and in a couple of minutes you'll be right as rain." Since the woman had hold of the back of Jesselynn's neck and was pushing downward, there wasn't much else she could do.

She shut her eyes and sucked in a couple of deep breaths. "I . . . I'm fine now, ma'am." As the patting hand released, Jesselynn sat back up to hear Lawrence telling his wife the story. It didn't sound any better the second time, worse in fact. Some of the slaves had been burned with the barns.

"You know where Miz Highwood is livin'?" Lawrence asked his wife as he leaned on his hands, arms stiff to prop him up.

"I might kin find out." The hesitancy in her voice gave Jesselynn an idea the woman knew more than she was letting on. "If I kin find her, where can she find you?"

"Ah, I'm not sure. You see, we just arrived here from Kentucky, and I was plannin' on stayin' with my kinfolk." Jesselynn knew her accent was going in and out but didn't seem to be able to do much about it. The shock had her stomach so tied in knots she could hardly swallow.

What will I do with the horses? Where can we stay? Can't go home until spring, and spring is a long way off from now.

Her legs gave way, and she plunked back down in the chair. *How can I feed all those people and the horses through the winter?* She didn't have to jingle her pockets to know how little money they had left.

Not near enough.

She got back to her feet. "I thank you for the information, and now I'd better get the other I came for and head on back." Mentally she rewrote the list. "I need five pounds of beans, same of flour and cornmeal, half a pound of salt . . ." She crossed off coffee and sugar. "And a sack of oats." The two mares would need extra feed for the next couple of months, since they were due to foal in early February.

"You want those oats rolled or—"

"No, regular is fine." She eyed the candy jars. Thaddeus and Sammy hadn't had any candy since halfway across Kentucky. She gritted her teeth. "And two sticks of that peppermint there." She watched as the two went about filling her order. *Eggs, I want an egg, and milk.*

"You know anyone could use a good blacksmith who can fix about anything, set wheels, shoe horses—?"

"You could check over at the livery down the street and to your right. There's a foundry in town too. He might want some help. Things been right busy since the army been in and out."

"Union or Confederate?"

"Union." He studied Jesselynn over his half glasses. "Why?"

"Just curious."

"You got slaves?"

Jesselynn shook her head.

" 'Cause some don't hold too highly with that. Could cause all kinds of trouble."

Jesselynn picked up the warning note in his voice. Did that mean her people were safe from slave traders here? Did she dare ask?

Like her daddy always said, "You learn more with a closed mouth and open ears."

"That'll be one dollar and seventy-five cents."

She brought out her five-dollar gold piece and laid it on the counter. "Know anyone wantin' the services of a good stud horse?"

"What's his breedin'?"

"Oh, this 'n that, but he throws mighty fine colts."

"I'm certain the military would be interested." He counted the change back into her hand.

"Most likely, but not for stud." Jesselynn gathered up her purchases and stuffed them into the tow sack she had with her. "We'll have to tie the oats on behind the saddle. That's my mule right out there." She nodded over her shoulder. Turning to the woman, she finished, "If you happen to see my aunt Agatha, tell her Zachary Highwood is lookin' for her. She kin write me a letter to the post office, and I'll pick it up there."

"Of course, young man, we'll do just that." She came around the corner of the counter as her husband left to get the grain. "Any message you want me to give her—if I find her, that is?"

Jesselynn nodded. "Tell her my daddy came home to die from the war and said we—I—was to come stay with her."

"All right. I'll do that. You know where the post office is?"

"No, ma'am."

She gave Jesselynn the instructions and closed the door after her. The bell tinkling overhead sounded as friendly as it had when she went in, but now the whole world was changed.

Clouds had covered the sun, and a chill wind picked at the edge of her coat and the brim of her hat, making her body feel as cold as her spirit.

Had Aunt Agatha even gotten the letter she'd written, the one that said Major Joshua Highwood had died and she was bringing the horses to stay at Hiram's? For a moment she wished she'd stayed out of sight and waited to see if the woman at the store had left to go find Aunt Agatha. She was certain she knew where Aunt Agatha was staying. Why would that be a secret?

Jesselynn kept watch over her shoulder as she crossed the prairie, meandering between farms and back to the willow-lined hollow where they'd sheltered the night before. The banks had been knee-deep in grass, so the horses were having a good feed. Maybe Daniel had even caught some fish in the creek. Now wouldn't that be a treat after their weeks of venison, rabbit, and more venison? The wild turkey that Benjamin brought in one day had disappeared faster than water on a hot stove. She'd kept a couple of the primary wing feathers for quills to write with and let Thaddeus play Indian with the others.

She whistled the three-tone greeting they'd agreed upon long before and waited for an answer before riding down the bank.

"What wrong?" Meshach stood at the mule's shoulder, staring up into her face.

"Hiram, the farm, all gone." Jesselynn shrugged and her shoulders sagged. "They said Aunt Agatha might be around. I'm sure she is, but the folks at the store weren't givin' her away."

"The farm?"

"Burned to the ground over a year ago. Why did no one write to us? I wondered why we didn't hear at Christmas, but . . ." She pleated the mule's brushy mane with her fingers. "Lots of times letters get lost during a war."

Like hers might have been. Maybe Agatha had no idea they were coming. She shook her head again and slid to the ground. "That's oats for the mares in the big sack. Ration it." She untied the tow sack from the saddle and slung it over her shoulder. Cursing the war and the men who started it, she plunked the sack of food in the wagon and looked around for Ophelia and the boys.

"Daniel got a mess of fish."

"Good thing. And we better be finding us a hidin' place. Most likely another cave."

"I take it you didn't have good news?" Sergeant White sat on the wagon tongue, rewrapping the bandage on his stump of a leg, his crutch at the ready beside him.

Jesselynn shook her head. "'Fraid not."

"How are you for money?"

Jesselynn stopped and turned to stare at him. "Why?"

"I got me some cash and I'd like to share it with you, since you been carin' for me and all."

Jesselynn stuffed her pride in her back pocket. "Paper or hard money?"

"Both."

"If it's Confederate script, it's not worth the paper it's printed on. Might as well start a fire with it, but the other, well . . ."

"Good thing you didn't have to cut this boot off." He pointed to his boot. "If you would do the honors."

Giving him a disbelieving glance, she did as he asked and handed him the boot.

He reached inside, dug in a slit, and brought out two gold coins. "The paper is in my pack."

"No, it's not."

"You didn't know where to look, and if the Confederates take over this area, the script might be worth something again. We can hang on to it." He reached toward her with the coins. "Here."

Jesselynn shook her head. "How will you get home without it?"

"How will I get home with it?" He pulled his hand back and stuffed one coin back in the boot, then handed her the other. "We'll split it, but if you need this, you tell me. Promise?"

Jesselynn took the ten-dollar gold piece and, hefting it once, dropped it into her pocket to mingle with the change there. That would help them for a while, but the winter stretched ahead like a painter about to pounce.

Barnabas set his boot on the ground and tried to stuff his foot in it, but the force sent him nearly tumbling over the side of the wagon tongue. Jesselynn jumped just in time to brace him. His head rested against her chest until between them, they got him upright again.

The look he gave her made her step back. "What?"

"Marse Jesse?" His voice came thick and hoarse.

"Yes." She took another step back.

"Okay, if that is what you say."

He knows. No, he doesn't. He can't. He knows.

But his gray eyes twinkled just the tiniest bit, and a smile quirked the side of his mouth, barely discernible with his beard but there nevertheless.

That night around the fire, Jesselynn clasped her hands, her elbows resting on her knees. She'd already told everyone what had happened in town, so continued. "Now the way I see it, we need to find a good warm cave to hole up in until we can go back home in the spring. Surely the war will be done by then." *Dreamer*. She ignored the accusing voice in her head to add, "Maybe Meshach can find work in town. Places are always in need of a good blacksmith." She studied the calluses on her hands. "We'll just have to live off the land." Glancing over at Jane Ellen, who sat wherever Ophelia put her, and down at the two boys, one sleeping on Ophelia's lap and Thaddeus leaning against her own side, she sighed. So many mouths to feed.

"I kin watch the young'uns." Sergeant White smiled at her across the campfire. "And I was a right good cook. So I'm sure losin' part of my leg won't change that once I learn to hobble better so's I don't tip over in the fire."

Meshach and Benjamin chuckled at that. "We save his hide mor'n once."

"So, tomorrow we're off to the hills to spy out a cave."

They all nodded.

"I kin still shoot, you know. If y'all want to leave me here with Ophelia and the young'uns."

Meshach and Jesselynn exchanged glances, then both nodded.

It took the four of them searching for two days to find a cave sufficiently large for them all and far enough away from any farms or main roads. It lay on the south face of a steep hollow several hours south and west of Springfield. There was plenty of pasture close by and not many farms, due to the roughness of the terrain.

Once they were settled in, Jesselynn took time to write letters, one to those at Twin Oaks, the other to her sisters in Richmond. After describing their journey so far, she asked if they had heard anything from Twin Oaks. She had really expected a letter from Lucinda to be waiting at the post office, but when Benjamin went in to check, there had been nothing for them.

> Please write soon. I must know how you are. Have you heard anything from Zachary? I keep telling myself that no news is good news, and I am grateful every time I read a casualty list and his name is not on it.
>
> Louisa, with all your gifts for healing broken creatures, I wish you were here to help us with Jane Ellen. She has not made a peep since that terrible scream when Meshach took her brother away to be buried. Sergeant White is healing up fine, getting around better on his crutch every day. I am as ever. Someday you'll have to try

wearing britches. It's hard to think that I will ever have to go back to skirts and dresses.

She thought of telling Louisa of her suspicions that the sergeant realized she is a woman, but the possibility of even a long-distance diatribe from Aunt Sylvania made her wish she hadn't said the latter.

She signed her name and, after waiting for the ink to dry, folded the letter and addressed the envelope. Daniel could take it into town in the morning. On a whim, she took her writing folder out to where Sergeant White was whittling on something and keeping an eye on Sammy and Thaddeus as they played in the sunshine.

"You want to write a letter home?" She extended the leather-bound case. "Perhaps your girl would like to know if you're alive or not too."

He took the case. "Don't have no girl." He paused and stared up into her eyes. "Yet."

Jesselynn felt a flash of heat from her heels to her head. *He knows.* She thought of challenging him on it but decided letting sleeping dogs lie might be wiser. He was comely, not handsome in the truest sense, but a fine figure of a man in spite of the crutch. Surely there was some young woman down in Arkansas who would be glad to hear from him.

The thought of his leaving gave her a curious hollow feeling. So many people came into her life and then left, one way or another. Each seemed to take a bit of her with them, till pretty soon there might not be anything left. And besides, Sergeant White was right nice to have around.

───────

"Now, remember, you get the mail, and you be lookin' out to see if anyone's watchin' you."

"Then you make sure to lose dem befo' you come home." Meshach finished giving Daniel the instructions for her. "An' you be watchin' out for bluebellies or sojers of any kind."

"Don't you go gettin' lost in Springfield either, hear?" After most of the hamlets they'd stopped at on their journey, Springfield seemed about as big as Lexington back home. Not that they'd ever gone there much, but still.

Jesselynn watched Daniel ride off whistling a tune and wished she were going instead. Surely they would at least hear from Aunt Agatha soon. With Meshach and Benjamin leaving to go hunting, the cave seemed huge. "I'll take the horses to graze." She glanced down to see the imploring look Thaddeus gave her. Her heart melted right then, even though time alone had been a prize. "And take Thaddeus along with me. High time he had a riding lesson, I'm thinking."

Thaddeus let out a squeal and threw his arms around her leg. "Me ride Ahab."

Ophelia giggled behind her hand, and Sergeant White had a hard time keeping a straight face.

"Thataway, boy. Start right at the top."

"You'll ride Dulcie." She took his hand. "Now, let's go."

"Bye, Sammy. Bye, Jane Ellen. Bye, 'Phelia. Bye, Sarge White."

Once outside the cave, Jesselynn scooped him up and set him astride the oldest mare. "Now you hang on to her mane, and I'll lead her real slow-like. All right?"

Thaddeus nodded, his grin so wide, his eyes barely showed.

Like all of the Highwood children, he seemed to be born to ride, his balance already good and his eyes dancing with delight. Even when the mare put her head down to graze, he stayed on her back, petting her neck and crooning his own version of the language between rider and horse. Dulcie twitched her ears, keeping track of everything going on around her. She raised her head at what sounded like a gunshot. When a second one followed close on the heels of the first, Jesselynn hoped it was Meshach and Benjamin and they'd gotten a deer.

After a while she lifted Thaddy down and gave him one of the biscuits she'd stuck in her pocket. A third shot some later and farther away sent chills up and down her spine. Was something going on that she wanted no part of? She hustled Thaddeus back up on the mare and, gathering the lead lines, took her charges back to the cave. She'd take them out later when she knew if she should be worried about the shots or not.

Sergeant White stood at the mouth of the cave, staring off to the southern hills.

"You heard them too?" Jesselynn lifted Thaddeus down and sent him into the cave.

"The first one was Meshach with the rifle, and the second was Benjamin with the repeater. Not sure about the third."

"It was farther away."

"I know."

Jesselynn hated playing the waiting game. She'd waited for her father and brothers more times than she liked to count. She'd waited for John and he'd never returned. She'd waited for her father to come home, and he'd died in her arms. Why were women the ones who waited?

The sun crept farther down the sky and still they waited.

Wouldn't it be easier to be like Jane Ellen and have no idea of time?

CHAPTER THIRTY-FOUR

Richmond, Virginia

Dear Jesselynn and Thaddeus,

I suppose I should address you as Marse Jesse, but I cannot seem to do that. I will address the envelope that way as you are already aware I did. First I will bring you up-to-date on the events here. The wedding was beautiful, and our sister was a lovely bride. She and Jefferson are so much in love that one can do nothing but be thrilled for them. Even Aunt Sylvania approves, and you know what a miracle that is. While the wedding wasn't the social event of the season, which it might have been had not there been deaths in the family, all the family and friends who attended did indeed wish them many blessings. Strange that even though Carrie Mae wasn't here much of the time, I miss her and know that our lives will never be the same again.

Not that there has been much sameness lately. Oh, sister, I long so for Twin Oaks and for our family to be together again. Thaddeus is growing up without us all to pet and tease and hug him as we were. Will this wretched war never cease?

I hope you are all settled at Uncle Hiram's by now and safe from the marauders I hear so much about. As if regular soldiers weren't enough.

Speaking of soldiers, we have several of the wounded from the hospital living here with us. Zachary is ready to use crutches, but without the right hand, this will take some thinking. We are trying so hard to keep him from slipping into a morose state like some of the others who have lost limbs. Like me, he feels he will be so much better when he returns to Twin Oaks. Did you know that until the war is over, he cannot even do that, or he will be shot? I pray daily *for an end to the battles, that we might all go home.*

I have news of my own. You remember the Lieutenant Lessling that I wrote about? He was one of the patients on my ward. He has asked if he might court me and had talked it over with Zachary before informing me. And here I was wondering if he felt the same as I do. Not that I always know what I am feeling, this is all so new and, at times, frightening. I can't wait for you to meet him. The sad thing is that he announced, nearly in the same breath, that he had been discharged and would be leaving for home in the morning and would return within a fortnight. A fortnight isn't really that long, I keep telling myself.

Aunt Sylvania is much improved now that the weather is cooler and she has "her boys" here to mother. She has taken over the reading in the afternoons, and some of the boys tease her until her cheeks are pink.

That is all from here. Your letters, few though they have been, bring such joy to us all. I commend you to our sovereign Lord's gracious care.

> *Love,*
> *Louisa*

P.S. Zachary told the surgeon general he didn't want his "wife" working in the hospital any longer, so I must find something else to do for the war effort.

My dear Louisa,

I miss your sweet face already, and I have been on the train for barely more than an hour. I was not able to take the one I had intended, as it was full of troops off to another front. Would that I could go with them, but the army says I am no longer of value. All that training at West Point gone to waste, thanks to an enemy shell. But I keep reminding myself that through the grace of God I am alive, and He has given me something to live for, after all—you. So many things I've wanted to say to you, but the time never seemed right, and I still cannot believe you return my feelings.

As soon as I straighten out things at home, I will return on the earliest train. Please write to me so that I may continue to have smiles in my life, the joy you so willingly share. I will mail this at the next stop, so it doesn't take so long to get to you.

> *Yours truly,*
> *Lieutenant Gilbert Lessling*

Dear Gilbert,

As the fortnight has come and gone and there has been no fur-ther word from you, I am praying that you are well and only so buried in business that you have no time to write. I treasure your letter and have read it so many times that the creases are working their way through the paper. I do hope you have received my other letters and that you are in better health each day. I ask our God to watch over you and bring you back safely.

Yours,
Louisa

"Can I bring you anything else?" Louisa stopped at the door to the parlor where Zachary and several other officers were visiting amid a cloud of cigar smoke.

"Nothing, thanks." Zachary waved his cigar, obviously waiting for her to leave before the conversation could continue.

What is he up to now? Louisa glanced back at the door that was now closed. "I know they are hatching something," she said aloud.

"What dat you say?" Abby stopped to ask on her way to take refreshments out to the men gathered around Aunt Sylvania and her open Shakespeare book.

"Just grumbling." Louisa set the tray down on the kitchen table and picked up a cookie to nibble on. While every morning on wak-ing she promised she would leave the lieutenant in God's strong hands, by afternoon she felt ready to fly apart. Why hadn't she heard from him again?

"You know that mail can't get through much of the time, and you know what God says about worry, so go knit socks or do some-thing helpful." She took her own advice and her knitting out to the front glider. If only Zachary would let her go back to the hospital where she felt useful.

After the three men left, tipping their hats to her as they filed past, Zachary called to her from the parlor.

Sure, he needs me to help him back to bed but sends me off with a wave of his hand when . . . Oh, stop feeling sorry for yourself, Louisa Marie High-wood. Others have things so much worse than you do. Put a smile on your face and kill that rapscallion brother of yours with a hearty dose of kindness.

She set her knitting back in the basket and stood, smoothing her skirts before she entered the house.

Zachary didn't look up when she entered the room; instead he stared out the window. From the look of him he wasn't seeing the jasmine vine that created a fragrant frame of white blossoms and green leaves beyond the curtains.

She crossed and opened the window to let the flowers' fragrance take away that of the cigar smoke.

"Come, sit here." He patted the horsehair seat beside him.

Louisa felt a catch in her heart. She crossed the room, never taking her eyes from his face. "What is it, brother?"

"I . . . I'm afraid I have bad news for you." He took her hand in his and finally looked in her eyes. "We have reason to believe that the train Lieutenant Lessling was riding on was the one blown to smithereens by the Yankees."

"Reason to believe? That means you have no proof." She hung on to his hand with all the power in her.

"No. No proof, but a certainty."

"Without proof, I will not believe it. The lieutenant gave me his word he would come back." *Lord, I cannot bear this. Unless you tell me, I will not believe.*

"Trust me."

Louisa got to her feet. "I . . . I think I need to be alone."

Dragging her feet up the stairs, she entered her bedroom and dropped down on the side of the bed. "He can't be dead, Lord. Wouldn't I have some sense if he were dead?"

"Trust me." The lace curtains moved gently in the air, as if puffed by a whisper.

"I've trusted you with everything, with everyone, but you take them away." Her eyes burned, the tears refusing to fall to cleanse this mighty trauma from her soul. "What else can I do?"

"Trust me."

The words seemed to hang in the stillness.

Louisa gritted her teeth and clamped her fingers into a fist until the skin broke. "I will trust you." Each word was ripped from her heart. "I will trust you, God, Father, S-Savior." A tear overflowed her now wet eyes and ambled down her cheek. "I will trust you, Jesus, my Lord."

The curtains moved again, and this time peace flooded her soul.

CHAPTER THIRTY-FIVE

Cave in southwestern Missouri
November 1862

The closer the sun slid to the horizon, the dryer Jesselynn's mouth grew.

Meshach arrived first, a deer carcass slung over his shoulders. Benjamin trailed him by several hundred yards, the deer on his shoulders heavy enough to make his slighter frame stagger with the weight.

When she shot Meshach a questioning look, he winked at her and whispered, "I offered to help, but . . ." His shrug said it all. He swung his burden to the ground.

Benjamin dropped his next to it with a *thwump*. The rise to the cave had him panting like a hound after a hunt. His deer sported two-prong antlers.

"Good, those horns can come in handy." Sergeant White's comment brought a wide smile, and Benjamin stood straighter. "And two hides. I see you brought me somethin' I kin do."

"Happy to help you, suh." Benjamin's beaming smile had pride written all over it. "Biggest deer I ever shot."

"Onliest deer you ever shot." Meshach clapped the younger man on the shoulder. "Let's get dem hung, and you can skin 'em." He looked around. "Where's Daniel?"

"Not back yet." Jesselynn hated saying words that immediately sucked the joy out of the moment.

"We better go lookin' for 'im."

"I was about to."

Meshach saddled one of the mares and Ahab. He slammed his rifle into the scabbard laced to the saddle and swung aboard, the look on his face grim enough to scare Sammy, who clung to Thaddeus. Meshach held an impatient Ahab steady while looking at Sergeant White. "Keep watch." He nodded to Benjamin. "Give him the rifle while you skin the deer."

Jesselynn mounted the mare and followed Meshach up the hill, then once out of the hollow, they nudged the horses into an easy canter that ate up the miles. They rode halfway to Springfield before they saw Daniel limping toward them.

"What happened," Jesselynn called, "the mule dump you?"

Daniel shook his head.

As they rode closer, they could see one eye was swollen shut, the cut on his head left a trail of dried blood down the side of his face, and he clutched one elbow to his side. One shirt sleeve hung by a thread.

"What? Who?" Jesselynn could feel rage bubbling and snapping in her midsection.

"Dey took de mule." He swiped blood and dirt from under his nose with his good hand and looked down at his bare feet. "An' my boots."

"They who?" Jesselynn dismounted and flinched at the close-up sight of his beaten body.

"Dey was fixin' to hang me for stealin' de mule, but some other men come along, and dey run dem off." He leaned against Meshach when he dismounted, and Meshach put his arm around the boy. "I tried to fight dem off, but one against three . . ." His voice trailed off, and he shook his head. "I'se sorry."

"I reckon you're more important than the mule anytime." Jesselynn gently pulled his arm away from his body, her lips tightening at the bruise on his side.

"Dey kick me. I never hurt so bad in my life." He dug in his pocket. "But dey din't take de letter." He thrust it into Jesselynn's hand and swayed on his feet. "Sorry, I'se gonna be sick."

Meshach held the boy's head with one hand and clamped the other around his waist until the retching finished.

"Ah, dat hurts." Daniel gasped.

"Broken ribs?"

"Cracked anyway." Meshach led Daniel over to Ahab, who, nostrils flared wide, skittered away at the smell of blood.

"Easy, son." Jesselynn held the stallion steady while Meshach boosted Daniel up into the saddle, then mounted behind him. She patted Daniel on the knee. "We'll get you right fixed up back at camp. Guess we better use some of that deer hide and make you a pair of moccasins to keep your feet warm."

"Thank you, Marse Jesse. You mighty good to dis black boy."

Jesselynn felt rage hot and sweet course through her as she followed the pair ahead. Who had taken the mule, and why did they beat Daniel so viciously? Pure meanness was all she could think of. Now, stealing the mule, that made sense, but beating someone half to death? And then stringing him up.

A picture of Cavendar Dunlivey beating one of the slaves sprang into her mind. That was when her father ordered him off the place. But she could still see the look in Dunlivey's eyes. He had enjoyed giving the whipping. Thinking back like that made her keep looking over her shoulder, her pistol at the ready.

"We kin track dat mule." Benjamin repeated his comment again. Supper finished, they were sitting around the fire before going to bed. "You know him hooves, Meshach. You shod 'im, after all. De right front, how it curve in? We go find dem and bring 'im back."

"No! There'll be no talk of trackin' the mule. Those men are killers. You want to end up like Daniel or worse?" Jesselynn nodded to the young man huddled under a quilt and whimpering in his sleep.

"What de letter say?" Meshach used the deerhorn to smooth the piece of wood he'd been working on.

"I forgot all about it." Jesselynn dug in her pocket and pulled out the envelope. Slitting it open with her finger, she extracted the paper and, tipping it, leaned closer to the light.

" 'Dear Zachary,

"Welcome to Springfield, although I am sorry I was not at home to greet you. The sad news is that Hiram died early on in the war, and some worthless scalawag burned us out. They do that a lot around here. All our horses were already gone, and several slaves died in the fire. I am living with a friend here in town, but since neither one of us has a husband for support, I have not even a room for you to stay in. Please come to visit me when you can.'

"She gives the directions and signed the letter, 'Sincerely, Mrs. Hiram Highwood.' "

Jesselynn looked up to find Sergeant White studying her across the fire. "Zachary is my older brother." She could feel her cheeks growing hot, surely from the fire.

He nodded and went back to his whittling. "When you goin'?"

"First thing in the mornin'." *Surely Aunt Agatha knows somewhere we can keep the horses over the winter. And maybe she's heard from the girls.*

"I go wid you." Meshach never looked up from his scraping.

"No, I'll be—" Jesselynn stopped when Meshach glanced over at the sleeper who came so close to leaving this life. "Thank you."

They had no trouble finding the house in the morning, but Jesselynn about choked when she saw the place. Disrepair hung over the house like a rent and rotten garment. Windows, doors, and porch all sagged, as did the gate to what used to be a picket fence. By the steps, one lone pink rose struggled to reach the sun. The nearby houses didn't look any better.

Meshach held the horses while Jesselynn went up to knock on the door. She waited and knocked again before she heard someone coming. The person fumbled with a lock on the inside, then peered around the barely open door.

"What do you want?"

The voice Jesselynn recognized, but the face bore only faint resemblance to the one she remembered. Once round with a habitual smile, this face had skin hanging off prominent bones and blue eyes that pierced rather than sparkled.

"Aunt Agatha?"

The door would have closed but for Jesselynn's quick thinking to put her foot into the opening. "Aunt Agatha, I know you were expectin' Zachary, but I'm Jesse, er, Jesselynn."

The woman behind the door gave her a once up-and-down look. "Young man, this is not funny."

"I'm not trying to be funny. I had to become Jesse to get us here safely. I promised my father—"

"And who is your father?" She might be living in dismal surroundings, but the starch had never left her tone.

"Major Joshua Highwood, deceased. My oldest brother, Adam, died in the war, and we have not heard a thing about Zachary. Mother Miriam died in childbirth, and I have little Thaddeus with me—er, back at the camp. I sent Louisa and Carrie Mae back to Richmond, where I thought they would be safe. Twin Oaks is—"

"Well, I'll be switched." The caricature opened the door a mite farther. "When and where was your daddy born?"

"Born in 1815 in the same bed he died in at Twin Oaks in Midway, Kentucky."

"Well, I'll be a—come right on in, child." A surprisingly strong hand reached out and yanked her inside to a hall that looked about even with the outside. She peered closely into Jesselynn's eyes. "Well, you certainly have the look of the Highwoods, but with those clothes . . ." Her nose wrinkled on the last word. "We'd better look through things and see if we can find something more appropriate to a young woman of what? Nineteen, or is it twenty by now?" All the while she talked, she dragged Jesselynn down the hall by the arm. "Leastwise you can have a bath."

Trying to stop her was like trying to harness a hurricane.

"Aunt Agatha, Aunt Agatha, wait." Jesselynn clamped a hand on the doorframe to bring the procession to a halt.

"Now what?" Agatha turned to look at her niece, only to shudder. "Britches! I can't believe a niece of mine is wearin' britches!"

At the moment, *that* niece was wishing she'd never come.

Jesselynn disengaged her aunt's stranglehold on her arm. "I have to stay dressed like this to keep me and the horses and my people safe. A woman in skirts would be fair game to any polecat out lookin' for sport. You know that."

"I declare, such talk. What would your dear mother say?"

My dear mother would be right glad her daughter was alive and in one piece. "And, Aunt Agatha, you must not breathe a word about who I am to anyone. You understand that? Not anyone."

"Why, land sakes, child, who would put two and two together anyway? I—"

"You have to promise me or I'll take my people and just fade into the backwoods where no one would know or care who I was." Jesselynn stood straight and leaned forward just the least bit. "It could mean life or death."

Agatha sagged, both inside and out. "Yes, I promise."

"Good. Let me go get Meshach. Is there somewhere we can tie the horses out of sight?"

"Why, why I guess in the shed out back. But isn't he one of your slaves?"

Jesselynn stopped in midstride. "No longer. I set him and the others free."

"Oh, why . . . ah . . . um."

Jesselynn turned back around so she could watch her aunt's face. "What happened to all your slaves, Aunt Agatha?"

"I sold them that didn't die in the fire. Other than the land, which will most likely go for taxes, that's all I had left. After all . . ."

Jesselynn held up a hand to stop the flow. "I'll go put the horses away."

"I mean, he can sit out on the back stoop, and . . ."

Jesselynn closed the door behind her. Obviously she and Aunt Agatha were about half a continent apart on the slavery issue. Maybe it was a good thing that they wouldn't be staying with her. *What about the woman she lives with? Where does she stand? And more importantly, who does she know?*

Right there she resolved to tell her aunt as little as possible. Their safety might depend on that.

"Have you received any letters from home or from Richmond?" Jesselynn and her aunt were now sitting in the parlor drinking tea. Meshach had gone off to the livery to see about a job as a blacksmith.

"Forgive me, child, I have. They went right out of my mind." She set her teacup down and pushed herself up with both hands on the arms of the chair. The sound of her knees popping and creaking could be heard clear across the room, let alone to the next chair.

"Aunt Agatha, let me. Just tell me where to find them."

"I should say not. I'm not too decrepit to do for myself. Got to keep moving after all. Why, that's what's wrong with Lettie, poor dear. She just gives up at times."

Jesselynn had learned about Lettie Copsewald while they were making the tea. She'd been having one of her bad spells and, after retreating to her bed, asked to not be disturbed lest the headache return.

"After she takes her bit of laudanum," Aunt Agatha confided, "she sleeps like a baby and wakes up the next morning feelin' more like herself again."

Aunt Agatha returned to the dim and dusty parlor where she had insisted they take tea and handed Jesselynn two letters, both from Richmond.

"Thank you." She kept her sigh to herself. What was happening at Twin Oaks? Lucinda had promised to write. Taking the sheet of paper from the envelope, she started to read, only to look up in guilt. "I'm sorry. Where are my manners?"

"You go right ahead. I'll just enjoy my tea while you catch up on the news. Oh, and that one on the top just came yesterday."

By the end of the few minutes it took, Jesselynn knew that Carrie Mae was engaged to be married, Louisa volunteered at the hospital, and Zachary was alive. That last she learned in the more recent letter. She put the letters down in her lap and fought the tears that threatened to break loose.

Zachary is alive. She wanted to dance and shout, but a glance at her aunt with her chin on her chest helped calm her to only a quick squeezing of her fists. *No matter how badly he is wounded, he can go home to Twin Oaks and start over. I'll take the horses home in the spring, and life will begin again.*

She ignored the voice that reminded her the war might not be over by then.

She read the letters again to savor every word and nuance. What had Louisa meant about her work in the hospital? Surely they didn't let young unmarried women take care of the wounded men. She read the paragraphs again. Certainly sounded like that was just what she was doing.

Whatever was Aunt Sylvania thinking of to let Louisa do such a thing?

The thought "let Louisa" made her eyebrows rise. How could she expect Aunt Sylvania to do what she had been unable to accomplish herself? She folded the letters and slid them back into their envelopes. The clink of her cup in the saucer brought Aunt Agatha upright.

"Isn't that good news?" She picked up her cup and wrinkled her nose when the tea she sipped was cold. "I must have slept a bit. Forgive my bad manners, please. When Lettie is unwell, I have a difficult time sleeping."

Jesselynn refrained from asking why and handed the letters back to her aunt. "Thank you for sharing them with me. I wrote the other day to tell them we were here safely." She heard a discreet rap at the back door. "I'd better be going. That is sure to be Meshach." She paused. "Is there anyone you know of, Aunt, who would let me keep the horses hidden on their farm until we can go home again?"

Agatha shook her head. "No one I would trust. I'm sorry, my dear."

Jesselynn said her good-byes, promising to return often, but not telling her aunt where they were camped. "If you need me, leave a letter at the post office, and whoever comes in to town will get it."

"Go with God, child. I just wish I could do more."

Jesselynn ignored the first part of the sentence and shook her head over the last. "I wish I could help *you* more." She looked around at the dilapidated house. "Perhaps we could come in one day and do some fixin' up, though. If it wouldn't offend Miss Lettie?"

"We shall see." Aunt Agatha stepped back from the horses and stared up at Meshach. "You take good care of her now, you hear?"

"Yessum, I hears." Meshach gentled Ahab and grinned when Agatha *tsked* at Jesselynn mounted astride.

Jesselynn waved one last time as they trotted down the rutted street. "Let's stop at the post office. Might be a letter from home."

All the way there she told him the news from Richmond and got a lump in her throat again at the sheen of tears in the big man's eyes at the good news.

"I'm right glad to hear that," he said. "Thank you, Lord above, for takin' keer of our boy."

Jesselynn rolled her eyes. Leave it to Meshach; he just didn't understand. Zachary making it through was luck, pure and simple.

"I have a letter here for Miss Jesselynn Highwood. Would she be any relation to you?" the woman behind the counter asked.

"Ah yes. That's my sister. I'll take it to her." Jesselynn took the envelope and studied the unfamiliar handwriting. "Thank you." She stuffed the envelope into her pocket and followed an elderly lady out the door. As she'd made the men promise to do, she glanced around but saw no one that seemed interested in her or what she was doing.

But once on the horses, she felt shivers run up her spine. Lucinda used to call it "someone walkin' on mah grave."

Before mounting she looked again, but everything around them seemed to fit.

"What wrong?" Meshach asked in an undertone.

"I don't know. Just feels like someone is watchin' me."

"Don' see nobody."

"I know. Me neither. Let's get outa here."

Once out of town, she opened the letter. A blank page stared back at her.

CHAPTER THIRTY-SIX

Missouri cave

"Why would someone send a blank page?"

"I don' know."

If Jesselynn had asked the question once in the last three days, she'd asked it a hundred times. While they had posted lookouts around the clock, no one had seen anything or anyone suspicious. They grazed the horses both morning and afternoon, and Meshach went hunting early every morning, returning with rabbits from the snares he set, another deer, and a couple of ducks. Those at the cave kept the fire going to cure the meat and worked at tanning the hides. Daniel wore his new moccasins, a gift from Sergeant White, with pride.

Barnabas, as he asked to be called, took one of the tanned rabbit pelts and created a pad for the stump of his leg, so he could begin to wear the peg that he and Meshach designed. While he couldn't wear it long or put all of his weight on it, the peg leg helped his balance.

"What if we carved me a foot and put a boot on it, then it would look more like a real leg."

"We kin try." Meshach studied the piece of wood in his hand. "Carvin' it ain't the problem. It'd be mighty stiff." With two fingers, he hung on to one end of the foot-long piece and bobbed it up and down. "Look, see how a foot walks. Needs to bend at de ankle." He leaned over and stroked the hair back from Jane Ellen's forehead.

Jesselynn often wondered how a man's hand so big and strong enough to shoe horses and all the other chores Meshach accomplished with such ease could still be so gentle with their silent girl.

Walking Jane Ellen had become Jesselynn's job, and as long as she held the hand that was becoming more clawlike daily and led her around, Jane Ellen walked. Otherwise she sat—and stared into nothing. They took turns feeding her, the boys chattered to her as if she were indeed listening, and Ophelia combed her hair and sang to her.

If Jesselynn allowed herself to think beyond the moment, she wondered if the young girl would just fade away and one morning they would wake up to find her cold and stiff, instead of warm and silent.

"What about a wire hinge or even a wooden one?" Barnabas took the wood from Meshach and outlined a hinge on the end of the wood. "Then notch up into the wooden leg."

"So, how you keep it from floppin' down when you walk?"

"Oh." The two went back to their carving and pondering.

Jesselynn took her sewing outside to sit in the sunshine. Sammy needed clothes for the winter, so she cut up one of her father's shirts and fashioned a shift for the black baby. She figured to make him a vest out of the rabbit pelts as soon as they were ready. The way Thaddeus was growing, she'd need material, or hides, to sew new pants for him too.

Ophelia had been down to the swamp and brought back cattail leaves for making baskets, along with stalks and roots for cooking. When she had a few minutes, she would sit down to weave again. "Babies sleepin'." She brought her work out into the sun to sit near Jesselynn.

A crow flew overhead, his raucous call causing Jesselynn to look up. A blue jay joined in the warning announcement.

Jesselynn's heart picked up the pace. She scanned the area she could see, set down her sewing, and stood to look up the hill above the cave. Nothing. She listened, but other than the breeze rattling the few remaining leaves, she could see or hear nothing. Nevertheless that feeling of being watched returned. Could someone be watching them and stay hidden? She examined the oak trees around them, one by one. Many had trunks large enough to hide a man, but who would dare come so close? They kept the rifles in plain view.

"What is it?" Barnabas stumped his way out to stand beside her.

"I don't know. It's just a feelin'." Jesselynn rubbed the back of her neck. "Guess I'm just spooked ever since that letter."

"Know anyone who could be lookin' for you?"

"Yes." *Should I tell him or not? And how can I without telling him who I really am?*

She continued scanning the trees, lingering over a broad trunk made even wider with a burl the size of a washtub. Now where would she hide if she were watching the camp?

"We need more wood. I'm thinkin' of tryin' to chop down one of those smaller trees."

"Choppin' wood puts lots of pressure on the knees."

"I know." He stood beside her, giving the trees the same once-over she did. He stumped along with her as she walked to the edge of the clearing where the bank sloped off down to the creek that threaded its way between the hills. Ridges and hollers, according to the locals.

"Jesse, mayhap I could be more of a help if I knew the whole story."

Jesselynn heard the caring in his voice. She knew if she turned around his eyes would be warm and his mouth curved in that gentle smile he had. Once or twice she'd even thought on what kissing him would be like. She straightened just enough to put a bit of distance between them.

"I know you're no lad."

"Umm." What could she say? Did she dare tell him?

"But I know too, you got yourself a mighty good reason to keep up the masquerade."

"I reckon what you don't know can't hurt you." *Or me either.*

"That's not always true."

"Maybe not, but I got to do what's best for everybody here."

"What about what's best for Jesse?"

"Jesselynn." *There, I did it.* "And the man who can do us the most harm is Cavendar Dunlivey. When my daddy kicked him off Twin Oaks and I turned down his proposal, he swore to get us all, including the slaves and the horses. While I've emancipated my people, he could sell 'em down the river if he caught them."

She shuddered inside at what he would do to her. "I'd kill him myself before I let him touch any one of us." All the while they talked, they both studied the surrounding area, rather than each other. But every particle of skin and clothing seemed charged, and she was sure sparks would snap if they touched.

Telling him let her stand a little straighter as he shared her burden.

"So, what will you do?"

"Hide the horses here through the winter. Then when the war is over in the spring, we'll go home again." The thought of seeing Twin Oaks when the infant oak leaves were pinking on the stems made her eyes water.

"What makes you think the war will be over by spring?"

"It has to be." She turned at the sound of the whistle that announced Benjamin was back with the horses. She whistled back and bumped into the broad chest of the man who'd been standing with her. The thought of leaning on that chest and letting him put his arms around her made her catch her breath. Not since John rode off so gallantly had she stood in the stronghold of a man's embrace.

She swallowed and stared at the button midway up his shirt. "I . . . I'd better go." Her hands itched to touch him.

"Jesselynn."

Ah, the sound of her name. So long since she'd been Jesselynn, it seemed a lifetime ago.

"Jesse." She stepped back. "Please remember that." When he reached to touch her hand, she sidestepped the contact. "I'd better get back to sewing if Sammy is to have something warmer to wear."

"We'll talk again."

"Oh, I'm sure we will." She swallowed the catch in her throat. *Could she love this man in the same way she had loved John? Did she really know what loving a man was like, since all she'd shared were a few kisses and dreams?* She stepped around him and returned to her sewing, stitching as fast as her thoughts swirled until she pricked her finger and a dot of blood glowed on the white cloth. The word she thought was not the one she uttered, which was a good thing because just then Thaddeus ambled out of the cave, rubbing the sleep from his eyes as she rubbed the blood from her fingertip.

That night before going to bed, Jesselynn stopped Barnabas at the mouth of the cave. "If you figured out that I'm . . . I'm not a man, is it that I am such a poor actor?"

White shook his head. "No. Don't worry yourself about that. One would need to be around awhile to figure it out."

"What then?"

"Little things, like your sewing. No man sews such a fine seam, and most men, especially young ones, aren't as tender as you with children or as gentle with the ill, like the way you care for Jane Ellen."

"Anything else?" She knew her tone was clipped, but the worry of it all sharpened her every which way.

"Well, ah . . ." His hesitation brought the memory back to her of when she'd helped him eat and drink, and the look on his face the one time he'd fallen against her chest.

"Good night, Sergeant White." She brushed past him and darted off into the trees, her cheeks flaming as much as she suspected his were, but he had a beard to disguise the condition.

"We'd better make another trip to town," Jesselynn said several days later, days she'd spent making sure she was always on the other side of the fire from Barnabas White. Being near him made it more difficult to think, and she couldn't afford herself that luxury. Even thinking his name made her feel soft inside.

"Kin we git some sugar or molasses an' maybe milk?" Ophelia looked up from hanging more venison over the drying fire. "De babies, dey need milk."

"I know." Jesselynn heaved a sigh. They all needed so many things, things she had taken for granted at home, like cloth and thread, flour and cornmeal, horseshoes and cowhide or pigskin to repair harnesses and bridles. One of the reins had broken the day before on the bridle Ahab wore. "Maybe if we get to Aunt Agatha's before dawn, the horses won't cause a stir." Oh, how she missed that mule right about now. No matter how they tried to disguise them, Thoroughbreds were Thoroughbreds, and anyone with a decent eye for horseflesh would spot them. If only they knew of a place outside of town where they could leave the horses and walk on in. And if Meshach got work at the livery, how would he get back and forth, or if he stayed in town, where?

Too many questions and no answers.

Instead of worrying about the possibilities, she took out paper and pen to write to her sisters. While she had as many questions for them as they'd had for her, none of them made a life-or-death difference. Now if only there'd be a letter from Twin Oaks at the post office, she would have one less thing to worry about.

The next morning after an uneventful daybreak ride, they tied the horses in the shed at Aunt Agatha's and rapped gently at the back door. Agatha answered the door, mopping her eyes at the same time.

"What is it, Aunt?" Jesselynn took her aunt's icy hands in her own.

"Lettie is so sick. I've been nursing her, but last night she took a turn for the worse. Please." She gave Meshach an imploring look. "Could you go for the doctor?"

"Of course he will. Where is the doctor's house?"

While Agatha gave Meshach instructions, Jesselynn crossed to the stove and checked the firebox. The fire was nearly out and the woodbox empty, but when she stepped outside, the woodpile was down to a few sticks. Checking the back side of the shed, she had to admit there was another problem: the two old women were about out of wood. If the temperature of the day was any indication, winter was shoving fall out of the way and taking over.

She'd have to set the men to cutting wood and bring in a wagonload, but that wouldn't help today. What could she do? Wasn't there anyone in this town who watched out for widow ladies? She picked up her load and headed back for the house.

Agatha met her at the door again. "I just don't know what more to do for her."

"I know. You've done the best you could." Jesselynn shaved a few slivers off the wood with the butcher knife on top of the stove and laid them over the few remaining coals. If she'd seen the ax, she'd have split a piece or two for fire starter. Opening the draft wide, she blew on the coals until a tendril of smoke rose, then another. She set the lid divider in place and then the back lid so the draft would work when she added the two smallest pieces. By the time the burners were hot enough to heat water, she could hear Meshach's boots on the back step.

"Doctor say he be right over." He caught his breath, then added, "Also ask why you not call for 'im sooner."

Agatha straightened as though she was about to fight, then slumped. "We have no money to pay a doctor, so we do what we can."

Jesselynn felt like crying for her, but more tears would only water the soup, as Lucinda was wont to say. "A cup of tea will help, I know."

"No tea."

"Coffee?"

A shake of her head. "And there's nothin' left to sell, neither. We already did that."

"What have you been livin' on?"

"The fruit and vegetables from our garden. The two hens left give us eggs. We manage."

"Good." The thought of an egg made her mouth get all set for the taste.

"But I've been thinkin' maybe some chicken soup would help—"

A rap at the front door stopped her in midsentence. "The doctor." Her slippers *flap-flapped* down the hall as she hurried to let him in.

"I'm goin' to de livery now, if you don' need me anymore."

"Not unless you can find something to cut up for firewood."

"Kin do dat tomorrer and bring it here in de wagon."

"I know." Jesselynn rubbed her forehead with the fingers of one hand. "You go on." She jingled the coins in her pocket. Should she buy wood for the women or scrape by on what was out there? The money in her pocket was all that stood between them all and . . . the thought didn't bear thinking about. She could at least have brought in some dried meat, if she'd known things were so bad here.

The doctor came out of the sickroom shaking his head. "Not much we can do but keep her comfortable. When a body don't want to live anymore, hard to keep 'em here." He shivered and came to the stove to rub his hands over the heat. "They let the fire go out?" he said under his breath to Jesselynn.

"About out of wood."

"Long on pride, these two, and short on sense." The doctor shook his head. "I'll get some wood over here sometime today."

"We can bring in a load tomorrow."

The doctor nodded. "You a relative?"

"Agatha's nephew from Kentucky. Thought to be safe here."

The doctor barked a laugh. "It's bad now but goin' to be worse, you mark my words."

"Worse?"

"Those hotheads down in Arkansas . . ."

Jesselynn didn't even want to ask him what he meant. Bluebellies, graycoats, no matter, she just wanted the war over so she could go home. She saw the doctor to the door, refusing to dip into their meager cash store to pay him, then returned to the backyard to see what she could turn into firewood to keep these two old ladies warm until the morrow. Since there were no animals, she tore off the manger and hacked it into stove-size lengths, likewise the posts and sides of the stall divider. That along with the remaining chunks of wood should serve them. The two hens eyed her, then went back to scratching in their pen. Since the grain bin was empty, Jesselynn brought in some garden refuse and threw it down for them.

Now she had all the old biddies cared for. The thought brought an almost smile. She went back in the house and set a pot of water to boiling to make soup out of dried beans, dried corn, fresh carrots, turnips, rutabagas, and potatoes, all from the cellar, along with a bit of cabbage. Again she wished she'd brought some of the dried venison along.

Agatha came out of the sickroom some time later and sank down onto a chair at the kitchen table. "She's sleeping, poor thing." She eyed the bottle of laudanum the doctor had left on the table. "At least she's not so restless. I could tell she was in pain, and at least now that can be helped."

Jesselynn watched her aunt straighten the saltcellar and smooth out the crocheted doily. She moved the medicine closer, then set it farther off again. Had the doctor told Agatha what he believed?

"You want me to spend the night?" She waited until she heard Meshach's boots on the steps to ask.

"No, no. You've done plenty, what with the wood and the soup and all. We'll be fine. Perhaps by tomorrow Lettie will be feeling much better."

She doesn't know. Good grief, what am I to do?

"You go on now. Your people need you worse than I do." Agatha made shooing motions with her hands. The vigor had returned to her voice, giving her almost as much a commanding presence as in earlier days.

"We'll be back with wood tomorrow, then." Jesselynn gave her aunt a hug and let herself be ushered out the door.

"No work here 'less I go to de army. But got a letter here for Sergeant White. Make him right happy." Meshach patted his pocket.

As they left town, that old feeling of being watched kept Jesse-lynn looking over her shoulder. *You'd think I'd be used to it by now.* But her interior muttering did nothing to dispel the feeling, so they returned to their cave a different way.

"Letter for you," Meshach said, handing Barnabas the envelope as soon as they got to the cave.

"Ah, from home." His smile widened. "A letter from home." He opened it carefully to save the paper and pulled out a single sheet. Only moments after beginning to read, he raised stricken eyes to meet Jesselynn's. "I've got to go home as soon as possible. My mother is desperately ill, and there is no one else to care for her. May I use one of the horses to ride to Springfield? I can catch the stagecoach to Fort Smith from there."

CHAPTER THIRTY-SEVEN

Missouri

"I'll be back," Sergeant White assured Jesselynn.

Why did those words seem so familiar? Jesselynn nodded. "Maybe you'll have to come all the way to Kentucky."

"No matter where, I'll find you."

She nodded again. "You just get your family taken care of." She stepped back when he reached for her. Two men hugging in public would cause all sorts of raised eyebrows, and she didn't want to draw any more attention to herself than necessary.

"I left you my address. You'll write?" The plea in his eyes tugged at her heart.

"And you? We'll miss you." *I'll miss you.* She didn't want to admit that to anyone, let alone herself.

As soon as he boarded the stage, she turned and headed back for Aunt Agatha's, where Meshach would be unloading the wood. *You will not cry!* She kept the order pounding out the same rhythm as her marching feet.

As soon as she'd checked with her aunt, who said Lettie was about the same as yesterday, she climbed up on the wagon seat and, taking the reins, headed the team out of town.

"De neighbors want to buy a load of wood," Meshach said after they were halfway back to the cave.

"Really? For how much?"

He named a price, and she smacked her lips together. "That will buy flour and beans."

"Miss Agatha, she send home some veg'bles." He motioned to a tow sack behind the seat. "An' three eggs."

Amazing, we actually think of the cave as home. She had realized that the day before when thinking the same thing herself. But this time there was no Sergeant Barnabas White to look forward to talking with. She stopped the next sigh in mid-exhale. Sighing could become a habit, a bad habit. If she let herself think of all the people who'd gone out of her life the last couple of years, the sighing would lead to crying, and no way was she going to let *that* happen.

"Maybe someone else would buy wood too." *If only they didn't have to use the horses as a team.* She wished they could have caught whoever stole their mule.

"Marse Jesse, I gots sumpin' to ask you."

Jesselynn glanced at the man sitting beside her. "So ask."

"Well, you heard Sergeant White talkin' wid us 'bout goin' west? Go on to Oregon for free land."

"Mmm. Guess I didn't pay much attention."

"I wants to do dat. Dey no niggers dere. Only black men free on their own free land. 'Phelia an' me, we wants ta be married, then up and go west." The final words came in a rush. "Sammy too."

"Oh." His words hit her like a dozen knife slashes. "You don't want to go home to Twin Oaks?"

"No'm. I wants land of my own."

She could hear the pride in his voice, the kind of pride she'd been nursing along so that he could become the man she knew he was.

"Would you wait until I get the horses home? Then I'd send you with my blessing."

"Yessuh, we would wait. Planned it thataway anyhow. I'd never leave you alone in dat cave."

"Good, that's settled, then. But if you and Ophelia want to get married sooner than that, I see no reason to wait. You could go to a minister in Springfield."

"I'll think on dat."

A scream from up ahead made her slap the horses into a trot. She pulled them to a stop near the top of the ridge and slung the reins around the brake post. Meshach was halfway down the hill before she crowned the ridge.

"Don't come any further!" The voice came from her worst nightmare.

"Now drop your gun or this nigger here won't have no head." Meshach did as ordered.

Jesselynn hid behind the tree with the huge burl and surveyed the scene below. She counted five of the roughest-looking men she'd ever seen, and Cavendar Dunlivey was the ugliest. How had she ever thought him handsome in those long-ago days at Twin Oaks? He wore a coat that once had been gray and cut for an officer, but now dirt warred with holes as to who owned it. His hat slouched over one eye, but the pistol he held against Ophelia's head glinted in the sunlight.

One man held a gun on Benjamin and Daniel, while two others were leading the horses out of the cave.

For an instant, Jesselynn was grateful they'd hooked Ahab up in the team, but that made no difference now. How could she get them out of this? She fingered the pistol she'd taken to wearing in her waistband and had drawn when she ducked behind the tree. She could get Dunlivey, but what about the others?

Jane Ellen sat where they must have dumped her, face slack, focusing on nothing. Sammy and Thaddeus huddled with Benjamin and Daniel. Looked like both the young'uns had been crying.

"Now, whar is she?" Dunlivey roared, nudging the mouth of the pistol under Ophelia's chin. Her eyes rolled white, and she whimpered, the sound such pure terror that Jesselynn drew back on the trigger. One shot and he would be gone.

"Who?" Meshach burned with a fire of his own, leashed only by a will that knew he'd be dead, and then what would happen to the rest?

"Miss Jesselynn Highwood, that's who."

"Don't never seen another woman here, boss." The man guarding the others called.

"She done gone back home." Meshach stood taller.

"And left that brat here. Naw, she's around." He poked the gun again. "Now whar?"

"Gone to her aunt's house." Benjamin drew back from the gun aimed at his head.

"Ah, then we wait. She's comin' back." Dunlivey lowered his gun, and Ophelia collapsed in a heap at his feet. He kicked her aside and strolled over to Meshach. "You 'member that beating

I owed ya?" He walked around the statue of ebony. "Answer me, niggah!"

The gun now dug into Meshach's neck.

"Yessuh."

One of the men who'd tied the mare to a nearby tree now reached down and picked up Ophelia, dangling her as one would a doll. "Now this here might be a fun plaything."

Meshach growled like an animal at bay.

Oh, don't move, Meshach. Wait, please wait. You remember Dunlivey. He likes to tease and torture. Hang on.

The man reached out and ripped Ophelia's dress down the front. She screamed and tried to cover herself. Meshach made a slight motion to go to her, and Dunlivey clubbed him over the head with his pistol. Meshach dropped like a steel weight.

"Watch 'im!"

One of the men shifted over to rest the tip of his rifle on Meshach's cheek.

Oh, God, what do I do?

"Let them all go, Dunlivey, and I'll come in!" Her voice rang with authority.

"Ha! I got them, and now you too."

Jesselynn aimed at the side of his boot. The shot rang out, and he jumped as if he'd been stung. "That wasn't a miss."

A string of curses heated the air.

"You want me to try again? Closer maybe?"

More curses. A snicker from one of his men.

"Let my people go!" Where had she heard those words before? The shot took off his hat.

Dunlivey nodded to his men. "Let 'em go. But we keep the guns. They won't go nowhere."

His men stepped back.

"Benjamin, get them outa there."

Like an adder striking, Dunlivey snatched up Thaddeus. "Now show yourself."

"Put him down. I told you I'd come in." Her heart pounded so hard she thought it might leap from her chest. *Not Thaddeus!*

"Let them all go, Dunlivey, or my next shot is through your heart." Her hand clutching the pistol shook so hard she couldn't have hit the cave wall.

"Show yerself!"

Thaddeus screamed. Jesselynn stepped out from behind the tree.

A shot rang out. Dunlivey dropped Thaddeus and clutched his belly that blossomed red with blood.

One of his men raised his gun, but before he could fire, Jesselynn's shot caught him in the shoulder and spun him around. The other three grabbed him and all disappeared into the trees.

Jane Ellen stood, feet spread, the gun in her hand now pointing at the ground.

"I'm gut shot." Dunlivey sagged to the ground, trying to hold his lifeblood in with spread fingers. "Don't leave me! You filthy scum, get back here!"

By the time Jesselynn got down to the clearing, Benjamin had an arm around Jane Ellen and held her as sobs rocked her skeleton body. Ophelia held Meshach in her arms, his head cradled in her lap. Sammy, tears streaming over his cheeks, toddled over to them, and Thaddeus drove straight for Jesselynn.

She scooped him up in her arms and rocked him, raining kisses on his cheeks.

"Someone, help me."

Jesselynn strode over to the clothesline she and Ophelia had hung and ripped a cloth off the rope. Tossing it to Dunlivey, she said calmly, as if she did this every day, "Fold that up and pack it in the wound. Might stop the bleedin'."

"The rest of you, let's get the things out of the cave. We can't stay here any longer."

Within half an hour, they were ready to load the wagon. As they went about their chores, no one looked at Dunlivey.

When they trudged up the hill with the supplies, he cried, "Give me a drink at least. Please give me a drink."

Meshach looked at Jesselynn, ignored her when she shook her head, and took a cup of water to the wounded man, who'd now managed to get himself backed up against a tree trunk.

"Dis only make it worse."

"You aren't goin' to leave me here?"

"Surely your men will come back for you." Jesselynn knew they wouldn't. Not the way they hightailed it. Knowing Dunlivey, he'd probably beaten each of them at one time or another.

He coughed. "You got any whisky?"

" 'Fraid not." She went back in the cave to see if they'd forgotten anything.

"All ready up here," Benjamin called from the lip of the ridge.

"Be right there." She took one more look around. *Take him into town and leave him at the doctor's. Surely you can do that.* Her mother's voice rang clear as if she stood right there. Jesselynn sighed. Yes, she could do that, even though he'd need a miracle.

"Ya can't go back, ya know."

She stopped and stared at him.

"I burnt it." His eyes slitted, and what might have been a laugh choked from his mouth. "I burnt Twin Oaks to the ground the night you left. You got nothin'."

"What about Lucinda, the others?" *He's lyin'. He's got to be lyin'.*

"Slaver got 'em."

"But they had their papers."

"Not after the burnin'." He coughed, and pink spittle bubbled from his mouth.

Jesselynn staggered. Twin Oaks burned to the ground. "You're lyin'!"

He dug in his breast pocket and tossed her something. She bent down and picked up her silver comb, half melted but still recognizable.

"Found that in the ashes."

She looked him in the eyes. His glee could mean only one thing. She rubbed the ashes off the comb, spun, and strode off.

"Shoot me, then. Put me out of this misery."

She looked back. "I've never shot a man and I won't start now." With that she strode up the hill to where the others waited. *Where do we go? What do I do? No matter what I—oh, God— what do I do?*

She stopped at the oak with the big burl and, taking a deep breath, turned around. "I'll send a doctor back for you." *There, Mama. I tried.* Each foot felt shod in granite. *Where, God, where do we go?*

She topped the rise as the fiery gold disc slipped behind the horizon. Oranges, pinks, purples, and magenta bled across the sky and burned the clouds to silver. Then the answer came.

"Where we goin'?" Benjamin handed her the reins.

"West. Soon as we can. West, where there's no 'niggers,' only black men as free as the land."

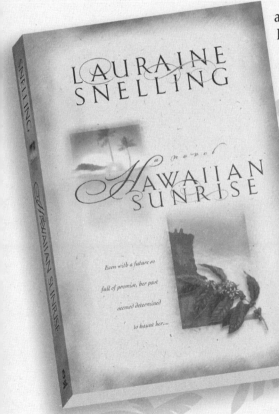